★　　★　　★

DON'T MISS THESE
STARBRIDGE ADVENTURES:

Book One: *StarBridge*
Book Two: *Silent Dances*
Book Three: *Shadow World*

The STARBRIDGE Series

STARBRIDGE by A.C. Crispin

STARBRIDGE 2: SILENT DANCES by A.C. Crispin
and Kathleen O'Malley

STARBRIDGE 3: SHADOW WORLD
by A.C. Crispin and Jannean Elliott

STARBRIDGE 4: SERPENT'S GIFT
by A.C. Crispin with Deborah A. Marshall

Also by A.C. Crispin

V
YESTERDAY'S SON
TIME FOR YESTERDAY
GRYPHON'S EYRIE (*with Andre Norton*)

A. C. CRISPIN
with DEBORAH A. MARSHALL

StarBridge
★ ★ ★ ★ ★ ★ ★ ★ ★ ★ ★ ★ ★ *Book Four*

SERPENT'S GIFT

ACE BOOKS, NEW YORK

This book is an Ace original edition,
and has never been previously published.

SERPENT'S GIFT

An Ace Book / published by arrangement with
the authors

PRINTING HISTORY
Ace edition / May 1992

ISBN: 0-441-78331-7

Ace Books are published by The Berkley Publishing Group,
200 Madison Avenue, New York, New York 10016.
The name "ACE" and the "A" logo
are trademarks belonging to Charter Communications, Inc.

PRINTED IN THE UNITED STATES OF AMERICA

10 9 8 7 6 5 4 3 2 1

This book is dedicated to Anne Moroz, a.k.a. "Saint Anne," patient listener, staunch friend, terrific writer, and a rock of refreshing calm we all cling to when beset by the storms of writers' uncertainty and general angst. Thanks for being a pal, Annie—and for making all those dinners!

Acknowledgments

As usual, many people helped me with the technical aspects of this book, because, to borrow the phrasing of one well-known doctor, "I'm a writer, not a scientist." With the caveat that any mistakes are assuredly my own, I'd like to thank:

Gwyneth Hannaford, nuclear engineer and knowledgeable s.f. fan. Gwen basically invented radonium, its evil twin variant, and the properties ascribed to both;

Chelsea Quinn Yarbro, for technical information on music and pianists. From Quinn I learned that a pianist sits in the percussion section while playing in a symphony, and what a threnody is (a piece written in memory of someone);

Henry Miller, archaeologist, who allowed me to visit a real dig;

Carol Theobold, archaeologist, who told me about banjos and thus inspired the "dowser";

Mary Frye, for checking (and correcting) my French;

Barbara Mertz, my favorite mystery author as well as a friend. Barbara generously loaned me an invaluable (and otherwise unavailable) reference book . . . Martha Joukowsky's *A Complete Manual of Field Archaeology*;

Sara Scott Peterson, psychologist, who gave many helpful suggestions during the final development of this novel;

And, of course, Dr. Robert Harrington, astronomer, of the U.S. Naval Observatory in Washington, D.C., who helped work out the dimensions and properties of the StarBridge asteroid. It was Bob who explained (in words of one syllable, so I could understand!) the fluctuations and gravitational irregularities that its odd-shaped mass would produce.

I would also be remiss if I did not acknowledge the editorial and writing help I received, because this book would never have been completed without it:

Kathleen O'Malley, my unsung co-writer on this book—as always, I couldn't have done it without you. May you live forever;

Merrilee Heifetz, my agent. Her faith in me pulled me through "hell week";

Ginjer Buchanan, "Honored Editor" of the StarBridge series, who helped immeasurably with character and plot development;

Laura Anne Gilman and Peter Heck, also of the Ace staff, who always lent a sympathetic ear during trying times.

—A.C. Crispin

CHAPTER I

♦

Interstellar Incidents

Cursing under his breath, Dr. Robert Gable trotted down the crowded corridors of StarBridge Academy toward his office. The first classes of the day were about to begin, and the slender, dark-haired psychologist had to dodge hurrying students from most of the Fifteen Known Worlds. *Of all the mornings to oversleep* . . . Rob thought, finger-combing his curly hair. *If I don't reach that shuttle before it takes off* . . . Glancing anxiously at his watch, he hissed a soft oath in Mizari. *Twenty-seven minutes late! Janet will be leaving any minute!*

There'd been a crisis during the wee hours of what Rob and the other humans on the asteroid still thought of as "night." One of the Drnian students, Shrys, had learned just after midnight that his clan-sib had died during a betrothal ritual, and Rob had been up for hours with the grief-stricken youth.

Both the human psychologist and the Drnian counselor, Parys, had had their hands full. Shrys was distraught, determined to do The Right Thing—offer himself as death-escort and companion in the NextLife. It had taken some fast talking to convince the student that he should consult with his family before making such an irrevocable decision. Rob and Parys had arranged priority transport home, then rousted Rob's Simiu assistant out of bed to pilot them all "up" to nearby StarBridge Station.

After Rob and Parys had watched Shrys shuffle forlornly down the boarding tube and into his ship, they'd trudged silently back to the *Fys,* the Academy's smaller shuttle. On the way back to the asteroid that had been his home for over six years, Rob had prayed silently that he'd see Shrys again ... knowing all the while there was a good chance that he wouldn't. The student's family might agree that Shrys would make a perfect death-escort.

Now, amid the hurrying horde of students, Rob cursed the seconds as they slipped away. *I shouldn't have gone back to bed at all,* he thought, chagrined. But at forty, a night of lost sleep took a far greater toll than it had at twenty, or even thirty. He'd lain back down, fully clothed, telling himself that he'd just close his eyes and rest for a few minutes ...

I'm late, I'm late ... The sounds of his rapidly moving feet seemed to echo in his ears as words. *Stop it,* he ordered himself disgustedly. *You sound like the White Rabbit!*

Rob rounded a curve in the carpeted, neutral-colored corridor that led to his office. He desperately needed to reach Janet Rodriguez, the Academy's Chief Engineer and pilot, who was even now readying the school's big shuttle, the *Martin Luther King, Jr.,* for the trip to StarBridge Station to pick up a group of new students. *I'm too late to reach the shuttle dome in time ... but if I can just call her before she takes off ...*

His strides came faster ... faster ... *I'll ask Janet to delay takeoff, then I'll try once more to reach Hing, see if she'll—*

Rob's thoughts broke off abruptly as he rounded another curve in the hall—only to find himself face-to-face with a flying Apis student!

The alien, who had been skimming along, minding her own business, swerved wildly to avoid him. Rob dug in his heels, stumbled, then caught himself, bracing one hand on the wall. He was terrified that he'd crash into her; if he did, he knew his weight would crush her brittle carapace and fragile wings.

Heart slamming, he regained his balance, hearing the meter-long beelike being buzzing at him reproachfully; she was too shaken to remember to key her voder with her antennae.

"A thousand apologies, Esteemed Ztrazz," Rob blurted in Mizari, the Academy's common language, making a hasty and apologetic bow. He was gasping with relief as much as exertion. "I'm terribly late, and I was trying to catch the shuttle before it takes off. Are you hurt?"

As she hovered before him, Ztrazz's antennae finally located the controls to her voder. Understandable Mizari emerged. "I am unharmed, Esteemed Rob," she said. "I should have been paying more attention to where I was flying, but I was conjugating English verbs." She glanced at him out of her enormous many-faceted eyes, and the doctor saw his own wild-eyed, rumpled reflection stare back at him, multiplied over and over. Evidently Ztrazz realized how shaken he was, for she added helpfully, "Would you like me to fly over to the shuttle bay for you and deliver a message?"

"Would you?" Rob knew she could make the journey in less time than it would take him to reach his office, unlock it, then activate his intercom. "Thank you so much, Ztrazz! Ask Esteemed Janet Rodriguez to hold the shuttle until she hears from me. I'm going to call her right now."

Without taking time to reply, the alien reversed course and sped off toward the dome housing the Academy's two shuttles, plus the small scooters that were used for individual or two-person travel across the asteroid's bleak surface. Rob sighed as he glanced at his watch again. *She'll catch her . . . I hope.*

The psychologist moderated his pace to a swift walk as he resumed his course. *Now, if only Hing is in her—*

Rob's dark eyes widened in surprise and relief as he rounded the last curve in the corridor, only to discover Hing Oun waiting for him, as though his wish to see her had somehow conjured her up. "Well, I'll be damned," Rob exclaimed, doing an exaggerated double take. "It's the late Hing Oun! To what do I owe this singular honor? Surely not the message I sent you two days ago—*or* the other message I left yesterday"—he shook his head slowly—"it couldn't be that you finally got around to listening to your messages, could it?"

The petite, almond-eyed young woman with the long, heavy braid of black hair tossed over one shoulder rolled her eyes. "Sarcasm isn't your style, Rob," she observed dryly. "You don't do it well." Then, pointedly glancing at her watch, she added, "Besides, you're the one who's late this morning. *And* making me miss my Interstellar Trade Contracts class, I might add."

"This is important. Have Professor Hathaway call me and I'll square it with her," Rob said, opening his door. He put a hand on the young woman's arm, ushering her into the office. Rob Gable was far from tall, but the top of the Asian student's head barely reached his chin. "I need a favor, Hing."

She grimaced theatrically. "Why do I all of a sudden feel like the fly being invited into the spider's den?"

"The idiom is 'web' or 'parlor,' not 'den,' " Rob corrected amiably. "Sit down," he said, waving at the visitor's chair. "I've got to call Janet first thing, then I'll explain."

Moments later the holo-tank on Rob's desk filled with the image of a strikingly attractive woman in her mid-forties. Janet Rodriguez was tall and athletically lean, with vivid green eyes. Her thick bronze hair was cropped stylishly short—much shorter than Rob's hair, which nearly brushed his shoulders—but the impression was anything but masculine. As soon as she identified her caller, she grinned, revealing strong white teeth. "Yeah, I'm still here. Ztrazz caught me just as I was completing my last preflight checks. I see by the Traffic Control log that you and Parys had the *Fys* out last night. Crisis?"

"Yeah," Rob said, then turning to Hing he mouthed, "Excuse me," and thumbed on the holo-tank's privacy field. "We had to send Shrys home. I just hope we see him again, Janet. His senior clan-sib died, and you know what that means."

"Oh, shit," Janet muttered, her expression darkening.

"We'll just have to hope his family doesn't decide Shrys would make a perfect death-escort," Rob said with a sigh.

"But that's not why you called this morning," she guessed.

Rob smiled wanly. "I need a favor, Janet. Hold takeoff for me while I talk to Hing Oun. I've got her in my office now."

"Those new kids are going to be docking in about fifteen minutes," Janet warned.

"I know. But this is important, and it won't take long—I hope. Listen, if Hing isn't there in . . . fifteen minutes, go ahead and prepare to take off. If I can't talk her into this . . ." Rob sighed, "I'll come up with you myself, okay?"

"Okay. I'm taking the big shuttle, of course."

"I'll tell her. Who's your orientation guide today?" Rob asked, glancing sideways through the shimmer of the privacy field at the dark shape that was Hing.

"Serge LaRoche," Janet said. "He's on the schedule."

The psychologist raised an eyebrow. *Serge, eh? That could prove interesting . . . should I warn Hing? No,* he decided after a moment, *it's none of your business. They're adults, remember?* "Okay. Fifteen minutes, Janet. Thanks."

"I'm waiting," she said, and cut the connection. Rob flicked off the privacy field and his brown eyes met Hing's even darker ones. The student's tilted, thick-lashed eyes and smooth, poreless skin were her best features—her mouth was too wide and mobile for symmetry, her nose too snubbed, her jaw too square. But Rob had seen her onstage, acting the part of a lovely but doomed woman, and had completely believed in the illusion of beauty she was able to create. Hing was one of the most talented actresses he'd ever seen.

"Thank you for waiting," he said. Taking in her wary expression, he smiled reassuringly. "Don't worry, Ms. Fly. I don't want a pint of your blood."

"Then what *do* you want, Doctor Spider?" she asked, sitting back, amused in spite of herself.

"I'm going to explain the whole thing to you," he promised. "Coffee or tea?"

"Tea, please."

The psychologist programmed the food selector in his office for a basket of muffins as well as Hing's favorite Oolong and his own coffee. Moments later he brought the tray back to his desk, and she helped him sweep aside some of the clutter.

Rob's sanctum was large, decorated in shades of tan, brown, and rust. A holo-tank dominated one wall of the space, and furniture designed for a variety of beings was pushed against the walls, ready to be moved into place to accommodate any visitor. On Friday nights, the place served as an impromptu theater, when Rob showed selections from his collection of antique films. Holo-posters from the "movies" hung on the walls, changing several times each day. At the moment *Casablanca, The Philadelphia Story,* and *The Attack of the Fifty-foot Woman* provided cheerful splashes of color.

Carefully balancing her cup and saucer, Hing turned sideways in her seat, draped one leg up over the chair arm, and relaxed with a catlike air of boneless grace. The vivid blue of her StarBridge jumpsuit clashed with the chair's rust-colored upholstery. "Okay," she said blandly, "talk to me."

Rob sipped his coffee, sighed appreciatively, then asked, "How would you like to have a new roommate?"

She shrugged. "I don't know. I've gotten used to having the whole suite to myself for the past six months. Now that it's my last year, I'm in and out a lot. We've just had tryouts for a new play, and I've got one of the leads."

Rob shook his head. "You try to cram three lifetimes into one, Hing. I don't know how you manage to keep up with your classwork."

She smiled cheekily. "But I do. You know I'll make a great Simiu translator. So . . . tell me about this hypothetical roommate."

Rob steepled his fingers. "Her name is Heather Farley, she's quite bright—*and* she's a very strong telepath, both as a projector and receiver. Abilities right off the scale." As he spoke, the doctor pulled up the girl's file, setting it to scroll slowly as he sat back, sipping coffee. "But she's got problems."

Hing raised her eyebrows, then nodded in silent comprehension why StarBridge Academy—with its extremely high standards for linguistic and diplomatic abilities, as well as personal integrity and stability—was interested in a "problem" student. Telepaths were all too rare—telepaths who were both effective receivers and projectors were extremely scarce.

The Cooperative League of Systems needed graduates from all three tracks at StarBridge Academy—translators like Hing who could communicate in several languages, interrelators who were trained to live on other worlds as ambassadorial or diplomatic personnel, and telepaths who used their skills when more conventional methods of communication failed.

In the past, telepaths, both human and alien, had proved invaluable in unknotting semantic Gordian tangles when problems arose in delicate negotiations between species belonging to the CLS. They also accompanied exploratory teams to the fringes of known space and beyond, to help establish peaceful communications with any newly discovered life-forms.

"Okay, so you've got a bright telepathic problem. Go on," Hing prompted. "Where do I fit in?"

"Heather's also the youngest human student—and, relatively speaking, the youngest student *ever*—to be admitted to StarBridge. I argued for her admission," Rob confessed, "because I was worried that if she didn't find something challenging to do with her skills, this girl would get herself into serious trouble."

Involuntarily, his eyes were drawn to the file, still slowly marching past. *Heather's skill with computers is undeniable,* the report from the Academy's Satellite School in Melbourne, Australia, asserted flatly. *Computer "tricks" played on teachers and other disliked authority figures occurred regularly until she came to us—for example, following her removal from her aunt and uncle's custody (instances of neglect and abuse are discussed under section labeled "Homelife"), Heather freely admitted that she "arranged" for this elderly couple, pillars in their fundamentalist church, to receive nothing but pornographic channels on their holo-vid viewer for weeks. Service technicians were unable to solve the problem, necessitating a memory-core wipe and replacement.*

Rob smiled reluctantly, shaking his head. He'd read and reviewed this file before, but he'd forgotten that bit. But his expression darkened at the next paragraph: *We do not know even now whether the power shutdown that plagued the school and delayed finals last year was sabotage . . . but only Heather, out of all the students and faculty, turned out to have complete backup cassettes of all data following the isolated power loss that managed to bypass all fail-safe levels simultaneously. When questioned about this, she told us she'd had a "hunch." Even the most painstaking analysis of the systems revealed nothing to link her with the shutdown. "System failure by unknown causes" remains the official diagnosis. But, still, we wonder . . .*

"Rob!" He jerked his head up, realizing that was the second time Hing had called his name.

"Sorry," he muttered, rubbing his eyes. "I missed out on my beauty sleep last night. What did you say?"

Hing regarded him over her teacup. "How old is Heather?"

Rob took a deep breath. "Eleven. Twelve at midterm."

The young woman groaned loudly. "Rob! What do I look like, a babysitter?"

"No, of course not," he hastened to assure her. "Heather will have to take responsibility for herself, just like any other student. But she needs a friend, Hing, and like many other kids, she's wary of authority figures. Like me." He spread his hands, palm up, and shrugged. "So I thought that someone the age of an older sister, someone who gets along well with just about everyone, might be just what she needs." He gave her a pleading glance. "C'mon, O Little Friend of All the World. Here's your chance to help someone out. It'll be good for your karma."

Hing smiled, albeit a bit reluctantly, at this reminder of *Kim,* an old book for which they shared a common fondness. Rob had shown her the movie version right here in this office, four years ago, when Hing was a freshman. Ever since then he'd kiddingly referred to her that way, after watching how easily she made and kept friends.

The student sighed, then nodded. Rob relaxed, realizing that he'd won her over. "She's had a rough time?" Hing asked.

Rob nodded assent, then hesitated, wondering what he could answer that would give Hing something to go on without compromising Heather's confidentiality. Another passage from the file caught his eye:

Heather Farley's telepathic index tops the scale. We cannot measure her innate ability. Extremely precocious intellectually, her intelligence approaches the genius range. This, coupled with

an artificial sophistication gained from her indiscriminate tele-
pathic contacts, makes her seem, at first encounter, older than
her years . . . Unresolved feelings of abandonment due to trauma
incurred from loss of maternal parent at age five have resulted
in stunted emotional development . . .

Maternal parent, Rob thought impatiently. *Why can't they*
just say "mother"? Her father, he remembered from his earlier
reviews, was still alive. If you could call it that. *. . . paranoid*
schizophrenic, with frequent violent psychotic episodes exacer-
bated by his telepathic ability . . . delusional, subject to hallu-
cinations . . . first institutionalized two weeks after death of his
wife, he has shown little improvement in the intervening years . . .
prognosis for recovery is poor . . .

Poor kid, Rob thought grimly. When he glanced at Heather's
birth date, he realized the girl was two months older than his
own daughter, Claire. Pity stirred in him again as he struggled
to find words to answer Hing. "Heather hasn't had it easy. Her
mother is dead, and her father—it's not possible for her to live
with him, for . . . health reasons. She lived with an aunt and uncle
for a while, but that didn't work out.

"Since then, there's been a succession of foster homes. She's
been shuffled around from pillar to post. After the mandatory
telepathic screening in school turned up her abilities, Heather
was offered the chance to go to Melbourne and try to pass the
profiles for StarBridge. She jumped at it, and she did very well
there. She's earned the chance to try to make it out here, and we
all want her to succeed."

Hing nodded slowly, and Rob saw from the expression in her
black eyes that she had indeed read between the lines of his
carefully worded explanation.

"So what does she need from me?"

"Mostly, a friend . . . someone like you, who's easygoing and
knows the routine. She'll need some leeway while adjusting,
but she'll be expected to follow the rules." Rob took another
swig of his coffee, then added, "What Heather needs, after the
time she's had, is stability in her life, and we'll try to provide
it here."

"Okay," Hing said, and for once there was no glint of laughter
in her eyes. "I'll do it. I owe you, Rob, like everyone else at this
school. You can count on me."

"Don't look so serious," Rob said, smiling at her gratefully.
"I'm not asking for your right arm. It's just that Heather's going
to need someone to show her around, keep an eye on her."

He buttered a muffin. "Someone . . . older, responsible, studious, trustworthy . . . a senior student who will be a good example, someone she can look up to . . ."

Hing had crossed her eyes and stuck out her tongue before he was halfway through. Rob chuckled. "Okay, yeah, I'm laying it on a little thick. Just be her friend, Hing. Help her out. Remember that if she makes it, with her telepathic abilities, she'll be a real asset to the school."

Hing nodded. Rob glanced at his watch, then made abrupt shooing motions. "Oops, that took longer than I thought. Hurry and catch up with Janet aboard the *King,* so you can ride back with the kid, take her under your wing, okay?"

She gave him a thumbs-up. "Tell 'em I'm on my way."

As she started out the door, Rob was seized again with the urge to mention that Serge LaRoche would be on that shuttle, too, but as he hesitated, she was gone with a last wave, and it was too late.

He shrugged and finished the dregs of his cold coffee, then poured himself another cup and hastily reviewed the end of Heather's file. *Early testing showed incipient megalomania coupled with a tendency toward compulsive fabrication . . .*

Psychologists' jargon, he thought morosely, taking a bite of muffin. *Why can't they just say that she's self-absorbed, extremely selfish, and lies a lot?*

Rob cheered up a little as he read the end of the Melbourne school's summary:

Since coming to Melbourne, there has been a definite and marked improvement. Heather's Social Adjustment Indices (especially the computer-linked tests) have risen significantly. Her telepathic ability, language aptitude, fluency in Mizari, and exceptional academic progress, coupled with her obvious determination to overcome her emotional problems, permit us to recommend her admission on a provisional basis . . .

"I just hope we can help this kid make it the rest of the way," Rob muttered to his small black cat, Bast, who leaped up onto his desk and stared interestedly at the remaining muffins. He put out a finger and rubbed the animal behind one ear, feeling as well as hearing the warm vibration of her purr.

Rummaging through his desk drawer, he unearthed a glittery ring made of a golden Mizari alloy that resembled a jeweled earclip. Fingering the telepathic distort thoughtfully, the psychologist sighed. *I hate wearing this thing. It'll give both of us a headache. But if it's necessary, so be it . . .*

Another thought made him smile. "We've got another secret weapon, Bast," he told the cat. "The only Avernian telepathic therapist in the galaxy. If Doctor Blanket isn't more than a match for Heather Farley, I'll swallow this distort."

Glancing at his watch again, he groaned aloud. "The faster I go, the behinder I get," he muttered. Keying his intercom, he instructed Resharkk', his assistant, to hold all calls, then resolutely dug into the files of the other incoming students.

Minutes later his intercom signaled. Someone had managed to override the lockout on his private line. "Shit!" Rob muttered as he answered.

The image of a young man with black, wavy hair and fine-drawn, handsome features coalesced. He flashed a wide, knowing grin at Rob. "I heard that," he said accusingly. "Is that any way to greet an old friend?"

Rob stared at him openmouthed, then laughed delightedly. "Jeff! I should have known. No one else could beat one of Janet's lockouts! Where have you *been*? It's been forever!"

Jeffrey Morrow was a former StarBridge student. He'd been nineteen back when the Academy opened, and was still the oldest freshman ever admitted. At the time, Rob had worried that Jeff was too old to adapt to alien languages and customs, but the young man's outstanding record at MIT and his single-minded determination had convinced the review board to accept him.

But over the next year, despite Morrow's hard work, it had become painfully obvious that he had no flair for languages. He was a whiz at math, and a magician with computers, but he couldn't even master Mizari, the official CLS language and the common tongue spoken at the Academy.

Rob had admired Jeff's persistence . . . but he'd admired him even more when the young man had finally accepted defeat and quietly left the Academy. He'd ached for the student as he'd watched Jeff swallow his pride and return to his father, owner of Horizons Unlimited, one of the largest human-run space engineering firms. Mike Morrow hadn't lost any time in triumphantly shoehorning his only son back into his engineering career.

"Forever's an exaggeration, but it's been more than a year since I've seen you," Morrow said. "I even managed to be on the crew that checked the radonium monitors six months ago, but they told me you were on vacation."

Rob nodded. "Mahree and Claire and I went to our cabin on Shassiszss. We had a great time, but I was sorry to find I'd missed you."

"How are they?"

"Fine. How is Angela?" Rob had been Morrow's best man, via holo-vid, at his wedding three years ago.

Jeff's features darkened, and his blue-gray eyes fell.

"What is it?" Rob exclaimed, alarmed.

"She's fine, that is, she's well, but . . . Rob, she left. She's divorcing me."

"Oh, Jeff, that's . . . I'm sorry to hear that," Rob said awkwardly. There wasn't any graceful way to respond to such news, he'd discovered that long ago. He chewed on his lower lip for a moment, then ventured, "Have you tried counseling?"

Morrow grinned crookedly, but it never reached his eyes; they were shadowed by pain and frustration. "Once a therapist, always a therapist. Rob, I wanted to go, but she wouldn't."

"Jeff . . . what happened? You seemed so happy . . ."

"I was never home, for one thing. And she wanted to start a family, and I'm just not ready for a big step like that." Jeff's mouth tightened. "I've got too much unfinished business to have time for a kid. I told her in a couple of years, but she didn't want to wait."

"I'm sorry," Rob said lamely.

"You can listen to me cry in my beer some other time. I know how busy you are. I just called to see about getting together for dinner."

"Dinner?" Rob stared blankly. "You mean you're *here*?"

Morrow nodded. "Close enough. I'm up at the station. Got a job to do."

"I thought you built space stations."

"I do. StarBridge Station needs an addition to its human-environment section, and I won the bidding war and got the contract. I'll be in and out over the next few months, making sure the job gets done right."

"That'll be great!" Rob said, careful not to let his first reaction show. He found it typically callous of Mike Morrow to send his son to oversee a job where he'd have to spend weeks staring at the site of his failure. He glanced at his clock, then shook his head. "Listen, Jeff, I hate to cut this short, but I've got a whole bunch of new kids coming in this morning, and I should go through these files one more time."

"I understand. We can catch up later," Jeff said. His gaze abruptly shifted, and he smiled faintly. "Here comes your shuttle. I recognize Janet's docking style. She used to give me heart failure every time she came in on manual like that. I was always sure that *this* time she'd miscalculated, and we were going to wind up splattered all over the station viewports."

"I know what you mean. About dinner . . . how about tomorrow?"

"Tomorrow is fine. I'll see you at eight. There's a new Japanese place up here. My treat, no arguments, okay?"

Rob grinned. "I never turn down a free meal." A sudden thought occurred to him. "By the way, Jeff, Serge LaRoche told me that H.U. funded the grant they received for the archaeological dig out at the Lamont Cliffs. You wouldn't have had anything to do with that selection, would you?"

Morrow shrugged. "I may have mentioned it to a few people."

"You did more than that," Rob said earnestly. "And don't think you're getting away without being thanked properly, Jeff. I know Serge and Professor Greyshine will want to tell you so in person, but . . . thanks. A lot."

Morrow glanced down, obviously uncomfortable at the mention of his generosity. "It was the least I could do, after my crew managed to move those artifacts while they were installing the new radonium monitors." He glanced back up at Rob with a wry smile. "Is your Archaeology Prof still cussing us for that?"

Rob shook his head ruefully. "Professor Greyshine is passionate about his work," he temporized. "But the grant no doubt helped."

"They still digging out there?"

"Every day," Rob said. "Since those were Mizari artifacts you uncovered, Ssoriszs has taken to hanging around the site, wanting to help any way he can."

Morrow laughed. "I'm trying to picture a Mizari using a shovel, but my imagination fails me." He nodded at Rob, then made a quick shooing-away gesture. "Get back to work. Don't forget, tomorrow at eight."

"I'll be there."

Hing Oun watched Docking Bay Six loom closer in the viewscreen, fighting the urge to cover her eyes. *This time we're not going to make it!* she thought, biting her lip. *I swear, we're going to—*

At the last possible second before crashing against the side of the docking cradle, the *King* straightened out, then came to a dead stop, perfectly aligned with the docking bay airlock. Hing let her breath out slowly, sagging back in her seat. *Someday, Janet*

Rodriguez, she thought. *Someday . . .*

Tight, speedy manual dockings were Janet Rodriguez's stock-in-trade, especially when she was late. There was a final soft lurch as their airlock mated with the station's, then they were docked. *How does she do it?* Hing wondered, shaking her head.

Unsnapping her seat harness, she stood up in the narrow aisle, pulling her blue StarBridge jacket on over her jumpsuit. Hing smiled, feeling a moment's flash of pride at her new fifth-year shoulder patches and collar insignia. The StarBridge logo—a rainbow bridge connecting two planets set against a star-studded background—was emblazoned on the back of her jacket, as well as on the pin she wore on the breast of her jumpsuit.

Softly humming an old Cambodian song her grandmother had taught her, she smoothed her hair, wishing for a mirror.

"Good morning," said a voice.

The young woman tensed, recognizing the warm baritone immediately. *Damn you, Rob Gable! I'll bet you knew Serge was on this trip,* she thought, even as she slowly turned to regard the man standing at the end of the passenger compartment, an uncertain smile flickering across his face.

Serge LaRoche was twenty-two, two years older than she. He was strikingly good-looking, with regular features, vivid blue eyes, and thick, ash-brown hair that he wore long and pushed back from his face. Tall—Hing's head had barely reached the top of his shoulder when they'd danced—LaRoche moved with an athlete's grace and balance. For two years running he'd been StarBridge's low-gee gliding champion.

"Serge!" she said, walking toward him, her hand out. Her theater training stood her in good stead, as she kept her features composed, showing only pleased surprise instead of the tension churning within her. "How are you?"

"Fine," he said, reaching out to shake hands. "It is a pleasure to see you again, Hing."

They had known each other for a long time; Hing felt, but did not react to, the inhuman smoothness and coolness of Serge's fingers as they grasped hers.

The memory of the first time they'd met filled her memory . . . she'd insisted on shaking hands, human style, instead of returning his Mizari bow. But, even though she'd already known that his hands were artificial, Hing hadn't been prepared for how inhumanly cool they were—and hadn't been able to conceal an involuntary wince.

Serge had grinned tightly, but his eyes had been filled with an old, cold anger as he'd held up his hands, wriggling the long, tapered fingers, letting her see the too-perfect cuticles, the faint sheen of nails that would never grow or chip. "Don't worry," he said lightly, with an ease born of many repetitions, "they were fed this morning."

"Oh, God," Hing stammered, her face flaming, "I'm so sorry! I didn't mean to—"

"Please . . ." His brittle composure softened, and a genuine smile replaced the strained grin. "Don't. It was my fault, I should have warned you."

"What . . . how . . ." she trailed off, stammering, even though she knew how it had happened.

"An accident with my parents' aircar, six years ago. I was fourteen." Serge had flexed his fingers, then snapped them. "They work very well . . . in some ways better than the original ones. I was very fortunate that the doctors were able to adapt Mizari technology so successfully when they made them for me."

Now, shaking his hand, all she could think about was how long it had been since they'd spoken or been alone together. Her heart had long since stopped jumping when she'd caught sight of him in the hallways, but you couldn't just wipe out six months as though they had never happened. "It's nice to see you, too," she said quietly, noticing that he still wore her gift, a small sapphire stud, in his left earlobe. She'd taken the ring he'd given her off the night of their breakup, and hadn't put it on since.

Serge smiled automatically at the pleasantry, but she could see the strain in it, and realized that he was far more nervous than she was. There was an eagerness in his eyes that made her drop her gaze and glance at her watch. "We'd better get going," she reminded him. "Those kids are probably swinging from the ceiling fixtures by now, waiting this long."

Serge nodded, then fell into step beside her in the featureless tube of the docking corridor. "Only the Simiu ones, if we are in luck," he said, matching her light tone. Although his English was extremely fluent, he spoke with the formality of one who is not a native-born speaker; despite his years at StarBridge, he'd never lost his Gallic accent.

Hing spoke French well herself, though she'd learned the language in Canada, and it had taken her months to get used to Serge's speech patterns and accent when he spoke his native tongue.

"What brings you to the station?" he continued. "Are you serving as an Orientation Guide now?"

"Heaven forbid," Hing said devoutly. "I'll leave that to you, I don't have the patience. No, Rob asked me to come up and meet my new roommate."

"Who is?" He checked the student roster he carried.

"Heather Farley."

Serge repeated the name to the Mizari voder he wore on his wrist, and Hing saw an image form on the tiny screen . . . round, freckled features, pale green eyes, and unruly carrot-colored curls. "She's rather young, isn't she?" Serge said.

"Only eleven," Hing replied. "I'm going to try my hand at being a role model." She grimaced.

Caught off-guard, Serge snorted, but managed to turn the sound into a fairly genuine-sounding cough. He was from Belgium, and his manners were perfect, touched with an Old European formality she'd always found charming. "So, what have you been doing these days?" he asked, evidently deciding that a change of subject was politic.

"Studying, trying to sandwich in a few extra credits in Simiu," she said. "I'm beginning to think I might like to work on Hurrreeah someday. Also, we're doing a new play, and I'm assistant director, as well as playing the embittered mother."

"Would I know it?"

"I doubt it. It's *They Don't Make Pennies Anymore,* by Eunice Goldberg. One of those really intense dramas that are a bitch to do, but if you do your job right, there won't be a dry eye in the house." She glanced up at him. "What about you?"

"I have been spending most of my time out at the dig with Professor Greyshine." His eyes flashed excitedly. "We might be on to something *very* big."

"Can you tell me about it?"

"We cannot say for certain as yet, because we still need more proof, but the Professor thinks that the artifacts we have in our possession may have been left by the Mizari Lost Colony. He believes they visited this asteroid after their departure from Shassiszss, over four thousand years ago."

Hing was impressed. "That's a long time . . ." she said. Four thousand years ago on Earth, the pyramids and Stonehenge were relatively new, slavery and war had characterized the most advanced human civilizations, and the great majority of people had spent their brief lives trying to propitiate the gods so they wouldn't starve or die of pestilence. By contrast, the large, reptilian Mizari had already possessed interstellar travel!

"This Lost Colony," she ventured, "don't they have any idea of where they went?"

Serge shook his head. "No . . . unless our site turns out to be that very clue. The preliminary dating we have done indicates that the time-span for these artifacts is right, but tests must be done in the lab before we will be certain. I wish we could uncover more artifacts. We've been at it for months, now, without locating a single new one. But the Professor says that often happens on digs—you make several discoveries, then weeks or months go by where you find nothing. It's odd, really . . . some things about this site simply don't add up . . . but, of course, this is my first dig, so I have nothing with which to compare it."

"I wish I could see a real dig," Hing said impulsively.

"Vraiment?" Even though he kept his voice casual, his slip into his native tongue revealed his excitement, his eagerness. Hing wasn't sure whether he'd noticed his lapse—people who habitually conversed in several different languages on any given day often switched back and forth in midsentence. But with Serge, she'd learned, such slips usually betrayed intense emotion and/or excitement. "I could arrange a visit."

Uh-oh, back off, Hing, she scolded herself. *Don't go giving him any wrong ideas.* "I'd love to go," she said cautiously, "but I'll have to see how rehearsals work out."

"I understand," Serge said, not meeting her eyes.

The silence between them hung heavy as they reached the end of the docking tube, then mounted the escalator to the station's multispecies lounge with its spectacular viewports. As they entered, Hing scanned the waiting crowd of new students for a flash of red hair.

The lounge was not really crowded, but it seemed filled because of the variety of beings waiting there. It looked like an *Intergalactic Geographic* documentary.

Hing caught a whiff of frying bacon, then the beach at low tide, followed by fresh blueberries as two Vardi engaged in conversation in their olfactory-based language. The two-meter-tall aliens, resembling giant stalks of purple-green broccoli, stood (since they weren't designed to sit) on the far side of the room. She was relieved to see that they were both wearing special voders so they could understand spoken language.

Next to the Vardi coiled a Mizari, his five-meter length filling his round, padded compartment. This one was golden-colored, with scarlet and black diamonds patterning his back and the masculine dorsal ridge. The tentacles haloing his wedge-shaped head barely stirred. Probably he was asleep, but with a Mizari's lidless eyes, it was hard to be sure.

A Heeyoon lay curled on a thick pad, long gray muzzle resting against furred forelimbs. The being's hot yellow eyes, long canine teeth, and bushy tail did nothing to dispel the lupine image. Heeyoons, however, walked erect, unlike Simiu, who moved on all fours.

The Asian student noticed that there was only one Simiu in the group—a burly male with a luxuriant chestnut mane flowing over his muscled shoulders.

Most of the room's considerable noise level came from the dozen human students who were clustered in front of the observation port, which provided them with their first view of StarBridge Academy, only forty kilometers away. The asteroid was shaped like an inverted, spindly cone, but from this distance, only the four lighted domes were visible, glowing against the blackness like white-gold coins.

Hing glanced quickly at each human face as they moved through the crowd to the opposite side of the lounge, conscious of the interested glances that followed them, taking in their jackets and uniforms.

Suddenly, beyond the viewport, a ship burst out of metaspace, trailing a muted explosion of rainbow colors. It was a magnificent sight, and no matter how many times she saw it, it always made Hing's heart beat a little faster. All her life she'd dreamed of going out into space to live, and sometimes she still felt as though she needed to pinch herself to convince herself she wasn't dreaming, she was really *here*.

When they reached the other side of the lounge, Hing glanced up at Serge. He shook his head at her. "I am missing one, by my count."

She nodded wearily. "Yeah, and I'll give you three guesses and the first two don't count as to the identity of our missing student." She looked at the doors leading from the lounge into the station grimly. "I'll go after her . . . you stall the crowd."

"Hurry," he said.

Hing made her way quickly into the human section of the station, figuring that was where the girl would have gone first. This area looked like a cross between a huge shopping mall and a spaceport, with arrival and departure boards flashing for attention. Shops lined the walls, and benches and food courts were clustered every few hundred meters.

If I were a kid just off a spaceship, where would I go? Hing wondered, then, on impulse, began checking the eateries. Hibernation made some people nauseated—others awakened ravenous. *And the younger you are, the quicker you tend to come out of it* . . .

Hing stuck her head into two fast-food places and drew a blank, but hit paydirt at the third, an ice-cream shop. There was a flash of red hair in the back, near the servos.

She went in for a closer look. Short—*even shorter than I am*— and rather pudgy, the girl in the back was intent on one of the food servos. Hing mentally compared her to the image in Serge's voder and nodded, satisfied that she'd found her quarry. *But what in the world is she doing?* the student wondered, watching the child. Heather had her pen in her hand and was muttering to it, never taking her eyes off the readouts on the servo.

"Hi," Hing said, trying not to sound too abrupt. "Need any help?" Heather ignored her. Suddenly the lights on the order terminal began to flash in time with the readouts scrolling past on the barrel of the girl's pen. Moments later the servo groaned, then delivered an enormous multicolored ice-cream concoction. Hing glanced at the screen on the wall, noting its charge readout: "Employee lunch—no charge."

"You must be hungry," Hing said dryly as Heather put the strawberry, fudge, and pistachio monstrosity down on a nearby table, then plopped herself down, spoon poised.

"Starved, if it's any of your business," the girl snapped. Shoveling a mouthful in, she smiled blissfully as her mood visibly improved. "Haven't eaten in four months," she added.

"You must have just come off a ship," Hing said blandly.

"Yeah, the *McIntyre*," the servo wizard admitted.

Hing pointedly tapped the "employee" readout. "Then you don't work here, do you?" she asked sweetly.

"And neither do you, lady." The girl gave her a contemptuous glance. Hing wondered whether the child had read her mind, or was just guessing. She was glad that the revealing StarBridge logo was on the back of her jacket. "You got a problem, or what?"

Hing's eyes narrowed. *Rob Gable, you snake-oil salesman, I'm never going to let you forget this.* "The problem is, what you just did is stealing," she pointed out evenly.

Heather shrugged. "Who the hell appointed *you* judge and jury, bitch? Who the hell do you think you are?"

Smiling evilly, Hing held out her hand. "Hing Oun, your new roommate at the Academy at StarBridge. Rob Gable sent me to escort you down to the school"—she glanced at her watch—"and if we don't leave *now,* we'll miss the shuttle."

Heather's mouth dropped open. A thread of hot fudge trickled out, rescued at the last moment by a swipe of her pink tongue. "Oh, *shit!*" she blurted. Her freckles disappeared as she blushed. "Uh . . . I'm sorry! I . . . uh . . . had no idea—"

"Obviously," Hing said dryly. "You won't have time to eat that. We have to go. The whole group's waiting."

"Just a couple of bites along the way?" Heather pleaded as she grabbed her dish and headed out the door after Hing.

"A couple of bites," Hing said as they reached the promenade level. "But it goes in the first recycler we pass."

"Okay . . ."

Hing did not glance around as they walked, concentrating on picking the swiftest, most efficient route back to the lounge. The considerably chastened Heather puffed as she kept up with the older student, but didn't complain.

When they got back to the lounge, Serge was already in midspeech. Hing, in the fore, waved unobtrusively at him and saw the worry line between his eyes smooth away. He nodded at her, still speaking in his flawless Mizari. " . . . be taking the shuttle down to the Academy in just a few minutes. We appreciate your patience, and apologize for the delay."

"He's *cute!*" Heather whispered in Hing's ear as Serge repeated his speech in English and Heeyoon.

Hing turned to her charge and smiled at the worshipful expression in Heather's eyes. "Serge is nice. I'll introduce you," she promised.

Heather gave her a speculative glance. "Did you ever go out with him?"

The older student shrugged noncommittally. "We dated, yes," she said, reminding herself to be patient with the kid.

Heather's pale eyes grew distant. "You did more than just *date* him," she said a moment later with a knowing grin. "A *lot* more."

Hing took a deep breath, reining in her temper. "Listen, Heather, I don't know what it's like for telepaths back on Earth, but here at StarBridge, there are rules about reading people's minds without permission. Please don't do that again."

The girl ducked her head, seeming genuinely abashed. "I'm sorry, Hing. Honest."

"Okay," the older student said. Glancing down, she noted that the child still held the melting remains of her ice-cream concoction. "I told you to pitch that," she said.

"You were going so fast I didn't have time to," Heather replied meekly.

"I *was* in a hurry," Hing admitted. Glancing around, she spotted a recycling chute in the nearest wall and pointed to it. "There's a chute over there."

"Okay," Heather muttered, and began threading her way through the crowd.

Hing turned her attention back to Serge, who was finishing up, " . . . and please make sure you have your carry-on luggage with you, then follow me." The crowd began flowing forward, moving toward the escalator and the docking tube.

"Hey!" That was Heather's voice, raised in indignant protest. Hing swung back around, catching a glimpse of that fire-brand hair. "Quit *shoving,* dammit! I almost—"

The girl broke off as she staggered backward, the ice-cream dish tipping disastrously. A moment later the deep roar of a Simiu voice raised in an outraged bellow filled the air, and Hing saw the big male Simiu sit back on his haunches, his violet eyes wide with surprise, then narrowing in fury. A lump of pistachio ice cream teetered over his right ear, then slithered down the side of his head, plopping into his perfectly groomed mane. The green streaks contrasted hideously with his chestnut fur.

With one hand, the Simiu brushed at the sticky mess, then stared horrified at his fingers. "You have dishonored me!" he snarled in his own language. To anyone who didn't understand Simiu, it sounded like the roar of a wild beast. "I demand the chance to regain my honor!" he growled, his enormous canine teeth flashing as his muzzle wrinkled in disgust. Bristling with rage, he advanced on Heather.

CHAPTER 2

♦

Excavations

As the furious Simiu stalked toward Heather, several human students began to titter nervously. "Shut *up*!" Hing commanded, pushing her way through the crowd. "You're insulting him!"

The laughter died away—except for Heather. She was still giggling as she backed away, eyes wide and fixed on the alien. "Hey," she blurted, "I'm sorry, but it's not *my* fault! Some asshole shoved me!"

"Heather, stop laughing, and *quit staring*!" Hing hissed at the girl. She grabbed the child's elbow, halting her. "Stand your ground, but don't show your teeth and *don't* stare at him—that's a challenge! Look down."

The Simiu's chestnut mane flared up from his head as he halted within striking distance of Hing and Heather. Deliberately, he wrinkled his muzzle, revealing his huge ivory canines, then raised one massive hand. It wasn't a full "challenge display," but there was no mistaking the implied threat. Seeing those teeth, that hand poised to strike, Heather gasped, suddenly terrified. Her mental "scream" tore into Hing's mind. *Hing! Help me! He'll kill me!* Only the woman's grasp on her arm kept the girl from bolting in panic.

Stand still, Heather, she ordered mentally. *I'll handle this. Calm down.*

Slowly, Hing let go of Heather, then stepped out in front of the child, between her and the Simiu. "Greetings, honored fellow student," she said quietly in her fluent Simiu. She was grateful for all the patient hours she'd spent mastering the clicks and growls of their speech.

Gracefully, fluidly, she made their ritual greeting gesture, touching her eyes, mouth, and chest, then extending her hand, fingers curled. She was careful not to stare directly at the alien. "I am Hing Oun. May I be honored with your name?"

The alien hesitated, then slowly, deliberately, squatted on his hindquarters, regarding her measuringly with his violet eyes. "I am Khuharkk'," he said finally. "And I am not honored at this moment. This rude, careless creature has insulted me, damaged my appearance, and *challenged* me."

The waiting lounge was utterly still.

"She is a child," Hing said. "What happened was an unfortunate accident, Honored Khuharkk'. Heather intended no dishonor nor disrespect. And, besides . . . how could someone so insignificant damage *your* honor?"

"She has dishonored me," the alien insisted. "She laughed at my disgrace."

"She intended no offense," Hing said, glancing behind her at the trembling girl. "It was an accident, and she is sorry."

"What concern is it of yours?" the Simiu growled. "Are you declaring yourself her honor-champion?"

"I trust that will not be necessary," Hing said quietly. *He's just embarrassed and mad,* she thought, hoping she'd gauged the alien correctly. *He won't push it to a real challenge.* "She is a child, and children need tolerance, is that not so? You have the opportunity to gain great honor here, by teaching this child the virtue of tolerance, starting with your own example."

"I am not convinced that she is capable of learning," the alien said, still sulky, but he was definitely beginning to relent; his flaring crest of mane relaxed. She felt a rush of relief.

"I promise that I will explain her error to her, and help her learn from her mistake," Hing said firmly. "In the future I am certain she will be more careful. May I have the honor of assisting you in restoring your appearance?"

After another long moment, the Simiu raised a conciliatory hand. "You have acted with honor, Honored HingOun. Consider the matter ended." Then slowly, respectfully, he made the greeting gesture to Hing. "I am Khuharkk'. I would be pleased to have you aid me with my grooming."

Hing turned and nodded reassuringly at Heather, who was still cowering behind her. "Stay here," she whispered. "It's okay now."

With Khuharkk' striding beside her, Hing turned and headed for the rest room. As she did so, she saw Serge, who was on the edge of the circle of onlookers. Catching her eye, he gave her an admiring smile and a quick thumbs-up.

"We'll be back in a minute," Hing said softly to him as they passed.

"We will wait," he promised.

Serge stood staring after Hing and the Simiu as they made their way through the crowd. Ruefully he shook his head. *She communicates so well,* he thought enviously. *I will never develop that rapport with aliens . . . or humans either, for that matter . . .*

It was more than the fact that Hing was majoring in the Simiu language. She had an undeniable knack with *people*—and it didn't matter whether those people were covered with flesh, fur, or scales. As he watched her turn the corner and disappear, feelings he'd thought dead for months welled up all over again, just as painfully as they ever had.

Serge swallowed, fighting down a surge of longing, experiencing again the hurt anger and terrible loneliness that had filled him that last night, when she'd packed her things and walked out of the suite they'd shared for six months.

The sound of a muffled sob made him turn. Heather Farley was standing in the midst of the muttering crowd, ice cream dripping down the front of her coverall. Angrily, she swiped at her tears with the back of her hand, leaving chocolate trails. Serge moved closer to her, unobtrusively waving the human students away. He whiffed an acrid, familiar odor as he reached her, and it was then that he noticed the dark stain between the legs of the girl's coverall and realized what had happened. *Pauvrette,* he thought, feeling a wave of pity.

Schooling his features, he gave no indication that he'd noticed her accident as he bent down to speak to her quietly. "Hello, you must be Heather Farley. I am Serge LaRoche. Are you okay?"

She shifted uncomfortably, legs pressed tightly together, blushing furiously. "Yeah, I guess . . ." she whispered. "But I—I've got this damned ice cream all over me . . ."

"Please, do not worry," Serge reassured her and, gently putting a hand on her shoulder, turned her toward the opposite side of the lounge from the direction Hing and the affronted Simiu had taken. He pointed. "There is a lavatory there, and you will also find a clothing servo inside. You go wash up. I will wait for you here. Okay?"

She nodded, not looking at him, and went.

Serge stood gazing after her, wondering why the devil the StarBridge Admissions Committee had decided to accept a child so young. Someone touched his arm, and he turned to find Janet Rodriguez. "Heard you had some excitement," she said dryly.

Nodding, he gave her a quick summary of what had happened. By the time he'd finished, Hing and Khuharkk' were heading toward them from the other rest room. "I have an idea," Serge said as they watched them make their way through the restless crowd of waiting students. "You and Hing accompany the group down to the *King* while I wait for Heather. On the ride back, you, Hing, and Khuharkk' ride in the passenger compartment. I will pilot, and keep Heather with me. That way we'll avert the chance of any further confrontations."

Janet nodded. "Good idea."

Quickly, without raising her voice, she herded the students together and, with Hing bringing up the rear, led them off down the docking tube.

They'd barely gotten out of earshot before Serge saw Heather returning. Face scrubbed, hair combed, she wore a freshly cleaned, dry coverall—and a black scowl. Her pale green eyes were as hard as jade marbles, and her mouth was a grim slash amid the freckles. "Where's that damned Simiu?" she demanded, glancing around.

"Khuharkk' and Hing have already boarded the shuttle," Serge replied. "Calm yourself, Heather . . . relax."

"The hell I will," she snapped. "The more I think about what happened, the madder I get. That damned . . ." she sputtered, "*monkey* was going to kill me! If it hadn't been for Hing—"

"Stop it," Serge broke in, his tone still quiet, but something in it made Heather obey. His blue eyes held hers. "Heather, if Rob Gable or any of the other instructors heard you speak about a fellow student in such a racist, demeaning manner, you would quickly discover yourself on the next ship back to Earth," he said flatly.

"You are at StarBridge, now, and you are expected to uphold the mission of the school—which is about establishing positive relationships between different species. You do not belong here if you cannot learn that." Seeing her pale, he spoke more gently. "I know Khuharkk' frightened you, and I am sorry for that. But you have to realize that you insulted him every bit as fully as if you had called him names before all the other students.

Appearance is terribly important to his people—you made him feel like a fool."

She took a deep, shaky breath, then her gaze wavered and dropped. "He had no right to growl and roar at me like that," she mumbled.

"He was speaking· in his own language. The Simiu tongue sounds like that to those of us who haven't learned to speak it," Serge pointed out. "Heather, I feel certain that Rob Gable and the Simiu counselor will discuss Khuharkk's behavior with him. But that is not your concern, understand?" He put a hand on her shoulder, gently. "I want you to promise me that you will not cause any further incidents—as much for your own welfare as for the Simiu's. Promise?"

She didn't look up. "I promise that I'll stay away from Khuharkk'," she finally said in a grudging tone. "I won't speak to him or go into the same room with him. Okay?"

Serge hesitated. "Eventually you are bound to find yourself in a situation where you must be polite to him," he pointed out. "StarBridge is a small asteroid."

The girl sighed, then she looked up, her green eyes direct. "I promise that if I ever have to speak to him again, I'll be completely polite," she said. "Okay?"

Serge nodded, relieved, and picked up Heather's small totebag. "That's fine. Now let's board that shuttle. We are a bit short of seats in the passenger compartment, so would you mind sitting up front with me while I pilot?"

She gave him a quick, incredulous glance, then began to smile. "Really? You mean it?"

"Mais oui," he said, giving her his most charming smile. "You are not subject to space sickness, are you?"

"Hell, no!"

Ssoriszs, the CLS Liaison for the Academy at StarBridge, lay coiled in the darkness of his room, far below the airless surface of StarBridge's asteroid, motionless and nearly silent. Only his breath came and went with the faintest of hisses. Lidless eyes fastened on the meditation disk before him, he willed the manipulatory tendrils haloing his head to stillness, then let his mind float free of all consciousness of his body.

The lack of light helped. Before him, the meditation disk turned lazily, barely seen holographic images swirling and flickering in its depths. The artists who created meditation disks swore that they did not place actual images of persons, places, or things into the depths of the disks. They maintained that the meditation disk only served to conjure what lay within the depths of the observer's own mind.

Ssoriszs saw spaceships in his disk.

He saw them frequently, more than any other vision. At times his dead lifemate's face would flash across his mind's eye, and sometimes the faces of his children that had gone to join her Beyond. Only rarely did Ssoriszs see the faces of the living.

Today, it was the ships again. A fleet of them, sleek and shining, braving the unknown stretches of the interstellar void. Ssoriszs knew who they were . . . Mizari who, millennia ago, had fled the homeworld of Shassiszss because they were not cherished, not wanted. Exiles, all of them, nearly four thousand years ago, now.

Including a full dozen of Ssoriszs' ancestors. The Esteemed Liaison was proud that he could trace his forebears back for over five hundred centuries. But there was one branch in his family tree that had been lopped off when barely more than a twig. Those ancestors had departed with what was now known as the Mizari Lost Colony.

Heritage, ancestors, and tradition were an important part of Mizari spiritual life. Those missing ancestors rankled Ssoriszs, making him feel incomplete, unfinished, in some small but vital way. What had become of them?

It was one of the elderly Mizari's fondest dreams to imagine that somewhere, in another part of this vast galaxy, he had relatives who were living and breathing offshoots from his family tree. Surely the Lost Colony was only misplaced—not truly lost!

He thought often of those so-distant cousins, imagining them alive and thriving, cradled perhaps in another of the galaxy's sheltering arms.

Centuries ago, the Mizari had begun the CLS when they had encountered first the Apis world, and then the Drnians. Now the ranks of the CLS had swelled to Fifteen Known Worlds. Trade flourished between the member planets, and despite inevitable conflicts, peace reigned. Ssoriszs frequently wondered about what his people had done when they had reached their unknown destination. What if the Lost Colony had somewhere established its own version of the Cooperative League of Systems? What if there was a rich flowering of culture and wisdom out there, somewhere?

In the eyes of his mind, Ssoriszs imagined the day when representatives of the two groups could finally meet, and talk.

There would be such a lot to catch up on—so much knowledge to be shared!

The elderly Mizari mentally pictured a youngster the same age as his only grandson—but as different from Zarshezz in mind and spirit as the night was from the day. This lad bore a strong resemblance to himself, with a pale green body and bold emerald and amber diamonds on his back. The image formed before Ssoriszs in the meditation disk, staring back at him with golden eyes that mirrored his own. Within the cells of both of their bodies would be a genetic signature traceable back to a common ancestor, long ago.

Greetings, he thought, mentally bowing to his imaginary cousin. *I am Ssoriszs, and I thank the Star-Spirits that they have allowed me to live to see this day! May I be honored with your name?*

And then they would converse, as Ssoriszs and Zarshezz had seldom been able to talk, openly and frankly. They would share knowledge and grow together in wisdom . . .

Ssoriszs did not smile—his mouth was not constructed for it—but his tendrils waved languidly and he hissed softly with pleasure as he imagined how it would be. Then, slowly, deliberately, he began bringing his consciousness back to normal functioning levels.

"Lights," he murmured finally, and the room, hearing even such a soft sibilant whisper, obeyed.

The Liaison's living quarters were furnished with padded rods and brackets protruding from the walls; Mizari enjoyed draping themselves over such extrusions. There were also several padded cubicles that served as resting places—his people's equivalent of chairs. In the bathroom, a refreshing hot mud bath waited in the large circular depression in the floor.

In addition to Mizari furnishings, Ssoriszs kept some off-world furniture for the comfort of visitors. There was an armchair for Robert Gable, and one of the padded, ottomanlike cushions that Chhhh-kk-tu favored, for Kkintha ch'aait, StarBridge Academy's Administrator. The three were old friends by now, having worked together for many years to make their shared dream of StarBridge Academy a reality.

Ssoriszs had excellent taste, as well as an eye for color; the suite was decorated in soft shades of green, gray, and rose. The silvery carpeting the Liaison now slid across was specially textured to provide the best surface for the gripping scales on his underbody.

Filled with a renewed sense of inner peace and resolve, Ssoriszs flowed over to the computer link. "Connect me with Professor Greyshine," he said.

When the Heeyoon's image cleared, Ssoriszs realized that his call had awakened the archaeologist from what had evidently been a most sound and enjoyable nap. Greyshine's greenish-yellow eyes were still slightly unfocused as he stared at Ssoriszs. "Greetings," he said after a moment. The slurred sibilants of Mizari were understandable but slightly distorted, produced as they were by a being with a long, furred muzzle. "Your pardon, Esteemed One. I was . . . resting."

"A thousand apologies," Ssoriszs said hastily. "I regret disturbing you. I was just wondering . . . what were the results of the additional dating tests you ran on the artifacts? Did they confirm our hypothesis?"

The Professor wrinkled his muzzle as he thought. "The artifacts that we have been able to date *are* from the correct time period," he admitted finally, then waved a forepaw at the Mizari to forestall his excited response. "Other tests are needed before I can definitively state that the objects found were brought to this asteroid by your Lost Colony, Esteemed One!"

The Mizari hissed softly. "Of course. I understand. But the possibility is growing."

"It seems to be, but I would not want to make premature assumptions," the Heeyoon said. His voice was gruff, deliberately quelling, but the CLS Liaison did not miss the answering flash of excitement in his eyes. *He, too, believes that we have found a vital link in tracing the fate of the Lost Colony*, Ssoriszs thought.

"What other tests will be necessary?" he asked aloud.

"We will need to test for ion patterning and magnetic resonances that would indicate the location of their manufacture on your homeworld. If we can pinpoint the location, that will help a great deal."

"Yes, yes it would," the Mizari agreed, restraining himself with an effort.

"But that will not be the end of the testing," Greyshine warned. "We must also attempt to definitively link the artifacts to artists and craftsmen who were part of the Star Seeker Sect."

"What kinds of tests would that require?" Ssoriszs asked.

"Examinations and computer analysis to check for makers' marks, for one thing. And some of the sealed items—such as the Sharizan globe—still contain air samples from the time of their making. We can look for traces of the incense traditionally burned by the Star Seekers during their daily devotions. But to extract samples of that ancient air will require a probe insertion, which is a delicate task that, no matter how carefully done, will cause unavoidable damage. I want the team of specialists from Shassiszss to handle that test."

"Damage the Sharizan globe?" Ssoriszs' tendrils waved in distress. "But that would be a tragedy!"

"Calm yourself, Esteemed One. The hole required for the test would be nearly microscopic in size . . . undetectable to unaided vision," the Professor assured him. "It would not ruin the aesthetic value of the globe. But I am a field archaeologist, I do not have the laboratory expertise to make a test on such a delicate object; I prefer to wait for those who do."

"That seems wise," Ssoriszs said, relieved. "I spoke to Rizzshor yesterday, and he assured me that their grant should be coming through any day now. Then it will take another week for the Mizari portion of the team to assemble and leave Shassiszss."

"That is good news," Greyshine said. "They will have better equipment than I possess. Better scopes, a full-size sifter, there are so many things we need! More equipment, more hands"—his muzzle crinkled mischievously—"or more manipulatory tendrils, as the case may be. Only then will we be able to do the most thorough job of investigating the site and uncovering any additional artifacts."

"It is regrettable that nothing has turned up except for the discoveries the engineering crew uncovered and moved," Ssoriszs said. "I am still puzzled that you have not found a star-shrine. The Star Seeker Sect should have had a star-shrine."

"It is entirely possible that they did have one, and we simply have not located it," Greyshine pointed out. "We have mapped and gridded only half the site, and analyzed less than half of that. Not to mention that there are many subsidiary caverns still unexplored. With only Serge as a full-time assistant, it has been slow work," he finished, sounding a bit defensive. "The only reason we are not at the site now is that he was called upon to serve as an Orientation Guide."

"I fully understand and sympathize," Ssoriszs was quick to reassure the Heeyoon. "If only I were trained, then I could be of more help to you!"

Greyshine cocked his head at the Mizari thoughtfully. "Esteemed One, I believe that you are more anxious for our discovery to be linked to the Lost Colony than I am." The Heeyoon's eyes were bright with curiosity. "And that strikes me as odd, for making such a discovery would insure my place among the great archaeologists of all time—Blackmoon Runner of my people, Zhoriszen among yours, Schliemann and Emerson of Terra. Why is this of such intensely personal interest to you, if I may inquire?"

Ssoriszs' manipulatory tendrils twitched with emotion as he regarded the other gravely. "You are correct as to my interest being intensely personal, Esteemed Professor. Proving a link between your dig and the Mizari Lost Colony would assure your future . . . but for me, it would return to me a piece of my past that I had thought forever lost. And we Mizari treasure our past . . . though that was not always so," he finished regretfully.

"Why *did* they leave?" Greyshine asked. "The records mention spiritual and ethical conflicts, but there was no mention of violence between the Star Seekers and the rest of your homeworld."

"Violence!" Ssoriszs shook his head—a gesture he'd picked up from Rob Gable years ago. "Thank the Star-Spirits, it never came to that, Greyshine. But the Seekers were ridiculed for their beliefs, made to feel unwelcome on their own world. Eventually they felt so unwanted that they elected voluntary exile from their world and their people." He sighed, his tendrils rippling mournfully. "Their departure marked a failure for my people, Professor. One of our worst."

The Heeyoon's tongue lolled slightly from his mouth as he listened, fascinated. "I have never before heard the story related from that viewpoint, Esteemed One. And, forgive me, but it seems a trifle . . . removed . . . from our time to cause you personal distress."

Ssoriszs hissed softly, ruefully. For a moment he was tempted to confess to the Heeyoon that his family was far away, removed from him in thought and spirit, as well as distance, and that he longed to discover new kin—to try again with them to forge bonds of blood, of understanding. He yearned for an end to his loneliness. But he only said, "I am very old, Greyshine, and the elderly often fixate on strange things—is that not true for your people, as well?"

"It is," the Heeyoon admitted. "It seems to be true for many different species. Young Serge reports the same thing among humans."

"I know," Ssoriszs said, straightening his body. He made a graceful wave of apology and dismissal with his tendrils. "Please accept my apologies for disturbing your rest, Professor. I will let you know the instant I hear from Rizzshor. In the meantime, good fortune in your digging."

"Many thanks, Esteemed One," the Heeyoon replied.

Ssoriszs terminated the connection, then thoughtfully made his way out of his quarters, down the hall of the instructors' wing, then into the lift. Reaching the surface level, he slithered along the corridors until he came to the Observation Dome. Coiling himself in the middle of it, he stared thoughtfully up at the profusion of stars—stars of all colors and degrees of brightness—wondering, for the thousandth time, whether the archaeological dig out at the Lamont Cliffs might solve the ancient mystery of the fate of the Lost Colony.

Silently, Ssoriszs invoked the Spirits of the Stars and the Sands, praying that it would.

Securely strapped into the copilot's seat aboard the *King*, Heather Farley watched Serge at the control panel, admiring the quick, deft fingers on the controls as he eased the shuttle out of the docking cradle. Suddenly her eyes narrowed. Something about the shape and texture of the young man's hands was . . . wrong. Heather frowned. The fingers—long and perfectly tapered. Too perfect. The skin texture—even-grained, without blemish. Again, too perfect. The nails, smooth and unsnagged—perfect.

The *King*, now free of the cradle, swung around in space, propelled by tiny taps on its steering jets, then Serge reached over to boost the shuttle's thrust as they eased away from StarBridge Station. As he did so, his sleeve pulled back a little, and Heather could clearly make out the spot above his wrist where the too-perfect covering ended and human skin began. The hairs above that spot were coarser, slightly darker, and crushed where the sleeve had rested.

But the hairs below . . . fine, golden, and perfect.

Suddenly Serge's hands froze on the controls, and Heather looked up to find his eyes fixed on her face. She'd been caught staring—there was no point in denying it. "Serge," she said quietly, "what—what happened to your hands?"

"I had an accident when I was a little older than you," he replied tersely. "I was working on my parents' aircar—the timing was a bit off—and I made a mistake. A big mistake."

"Oh, shit, I'm sorry," she whispered. Usually, she couldn't have cared less about other people's tragedies, but Serge had been so *nice*—and he was so handsome. It hurt her to think of how it must have been, but she could see it wouldn't be a good idea to ask. Instead, Heather *reached*—

—and encountered his pain, as raw and fresh as the day it had happened, the pain that lay buried in his mind, far below the conscious level. For a moment she was *there,* on that fateful day, she *was* Serge, hearing the hissing sputter, then seeing the sudden white-hot flare from the engine. A heartbeat later she/he was staring with disbelieving horror at two charred, oozing horrors that had replaced her/his hands. Pain seared along the deepest fibers of her/his mind, pain that was every bit as white-hot and blazing as the original blast.

Pain . . .

As the echo of that agony resonated in Serge's mind, Heather quickly withdrew, not wanting to share any more of that particular memory. Despite her inward wince, she was experienced at keeping knowledge gained by telepathic snooping off her face.

But Serge was staring at her, startled. *Did he feel that?* she wondered, but no. Touching the surface of his mind lightly, she was reassured—and amused—to find that it was her language that had startled him. "I'm sorry, I shouldn't have been staring," she amended.

"That's okay." Serge shrugged. "I should have warned you."

I know why you didn't, Heather thought. *You can't stand to talk about it, any more than you can stand to think about it . . .*

As she cast about for a way to change the subject, the viewscreen suddenly lighted up. A heartbeat later a ship burst out of metaspace in a rainbow blossom of colors. Heather gasped in astonished delight. "That's beautiful!"

"When I first came to StarBridge, one of the things I missed most about Earth was sunsets," Serge confided, setting their course and speed. He smiled reminiscently. "I still miss them, but now I would miss that sight even more if I went back to Earth."

"Where are you from?" Heather asked, sitting up a little straighter. Never in her short life had an eligible male paid this much attention to her, much less anyone like Serge. He was different . . . older, polite. Real class. His faint continental accent was exotic, charming, especially in light of his mellow baritone. Not to mention his looks . . .

"Eurostate. Belgium province," he said, then glanced over at Heather as he completed the last of his navigational checks, then switched on the automatic. "And you?"

"OldAm."

"Which metroplex or city?"

Now it was Heather's turn to shrug. "I was born in Baltimore. After that, it was Kaycee, Deecee, Seattle . . . then New York, just before I left for Melbourne."

He glanced over at her quickly, and without even extending her telepathic sense, Heather could read his surprise, then a surge of pity. The emotion angered her, though her expression remained neutral. *I don't want your pity,* she thought, *and you can take your bleeding heart and shove it up your—*

"Look!" Serge was pointing. "There is StarBridge in the center of the viewport. That is your new home, Heather."

The girl stared in fascination, forgetting her irritation. Star-Bridge Academy showed as several large lighted circles in the middle of a dark, irregular mass whose shape was only discernible because it blotted out the background stars.

Home, she thought, *could it be?* She bit her lip, then smiled without humor. *At least I'm billions of klicks away from Aunt Natalie and Uncle Fred. They'll never leave Earth, those chickenshit assholes. And I'll never go back. At least I've seen the last of them.*

"How big is the asteroid?" she asked.

"It is cone-shaped," Serge replied, "and the part we are viewing is the wide, flat top of the cone." He traced an irregular shape in the air. "The surface where the Academy is located is about two hundred and seventy kilometers across. Those four domes are the shuttle dome, the Arena—which is an auditorium that can be converted for all kinds of sports—the botanical garden, and the Observatory Lounge. But most of the school extends deep underground."

Heather's eyes narrowed. "Hey, I see more lights, little ones. What's over there?" She pointed to a spot to the left of the school.

Serge smiled. "That is our archaeology dig. I have been helping Professor Greyshine excavate some caves in the Lamont Cliffs about twenty kilometers from the school." Enthusiasm tinged his voice. "We are hoping to make some exciting discoveries."

"Yeah? Like what?" She remembered reading articles in *Intergalactic Geographic* about archaeological sites. Frankly, it didn't sound like much fun, all that digging and sifting.

"More artifacts, for one thing," Serge said.

"You mean you've found some already?" Heather's mind was off and running, presenting her with vivid images of Tutankhamen's famous golden mask and other treasures she'd seen on holo-vid programs.

"Unfortunately, we didn't uncover them ourselves," Serge admitted. "The engineers who come to StarBridge to monitor the radonium deposits actually found them—in some cases, they literally stumbled across them. They opened up a cavern to install some new monitors, and there they were, lying half-buried in dust. Our tests indicate those objects are almost five thousand years old." Serge's handsome features darkened. "Unfortunately, in their ignorance, the engineers picked the objects up and handled them, so much valuable information about them was lost."

"Why?"

"If a find is moved, the archaeologist loses the chance to study where it was lying, and how. A trained person can examine an object in situ and tell a great deal about how long it has been there, whether it was deliberately buried or simply discarded . . . things like that."

"What kind of stuff did you find?" Heather was still clinging to her vision of bejeweled goblets and golden idols.

"Six artifacts—so far." Serge hesitated, but seeing that her interest was genuine, he shrugged and said, "I suppose there is no harm in telling you. We have been waiting for the archaeological team from Shassiszss to officially unveil the finds, so this must stay between ourselves, okay?"

Heather solemnly crossed her heart.

"There is a Sharizan globe, which is a small diagnostic instrument resembling a crystal ball. It's surrounded by a silvery rim of circuits and instrumentation. Mizari still use them in eye examinations. Sharizan globes have bioelectronic components built into the rims of the magnifying lenses, and they can analyze the cellular structure of the Mizari eye. The globe is beautiful as well as useful."

Heather held up a finger. "That's one."

"There is also a partial casing from a Mizari environmental field—what they use instead of spacesuits, you know?"

Heather nodded. "I've seen them."

"It is simply a piece of the Mizari building alloy, with ripped edges. From examining it, we are speculating that the chamber may have been subject to explosive decompression at some time. Which may explain why the artifacts were not retrieved—they escaped, then never reopened that cavern." He made a minute adjustment to their course. The asteroid was growing ever larger in their viewscreen.

"The number three artifact," he continued, "is the Slee-kar, an ancient ceremonial tracing tool used in Mizari religious rites. It looks rather like a blue-bladed dagger, but has no hilt. There is supposed to be a carved, curved grip, but that has broken off, and we have not yet found the second piece."

"Do you think you will?"

He sighed. "I do not know. I am beginning to doubt it. There's also a songharp, one of the ceremonial-style ones. It is intact, fortunately, and quite beautiful, but the top is bent."

None of Serge's precious artifacts sounded all that valuable to Heather. *But maybe he's saving the best for last.* "What else?"

"A can of ration pellets and a fragment from a traveler's waste-disposal bag," Serge finished, then glancing at Heather's crestfallen face, he laughed softly. "Not very glamorous, those last two, are they?"

"No," the girl admitted. *Frankly, none of them sound glamorous,* she thought sourly. "What's the songharp like?"

"Very similar to modern ones, actually. But this one was made by a master craftsman, we believe. Sallzor lived thousands of years ago, and was one of the most famous songharp makers ever. Rather like the Mizari version of Stradivarius."

"Who?"

"A famous violin maker who lived hundreds of years ago on Earth. Some of the violins he made are still in use in orchestras. They have a tone that remains unmatched."

There was something in his voice as he spoke of musical instruments . . . a hint of some old hurt, old longing. Heather was sensitive to nuances and hidden meanings—she'd had to be, because Uncle Fred had an explosive, unpredictable temper. She watched Serge closely. "Can the songharp still be played?"

He shrugged. "Perhaps . . . if the warped top could be straightened, or if it could be tuned to compensate . . ."

"Have you ever played one? You play, don't you?" she asked, certain that she'd guessed right.

For the first time since she'd met him, Serge's eyes narrowed with anger. "Heather, have you been reading my mind?"

The girl shook her head vigorously. "No, Serge, I swear I haven't!" *And I didn't,* she thought, mentally crossing her fingers, *at least not about this . . . yet.* "It was just that . . . there was something in your voice when you spoke about music, and I thought . . . I wondered . . ."

Slowly his tight shoulders relaxed, then he nodded. "You are very perceptive," he said quietly. "I used to play songharps, and other instruments. But that was a long time ago. I don't play these days."

It was there, on the surface of his mind, a memory . . . Heather touched it effortlessly and received a sharp image of a younger Serge, wearing a funny outfit with a long-tailed black coat and a white bow tie, walking onto a stage. Spread out before him was an excited, glittering audience, applauding as he bowed, then hushing quickly as he seated himself at a shining grand piano in the center of the stage. He raised his hands, concentrating, feeling the music flow through him, his mind filled with the liquid beauty and passion of Rachmaninoff, his fingers tingling with anticipation. Then, bending forward, he touched the keys, and was enveloped by the music, the music . . .

Heather blinked herself back to reality. Serge, concentrating on the controls again, hadn't noticed her lapse. She was shaken by the intensity of that memory. *Damn, that's awful,* she thought. *To be that good, and then not be able to play again . . .*

"Is it hard work, digging in those caves?" she asked after a moment.

Serge hesitated. "Not exactly. We have instruments that do much of the physical work. We no longer have to do much actual digging. But we must be very careful, because we are working above one of the largest deposits of radonium in the whole asteroid."

Heather knew that radonium was the stuff that powered spaceships and space stations. Everyone knew that, just as everyone knew that the Mizari had donated this asteroid, with its valuable radonium deposits, as a site for StarBridge Academy. The school had deliberately been situated out in deep space, rather than near any planet, because the Academy was supposed to remain independent of political influence.

"Isn't that dangerous?" she asked, feeling a tinge of anxiety for Serge. "Radonium isn't something that you can take chances with. You could get radiation poisoning, or cause an explosion."

"We are very careful," Serge reassured her. "Radonium is not terribly dangerous. It is radonium-2 that is so hazardous and volatile. And the radonium at StarBridge is stable; they monitor the deposits constantly."

"But if you're right on top of it—"

Serge smiled at her. "Do not concern yourself, Heather! We truly are very careful. The radonium deposit is, at a minimum, five meters below the floor of the cavern, and we are shielded by solid rock." He pointed to the viewscreen. "You are missing our final approach."

Heather watched in fascination as the *King*, now controlled by the docking guidance beam, swooped toward the surface of the asteroid. She tensed as the shuttle seemed to drop too close to the jagged, crater-scarred surface, but a second later they were gliding slowly into the hangar dome, then settling gently to a perfect landing.

Serge finished shutting down the controls, then keyed the intercom. "Welcome to the Academy at StarBridge. Passengers may unstrap at this time. Please check that you have all your carry-on bags or containers before leaving the shuttle."

Heather released her safety harness, then started to stand up, but Serge raised a hand to forestall her. "One moment," he said. "If you will wait for me to finish the last of my systems shutdowns and my log entry, I will help you find your assigned room."

He really likes me! He wants to spend more time with me! Heather thought for an exhilarating instant, then she glanced at the viewscreen again and realized why he'd made his offer. The screen now showed the shuttle's ramp, and Khuharkk' and Hing were just debarking. *Shit,* the girl thought disgustedly, *he just wants to keep me away from that Simiu. He doesn't want any more trouble.*

Serge had followed the direction of her gaze, and when he turned back to regard Heather, his blue eyes were intent. "Heather . . . remember your promise."

She hadn't forgotten her carefully worded statement. *Oh, I remember, Serge,* she thought, expertly concealing the anger still seething within her. *And I'll keep that promise—to the letter. But, fortunately, I don't have to speak to Khuharkk' or spend a single nanosecond in his presence to get my revenge. That damned monkey will be sorry he ever left his homeworld, and that's a promise, too.*

Heather Farley smiled sweetly at Serge. "I remember," she said, tracing her fingers across her flat chest in a quick X. "Cross my heart."

CHAPTER 3
♦
Plans, Grids, and Plots

Serge had a difficult time getting through his Intro to Archaeology course the next morning. Usually he enjoyed teaching—and was good at it—but today it was a real effort to concentrate on his students. He kept seeing Hing's face in his mind, remembering how she'd confronted Khuharkk' . . . so calm, yet resolute.

Intro was a popular course, and he'd been assigned one of the large classrooms that was half laboratory. Normally, Serge and his class spent much of their time in the laboratory, but today the students were presenting their first reports of the term, so they met in the classroom portion. Serge sat in the back, listening, keying notes for grades and ideas for tests into his computer link, resolutely not glancing at his watch.

The Mizari who had been giving his report on the development of Egyptian art during the reign of Akhenaton finally finished with a last flourish of his manipulatory tendrils, and Serge straightened, nodded. "Thank you, Sarrhezz. I have seen Tell-el Amarna, the Heretic Pharaoh's city and final resting place, and you gave a very vivid and accurate portrait of it. Your visual references were particularly effective." He glanced around at the class. "Who wishes to be next?"

Lisa Castillo, a tall, heavyset girl with sparkling dark eyes and curly brown hair, waved her hand. Serge nodded to her, and she rose and launched into her report, which compared early Terran pottery types from the Old World and the New. She'd done a nice job researching the subject, her visual presentation was outstanding, and the accompanying text gave just enough information to be interesting and lively. Unlike some students, she didn't bury her audience in dry facts and figures. She'd even taken the time to shape and fire a fairly good replica of a Nasca vessel to illustrate one of her points.

The last student to speak was Nightsinger, a Heeyoon. He reported on recent excavations on Drnia that had uncovered a totally new dynasty that had flourished three thousand years ago. Serge noted that the material was well researched, but that the organization needed work. Nightsinger was bright and creative, but he tended to be scatterbrained. Serge listed suggestions for improvement and made a note to call the student in for a conference.

As Nightsinger returned to his pallet on the floor, where he sat on his haunches, ears pricked alertly, Serge walked up to the front of the class and raised a hand for attention. "Thank you, Nightsinger. It is always exciting to hear about brand-new discoveries in the field. The dig at Kal-syr is helping to write a new page in Drnian prehistory."

He paused to be sure he had their full attention. "I am certain that all of you recall our last session, when Anatoly asked whether our class could visit the Lamont Cliffs dig, as the Intermediate and Advanced Archaeology classes have done. After conferring with Professor Greyshine, he and I have decided that a field trip to the Lamont Cliffs would be beneficial for this class, also."

The students' reaction was gratifying and immediate. Khuharkk', here on his first day of classes, voiced his approval with several barking yelps. The two Mizari hissed softly, their fangs folded back. The humans clapped and stamped their feet.

After a moment's noisy approbation, Serge waved again for quiet. "I am glad that you are pleased. We will announce the scheduled date by the end of this week. However, I must caution you—anyone wishing to go on this trip must first have passed the minimum spacesuit competency requirements." He went on to detail the requirements, then advised any students that needed certification to schedule lessons and testing with Janet Rodriguez.

By the time he was finished, class was over. Free at last! Serge hastily thrust his notes and computer link into his case, then plunged into the crowded corridor. Yesterday at about this time he'd escorted Heather to her room, and it would only be natural, he told himself, for him to stop by and see how she was doing.

He crossed his fingers that Hing would be there, too.

Last night he'd barely slept at all. Memories had filled his mind, repeating over and over in a chaotic whirl of images. The first time he and Hing had met, at the Spiral Arm, the Academy's student hangout. The time that she'd done Lady Macbeth and he'd designed and constructed the scenery for the play. Their first kiss, backstage after opening night. Dates, walks in the botanical garden, trips in the shuttle up to StarBridge Station for dinner or a show, shopping together, the time he had won the low-gee gliding championship for the second year running and Hing had come running up to him as he'd stood clutching his trophy . . .

Most vividly of all, he recalled the first time they'd made love. Self-conscious about his hands, he'd been afraid to caress her skin or even touch her clothes to undress her, though he'd known that was what she wanted. It was his first time, and she had to have realized that—just as he'd been sure that it *wasn't* her first time.

As he'd hesitated, she had kissed him tenderly, solemnly, then gave him an impish grin and ostentatiously linked her fingers behind her neck. "No hands," she announced. "Anyone using hands loses the game."

"What game?" Serge asked, amused despite his apprehension.

"The one I just invented," she declared, leaning toward him. Slowly, hesitantly, Serge followed her example . . .

They hadn't been able to play the "game" long, but by the time they abandoned it, laughing and gasping, it hadn't mattered anymore. Things had been fine—better than fine. Wonderful. Serge had never felt so *right,* so in accord with the universe. It had been like playing perfect music . . .

But step by step with the good times, the bad memories had kept pace, making him toss and turn; words he should have said, things he should have done, statements and accusations he would give anything to take back. He'd been a fool to let her go, to drive her away, a stupid, stupid fool, and that lesson, learned every night for the past six lonely months, was not one he could or would forget.

But yesterday, Hing had smiled at him, at first diffidently, then, when he'd escorted Heather to her room, with real warmth. And for the first time, he'd thought that maybe it didn't have to be over . . . maybe, if he were patient, more willing to share, maybe he could get her back . . .

Maybe . . .

Checking his watch, Serge muttered a Heeyoon imprecation under his breath (roughly translated it meant: "may parasites torment thee in midsummer") because he was running late. Quantum Physics started in fifteen minutes, and the class was not one he could afford to cut. He quickened his stride until he was nearly running down the corridor.

Even though his official status at StarBridge Academy was Assistant Instructor, Serge still attended classes at the Academy—though he'd stopped kidding himself over a year ago that he'd ever become an interrelator. He'd had to recognize that he simply didn't have the empathy, patience, and stability to live on an alien planet as a career diplomat . . . even though his language skills were excellent and his grades in the top five percent.

For one thing, the young man's Social Adjustment Index was too low, and for another, Doctor Blanket said he wasn't ready to take on an assignment. That had clinched it, because no would-be interrelator graduated from StarBridge until Doctor Blanket pronounced him, her, or seloz (the Mizari pronoun that was used for neuters) ready.

At first Serge had considered leaving the Academy, but there wasn't anything else he wanted to do. His parents had never forgiven him for not pursuing his music career; he couldn't face returning to their silent recriminations. In his years at StarBridge, the school had become home . . . Rob, Janet, and the other staff were now his family.

So Serge had stayed on, serving as an Orientation Guide (the best one they'd ever had, Rob had told him). His interest in archaeology (he'd minored in it) had led to his becoming Professor Greyshine's teaching assistant when the Heeyoon had arrived a year ago. He'd done so well that for the past eight months Serge had been teaching the intro-level courses himself. Following Horizons Unlimited's discovery of the artifacts, both archaeologists spent every free moment out at the dig. For the first time since his accident, Serge had felt that he was making a real contribution.

As he neared Hing's room, Serge had to force himself to keep striding quickly. His heart was pounding, and not from the brisk walk. *Perhaps she's not here . . .* It was possible, though he'd checked her schedule, and knew there were no play rehearsals held this early in the day. *Perhaps she'll be angry when she sees me . . . perhaps she will think I am pushing her . . .*

Giving himself a mental shake, he keyed the door. *She was glad to see me, I know she was. Just say hello, and inquire how*

Heather is . . . she cannot possibly think you are overstepping by merely asking . . .

"Who is it?" the intercom inquired. It was Hing's voice, and Serge's mouth went suddenly dry as he identified himself.

The door slid open halfway, and she was there, her hair, not yet braided for the day, flowing over her slender shoulders and down her back like an ebony waterfall. "Hi," she said with a faint smile, but there was a wary gleam in her dark, almond-shaped eyes.

"Hello," he said. "I stopped by to see how Heather is doing. She had quite a shock yesterday, when Khuharkk' came at her. Is she here?"

"No, Dr. Rob asked to see her this morning, and she's there now," Hing said, signaling the door all the way open, then waving him in. "She seemed fine by last night . . . and this morning she was bouncing around, all excited about being here. You know how resilient kids are. Would you like to sit down? Do you have time for a cup of tea?"

"Of course," he lied.

Hing was wearing a silky robe made of Apis spider-silk, pale silver in color, with exotic alien blossoms in shades of pastel green and saffron rippling across it. Within its folds, she looked even smaller and more delicate than usual. Serge sat down on the couch in the living room and sipped the tea she gave him.

"You were wonderful yesterday, with Khuharkk'," he said, his eyes finally meeting hers. "That could have been a nasty incident, but you handled it so calmly."

She smiled wryly. "One of my better performances. My heart kept wanting to sink into my shoes. Khuharkk' was really pissed, not that I can blame him." Her smile broadened into a grin, then she giggled as if she couldn't help it. "Poor Khuharkk'— his expression when that ice cream slid down his mane—"

Serge shook his head. "Pistachio is definitely *not* his color," he agreed, and they both laughed ruefully. He finished his tea, and put the cup back on the table, careful, as always, not to exert too much pressure on the fragile china. When he'd first been learning to use his artificial hands, he'd broken half of what he touched.

"You mentioned wanting to see the dig," he said, carefully casual. "How about next week? The Professor and I have decided to take my Intro class out on a field trip, and some experienced help would be welcome, to keep an eye on the freshmen. Some of the students have barely passed their basic spacesuit tests."

Hing considered, then nodded. "Sure, I'd like to see the dig. And I'll be glad to help you out."

He nodded, keeping the exultation he felt under control. *Be light, casual,* he cautioned himself. *Don't push, don't push . . .* "Excellent," he said, and rose. "The tea was delicious. Thank you. I will call you later today with the exact date and time, if that is okay."

"That's fine," she said, "I'll be looking forward to the trip."

Outside the door, Serge glanced at his watch, realizing that there was no way he could make his Physics class. And there was an exam day after tomorrow. *But it was worth it,* he thought, grinning. *Definitely worth it!*

"Hi, Heather."

The girl looked up from the viewmag in the assistant's outer office to see a short, slender, dark-haired man standing in the doorway, smiling at her. She'd never met Rob Gable before, but she recognized him immediately—almost any human would have. "Dr. Gable!" she blurted, jumping up. Heather was surprised to find herself nervous; but then again, she'd never met anyone famous before.

He waved her into the office. "Dr. Gable is my dad," he corrected her pleasantly. "Don't make me feel any older than I do already, okay? The students call me Rob, or Dr. Rob. Sit down, won't you?"

Heather sat down before the cluttered desk, then glanced cautiously around her, taking in the small black cat curled on the other visitor's chair, the huge holo-tank on the wall, and the holo-posters . . . *I Was a Teenage Werewolf, Gone With the Wind,* and *A Night at the Opera.* She'd read *Gone With the Wind* while she was at Melbourne, but had never heard of the other two.

Rob instructed his Simiu assistant to hold his calls, then closed the door and walked over to her, his hand out. "I'm pleased to meet you," he said as she timidly shook with him.

"It's an honor to meet *you,*" she replied, looking up at him, thinking he wasn't bad-looking, for an old guy. It was funny, but she'd thought he'd be taller. "Even when I knew I was going to get the chance to come here, I somehow never really thought I'd get to meet *you*—in person, you know."

He chuckled. "We'll be seeing a lot of each other. I see a lot of all the freshmen. Would you like something to drink?"

"An orange soda?" she asked, and he nodded and keyed the servo. Moments later he handed her the glass. Heather cocked her head as she looked up at him. "With all the holo-posters in here, I'd have expected to see one from the *First Contacts* vid," she said demurely.

Rob grimaced. "I'm still trying to forget about that one," he said, shaking his head ruefully. "I'll never live it down. Everyone's still kidding me about the actor who played me."

"Trey Leonard doesn't look a bit like you."

"No kidding. Tall, blond, with muscles on top of his muscles, and all the emotional range of an artichoke—they couldn't have found anyone less like me if they'd put out a planet-wide casting call." He stroked the cat, who'd jumped up into his lap, and when he looked up, Heather knew that the pleasantries were over; it was time to get down to business. "So, what do you think of the Academy?"

She gave him a winning smile. "It's great, Dr. Rob. I'm glad you picked Hing to be my roommate . . . she's been really nice to me."

"I'm glad you like her. Almost everyone does," he replied. "Have you thought about what you'd like to accomplish here, Heather?"

She was slightly taken aback. "Accomplish? You mean, what I'd like to do when I graduate from here?" To Heather it seemed like a foregone conclusion that she *would* graduate, assuming she decided to stay—after all, she was a powerful telepath. They needed her.

Rob nodded.

Heather shrugged, bewildered. "I'm a telepath. I'll become a deep-space explorer, right?" She leaned forward, careful not to seem *too* ingratiating. "I've always dreamed of deep-space exploration, ever since I read Mahree Burroughs' *First Contacts*—I've read it at least three times!"

"Really?" he said neutrally, and Heather, meeting his dark eyes, felt her smile waver. *He's not buying the bullshit,* she thought. *What does he want? What's he fishing for?* She reached out to scan his surface thoughts—

—and hit a blank wall, filled with a roaring mental "noise." Heather gasped softly, recoiling, and the glass in her hand tilted, slopping cold soda over her fingers. Behind that wall, the girl could sense the psychologist's mind, but it was impossible to read anything from it, with that "noise" resounding in her head.

Heather pulled back until she was safely inside her own mind again, wincing from a sharp headache that sprang up. "Oh, look what I've done," she gabbled, putting the glass down and mopping at the spill she'd made. "I'm sorry. I shouldn't have been so clumsy."

Rob Gable watched her grimly. "Heather," he said finally, "look at me."

The girl took a deep breath, then sat back in her chair, forcing herself to meet his gaze squarely. Rob's eyes narrowed as he slowly, deliberately pushed his dark, curly hair back from his face, revealing his left ear, which bore a small, glittering earcuff. "See this?"

She nodded.

"Do you know what it is?"

Heather had a sinking suspicion, but she had never seen one before, only heard of them, so she shook her head. The headache had eased off, but still throbbed dully behind her eyes.

"It's a teledistort," Rob told her. "It protects my mind from unwanted telepathic contact. I hoped when I put it on a few minutes ago that it was an unnecessary precaution."

Oh, shit! Caught cold! It was a struggle to keep her resentment and anger from showing on her face, but she schooled her features to meek apology. "I'm really sorry, Dr. Rob. I know I shouldn't do that, but I got into a bad habit of scanning people automatically, back when my uncle Fred was being so mean. Sometimes I could sense when he was going to hit me in time to get out of range."

That ought to make him feel pretty shitty, she thought smugly. It was actually half-true . . . her telepathy *had* saved her from a slap or a boxed ear more than once in the past, when she'd been living with Uncle Fred and Aunt Natalie. But Heather had been an accomplished telepathic snoop since before she'd learned to read.

Rob's grim expression thawed slightly. "I can understand how that kind of habit could get started, considering the unfortunate circumstances. But"—he leaned forward, his eyes holding hers—"it's got to *stop,* understand?"

"Well, sure . . . I . . ." she found herself stammering again. *Damn you, Heather, get hold of yourself,* the part of her mind she thought of as her "survivor-self" (because that's what it helped her do) barked. *You can't let this shrink push you around!* "I understand," she said more composedly.

"I had a great-aunt who was telepathic, and my daughter, Claire, is a telepath," Rob said, "so I know something about how an ethical esper is supposed to behave. I'm sure they taught you at Melbourne that it's wrong to read someone's mind without their knowledge or permission, right?"

"Yeah," Heather muttered, looking down at her hands, which were clasped in her lap.

"We have the same rule here. You'll be starting classes tomorrow, and the teachers in your Telepathic Techniques course will be emphasizing that rule. We're a small community here, living in fairly close quarters. It's important that everyone respect the rights of others." He smiled faintly. "Don't forget that certain aliens can sense indiscriminate telepathic snooping, as most humans can't. And if they sensed it, they'd be rightfully furious."

"Really?" Heather was startled; she'd never heard that before. "Which aliens?" *Could it be the Simiu who can do that?* But no, she hadn't sensed any telepathic awareness in Khuharkk' yesterday—only his anger, which she couldn't help "reading."

Rob smiled faintly. "I think it might be better if I didn't spell that out for you," he said dryly. "At least, not yet. Right now, I'd like to discuss what happened yesterday between you and Khuharkk'."

Heather felt a sullen anger bubbling inside her, but forced herself to remain impassive. "I'd like to hear about what happened from your point of view," Rob continued. "I'll be talking about all this with Khuharkk' later, and I'll get his version then."

She hesitated, biting her lip, and the psychologist added, "I'm not asking so I can scold you or punish you, believe me. Janet wasn't there when the incident happened, and I haven't had time to talk to Serge or Hing."

"Do you have to talk to Serge?" she blurted. Heather didn't want the young instructor telling Rob that she'd pissed herself like a baby. Not with what she was planning to do to Khuharkk' . . .

"That depends," he said, and sat back, clearly waiting.

"I had this ice cream . . ." Heather began, then went on to give the counselor the whole story, as accurately as she could, up until the point where she'd wet herself, realized that Serge had noticed, then mentally promised herself that Khuharkk' would pay for what he'd done. She left all that out, of course.

When she was done, Rob nodded thoughtfully, then said, "Do you understand why Khuharkk' was so angry?"

"I think so," Heather said. "Hing explained last night how Simiu regard anything that makes them look stupid or foolish as an insult and a threat. She also told me that this"—she opened her mouth to mimic laughter—"is like a red flag to a Simiu. It's the way they challenge each other."

Rob nodded. "I'm glad she explained. Understanding other species so we can improve communications between the Fifteen

Known Worlds is the entire mission of this school. You've had a firsthand chance to see how messed up things can get when misunderstandings occur. We work to prevent problems like that, on a planetary as well as an individual level. And telepaths are very important in helping us understand and communicate."

Heather relaxed slightly. It seemed as though Rob wasn't going to lecture her too much, which would have been boring, as well as useless. "I know," she replied. "That's why I was glad to come here. I really do want to be a space explorer when I grow up." *That was just right,* she congratulated herself. *Not too gushy, but enthusiastic . . .*

The psychologist regarded her steadily. "Only the best, most stable telepaths are selected to go out on the deep-space vessels," he said finally. "But having that dream gives you a goal to work toward, which is all to the good. Helping you set goals and work to achieve them is part of my job. Which brings me back to your curriculum here." Rob pressed a button on his computer link, and scanned the holo-tank. "Is your class schedule okay? You're not going to change anything?"

Heather shrugged. "No, everything's fine," she said, wondering what he was leading up to.

"You've got a long break between your Intro to Nonhuman Telepathy class and Intro to Calculus," he said. "I'd like us to meet twice a week, right after that Telepathy class. Would that be convenient?"

"You mean meet for counseling sessions," Heather said flatly. *Oh, shit, I've had enough therapy to last me forever!* she thought disgustedly.

Rob nodded. "I see most of the freshmen on a regular basis," he replied blandly.

"You see *all* the freshmen twice a week?" she asked with more than a hint of sarcasm.

"When necessary," he said evenly. "We'll just spend time together, talking, playing games, maybe watching some of my old movies." He smiled at her. "I've got one I bet you'll like. It's about a kid who can do anything with computers because he's got a computer link in his brain."

Shit! Heather barely restrained herself from leaping out of her chair and bolting from the room. *Does he know? But how could he?* A moment's consideration convinced her that there was no way Rob Gable could know. No, it had been nothing but a shot in the dark, coincidence. *Don't forget all those "pranks" you played back on Earth, using computers. This shrink just did his homework, reading the files . . .* Her heart subsided in her chest.

Managing a feeble smile, she said casually, "I like computers. And I'm good with them. They're really simple to deal with, compared to people." Heather glanced down. "They never yell at you or beat you when you make a mistake, either."

"I know you've had a rough time of it," Rob said, and his dark eyes were sympathetic. "But you strike me as the kind of person who doesn't let adversity stop her. Now is your chance, Heather. Things can be different here at StarBridge. I argued that after you'd made such excellent progress at Melbourne, you deserved this chance. We all want you to succeed, believe me."

He took a deep breath. "But . . . Heather, I have to remind you that your admission is provisional, and whether you stay will depend on *you*. I'll help you as much as I can. I want you to come see me if you have any problems, or just need to talk. Hing is also a good listener, as you've probably already discovered."

Heather realized with relief that the interview was drawing to a close. Most of the time she found it easy to fool adults, but Gable was smart . . . and disconcertingly observant. "Thank you, Dr. Rob," she said gravely. "I appreciate your help. I'll try not to let you down."

"We need strong telepaths, Heather. Just like we need people like Hing to translate and Khuharkk' to become interrelators."

The girl stiffened at his mention of her nemesis. "Are you going to make me apologize to him?" she asked bluntly. She'd been surprised that he hadn't demanded it immediately. Adults were like that.

"No," Rob said. "I'm going to leave the decision about that up to you. If things go well, and you really begin to fit in here, one of these days you'll *want* to tell Khuharkk' that you're sorry. Just as I think that one of these days Khuharkk' will feel that he should apologize for frightening you. But it'll mean more if you both reach that decision on your own. When that day comes, let me know. When both of you are ready, I'll set up a meeting."

You'll wait until hell freezes over, then, Heather thought, but she kept her gaze candid and steady as she nodded.

Rob keyed a notation into his computer link, then stood up to indicate the interview was over. "Thanks very much for coming, Heather. I'll see you on Thursday, right after your Telepathy class, okay?"

Heather nodded and rose in her turn. "Okay, Dr. Rob."

• • •

That same afternoon, Serge and Professor Greyshine took one of the small skimmers out to their dig for a couple of hours of excavation.

The caverns where the artifacts had been discovered lay beneath the jagged peaks known as the Lamont Cliffs, named after the *Désirée*'s famous Captain. These mountains had existed for millennia—far longer than the asteroid had *been* an asteroid. The mountains and the caverns beneath them were the only features that were known to have survived intact from the time when the StarBridge asteroid was still part of a living planet.

Approximately two hundred fifty million years ago, a stray comet had crashed into a medium-sized, oxygen-nitrogen atmosphered world, shattering it. The remains of that ruined world still orbited Shassiszss' sun, much as the asteroid belt between Mars and Jupiter orbited Sol. The Mizari had begun mining their asteroid belt nearly seven thousand years ago. The asteroids were, to varying degrees, rich in radonium, the substance that generated tremendous amounts of power—enough to propel spaceships into metaspace.

The asteroid that the Mizari had donated for the site of StarBridge Academy was one of the largest; it contained enough radonium to power the school for ten thousand years.

Nothing could have seemed more lifeless, more barren, than this airless cone-shaped chunk; pitted by impact craters, slagged by the fires of its ancient catastrophe, it had a stark, rugged landscape with an eerily close horizon.

The asteroid's natural gravity was only one-tenth gee, even less than Earth's Moon. Due to the irregular shape of the rock chunk, the gravity fluctuated slightly, depending on one's location. At times it would seem to a person standing on the surface that he or she was leaning to one side or the other in order to remain upright—an extremely disconcerting experience, requiring special adjustment and coaching when wearing a spacesuit. Serge was used to it after five months of work, and still he had to fight the tendency to overcompensate, lest he topple over.

The young teacher and the Professor had pressurized and thrown up an artificial gravity field in the two main caverns. Otherwise, their surveys and excavations would have been extremely difficult if they'd been hampered by helmets and heavy gloves. Other caverns opened off the ones they'd pressurized and sealed off with temporary airlocks, but the two archaeologists were limited in money and equipment, so they'd been forced to confine their explorations to the areas where the Horizons Unlimited engineers had discovered the artifacts.

After cycling the airlock that protruded slightly from the rugged cliff face, Serge and Greyshine stepped into the main cavern and removed their pressure suits. Automatically, they checked the artifacts beneath their faintly glowing stasis fields. All the protective fields were functioning normally. Serge stared down at the songharp for a long moment, his eyes caressing its graceful lines. The musician inside him longed to touch its chords, coax sweet piping notes from its carved neck and graceful body.

Resolutely he suppressed that urge, and walked away from the artifacts, out into the cavern. It was a large one, fifty meters long by nearly thirty wide and twenty high. The floor of the place was fairly smooth, covered as it was by the glassy, fused silicate. In contrast, much of the ceiling was gouged and irregular, studded with the remains of stalactites that had broken off during the long-ago cataclysm. The walls were brownish-orange, with extrusions of a dark gray basalt running through them.

The slagged rock in the cave was the result of melting that had occurred during the destruction of the planet. The ancient impact had seared the doomed world, turning most of its exposed surfaces to a silicate layer between ten and twenty centimeters deep.

Serge lifted aside the proton magnetometer (affectionately known in English as a "banjo" because of its shape) and took the portable sifter out, then stood a moment surveying their site with mingled affection and frustration. They'd worked so hard, yet they'd barely made a good start on the excavation!

Marking off the cavern's rocky floor were stakes with bright-colored cords stretched between them to measure off four-meter-square grids. Each square was separated by a balk of raised soil that served as a walkway and additional divider. In the middle of the cavern ran the exploratory trench, which Serge and the Professor had cleared to a depth of one meter.

Careful not to knock soil into the already excavated grids, Serge walked along the balk to grid number LC-C1-16 (which stood for Lamont Cliffs, Cavern One, Grid #16). He'd only begun this grid the day before and had barely cleared it down to the earth and rock-dust level below the patches of slagged silicate.

Kneeling down beside the area he'd left off the day before yesterday, Serge powered up the sifter and set to work. Across the cavern, Greyshine worked on extending the exploratory trench another meter.

Serge's sifter, like many technological marvels, was originally a Mizari invention. The small vacuuming unit sucked up soil and analyzed it, even as it probed electronically four centimeters into the packed ground, searching for any artifacts, no matter how small.

Glancing at the analysis scanner, he noted that he was still in the diatomaceous layer of pale gray soil. The chalky, microscopic remains of planktonlike sea creatures gave it its light color. The sifter analyzed the soil, but found nothing but soil within its range. No bone fragments, artificial materials, splinters of wood or metal . . . nothing. Serge was disappointed, but hardly surprised; the magnetometer would have picked up any objects larger than four or five millimeters.

Strange to think that this was once the ocean floor of an alien sea on a planet in the Serenity Sector, he thought, moving the sifter to his other hand to begin the right side of the grid square. *I wonder whether the caverns existed when this soil layer went down, or whether they came later, after the mountain range pushed up out of the sea?*

Glancing over at the Professor, Serge saw he was bent over the songharp, comparing its designs to a display on his computer link. The alien was tall, standing more than a head higher than Serge, who was tall for a human male. With his sharp, pricked ears, luxurious silver-gray coat, and long muzzle surrounding sharp teeth, Greyshine could have auditioned to play opposite Little Red Riding Hood—though his forehead was higher and more domed than any Terran lupine. Humor and intelligence softened his greenish-gold eyes, and his bipedal stance also helped dispel his wolflike aspect.

"Greyshine" was the literal English translation of the soft whine that was his name. During their time together, Serge had learned to speak Heeyoon, and since the Professor knew no human languages at all, they either conversed in Heeyoon or Mizari when they talked. Catching the human's eye, the alien turned off the computer link and came over to squat beside Serge on the balk, watching as he sifted.

"I should be able to finish this square today," the man said in Heeyoon. "Even though this portable sifter makes the work go slowly." He massaged his forearms, grimacing as sore muscles complained. *How fortunate that my hands don't tire,* he thought sardonically, hating the feel of artificial flesh against the livir

"You have been spending many hours out here alone, Serge," the Professor said. "Do not think I haven't noticed your dedication. You're working too hard."

"I want to uncover an artifact that we can claim as our own discovery," Serge said, frustration edging his voice. "It disturbs me that every one of these finds was handed to us like a gift by those idiotic engineers, who knew no better than to move them!"

Greyshine sighed gustily. "You must be prepared to accept failure, Serge. All of our neutron scans have indicated that both these cavern floors are now empty. The only reason we are even using the sifter is to eliminate the possibility that some tiny fragments have not shown up on the neutron scans."

"I wonder why the Mizari abandoned the artifacts," Serge said thoughtfully. "Even if there was an accident and the cavern depressurized, they could have come back in wearing protective fields and retrieved their belongings."

"Impossible to say," the Professor stated the obvious. "Perhaps there were fatalities associated with our supposed accident, and they felt these caverns were ill-omened."

"If that's the case, then I wish they had left the bodies," Serge said, realizing after he'd spoken how ghoulish that sounded, but knowing that the Professor would understand what he really meant. "Finding skeletons would be conclusive proof."

"Indeed it would," the Heeyoon agreed. "But life and archaeology seldom have such easy solutions, Serge. We may conjecture and theorize until the stars freeze over, and we will unfortunately never know for certain. That is the nature of the work."

Absently, the Professor examined his clawed, stubby fingers that resembled a dog's paw—except they were far bigger, and the digits were elongated. One of them was opposable, the equivalent of a human thumb. "I have scratched myself," he muttered, licking the injury clean as fastidiously as any house cat. "I have been examining the marks around the cavern entrances and on the floors, and there are indications that they had begun to improve this chamber and the other one . . . some of this smoothing is clearly artificial, not caused by the cataclysm."

Serge had a feeling the alien had something else he wanted to say, but was unsure of how to broach the subject. His comments had a rather abstracted air. For a moment he was tempted to ask Greyshine bluntly what he had on his mind, but he decided to bide his time. "If they were fusing the chamber floors so as to create a smooth surface for them to glide across, that would explain why the artifacts were partially embedded in the slag," he replied. "At least . . . they were partially embedded before those fools moved them," he added sourly.

"Yes."

"Can we identify the type of equipment they would have used, and use it to provide another dating check?"

"No," Greyshine said. "Unfortunately not. The sheltered location and the vacuum makes it impossible to tell whether the fusing and pressurization attempts were made three weeks ago, three months ago, three thousand years ago—or three million. Mizari equipment and techniques have simply not changed that much for thousands of years. They have been civilized and technologically advanced far longer than your people—or mine."

"We could open one of the other caverns and begin excavations," Serge suggested hopefully.

The Professor wrinkled his muzzle, revealing his sharp ivory fangs. "The cost, I am afraid, would be prohibitive. If only Horizons Unlimited would give us another donation, we could work on pressurizing Cavern Three."

"Rob mentioned that he will be having dinner with Jeffrey Morrow tonight," Serge said. "They are friends, and Rob knows how much we need funding. Perhaps he will let Morrow know that we need another donation."

"Perhaps . . ." The Heeyoon trailed off, then gave Serge a sideways glance. The human eyed him warily, knowing the alien was finally about to voice what was on his mind. "Incidentally, as I was waiting beside the entrance to the shuttle dome, I noticed Hing walking with you, did I not?"

Serge felt the hot rush of blood to his cheeks and silently cursed his Teutonic ancestors. He should have known. Greyshine, like most Heeyoons, was an incurable romantic and a relentless matchmaker. "Earlier today, I invited Hing to accompany us when we took the class to see the dig. Then, later, I saw her again in the Spiral Arm and took that opportunity to give her the particulars about the field trip," he explained, not looking at his companion. "It saved me a call. Afterwards, she just happened to walk along as I was heading for the hangar, because she was going to the theater for a rehearsal, and it was on her way."

"She has agreed to accompany us to the site?" The alien cocked his head at the human, his eyes gleaming with interest.

"She told me yesterday that she was interested in seeing the dig," Serge said, careful to keep his tones casual. "And we c‡ always use another senior student to help shepherd the Intro class, so I invited her to come."

"She is most welcome, of course!" Greyshine said. "Do not sound so defensive, Serge. I was simply pleased to see the two of you together today. Perhaps you will become mates again?"

"Uh, Professor . . ." Serge began, but the Heeyoon was off and running now, his eyes shining. "Together, you belong together! You make such an attractive couple—you with your pale headfur and eyes like the midday sky on my world Arrrouhl, she with headfur the color of a starless night, and eyes as black and sharp as the ice in the Dark Oceans of my world's second moon . . ."

"Professor . . ."

Oblivious, the Heeyoon went on cataloguing Hing's virtues. "Never forget, Serge, that mere beauty is fleeting, but Hing's quick wits and kind nature are worth far more in the end than shiny headfur and bright eyes, lad. I am growing older, and so is my mate, Strongheart, but in our love we will always be young." He looked straight at Serge. "You and Hing would make fine pups together, my young friend. Both of you have strong teeth, shiny eyes, good minds."

The human shook his head. "Simply because Hing agreed to come out to the site and assist us in chaperoning the freshmen around does not mean we are anything more than friends, Professor!"

"But I saw her eyes, as she stared longingly into yours . . ."

"For perhaps two nanoseconds!" Serge snapped his fingers sharply. "You call *that* 'staring longingly'?" All at once he found himself laughing. It was impossible to be angry with Greyshine; he was so innocent in his matchmaking. "Professor . . . if Hing will have me as a friend, that would be wonderful. I don't dare hope for more," he said, knowing he *was* hoping . . . he was unable to stop himself.

The alien wasn't deceived. "But if you could win her back, you would be happy again, Serge," Greyshine insisted. "Don't think I haven't noticed how lost you have been without her."

"I miss her, yes," Serge admitted. "But I do not intend to wreck my chance of regaining her friendship by pushing her. If, over time, she grows interested in renewing our old relationship, I'll know."

"Time . . . yes, your species has time to take such a leisurely, no-pressure approach to mating," the Professor sighed. "With my people it is different. We must, as your human poet put it, seize the day—the moment! But your people have such splendid adaptations in your reproductive habits." He sighed again, longingly. "What a delight it would be to have an ever-receptive mate, unbound by the dictates of her estrus cycle! To be able to mate as often as one chooses, ah, that would be bliss!"

" 'Those who rush, leap on the shadow and miss the prey,' " Serge cautioned dryly, quoting an old Heeyoon proverb that Greyshine had taught him. "Or, as my people put it, 'Don't jump to conclusions.' Humans make things complicated in other ways. It is definitely not as easy as it seems."

"I suppose not," Greyshine allowed. "And while it is true that mating as one chooses, rather than experiencing a mating season or drive, is a titillating concept, it is sad that you humans will never feel the flood of seasonal passion that my species does."

"We feel passion," Serge protested, smothering a grin. "You have read more human love poetry than I have, and you are always telling me how amorous human poetry is!"

"That is true," Greyshine agreed meditatively. "Donne, Shakespeare, Rilke, Lady Murasaki, Sappho . . . your species writes most eloquently of the heart and its passions."

"The heart and its passions," Serge said firmly, "should be relegated to the proper time and place. At the moment we have work to do."

"True, true." Greyshine rose to his feet. "But I will be crossing my claws for you, to paraphrase a human idiom I have heard Kkintha ch'aait use."

"Thank you, Professor," Serge said warmly, and went back to work.

Twenty minutes later their computer link buzzed softly, signaling an incoming message. Greyshine took the call. Absorbed in trying to finish his grid before quitting time, Serge paid no attention to the alien until a soft whine of distress made him turn off the sifter and hurry over to his friend and mentor. "What is it?" he demanded, seeing the alien's flattened ears and downcast expression. "What has happened?"

"That was a message from Esteemed Rizzshor," the Heeyoon said bleakly. "The Mizari Archaeological Society has decided to send Rizzshor and his assistant to inspect the site, before dispatching the entire team and funding a full-scale dig. Rizzshor will be making a preliminary survey and digging test trenches in two more of the discovered caverns. But if no further artifacts are discovered, further funding, he says, will be denied."

"But the chances of their finding more artifacts in just two trenches, in two caverns picked at random, are probably negligible!" Serge protested. "They can't do this to us! We have worked so hard!"

"I know," Greyshine said sadly. "But don't despair, Serge. It is entirely possible that the test trenches in the two caverns will turn up something. All it would take would be one small indication—anything, even a broken string from a songharp!"

"And if nothing turns up? No more funding! It takes funding to make discoveries!"

"We can still keep working," the Professor pointed out. "And there are other sources of funding I can apply to receive."

"Certainement," Serge muttered bitterly, knowing how remote was the chance of their receiving human or Heeyoon funding if the Mizari turned them down. *Mon Dieu,* he thought, turning away, his shoulders sagging. *What will we do?*

Hours later, Heather Farley huddled behind a *balon*-wood sculpture of a Simiu that marked the entrance to the Simiu-adapted wing on Level Three. Hot, damp air surrounded her, but despite her discomfort, she remained still . . . waiting.

Waiting was always hard, but she could do it when she had a good reason to wait. Like now. Anger twisted in her stomach like a gigantic parasite. She could sense Khuharkk's mind; the Simiu was only a few doors away. His consciousness was open, unguarded, as he concentrated on his Spatial Physics problems.

Let the punishment fit the crime, Heather thought, glancing at her watch for the dozenth time. Who was it that had originated that saying? Well, in just a few minutes, the old proverb was going to come true.

Leaning back into the safety of her niche, she sent a mental inquiry into the room that lay only meters away. She'd discovered that grasping an alien's thoughts wasn't easy—naturally, each species thought in their own language, at least on the conscious levels, and "translating" presented problems. But she'd been practicing ever since she'd left Earth, aboard the S. V. *McIntyre,* which had carried a number of alien passengers, and now at the Academy itself. When Heather concentrated, she could figure out what Khuharkk' was thinking, in a general way. It helped that the Simiu had a very ordered mind.

A slow, anticipatory smile animated the girl's freckled features as she mentally "eavesdropped" again. Khuharkk' was getting sleepy; his eyelids were drooping. Heaving a deep sigh, he signaled his computer link to "save," resolving to get up early tomorrow to finish the last few problems. The Simiu rose from his desk, stretching thankfully. His thoughts brightened, grew easier to read as he anticipated the warmth of his sleeping pallet, the comfort of his nightly grooming ritual.

That's right, hairball, his unknown observer thought, narrowing her eyes, *you're tired . . . sleepy . . . so tired . . .*

Heather knew she couldn't really influence a living being's thoughts, of course—no one could. She could "read" thoughts and emotions, and project her own thoughts into a receptive mind to communicate, but "mind control" was not among her abilities. *Which is too damned bad,* she thought sourly. *My life would be a lot easier, wouldn't it?*

Pulling her computerpen out of the pocket of her green StarBridge jumpsuit, she turned it over in her hand idly. Too bad people weren't more like computers. Artificial intelligences were so reasonable, so direct and simple, just explain what you wanted them to do, in terms they understood, and they were always happy to oblige.

And computers never yelled at you and nagged you to clean up your room, like Aunt Natalie. They never called you an "Abomination," the way Uncle Fred had. Thinking of Uncle Fred made Heather scowl blackly. Too bad she hadn't been able to *really* get that old creep for what he'd done to her . . .

An involuntary shudder wracked her small, stocky form as she remembered the vicious slaps, the wrenched arms and wrists, the yelling, the cursing, the name-calling. As she'd grown, he'd begun hitting harder, then one fateful day he'd used his fists, only stopping when Heather's head had snapped back against the wall, knocking her out.

Uncle Fred had warned his niece not to go to school the next day, but Heather had sneaked out and gone anyway. The school nurse had taken one look at the child's torn, swollen lip, the two black eyes, and the lump on the back of her head, and had pounced on Heather. After she'd questioned her, she'd called in the authorities, and then the cops had been on Uncle Fred like stink on shit.

What an uproar there'd been! Before she knew it, Heather had been made a ward of the court, and deposited in a foster home. At least no one had hit her there. They'd even tried to be kind, but they'd been nervous around her, afraid she'd read their minds. Telepaths made most "normal" people nervous.

After she'd run away from the Morgans, they'd put her with another family. But it hadn't taken her long to realize that the youngest child, far from fearing her as a telepath, was developing an unhealthy craving for telepathic contact. TSS, they'd called it, Telepathic Stimulation Syndrome. It was rare, but not unknown. In some individuals telepathic contact stimulated the pleasure centers. These people often grew addicted to telepathy and would do almost anything to stay in contact with telepaths.

At first, Heather had been pleased that Pamela had wanted to spend all her time with her younger foster sister. But then, when Pam had insisted that Heather should only communicate with her telepathically, and had become jealous of the child's time and attention—fiercely, irrationally jealous—Heather had realized the bitter truth. Pam hadn't cared about *her* at all. Any telepath would have done. She represented nothing but a way for Pam to feel good. So she'd run away again.

And finally she'd been taken to Melbourne, following extensive telepathic testing. Everything had been different then. It was there that Heather had discovered her true gift, her destiny, as she sometimes thought of it.

No, she couldn't control people, no matter how much she wished she could. But computers were different. She'd always been good with them, but last year, Heather had discovered that she, alone of all the telepaths she'd ever encountered or heard of, could telepathically link with computers—and control them.

Organic-based memories had been standard in computers for a hundred years, mimicking the speed and complexity of human thought processes. Heather's discovery that she could telepathically link with and influence an AI had happened during her first months at Melbourne. She'd been working on a tough trigonometry problem, getting nowhere fast. Finally, in frustration, the girl had directed her thoughts at the computer. She'd imagined her mind reaching into the machine and *forcing* it to render up the correct solution, despite the constraints of the teaching program she was currently using—one programmed *not* to reveal the correct answer unless directed to do so by the supervising professor.

Instead of the lack of contact she'd expected, Heather had actually felt herself link into the computer's "mind." She'd sent her telepathic command racing along pathways of artificial neurons, searching out the vital area in the program, and suddenly she was there, at the critical spot. With a sort of mental "push" (actually it was more like a poke), Heather had changed the programming from a "no" to a "yes"—caused a temporary override. Her mind had reached all the way past the language-based programming, clear into the binary thinking processes of the AI. Deep in its "mind," Heather had changed a binary "off" to an "on."

Scant moments later Heather had blinked herself back to awareness of her surroundings, and found herself in her seat before her holo-tank. In its glowing depths, the solution to her trigonometry problem was neatly spelled out.

With careful exploration and practice, she'd honed her gift. Usually, Heather was such an experienced hacker that she didn't need to reach inside a computer's mind or memory. Tricks like getting that free sundae were easy. But every so often, the computers needed that little extra "push"—the mental poke that only she could manage.

Heather shifted her attention back to Khuharkk', who had begun grooming himself. *C'mon, furball, hurry up!* she thought.

But Khuharkk' was as fastidious as most Simiu were reputed to be. Slowly, painstakingly, he washed himself with his tongue, then combed his fur with his thick fingernails. Glands beneath his nails secreted a substance to keep his luxurious coat soft and shiny. As soon as his personal grooming was attended to, Khuharkk' took several minutes to tidy up the room where he and another Simiu student were quartered.

What a pain in the ass! Heather thought disgustedly. *Aunt Natalie would have loved this jerk—if he'd been human, that is . . .* Aunt Natalie had been petrified of aliens, claiming that they were going to take over Earth "as soon as our backs are turned." *The bigoted old bitch,* Heather thought, picturing her aunt's reaction to finding herself on an airless asteroid with hundreds of aliens. The girl smiled evilly. *Too bad there's no way to swing that . . .*

Hearing footsteps, she tensed, crouching behind the statue. Two human students passed the entrance to the Simiu wing, but they were deep in conversation and neither glanced up. Heather's heart was slamming in her chest, and she was tempted to bolt back to her room and forget the whole thing. She half rose, then Serge LaRoche's face rose before her eyes. Heather experienced again that awful moment when she'd read his mind and discovered that he *knew* she'd pissed her pants.

Slowly, she settled back down, her mouth set in a grim line.

Almost time, she thought, checking on Khuharkk', who was cleaning his teeth. *One final computer check . . .*

With practice she'd learned to enter the computer's "mind" even from remote peripherals. Now, staring at her computerpen, Heather let her consciousness extend, tracing along the linkage of the pen, until she was in the mainframe, tracing the pathways to the environmental systems. Yes, the alteration she had programmed to affect Khuharkk's quarters was ready to be activated, then erase all trace of its presence an instant later.

She concentrated again on Khuharkk', who was giving loving attention to the huge ivory canines that had frightened her so badly when he'd bared them and advanced on her. *Soon . . . soon . . .*

Moments later he was finished, and his attention shifted to the last of his presleep rituals. Heather could feel the vicarious pressure in her bladder, her bowels . . .

Khuharkk' positioned himself on his toilet.

Poised, hardly breathing, Heather touched her mind to the environmental computer's, and reversed one vital command in the sanitation system's disposal system.

Khuharkk' pushed the waste-disposal button.

A bare instant later a Simiu's outraged shriek reverberated through the corridors, loud despite the soundproofing. Hysterical yammering, then other howls, followed.

Rising to her feet, Heather stepped out of the niche, tucking her pen into the pocket of her jumpsuit. She walked quickly until she reached the main corridor, then sauntered away, smiling.

CHAPTER 4

◆

Alarums and Excursions

"To friendship," Jeff Morrow said, raising his cup of sake with a flourish. Behind him, a miniature waterfall splashed into a streambed pebbled with colorful stones, where fish vivid as living jewels swam lazily. Paper screens with carved frames gave diners an illusion of privacy, and twelve-tone music *plinked* softly in the background.

Seated on a cushion before the low, lacquered table, Rob Gable raised his cup of green tea. "To friendship," he echoed. "Long may ours endure."

"Hear, hear," Jeff responded solemnly, then emptied his cup.

Rob drank his tea, then scooped up a cucumber roll in his chopsticks and popped it into his mouth. "Best I've had in years," he said as soon as he could speak coherently. "Try the *futo-maki*," he urged, capturing one himself. "If I keep this up, I won't have room for the tempura."

Jeff sampled the sushi and nodded agreement. "So tell me, how is everything going at the school?"

"Hectic," Rob sighed. "It's always hectic when we get a new shipment of freshmen in. The kids are homesick, they need lots of reassurance, course and schedule changes, personality conflicts, culture shock . . ." He shook his head ruefully as he cautiously sampled a bite of pickled ginger. "After a month or so, they'll have adjusted, and things will calm down, as much as they ever do. Running StarBridge reminds me of that old Chinese curse: 'May you live in interesting times.' "

"What are the new kids like?"

"Great, most of them. It's a real boost to see their enthusiasm, their idealism. Almost makes me feel young again," he said wryly.

Morrow snorted. "You're the biggest kid down there, Rob, don't think you can bullshit me." He balanced a California roll between his chopsticks. "You said 'most' of them. You've got a problem child?"

Rob nibbled thoughtfully on a *tamago*. "I don't know yet. I've got a kid who's a helluva hard case. I just hope we'll be able to reach her . . . because if we don't she could wind up in real trouble."

"Trouble how?"

"Drugs, maybe, or promiscuity . . . she craves affection and approval, though she doesn't realize it. I can picture her as a drugged-out joygirl in some spaceport." He shook his head. "But it's even more likely that she'd get into computer crime. She's one of the cleverest hackers, by all reports, ever to attend StarBridge." He grinned at his friend. "Since you, at least."

"Sounds like she's quite a risk. Why take it?"

"Because she's one of the most powerful telepaths we've ever discovered."

Jeff blinked. "Really? Projector or receiver?"

"Both."

"No wonder you're sticking your neck out."

"I just hope I've done the right thing . . ." Rob said, smearing a blob of green horseradish over the end of another cucumber roll, then popping the whole thing into his mouth. Moments later, his eyes widened. Swallowing hastily, he reached for his tea, drained the mug, poured another, and emptied that. "Whew!"

Jeff chuckled at his expression. "Cleared your sinuses, eh, Doc?"

"I'll remember that the next time I get a cold," Rob gasped. Just then their waiter arrived, with the *miso* soup. Both men raised the bowls to their mouths, sipping appreciatively.

"So how are the nonhumans doing . . . Esteemed Ssoriszs, Kkintha, Hrasheekk', and that new one, the Heeyoon archaeologist you mentioned the other day . . ." Jeff's brow wrinkled as he groped for the name.

"Greyshine," Rob supplied. "They're all fine. I saw Hrasheekk' today and mentioned I was seeing you, and he said to tell you he sends you greetings."

Jeff smiled. "Is he still making the kids hustle through their workouts, screaming like he's possessed when they slack off?"

Rob chuckled, nodding. "When Tesa Wakandagi was here, she gave him a name that, in sign, meant 'Dr. Noisy.' It fits so well that I have to bite my tongue to keep from using it to his face!"

"Tesa . . . just one of your graduates who has made the news," Morrow said. "Gaining Earth full membership in the CLS practically single-handed. She still on Trinity?"

"You bet." Rob smiled reminiscently. "It would take a null-grav booster to get Tesa off her adopted world. She loves being an interrelator."

"What about Mark Kenner, the one who got the hostages free? What's he doing?"

"Serving as the interim interrelator to Elseemar. He'll be back at school in another six months. I don't know whether he'll decide to go back to Elseemar, or go on with his original major, Mizari. I'm also getting another celebrity on the next ship—Cara Hendricks. She and Mark were together on Elseemar."

"You mean the journalist? The one who won the Pulitzer for her coverage of that hijacking?"

"The very same," Rob said proudly. "She's decided she wants to be an *interstellar* journalist, and a CLS internship as a translator would be a good starting point."

"She's right about that!" Jeff pounced on the last *futo-maki*. "And then there was that young Chhhh-kk-tu who conducted the arbitration between those two Simiu clans that had declared death-challenge on each other."

"Partha kel'chon," Rob supplied. "Yeah, he did a fantastic job."

"Rob, that's an impressive success rate. You have every right to be proud."

Rob nodded. "Yeah, but—" he broke off, not wanting to get into a sensitive subject.

Jeff knew him too well to let him off the hook. "Yeah, but *what*?" he prodded. "What were you going to say?"

The doctor sighed, realizing that he'd been backed into a corner. "Naturally I'm proud," he admitted. "But, Jeff, the picture isn't as rosy as it might appear from the outside. We've had cost overruns, and the CLS Council is kicking about funding. They point out that we're not graduating as many students as we'd predicted."

Morrow nodded sympathetically. "I've seen articles on the subject. The CLS reps point to the high dropout rate, and claim the school isn't paying off the way it was supposed to."

Rob toyed with his chopsticks, chasing grains of rice around his plate. "Believe me, I'm aware of the criticism, and to an extent, it's justified. I keep hoping we'll be able to improve that dropout rate. We're refining our testing methods, trying to pare it down. It's discouraging that some of the best and the brightest just don't graduate, for one reason or another." Serge LaRoche's handsome features flashed across his mind and he frowned, shaking his head. "I feel awkward, discussing this with you . . ."

"Rob"—Jeff leaned forward earnestly—"I appreciate your tact, but quit trying to save my face when it doesn't need saving! I made my peace over dropping out long ago, and I'm happy with my life as it turned out, I assure you!" He grinned wryly. "I'm a millionaire in my own right now—no way I could've done that if I'd stayed at StarBridge, right?"

"Brother, you are *so* right!" Rob agreed, smiling with relief. "You should see my bank balance!"

"Yeah, I know about that pitiful excuse for a salary they give you. It was in those Public Information records when we gave those archaeologists their grant. Talk about insulting . . ." He grimaced.

Gable shrugged. "Don't worry about me, I'm fine. What do I need with money out here? Hardly anything to spend it on! Years ago I transferred half my holdings over to my sisters, who have six kids between them. Uncle Rob is putting his nieces and nephews through school. The rest is in trust for Claire."

"If you went back to Earth, you could run for President, Rob," Jeff said earnestly. "I'll finance your campaign. You'll win in a walk, no contest. President of Earth—how does it sound?"

Gable stared at him, appalled . . . then, slowly, Morrow's poker face melted, and both men burst out laughing. "Not me," Rob sputtered finally, gasping for breath. "Not after seeing what Mahree went through when she was Secretary-General. They're trying to talk her into another term, but she's holding out—so far. President of Earth? Hell no, not me!"

"But the money, the prestige . . ." Jeff urged, still chortling.

"Prestige be damned, and I don't need the money," Rob said dryly. "Thanks, but no thanks!" Sobering, he changed the subject. "Speaking of money, about that grant H.U. gave the archaeologists out at the Cliffs . . ."

"Go on," Morrow encouraged.

"If you folks have any more grant money floating around that hasn't been assigned, Ssoriszs got some bad news today. The Mizari Archaeological Society is backing off from their promise. They want to send someone out to evaluate the site, but they're no longer talking about a full team. Professor Greyshine says he'll carry on as best he can, but he and Serge need to pressurize more of the caverns. That takes equipment—and money. If they can't do that, they'll have to stop."

Jeff shook his head. "After all that work? We can't let that happen!" He considered for a moment. "I believe the grants have all been apportioned, but I'd be willing to help with a private contribution. It would be tax deductible, right?"

Rob's eyes widened. "Jeff, that's—that's extremely generous of you!"

Morrow shrugged. "I don't have time to spend half of what I've got—I'm too busy working. Tell Greyshine that my assistant, Helene Majors, will be in touch to see what he needs so they can generate some figures."

Rob started to thank him again, but was interrupted by the waiter arriving with the tempura. Jeff waved aside his friend's gratitude. "I'd rather spend it on something like this than some charity back on Earth that has a board of directors earning fat salaries. You know how important StarBridge is to me . . . always will be."

The doctor nodded as he dipped a shrimp (*real shrimp, imported from Earth, this meal is costing Jeff a fortune,* he thought) into one of the sauces and raised it to his lips—

—just as the telepathic summons reverberated in his mind like a sudden shout.

<Rob!>

Doctor Blanket? the psychologist thought incredulously. He'd never known that the Avernian's telepathy could reach so far. Oblivious to his startled companion, to the shrimp that had fallen into his lap, Rob shut his eyes and concentrated. *Doctor Blanket, what's wrong?*

<Rob, there is trouble here at the school. One of the students, a Simiu named Khuharkk', has been terribly frightened . . . I cannot read past his hysteria to discover why, but Janet is concerned about the environmental computers, she wishes she could reach you, but she knows you are not on the asteroid . . .>

The environmental systems! Oh, shit! Rob leaped to his feet, barking his shins on the low table and wincing. "Jeff, I'm sorry, but I've got to get back to the school—something's wrong—"

"What? How do you know that?" Morrow stared, bewildered.

"Doctor Blanket just contacted me. There's some kind of environmental problem. I'm sorry about dinner, but—"

"Don't worry about me!" Jeff broke in, waving at him reassuringly. Despite his words, some emotion flashed in his eyes that Rob couldn't read. Annoyance? Irritation? No, it was stronger than that, but now wasn't the time to pursue it. Rob's concern for his school filled his mind with a terrible sense of urgency. *The environmental system! Oh, God!*

"I've got to get to a phone, call for the shuttle to come pick me up . . ." Rob said over his shoulder, already striding toward the entrance and the computer links. "I promise, Jeff, I'll make it up to you . . . the next time is on me, but I—"

"Quit apologizing!" Jeff ordered crisply, catching up to him at the entrance and grabbing his arm. "Just hold on for a second, Rob! Stop!"

The doctor obeyed, watching as the engineer spoke briefly into a small comlink he took out of his pocket. "There, it's all arranged. You don't have to wait for your shuttle, one of the H.U. pilots will take you down. He'll meet you in Docking Bay Four-B, okay?"

"Four-B," Rob repeated. "Thanks, I really appreciate this," he said, extending his hand.

Morrow's grip was strong and reassuring. "Call me," he said, his handsome features creased with worry. "I'll be wondering what's up until I hear from you."

"I will. Thanks again, Jeff. I wish . . ." The doctor smiled and shrugged. "No rest for the wicked."

Morrow smiled faintly. "That place owns you, body and soul, doesn't it?"

Rob rolled his eyes. "At least it's never dull!" With a last wave at Morrow, he dashed down the corridor toward the docking bays.

Once aboard the shuttle, Rob used the small ship's communications equipment to call his assistant, Resharkk'. The Simiu informed him that the Academy was currently on "environmental alert" status—students were required to strap on one of the emergency beltpaks designed by the Mizari. These small units generated a protective field that could maintain air supply and pressure to sustain the wearer for thirty minutes—in theory, long enough for the individual to reach a securely pressurized area. They were also supposed to activate the location transmitters built into their student pins.

But these measures were strictly precautionary, Resharkk' emphasized. He'd just spoken to Janet Rodriguez and she'd told him that the threat to the Academy's environmental computers appeared to be confined to the waste-disposal unit in Khuharkk's quarters. Somehow, the Simiu reported, the student's toilet had reversed itself.

"It *what*?" Rob said incredulously. "How could that happen?"

"Unknown, Honored HealerGable," Resharkk' said, his violet eyes very grave.

"Can you connect me with Janet?" Rob asked, then glancing out the viewport, he amended, "Never mind. We're almost there. I'll talk to her soon. Where exactly is Khuharkk' now?"

"In the infirmary, Honored Rob," the Simiu said.

"I'll go there first."

Rob hurried through the corridors, conscious of the knots of tense students who crowded together, whispering. Each of them wore one of the small beltpaks. "Take it easy," Rob told the groups he passed. "Think of this as just another drill. The beltpaks are just a routine precaution. The pressure is fine. Everything's okay."

Reaching the infirmary, Rob went in and the human physician, Dr. Rachel Mysuki, admitted him into the examining room. Khuharkk' was there, having just emerged from the shower. Simiu hated to get wet, with good cause; the student's luxuriant coat was a stringy, soggy mess that would require hours of combing and grooming to restore.

Rob struggled with the guttural growls, shrill whines, and sharp clicks of the language. "Honored Khuharkk' . . . what happened?"

The student blinked at Rob, his violet eyes still glassy from shock, then slowly shook his head. "I do not know, Honored HealerGable. One moment everything was fine, then next . . ." He shuddered deeply.

Rob watched as Dukeekk', the Simiu counselor, and Frikk'har, Khuharkk's roommate, labored over the stricken student, drying his fur while offering deep-throated rumbles of reassurance. He struggled to translate the Simiu's soft whines of distress:

"Dishonor . . . ultimate dishonor . . . if my family knew . . . I cannot bear this, I cannot! Why did this have to happen to *me*? I am dishonored, besmirched . . ."

"Khuharkk'," Rob said, waving a hand to get the victim's attention. "Did you have any warning? Any sound, any . . . odor?"

The student shook his head, his whines and yips of distress finally quieting. "None, Honored HealerGable. No warning. Suddenly I was surrounded by . . ." He shuddered, his usually upstanding crest drooping limp and sodden. "My honor is destroyed, Honored HealerGable. Everyone knows what happened to me, how degraded I am. I cannot bear for them to know of my disgrace! I must leave here immediately."

"Honored Khuharkk', your honor is not compromised. Everyone knows that what happened was in no way your fault!" Rob insisted. To demonstrate his respect, he made a deep Mizari bow to the student. Straightening, he gave the Simiu counselor a meaningful glance. "Dukeekk' knows that, don't you?"

"Your honor is intact, Honored Khuharkk'," the older alien said, picking up on her cue. "I assure you that in *my* eyes you are no way diminished."

"I also know that your honor is intact, FriendKhuharkk'," Frikk'har maintained stoutly, patting his roommate's shoulder comfortingly. "And I will personally challenge anyone that dares say otherwise!"

"So will I," Dukeekk' added.

"So will I," Rob said. "And I'd like to see anyone defeat *me* in the Arena of Honor!" He raised a clenched fist and flexed his biceps ostentatiously. As he'd hoped, the idea of a human defeating a Simiu in a bare-hands fight was so ridiculous that Dukeekk's and Frikk'har's muzzles wrinkled and they snorted softly with amusement. Even Khuharkk's eyes brightened with a gleam of humor.

"Honored HealerGable," he said gently, "you have made your point. Very well, I will stay."

"That's the spirit!" Rob said. Then he turned without further ado and left. Simiu greetings were prolonged and traditional, but leave-takings were not—it was perfectly polite to simply walk away once a meeting was concluded.

Rob's next stop was Khuharkk's quarters. As he entered the Simiu-adapted wing, Rob followed an ever-thickening trail of slimy, odorous debris that terminated in foul smears, clumps, and spatters as he reached the stricken student's room. A small crowd still gathered outside, but most of the students had gone back to their own rooms. Shooing the stragglers away, Rob keyed open the door and found Janet Rodriguez in Khuharkk's sleeping room, intently working at the computer link.

"Rob!" she exclaimed, relief lighting her weary features. "How is Khuharkk'?"

The doctor wrinkled his nose at the stench within the confines of the room. "Physically, he's fine. Emotionally . . . shaken, very shaken. But I believe I convinced him that everyone will understand that this was an accident, and that it doesn't impugn his honor." Glancing down at the smears on the floor matting, he shook his head. "Janet, what the hell happened?" At her sardonic glance, he waved a hand at her. "Yeah, I know it's obvious *what* happened. Somehow the waste-disposal cycle in Khuharkk's bathroom reversed itself after he'd . . . finished using the facilities."

She frowned grimly. "It's worse than that. Somehow, all the school's wastes for the *entire evening* failed to reach the energy recycling unit, and instead got shunted into this line, and then reversed when Khuharkk' flushed the unit."

Rob's eyes widened. "That's impossible!"

"It should be," Janet said stonily. "That's what scares me."

Rob strode across the room, heading for the bathroom. The Chief Engineer shook her head at him. "I wouldn't. I haven't activated the cleaning servos, yet. It's pretty bad . . . I lost my supper."

"I'm a doctor," Rob reminded her curtly. "One time I had to autopsy a week-old—"

The psychologist broke off with a gasp as he stepped inside the bathroom, then he clapped his hand over his mouth and nose, feeling the sushi lurch in his stomach. Even a single whiff made his eyes water. Pinching his nostrils shut, breathing through his mouth, Rob forced himself to hold his ground for a moment.

Bodily wastes from human and alien students splattered the ceiling, walls, and fixtures in grotesque, bas-relief sculptures radiating outward from the toilet. Brown, indigo, crimson, white, green . . . Rob had never realized that excrement came in so many colors and textures. Janet's abandoned supper didn't help matters any.

"Oh, my God . . ." Rob whispered. Gagging, he backed up, then retreated hastily to the entrance to Khuharkk's quarters. Bracing himself in the doorway, he drew a deep, grateful breath of blessedly recycled air.

"Thanks for not saying 'Holy shit,' " Janet said dryly, joining him.

"No wonder Khuharkk' was hysterical!" Rob gasped, wiping his eyes. "How could this happen? And most importantly—does this indicate that there's something wrong with the environmental systems?"

Janet shook her head, her short reddish hair standing on end, as though she'd been tugging at it. "It wasn't a mechanical failure, I know that. Somehow the computer glitched and caused the sanitation system to reverse. My checks indicate that everything—including the waste-disposal system—is running normally again."

"A computer glitch caused *that*?" Rob was aghast. "How? Why? Can you trace it?"

"I've been trying. As to how, there's no indication in the system. I'm going to check everything again—to the extent of getting a binary dump, if I have to. But I have a feeling I'm not going to find anything." Janet's green eyes narrowed. "Rob, I can't prove it, but my gut instinct tells me this was sabotage."

"Sabotage?" Rob's mouth went dry. "But—but . . ."

"I know it doesn't make sense, but I can't shake the feeling."

"Not everyone is in favor of the Academy," Rob said slowly. "There are anti-StarBridge factions on most worlds, I'd guess. But if some terrorist wanted to harm us, why do something like this? Why not tamper with the water, or the food—or, God forbid, the air? Blowing sewage out of one toilet isn't life-threatening, it's more like a practical joke, a prank . . . wait a minute, a prank . . ." Rob ran a hand through his hair, thinking hard. "Pranks using computers . . . oh, no . . ."

"What?" Janet seized on his words. "You think this was some kind of practical joke?"

"In a bizarre way, the punishment even fits the crime—an eye for an eye, a bathroom accident for a bathroom accident . . ." Rob muttered, his mind racing. His eyes met Janet's, holding her gaze. "Suppose this was a prank," he said slowly. "Or revenge, aimed at Khuharkk'. Is it possible that somebody programmed the system to cause this?"

"Without leaving a single trace of meddling?" Janet was skeptical. "I don't know, Rob, that's asking a lot. Tampering by hackers is usually detectable, and I haven't seen any sign of that."

"But is it possible?" he repeated tensely.

"I'd like it to be possible," her voice was quiet. "Believe me, I'd much rather conclude that somebody managed to bypass the multiple levels of fail-safes and traps I programmed into these systems than believe that the whole incident is accidental, and that those multiple fail-safes coincidentally went down at the same time." Her eyes searched his drawn features. "You think someone did this deliberately? Supposing someone could engineer this—though I have trouble imagining *how*—*who* would do this? And why?"

"I think it was a kid named Heather Farley," Rob said bleakly. "And, like you, I don't have any proof . . . just my gut reaction."

"That little kid?" Janet was startled. "You mean the girl who nearly got slugged by"—her eyes widened—"by *Khuharkk'*, that's who!" She put a hand on Rob's arm, shook it excitedly. "Did Serge tell you that she wet herself when Khuharkk' came at her?" Rob nodded grimly. "Damn, it fits, doesn't it! But how? How could she manage it?"

"I don't know how," the psychologist said. "But you ought to see her file." Briefly, he recounted some of Heather's more spectacular bits of computer chicanery—including the "systems failure by unknown causes" that had plagued the Melbourne Satellite School. "This sounds like more of the same," he finished.

"But there's not a shred of evidence that she did this. And I can't even begin to imagine *how* she did it—if she did it." Janet glanced at the ugly trail leading up the hall and shuddered. "If you're right, and Heather Farley did this, she's dangerous, Rob. I helped install the systems here at the Academy, and believe me, we anticipated that someday some bright young hacker might try to mess around with the life-support systems to show off. Heather should have tripped several traps on her way in—but she didn't."

"And?" Rob said, knowing the answer, but wanting to hear her say it.

"And if she can do this, she could get into the other environmental systems. The food, the water . . . the *air,* Rob. If she can bypass all those safeguards we put in these systems, she could cause a pressure drop, too."

A chill ran down Rob's spine. "The thought of that makes me want to expel her, stick her on the next Earth-bound transport. But without proof . . ." He shrugged. "What if I'm wrong? That would be a terrible injustice."

They stood in silence for a minute, frustrated and more than a little frightened. "So what now?" Janet asked finally.

Rob sighed. "Activate the cleaning servos, I guess. Then go over those dumps with a fine-toothed comb."

"It'll take me several days, at least."

"I know. But keep at it. If you discover even a shred of evidence that this was sabotage, I'll confront Heather, see if I can rattle her a little." He bit his lower lip, then shook his head. "Maybe I should ask Doctor Blanket to scan her. Then we'd *know.*"

Janet raised her eyebrows at him. "That's not ethical, Rob. We're supposed to set a good example—not let the ends justify the means."

"I know," Rob said wearily. "But remind me about ethics when we're all trying to breathe vacuum, why don't you? If this kid is unbalanced, there's no telling what she might do."

"We don't have any proof," Janet reminded him. "Hold off and let me do those checks."

"Okay. Maybe just dropping a hint or two would be enough to make her betray herself. But I'm not going to bet on it with this one, she's a tough little customer."

Janet turned to look back at the excrement smearing the floor matting outside the bathroom door. "No shit," she muttered sourly.

CHAPTER 5

♦

Siteseeing

Serge stood in the locker near the hangar dome, sealing his pressure suit while keeping one eye on his class. Many of them had finished suiting up, but some were still struggling with recalcitrant fastenings and seals—except, of course, the Mizari students. They shimmered, surrounded as they were with the radiant energy fields their race had developed in lieu of garments to protect against vacuum.

When he and the Professor had first begun working out at the dig, Serge had invested his entire savings to purchase his own pressure suit, tailored to his exact height and weight. It was a metallic ice-blue, standard color, but in anticipation of this field trip, he'd emblazoned scarlet lightning bolts on the upper arms, across the chest and back, so he'd be instantly recognizable to his students.

Leaving his helmet and gloves lying on the bench, the young instructor clumped across the room to where pretty, brown-haired Susan Whiteman was struggling to put on her helmet. "Allow me," he said, taking it and settling it on her head. "Next time, put the helmet on *before* you put on the gloves. That way, it's much easier."

Grasping the helmet, he turned it slightly, then clicked it into place against the collar of her pressure suit. Fastening the safety seals, he peered into the bulbous transparent faceplate, squinting at her face behind the glare of the overhead lights. "Commence your suit-check!" he cried, raising his voice so she could hear him.

"Who is your suit partner?"

She pointed to Howard Weinberg, a slight, dark-haired student with a beard. The young man was apparently ready, but as he saw Serge watching him, he pointed at his face, then grimaced behind his faceplate. Serge understood the student's discomfiture immediately; his beard was rasping and prickling against the suit controls as he attempted to activate them using his chin or his lower lip. *I should have warned him about that,* Serge thought, remembering his experience with facial adornment inside a helmet. With his fair coloring, it had taken him a long time to grow that beard, but he'd removed it without a second thought the instant he got back to his quarters.

Leaving Howie and Susan to complete their suit-checks, he put on his own helmet (but not his gloves), then went down the line of students, checking fastenings here, seals there. As he reached Professor Greyshine, the teacher glanced down at him, his eyes bright. Heeyoon helmets were shaped like blunted eggs, with the long, rounded portion of the oval extending outward from their faces, to accommodate their long muzzles. Greyshine's helmet, unlike those of human design, was completely transparent.

The Professor activated their private frequency: "Where is Hing, Serge? If she is going to accompany us, she should be here by now."

Serge sighed. "She is late, *comme d'habitude,*" he said, hoping that it was true and that she hadn't simply changed her mind. *Hing would not do that,* he argued mentally. *She may be scatterbrained at times, and chronically late—but she would never break a promise.*

As if in response to his thoughts, the door slid open, and Hing hurtled in like a shuttle leaving the dock. Her cheeks were flushed as she waved at him, mouthing "Sorry I'm late," then dived for the suit lockers, pawing through their contents to find one small enough to fit her.

Serge watched as she stepped out of her shoes, then shucked off her blue StarBridge coverall, leaving her wearing the black, one-piece leotard and tights designed to prevent clothing wrinkles from chafing a spacesuit wearer. After years of ballet classes to improve her balance and coordination onstage, she was boyishly slender. Her hips and rear had almost no padding, but her stomach, much to her expressed disgust, would never get quite flat. Her small, firm breasts jiggled as she stepped into the spacesuit and began tugging it up. It was chilly in the suit locker, and her nipples were clearly visible beneath the snug garment. Serge swallowed, unable to stop a rush of memory. *Stop that,* he reprimanded himself sternly. *Of all the times to think about sex!*

He waited until Hing had slipped her arms into the sleeves before he went over to help her fasten the final seals. "I'm sorry," she gasped as soon as her helmet was on and she'd activated her radio. "Play rehearsal ran overtime. You can draw and quarter me, I deserve it."

"Draw and quarter?" he repeated the English phrase carefully to make sure he had it right. "I haven't heard that expression before."

"Tear me limb from limb," Hing translated, grinning.

"There is no cause for concern," he hastened to reassure her. "Most of the students are only now finishing their suit-checks."

Quickly Serge and Hing ran through their own checks, verifying that seals were tight, their air paks were full, and that all interior displays were properly activated.

As soon as he was finished, Serge activated the universal frequency. "May I have your attention, please, class?" A moment later he continued, "Now we will form a line and walk through the hangar dome and out to the *Morning Cry.* Everyone stay with your suit partner, please, and remember—this asteroid's natural gravity is only one-tenth Terran normal—even less than that of Earth's Moon."

He paused, then continued grimly, "You will feel so light and floating that almost everyone is tempted to try a jump, but I beg of you, *don't*! It will be hard enough to keep your balance with both feet on the ground, because of the asteroid's irregular mass. The gravity forces here fluctuate slightly, depending on where one is standing. That can make people feel as though they are being pulled sideways, when actually they are standing up straight. It can be extremely disconcerting—and can cause you to lose your balance and fall."

He regarded them grimly. "One of the few casualities that ever occurred here at StarBridge Academy happened when one student wagered with another that he could jump high enough to achieve escape velocity—which, I assure you, is impossible, even at one-tenth gee—but the student actually attempted it. He jumped about a hundred meters high. Unfortunately, when he landed, he ripped his suit on the edge of a crater and decompressed. By the time the rescue team found him, the body was frozen *solid.*"

The new students murmured and shuffled; they hadn't heard the story until now. "So please—no leaps, no jumps. Okay?"

A general murmur of assent followed.

Once through the first airlock, Serge led them to the outer hangar exit. "Enter, please," he said, opening the inner door of the airlock leading onto the asteroid's surface. Hing and the Professor brought up the rear as the excited crowd jammed into the big supply lock. "Now I am going to depressurize the lock, at the same time reducing the gravity to the one-tenth gee outside."

Within moments, as the air was sucked out, Serge began to feel lighter. Gradually he decreased the gravity, until it matched that of the asteroid. "Is everyone okay?" he called, hearing muffled giggles and murmurings over the radio frequency. "Thumbs-up if everyone is A-okay!"

Seventeen thumbs were raised, plus two Mizari tentacles. Serge smiled, seeing that Khuharkk' had solemnly raised both his thumbs on his right hand.

Despite the many times he'd been out on the surface, Serge's pulse quickened, as it always did, when he keyed open the outer door. It was exciting but unnerving to think that the only thing standing between oneself and hard vacuum was a thin layer of plas-steel fabric.

Glancing up, he was struck once again by how extraordinarily brilliant and *alive* the stars were, viewed through the faceplate of a spacesuit. Unwinking, they hovered like myriads of sapphires, rubies, sunstones, and diamonds, a scattered treasure so vibrantly close that Serge fancied he could stretch out his gloved hand and gather them up.

"Please follow me," he said, starting forward. "Move slowly. Human students, flex your knees, keep them bent, and keep your feet fairly wide apart . . ."

At one-tenth gee Serge weighed only 6.53 kilos, but his body mass remained the same, so he moved carefully. The closest analogue was trying to walk underwater. Keeping his knees bent, he did a queer little step that was a cross between a skip and a shuffle as he led the way to the ship waiting for them a hundred meters away.

The *Morning Cry* had once been a luxury vessel, designed to ferry passengers at sub-light speeds from the Heeyoon mother world to its six moons. Its engines were still in decent shape, but it was no longer pressurized—after the Heeyoons had donated it, Janet Rodriguez had stripped out the seats and substituted handholds and restraining straps to make more room for passengers.

Serge reached the ship first, as he'd planned, and checked to see that everything was ready. It was, so he stood beside the ramp, beckoning his cautiously moving students forward.

"Look!" Hing, who was in the forefront of the column, suddenly pointed up. Serge followed her finger to see a ship emerging into realspace in a silent explosion of color. The sight was breathtakingly beautiful, and the visual image echoed inside Serge's head as rich chords—a sustained E-minor, then, as it dispersed into the blackness, an A-minor. He could see the notes on sheet music, hear the opening notes of a symphony, the Starburst Symphony . . .

He'd heard it before, in his mind—first that opening chord would be a triumphant blare of trumpets, fortissimo, then the woodwinds would come in to help the chord alter and fade, as the rainbow colors had faded—

No! Serge thought angrily, looking back at his students, pushing the music and its siren lure away. No matter how he tried to forget, notes that he could no longer translate into beauty kept intruding into his mind, his heart. His mouth a grim slash, he forced himself to concentrate on his students, helping each of them up the ramp until all were safely aboard.

Once all the students were belted into place, Serge turned off his radio and touched his helmet to Hing's so they could speak privately. "If you would like to ride up front, it is cramped, but the view is spectacular."

She hesitated, and for a moment he was afraid that he'd overstepped, but then she smiled, nodded, and followed him into the control cockpit. "This will be close quarters," he apologized as they squeezed in together. "This cabin was designed for one Heeyoon pilot."

There was just room enough for her to squat down and brace herself beside the pilot's seat. Serge had to wriggle to fit into it; it was designed for a Heeyoon's narrower hindquarters, padded and shaped to fit people who had tails. But he was used to the old ship. Responsive to his commands, the *Morning Cry* rose obediently on her belly-jets, hovered some twenty meters above the surface, then glided forward over the slagged, crater-pocked terrain.

Hing leaned forward to peer out of the viewport, watching the surface as the running lights spotlighted it in quick flashes of reddish-brown, gray, and black slag. "It's hard to believe that living things once grew down there," she said softly. "Have you found any fossils of large animals dating back to when this asteroid was part of a planet?"

"A few," Serge replied. "The plant and sea life had progressed to a level similar to Earth's during the Miocene. We found tiny charred and fused bone fragments in the slag covering the cave floor. Nothing large enough to give us a picture of the creature."

In the distance he could make out the Lamont Cliffs, visible only because their jagged edges blocked out the stars on the eerily close horizon. "Fused bone fragments?" Hing's voice held surprise. "Oh! Burned and fused during the comet's impact, you mean."

"That, too," Serge replied. "But last week Greyshine discovered that someone—presumably the Lost Colony—deliberately vaporized the top soil and rock levels in the caverns, smoothing them out."

"Which would destroy any fossils."

"On the top levels, yes. Besides," he added, "Greyshine and I are archaeologists, not paleontologists. If the Mizari change their minds and send a complete team to investigate, one of them will undoubtedly be someone with fossil experience, someone who will be able to tell more than we can from those fragments. Until that time, we must confine ourselves to collecting and preserving them."

"Change their minds?" Despite his effort to keep it level, she'd heard the bitterness that tinged his voice.

"There is a good chance that the Mizari Archaeological Society will not fund the dig further . . . *c'est bien dommage,*" he admitted heavily. "They are sending Esteemed Rizzshor and one assistant to make an evaluation. If they decide against us . . ." he trailed off.

She was distressed for him. "Oh, Serge, I know how disappointed you must be! You were counting on the Mizari to help, weren't you?"

"We were," he replied, struggling not to sound curt. It was not easy for him to talk about something he felt so strongly about, but in his sessions with Rob Gable in the past months, he'd painfully learned that if you expected people to share with you, you had to start by giving something of yourself. "But it may not be the end— Jeffrey Morrow has promised to give us some funding personally, so we can continue, at least for the moment. We will be opening up more caverns, because the two we have worked on to date seem to be, as miners put it, 'played out.' "

"I've got my fingers crossed for you," she promised, shifting restlessly in the cramped space.

"We are nearly there," Serge said, pointing to the mountain peaks that were now blotting out wide swaths of stars. "But if your legs are tired, you could go back to the passenger cabin."

"I'm okay," she assured him.

Serge was tempted to ask her whether she wanted to sit on the arm of the seat beside him, but he resisted. He thought he was making progress in getting back in Hing's good graces, and he didn't want to spoil it.

"So, how is your play?" he asked, after a moment, changing the subject.

"At the moment, we're still learning lines. The director's having academic problems, and he may have to drop out. That'll leave me holding the bag," Hing said ruefully. "Talk about bad timing!"

"You would make a gifted director," he reassured her. "You have had a great deal of experience by now."

"Maybe, but I'd rather make my directorial debut in something I don't have a part in," she said. "And this part, it's a real challenge! It may be the hardest I've ever done. It's difficult, playing somebody old and embittered. Mara is a character who won't let anyone get close to her . . . and now she's alone, and facing the end of her life, and she's beginning to regret, but she doesn't know how to reach out to others."

Serge winced inwardly, wondering whether Hing was trying to twist the knife. Toward the end of their time together, she'd complained that he held people at arm's length, wouldn't let anyone get really close to him. She'd tried to persuade him to open up to her about his feelings, talk about his music, his lost hands, but he'd rejected every such attempt with stony silence . . . and worse.

For a moment he tensed, but then, as Hing chattered on, giving him a complete character sketch of Mara and her history, Serge realized there were no hidden agendas in what she'd said; it was his own guilt that made him hear a silent comparison and accusation.

Vainly, he racked his brain for some way to bring the conversation back to a more personal level when Hing lapsed into quiet once more. "By the way, how is Heather?" he said finally. What he really wanted to know was, "Are you seeing anyone?" but he couldn't figure out a way to make *that* question sound casual.

"She's fine, except that environmental drill we had the night Khuharkk's john blew up really scared her. The poor kid went absolutely white when the alarm went off, and she's been subdued—for Heather—ever since."

"It is frightening to truly realize that there is no air outside," Serge said, gesturing at the viewport. Slowing the *Morning Cry,* he checked his position on the computer map grid, heading the ship for McAuliffe Pass. Stars suddenly winked into view between Shrann Peak and Greendeer Peak—they would enter the pass in moments.

"That's true," Hing said hesitantly, "but somehow I don't think that's the whole story. Heather's a funny kid . . . she talks a lot, but not much about things that really matter to her. I'm trying to be her friend, and I can tell she likes me, but she doesn't trust me. I don't think she trusts anyone—it's sad, a kid that age."

"I like her," Serge surprised himself by saying. "She is . . . tough. What is the English expression . . . spunky, *non*?"

"Spunky, *oui*," Hing agreed, and he could hear the impish smile in her voice. "She likes you, too. *Beaucoup*. How do you feel about younger women?"

Repressing a groan, Serge turned to glance at her. "You are joking, *non*?"

He could see her grin behind her faceplate. "*Non*. She has a terrible crush on you, so be kind, Serge."

Chuckling weakly, Serge shook his head and turned his attention back to his controls. "Being kind is not something I do very well," he said, recalling some of their arguments. *And neither is commitment . . . or intimacy.*

"*Au contraire.* You're very kind, Serge," Hing said quietly, a note of fierceness in her voice that surprised him. "I've always known that."

It was the most personal remark she'd made to him since the breakup, and Serge wanted desperately to pursue it, but by that time they were through the pass and approaching the landing lights outside the caverns. *Zut!* he thought disgustedly. *Speaking of bad timing—!*

What am I going to do about Serge? He wants to try again, I can tell. But what do I want? Hing wondered as she stood with Professor Greyshine aboard the *Morning Cry,* waiting to debark. Ahead of her the line of students shuffled slowly forward as Serge helped them down the steep ramp, doubly difficult to negotiate in the irregular gravity.

Frowning, she remembered what it had been like that last week they'd been together. Frustrated by his casual assurances of devotion, Hing had confronted Serge, pushed him, demanding that he talk, as she desperately tried to discover what lay beneath the surface. For days she'd struggled to penetrate that good-humored mask he turned outward. The results had been disastrous . . . first he'd tried to laugh off her demands, then he'd lapsed into sullen silence, and finally he'd lost his temper and shouted bitter recriminations, then withdrawn completely. Hing had packed and left the next day.

I was wrong to push him so hard, she thought, shifting uneasily in the uneven gravity that made her right side feel slightly heavier. *I should have realized how much he cared, not tried to make him say things he wasn't ready to say.*

But revealing how he really felt had been nearly impossible for Serge. It was as though all his deepest emotions were inextricably tied in with the anger that lay smoldering far below the surface . . . like a deep river of magma, it bubbled and seethed, and occasionally frightening glimpses of it broke through.

His lost hands . . . his lost music. Serge's anger over his accident and its results was slowly poisoning him, had already poisoned a relationship that Hing admitted to herself might have become very serious indeed.

She'd been a heartbeat away from loving him, but something had held her back . . . somehow she'd instinctively sensed that Serge wouldn't truly be capable of a deep and caring relationship until he made peace with his past.

And now . . . what?

Maybe this time we could make it work, she thought, feeling a spark of longing. She knew that Serge had been seeing Rob Gable intensively ever since their breakup, and she knew Rob well enough to know that Serge wouldn't be able to stonewall the psychologist the way he'd stonewalled and rebuffed her. *Maybe now it would be different . . .*

But she didn't want to risk being hurt again. When she and Serge had broken up, she'd been depressed for weeks. She'd—

Someone nudged her gently, breaking into her musings, and Hing realized with a start that all the students were down the ramp, and Serge was holding out a hand to steady her. "Oh, I'm sorry!" she gabbled, flushing and placing her gloved hand into his. "Sorry, I was . . . uh . . ."

As she trailed off, concentrating on picking her way down the ramp, Serge's voice came over the frequency they'd selected for "private" communication. "Rehearsing your lines, yes? I know you too well, you see."

She smiled, relieved that he hadn't guessed the direction of her thoughts. "You want me to bring up the rear?"

"Please. Call me immediately if anyone has a problem."

Turning, he led the way toward the cliff wall about a hundred meters away. A spotlight, its beam sharp as a blade without atmosphere to soften and diffuse it, illuminated an airlock set into the rocky face of the cliff at the foot of Greendeer Peak.

It was the first time Hing had been to the mountains, though she'd taken several walks on the surface of the asteroid during her time as a student. Watching her step with one part of her mind, she glanced around her. Aside from the lighted airlock opening ahead, the starlight provided too little illumination to permit a real view. Only glimpses of the peaks tantalized her, looming sharply over the little party in their pressure suits.

"Professor, how were these caverns formed?" Hing asked, using the universal channel so all the students could hear his reply.

The Heeyoon hopped over a slagged hummock, then floated ever so gently down to the ground again before replying: "This cavern was formed by the action of water against rock and limestone, roughly a billion years ago. It is fortunate that it survived the cataclysm that tore its world apart. We will be visiting the large cavern where the original artifacts were found, plus a smaller one a short distance from it. Everyone please stay together, because there are many caverns, and most of them are not pressurized. If anyone became lost, it could be very serious indeed."

Hing thought of *Tom Sawyer* and Injun Joe's fate, and resolved to stick close to the others. Serge led the first group into the airlock, and Hing and the Professor waited with the remaining students until the light flashed, indicating the lock was ready to use again.

The air cycled through, the indicators flashed go. "There is a Mizari-normal gravity field within," the Heeyoon told them. "Everyone please tread carefully."

Hing felt the gravity shift as she stepped over the threshold, grabbing her like glue, but she was so enthralled by what she was seeing that she barely noticed. *It's beautiful!* she thought delightedly.

She'd always loved caves and caverns. As a child growing up in Montreal, she'd visited most of the major caverns in North Am. She had vivid memories of the stalactite organ at Luray Caverns, the tiny freetail bats nesting in the ceilings of Carlsbad Caverns, and the magnificent cathedrallike vastness of Mammoth Cave.

But she'd never seen anything quite like this place!

Red-gold stalactites, broken but still huge, reached down toward the stubs of blue-gray stalagmites in a cluster to her right. Flowstone snaked its sparkling way across a ceiling that vaulted upward into darkness.

Serge and the Professor's grids marked out even squares on the slagged, black-splotched floor, but their excavation covered only a fraction of the total area in this one cavern alone. *No wonder they need a whole team!* Hing thought, realizing what a huge task Serge and the Professor had tackled. Thoroughly excavating even this one chamber would take them months . . . years, perhaps.

Against the far wall, protected by glowing protective fields, were the artifacts. Serge waved them in that direction. "Everyone please remove your helmets," he told them. "This area is pressurized. Do not forget to turn off your breathing paks, so we can conserve them while we are here in the cavern."

Hing removed her helmet and turned off her pak, then followed Serge and the Professor over to admire the artifacts. When they came to the songharp, Hing glanced over at Serge and asked quietly, "Has anyone tried to play it?"

For a second she glimpsed temptation in his expression, then he shrugged and looked away. "No. It would be too much risk to handle it. The years have probably made it brittle."

"Esteemed Ssoriszs believes that these artifacts were left by our Lost Colony," one of the Mizari students said. "Do you believe that is true?"

The Professor hesitated. "I am reserving judgment," he said finally. "Although the indications so far are favorable. Strontium-rubidium dating confirms the artifacts are from the same era as the Lost Colony. But I want to know *where* these artifacts came from, as well as *when* they were made."

"How can you determine that?" Susan asked.

"Several of these artifacts are made of a ceramic alloy that was central to Mizari manufacturing four to five thousand years ago," Professor Greyshine replied. "Experts will be able to determine their exact place of origin by tracing their magnetic resonances."

A Simiu student standing in front of Hing raised his hand, and she recognized Khuharkk'. "How does that work?" the Simiu asked.

"You will recall our class discussions concerning dating techniques and location pinpointing," Serge said. "Any planet that has a defined magnetic field, such as Hurrreeah, Shassiszss, or Terra can use this type of magnetic 'signature' of origin."

Professor Greyshine pointed to the songharp with its iridescent surface, its scrolled insets, its jeweled frets. "When this—and each of the other artifacts that contain this ceramic alloy—was fired, they all became slightly magnetized. The electrons lined up in patterns that paralleled those of its surroundings. Mizari archaeologists have programs that will compare the magnetic fields known to exist four thousand years ago with those of these artifacts and attempt a match. If they match up to the time *and* the location of the Mizari Lost Colony, then we will know with certainty that they passed this way."

"How will they know which is the correct pattern?" Hing asked.

"Much is known about the Mizari expedition now called the 'Lost Colony,' " the Professor said ruefully, "except, of course, for their ultimate fate. They obtained all of their supplies from a specific manufacturing area located in their southern hemisphere. The magnetic 'signature' will be very clear."

"There are other tests that will also be conducted," Serge added, "but the magnetic tests are among the most important. If you'll recall our session last week on identifying falsified and stolen black-market artifacts, this technique has been frequently used to uncover fakes as opposed to stolen treasures."

After a brief demonstration of the sifter and the other excavation tools, Professor Greyshine instructed them to put on their helmets, indicating another airlock within the chamber. "We must go down an unpressurized tunnel. Taller students, please be cautious. The ceiling is quite low."

The group passed through the airlock and into a narrow, low passage, illuminated by battery-powered lights every ten or fifteen meters. Hing was short enough to walk upright, but many of the students—including the tall Heeyoon—were forced to bend down and keep their heads tucked like turtles.

The tunnel narrowed even farther, until they were walking single file. Hing was not usually claustrophobic, but even she felt uneasy as the walls and the ceiling seemed about to close in on them, trapping them. "Only a few steps more," Serge called out reassuringly, "then you will be able to walk upright."

As he'd promised, the passageway widened out, and suddenly they were facing a branch-off and another airlock. "In here," Serge said, standing in the mouth of the side tunnel and gesturing them past him, thus forestalling anyone deciding to embark on any side trips.

This airlock held only a few individuals, so it took the group several minutes for everyone to get into the small cavern. Hing, still bringing up the rear as requested, was in the last party to go through. Gravity made her feel stumble-footed again as she stepped over the threshold, took off her helmet, then looked around.

Before her, frozen calcite waterfalls glimmered like ghosts beside vast columns and other formations of fused rock. A sheet of dark flowstone overhead looked like a horse's head thrown back, bugling silently into the eons. Hing smiled wryly to herself as she imagined a tour guide pointing it out and calling it "The Black Stallion."

This chamber did not have the slagged floors and walls of the other. *It must have been protected when the comet hit,* Hing thought, *because it's so much deeper inside the mountain than the big cavern.*

She inhaled the air, tasting the dry, chalky odor of ancient rock, and wrinkled her nose.

This chamber was approximately twenty meters by thirty, and roughly ellipsoid in shape. At the other side of the chamber another airlock, a tiny, one-person job, was inset into the wall. Serge explained that the tunnels beyond continued an unknown distance into the mountains. Along the right wall, three-meter-wide crevasses in floor and wall marked an ancient split in the rock. As Hing followed the students past the rift in the floor, she looked down, seeing a Mizari protective field generator resting on a small ledge approximately five meters down. The artificial gravity and pressure only extended down as far as that ledge; below that generator was the asteroid's normal hard vacuum and one-tenth gee.

The Professor gestured to the floor, which had only a few grids marked off. "We only began excavations here last month," he said. "The ration pellet container and the waste-disposal bag fragment were found in this chamber, approximately where those two grids"—he pointed—"have been excavated."

Hing stared around her, trying to imagine what it might have been like here four thousand or so years ago, picturing Mizari gliding along these dusty limestone floors, their scales crunching the dust, tracing it into swirling patterns.

Suddenly she stiffened, then grabbed Serge's arm. "Serge, look!" she whispered excitedly. "Something up on that ledge is reflecting the light!"

The young instructor followed her gaze, but couldn't see anything until he did a half-knee bend, hunkering down to her eye level. *"Mon Dieu, vous avez raison!"* Serge whispered. "And see the ridge leading up? It has been artificially flattened and smoothed, like a Mizari ascension ramp!"

About three meters above them there was a dark depression in the cave wall; it resembled the mouth of a minuscule cave. A flattened ridge of rock lay beneath it, angling upward from the cavern floor. Deep in the blackness, something glimmered softly.

"I see it!" Hing said, still clinging to his arm. "Could they have carried something up there?"

"Professor!" Serge cried, waving an arm, then gesturing for emphasis. "Voilà! Look up there! Hing saw it first!"

"What?" The Professor squinted and weaved, trying to see what had attracted their attention.

Khuharkk' sat up on his hindquarters, his violet eyes widening.

"I see it, too! Crouch down, Professor! There is something shiny up there, along the wall just inside that tiny cave."

"By the Teeth of my Ancestors," Greyshine muttered, his eyes narrowing to slits. Absently, he skirted the edge of the crevasse in the floor, then trotted over to the base of the rock ramp and peered upward. "Here we have been looking so hard at the ground—what is on it and beneath it—that we failed to examine what might lie above. Serge"—his voice grew suddenly shrill—"I believe Hing has discovered our missing star-shrine! More evidence that we have indeed found a link to the Lost Colony!"

The class began applauding excitedly. Hing, grinning, stepped forward and curtsied, just as she would have taken a bow on opening night.

The Professor's sharp canines gleamed as he yipped wordlessly with excitement. When the clamor died down, he eyed the little opening measuringly. "Serge, hand me the camera and the neutron emitter," he ordered. "I am going to climb up there."

"Are you sure you should?" the young man said doubtfully, handing the alien the requested pieces of equipment. "It's quite steep. Perhaps we should go back to the other chamber for an anti-grav climbing unit."

The Professor laughed, a great roaring bark that echoed around the chamber. "My people are the most surefooted of the Fifteen Known Races, Serge, and as a youth, my hobby was ridge-strolling." Placing the neutron emitter in his mouth (he looked for all the world like a German shepherd Hing had had as a child), he clipped the minicam to the belt of his suit, then began scrambling up the narrow rock ramp on all fours.

Hing watched, fascinated, as he reached the tiny ledge, then bent forward into the mouth of the cave, the stumpy shape of his tail hanging over the brink. "It is!" he shouted, busily filming. "The star-shrine! And a beautiful one at that . . . definitely the work of a master artist!"

Hing had heard of the star-shrines . . . the Star Seekers had worshiped the cosmos in all its expanding glory, but in order to show the proper humility, they had created small representations of star-scapes for use in their devotions, not presuming to gaze upon the actual stars during their religious ceremonies. Star-shrines were like tiny planetariums, and often the "stars" were made from inlaid precious and semiprecious stones.

"Is it jeweled?" she called.

"Yes, I see sunstones, firestones, icestones . . . oh, it is a wonder!" Professor Greyshine put down the camera and picked up the neutron emitter. "I will use this to discover whether anything is stored behind it. Sometimes the Star Seekers secreted records behind their star-shrines, and the neutron emitter will reveal any such storage places. An early version of this instrument was used to look for hidden chambers in one of the pyramids on Earth's old Egypt, centuries ago," he added, then turned with the camera in hand. "Here, Serge, take this," he instructed, placing it on the ledge beside him.

Serge started forward, but Khuharkk' was already there. "Allow me," the alien said, and before the young instructor could protest, the Simiu was scampering up the narrow ramp as agilely as if he moved on a level floor.

Greyshine had already turned back to his discovery, neutron emitter in hand. He switched it on. "First I must—"

The alien broke off as an alarm abruptly began shrieking. "Radiation warning!" a computerized voice announced. "Radonium-2 levels dangerous to most life-forms detected in this area! Vacate immediately!"

"Helmets on!" Serge yelled. Hing fumbled with hers, her heart slamming. As soon as she could see again, she looked back to see Serge, his helmet still in his hands, his voice now muffled and distant. "Professor, you must put on your helmet!" he shouted. "Come down at once!"

Hing's radio frequency echoed with a loud babble of mingled curses, frightened questions, and panicky exclamations. "Everyone stay calm," she commanded, her voice cutting through the cacophony. "These suits are shielded against radiation, remember? We're going to leave right away, but we're going to do it in an orderly fashion, as soon as the Professor is safe. Remember your emergency drills! Now quiet down and keep this frequency clear!"

Blessed silence ensued.

Serge, put on your helmet! she urged him mentally, realizing that he was probably inhaling contaminated air with every breath. But if he did that, he'd no longer be able to communicate with the Simiu or the Heeyoon, still high above him. "Khuharkk', if you back down, I will guide you," he urged, his voice calm and steady. Putting up his hands, he began coaxing the alien backward. "Professor Greyshine," he repeated urgently, "come *down!*"

"But the star-shrine—" Hing could barely hear the archaeologist's protest. Then, evidently deciding that he had no alternative, the alien instructor began crabbing sideways, trying to turn so he could begin his descent—

—until his hand slipped!

Hing gasped in horror as the Heeyoon's heavy body lurched, then skidded. An instant later the Professor was falling, slamming into Khuharkk', tumbling toward the humans. Hing screamed involuntarily as she threw herself to the side, grabbing at a flailing arm or leg. Her gloved hand skidded over the slick material of his spacesuit, finding no purchase, no hold . . .

The Heeyoon's frightened yelp rose above the still-wailing alarm and the computer's repetitious warning as he landed on the brink of the crevasse; then, with a final howl of agony, the Professor disappeared over the edge.

CHAPTER 6
◆
Over the Edge

Heather leaned back in her chair and closed her eyes, trying to relax. She was sitting in a study cubicle in the spacious StarBridge library, waiting for her tutor in alien telepathic techniques to arrive. The child was supposed to be meditating, clearing her mind, but her thoughts churned restlessly, images forming behind her closed eyes.

Images . . .

Khuharkk's yelping, gibbering form, trailing filth from his matted hair, bolting headlong down the hall, nearly knocking her over. Heather had barely begun to savor her victory before she'd been startled by the blare of the emergency alert. She'd wandered aimlessly until one of the seniors, a Chhhh-kk-tu, grabbed her and strapped her into one of the Mizari beltpaks, showing her how to activate her location transmitter.

Heather had never envisioned her prank causing such a furor. Students had milled anxiously in the corridors, whispering that the environmental systems were all tied in together, and that a problem with one might affect all the others. Her mouth dry and heart pounding, Heather wondered whether her meddling had caused additional systems to overload or short out. By the time the "all-clear" had been issued, she'd been so scared she was on the verge of confessing everything.

Images . . .

Rob Gable's well-drawn features replaced Khuharkk's draggled

form in her memory. Heather had discovered the psychologist
leaning against the wall near the entrance to her Advanced Mizari
class the next day. When he'd spotted the girl, he'd beckoned her
over. "Hi, Heather," he'd said, his usually warm smile noticeably
absent. "How are you doing?"

The girl smiled uncertainly and shrugged. "Oh, fine, Dr. Ga—
uh, Dr. Rob. How are you?"

Rob's dark eyes never left her face as he folded his arms across
his chest. "Not so good, Heather. I didn't sleep very well last night.
I was worried about the environmental systems. One failure can
lead to another, you know . . ." He leaned forward, and for a second Heather tensed, thinking he was going to grab her shoulders
and shake her. "You *did* know that, didn't you?"

Oh, shit, he knows I did it! Heather thought frantically, *I don't
know how, but he knows!* She almost blurted out the whole story
then and there, but fears of going back to Earth, of being returned
to Uncle Fred, had stopped her. Biting the inside of her lip, she
forced herself to say quietly, "Yeah, I know. I was really scared."

"I'll bet you were. So were a lot of other people," Rob said
grimly.

"Do you have any idea how it happened?" Heather asked,
wishing she dared to search his mind to find out what he knew.
But she'd abandoned the idea of a telepathic probe the moment
she'd noticed the jeweled earcuff he was wearing. The tiny thing
was almost concealed by his hair, and so pretty that it might have
been mere ornamentation, like the small ring of Rigellian opal
Rob wore in his left earlobe—but Heather was willing to bet it
was another of those damned distorts.

The psychologist hesitated for a long second before replying. "I
hate to tell you this, Heather," he said finally, "but we're pretty
sure the whole thing was due to sabotage. Computer sabotage."

The child's stomach lurched sickeningly. *Calm down!* her
survivor-self ordered sharply. *If he had any proof, he wouldn't
be playing cat and mouse. And you know you didn't leave any
traces of tampering behind.* "That's awful!" She managed to
register an appropriate amount of shock. "Who could have done
such a thing?"

Rob smiled coldly. "That's what I lay awake last night asking
myself. It must have been someone who is awfully good with computers. I'm just hoping that the guilty party will come forward. Or
at least have the sense not to tamper again. It would go hard with
him, her, or seloz," he said. "*Very* hard." His dark eyes were so
cold she had to repress a shiver.

"I'll bet," Heather agreed fervently. "Uh, listen, Dr. Rob, I've got to get to class. If I hear anything, I'll let you know."

Rob bared his teeth in a smile that had nothing of good humor about it. "You do that, Heather. Thanks a million." As she'd stood watching him, he sauntered away. Just before he turned the corner, Rob reached up and pulled off his distort, and immediately Heather caught his thought—the thought he'd *wanted* her to catch. *And I'm sure Khuharkk' would be highly interested in knowing, too . . .*

Now, sitting in the library, Heather's throat tightened as she envisioned the Simiu, what he'd do to her if he ever found out who had caused his disgrace. Heather swallowed, gulping back nausea, remembering Khuharkk's huge fangs and massive, sinewy hands. *He'd rip me in two . . .*

The day of Rob's not-so-veiled warning, Heather had been so upset that she'd cut class and practically run down the corridor in the opposite direction, her heart slamming painfully in her chest. It had taken two ice-cream sundaes at the Spiral Arm, StarBridge's student café and hangout, before she'd regained her equanimity.

Despite her fears, Rob hadn't pursued the issue, and within a few days, the sewage-reversal incident seemed to be mostly forgotten, except for a rash of scatological jokes a few humans took relish in repeating—always carefully out of Simiu earshot, of course.

But Heather didn't forget. Her life wouldn't be worth a kilo of comet dust if Khuharkk' ever found out who had sabotaged his john, and she never lost sight of that unpleasant fact. She needed money, money she could use to make a quick getaway, money to take her to another world, because, no matter what, Heather wasn't going to let them ship her back to Earth! Hell, no!

So, for the past few days, the girl had been working on a plan that would give her a tidy nest egg, hidden away in a place where no one could trace it. Soon she'd be ready to put Phase Two of her scheme into effect, and then it wouldn't be long before she'd have enough for a ticket to one of the colony worlds, and plenty to live on until she could find work.

But I hope I don't have to leave, she thought wistfully, surprising herself. She *liked* it here at StarBridge. This school challenged her active mind. She actually found herself looking forward to some of her classes. *Don't forget, there are other schools,* she reminded herself, then she sighed aloud. *Other schools, yeah, but only one Serge LaRoche. And only one Hing.* The thought of never seeing them again made her bite her lip and wish, for the first time, that she'd just let bygones be bygones with Khuharkk'.

Serge . . . his handsome face filled her mind, and Heather smiled dreamily. Serge, as she'd known from the first moment she saw him, was definitely a class act—a real gentleman. And she loved him, loved him as she had never loved anyone before.

Heather's feelings were so new, so strong, so intense that they scared her. She would have died rather than admit them to anyone, and only in her innermost fantasies had she even dared to dream that Serge would ever love her in return. It was enough for the girl that he was nice to her, waved and smiled when he saw her, talked to her as though she were a grown-up, instead of patronizing her like most older boys. Heather knew, from cautiously probing his mind, that Serge genuinely *liked* her—and that was more than she'd ever believed possible.

She didn't even feel jealous of Hing—at least, not much. Heather was a realist, and didn't delude herself about the odds against Serge ever being attracted to her as a girlfriend. The difference in their ages—eleven whole years!—seemed a century to the child . . . a gulf so great it could never be bridged.

Besides, she admired Hing. If Serge had to be in love with another woman, Heather concluded, Hing was the only person she'd met so far who came close to being worthy of him. She wasn't pretty enough, and her figure wasn't perfect, but she was smart and talented, and her cheerful friendliness was contagious. The Cambodian student was also genuinely interested in her younger roommate, and this was such a new experience that Heather found it impossible to resist. Hing really *listened* when the younger girl talked. *If I could have had a big sister,* she thought, leaning her head back and lazily twirling in her chair, *I'd have wanted one like her . . .*

Heather knew from her cautious peeks at Hing's thoughts (she hadn't dared to really probe; Hing was sensitive to mind-touches) that the older student saw her more realistically than anyone she could remember—and, wonder of wonders, Hing still liked her! Heather was warmed by that knowledge—it had proved a bulwark against her initial homesickness for Earth, her ever-present loneliness.

Yesterday she'd had her usual appointment with Rob, and Heather had been "as nervous as a harlot in church," to quote Uncle Fred, but Rob had not alluded to Khuharkk's "accident." Instead, he'd asked Heather about her earliest recollections, whether she remembered her mother and father at all. The girl had been asked these same questions so many times that it was easy for her to give relatively truthful answers without letting what she was saying penetrate on any emotional level . . . though she'd quickly sensed that Rob Gable wasn't going to be content to leave it there—and she'd been right.

He'd been particularly interested in her father. "Your father is telepathic, it says here. Did he ever communicate with you telepathically?"

"I don't remember." Heather shook her head, feeling suddenly uneasy. "It was so long ago. Six years, almost."

Rob had smiled ruefully. "Wait until you have to try and remember things that happened two or three decades ago, instead of a few years. Tell me, do you have any memories at all of him before your mom's death?" he prodded. "Anything at all?"

Heather's cool detachment had faltered slightly as she'd answered honestly, "I think—I think I remember him buying me an ice-cream cone one time. At the park."

"Tell me about it."

"I don't remember anything else. Just that it was an ice-cream cone, and that he bought it and handed it to me."

"What flavor?"

Heather had given him a look that mingled surprise and exasperation. "How the hell—I mean, how should I know?"

"You'd be surprised how many times tactile memories can trigger others."

"Well, I don't remember," Heather had said curtly.

But now, sitting in the library, remembering yesterday's session, she suddenly *did* remember. Peppermint. She could see the pink and white swirls. Peppermint. Her mind was suddenly full of the memory-taste, sharp, cloyingly sweet . . .

Daddy handed the cone to her, its sticky pinkness dripping down the white napkin; she'd clutched it so hard the cone had cracked, but she'd eaten it anyway, lick-lick-lick, yum, yes. Good . . .

Daddy smiled, smiled so wide. His teeth were white as he smiled at Heather, then he smiled at Mommy and Mommy smiled back. Mommy was so pretty, her red-gold hair curling softly, smelling like flowers, her blouse the color of the sky above the park. The park was green and smelled all growy like gardens. Flowers everywhere, and someone had a puppy, it wanted to lick Heather's ice cream and she was willing but Mommy said no, which was the word grown-ups knew best . . . lick-lick-lick, savor the taste, savor the moment, yum, yes, it was good to be here with Mommy and Daddy . . .

Mommy thought it was good, too, her mind was warm and sweet like the runnels of ice cream dripping off Heather's chubby fist. But Heather knew better than to touch Daddy's mind, because there was a bad spot inside, and she was scared of it. Daddy could talk without moving his mouth just like Heather could, and they used to talk together like that, and that was the most fun of all. But lately, Heather wanted only to mouth-talk with Daddy, because the last time they had mind-talked she had touched the bad spot and she never wanted to touch it again, no, no!

Touching the bad spot had been like the time she'd bitten into the pretty pale orange fruit Mommy called "ape-ri-cot" and there had been a black oozy place inside, smelly and soft and squooshy, yuck! And Mommy had said the fruit was sick inside, bruised, and had thrown it away.

So Heather was too scared to tell about the bad spot inside Daddy, because he was still her daddy and she loved him; she didn't want anyone to throw him away. But she couldn't help knowing sometimes that the bad spot was there, and it was growing. More and more of Daddy's mind was getting bruised; Daddy was always afraid of what was inside his head, but he didn't want anyone to know what was there, or how scared he was. Heather knew that Daddy sat alone at night, fighting the bad spot and the things it told him, the things it showed him—things Heather had glimpsed just that once and never wanted to see again.

Daddy was scared, so scared it made Heather want to cry, but she knew he loved her . . . he loved Mommy, too, even though sometimes they had fights, but today everything was good, the bad spot was far away, and the ice cream was—

A gentle, wordless greeting touched her mind. Heather jerked upright in her seat, her eyes snapping open to see her instructor before her. Correction—instructors, plural. Shadgui were a symbiotic organism, and thought of themselves as "we."

The "Shad" portion of the symbiont was a large, hairy being with only vestigial depressions in his face that once, ages ago, had been his species' eye sockets. More than two meters tall, the massive, slothlike creature dwarfed most humans, and especially Heather. Nestled on the Shad's huge shoulder and actually linked to the hairy creature's body by a complex biochemical bond was the "Gui" portion of the organism; a small, red-skinned toadlike being with bright button eyes that "saw" for both of them.

The Shad's mouth moved, and carefully articulated Mizari emerged. "Are you ready for our lesson, Heather?"

The girl nodded, then, knowing that Shadgui preferred telepathic communication, expressed her assent mentally.

Approval flowed from Kaross as the Shadgui settled himself into the slinglike support his species used in lieu of seats. "We will work today on nonverbal communication, which is vital when making a First Contact. You expressed interest, we believe, in becoming an explorer?"

Yes, I did, Heather replied silently.

"Very well. Let us begin with identifying basic emotions shared by most of the species inhabiting the Fifteen Known Worlds. Are you ready?"

Heather expressed her agreement wordlessly, then tried to make her mind as blank as possible. A moment later she felt the muscles at the back of her neck tense, and stiffened warily in response to the emotion brushing her mind. "Fear?" she said aloud.

"Not quite," the Shadgui said. "We were projecting caution. Fear is less reasoned, less intelligently alert. Are you again ready?"

Yes, Heather thought. *Go ahead.*

Almost immediately her mind felt a tendril touch of warmth, and she found herself smiling. *Love?* she guessed.

Close. We were projecting goodwill. Here is love.

The warmth intensified, filling her with a glow like sunshine on a warm spring day. She felt buoyed up with hope and happiness, until her throat tightened with the unaccustomed emotion.

Do you sense the difference?

Oh, yes! Heather looked over at Kaross gratefully, still filled with the intensity of the alien's emotion. *I—*

—Fear!

Sharp, panicky *terror* engulfed Heather's mind with the force of a mental hurricane. The contact lasted for only a moment, but that instant of profound rapport left the girl gasping and shaking. Heather leaped to her feet with a muffled cry. "Omigod! Oh, no!"

What is it? What is wrong? Kaross demanded, hoisting his bulk out of his sling with more alacrity than his lumbering appearance indicated.

"Oh, shit, something's wrong!" Heather was shivering with reaction. "Esteemed Kaross, it's Hing, my roommate!"

"What is wrong? Where is Hing?"

"She's on a field trip out at the archaeological site this afternoon—and something's gone wrong out there!"

"She sent you a message?" The Shadgui was plainly skeptical. Heather couldn't blame the alien—most telepaths couldn't send or receive thoughts over distances of a hundred meters, let alone ten or twenty kilometers.

Heather fumbled for words. "Not a message, not words. Just a moment when I sensed what she was feeling, and she was terrified. She's in a closed-in place, surrounded by rock walls, and something terrible happened!" She concentrated, closing her eyes, reaching, groping . . .

The alien's mind intruded. *Can you still sense her?*

"Yeah . . ." Heather whispered slowly. "Yeah, I can . . . it's like a nagging headache back there. She's still scared. Something is wrong. She's in danger."

The Shadgui regarded her with those little button eyes in the Gui's warty red face. "If you are indeed sensing your friend, your range is most impressive, Heather. We have not heard of any telepath except Esteemed Doctor Blanket who can receive over such a distance."

"I know it's a long way, but I'm sure I'm reading correctly!" Heather insisted, jiggling with impatience. If Kaross refused to believe her, would anyone? "Please, Esteemed Kaross, we have to get help out there!"

"Your record shows a history of what humans call 'pranks,' " Kaross said quietly, using the English word. "We trust this is not one of them."

Frustrated and furious, Heather hurled a wordless message at the alien. *Damn you, I'm not screwing around this time! It's real! Do something!*

The Shadgui regarded her for a long moment, the little Gui's eyes as bright and unblinking as a doll's. Then the alien abruptly turned to the terminal built into the desk of the study cubicle. "Connect us with Administrator ch'aait immediately," the symbiont commanded. "It is an emergency."

Time slowed, s-t-r-e-t-c-h-e-d, thinning like pulled taffy, and it seemed to Hing that hours had passed since she had helplessly watched Professor Greyshine disappear over the edge of the crevasse. She crouched in frozen horror, unable to think, speak, or move, hearing herself whimpering like an injured puppy, but unable to stop. Her mind felt encased in plas-steel. *Did I imagine it?* she wondered numbly. *Did it really happen? Oh, God, let it not really have happened! Let me be dreaming!*

Greyshine, she thought sickly, must already be dead. The Heeyoon hadn't been wearing his helmet, and without it, the alien would have literally burst the moment he plunged through the protective field that kept the air and gravity within the small cavern from escaping into the asteroid's natural vacuum. The Mizari field, designed to contain air, would never stop a hurtling body.

Dehydrated blood and fur must now coat the sides of the crevasse, freeze-dried instantly in place. The body would be—

"Hing! Are you hurt? Hing!" A hand grabbed her arm, shook her violently. Hing looked up dazedly to see Serge beside her. "Are you hurt?" he yelled, having to shout so she could hear him through her helmet. Slowly she shook her head from side to side, unable to speak.

"Then get up. I need your help!"

The student's mind teetered on the edge of total mindless panic, much the way Professor Greyshine had hung on the brink of the crevasse for that endless, heart-stopping instant. She stared up at Serge, then slowly she drew a deep breath . . . another . . . and forced back the horror, steadying her mind the way she did before she walked out onstage on opening nights. *If I can't be cool and collected, at least I can **act** that way,* she told herself. "The Professor's dead." Her own voice was flat and toneless as it reverberated within the confines of her helmet.

Serge nodded grimly. "But we have a responsibility to make sure the students are safe." Tugging at her arm, he helped her up.

Hing's legs trembled so hard that Serge had to steady her, but a second later she was able to stand on her own.

The radiation warning sounded in the cavern again, jerking her back to reality. "Serge," she yelled, pointing at his head, "you need to put on your helmet! You could be inhaling contaminated air with every breath!"

Quickly Serge placed his helmet on his head, clicking it into place. "Attention, everyone," he addressed his class, who stood clustered near the airlock, frozen with shock. "We are in the midst of a crisis, but we must all stay calm. I want all of you to leave this cavern immediately, for your own safety, and wait for us in the main cavern."

"Where are you going to be?" demanded one of the students, a young, bearded fellow who was standing with his arm around a girl.

"Hing and I will stay behind to recover the Professor's . . ." he broke off and amended, "to attempt to recover the Professor. Quickly now, into the airlock, all of you."

A chorus of volunteers to stay and help filled their radios, but Serge was adamant. "No, and that is final. You can help best by going back to the main cavern. There is a communicator there, and you will be able to call the school and request assistance."

Serge hesitated for a second, and Hing heard him muttering to himself. " . . . *quinze . . . seize, dix-sept, dix-huit . . . l'un nous manque*—**has anyone seen Khuharkk'?**"

The students shuffled and muttered. Hing swallowed. "He fell," she said, her voice thin and shaky. "He was falling toward me. Do you think he—" She broke off, unable to voice the thought aloud.

Serge turned slowly, surveying the small cavern, but there was no sign of the Simiu student. "Did anyone see him fall over the edge?" he demanded.

Nobody had, but the crevasse was over ten meters long; it extended across half of the cavern floor. And everyone's eyes had been fastened on the Professor. "We will look for Khuharkk', also," Serge promised bleakly. "At the moment, I would like you, Sarrhezz"—he pointed to the oldest student, a Mizari senior—"to make yourself responsible for escorting the group back to the main cavern and seeing that they stay there. Okay?"

Behind his protective glow, the alien inclined his tentacled head. "I will see them to safety," he promised.

"Susan and Howie." Serge nodded to the human students who stood close together, the young man's arm around the girl. "You will please make yourselves responsible for contacting the school and giving them the Mayday," he said, giving the slang term its original French pronunciation. "Okay?"

Together, they nodded.

"Now, please go," Serge ordered. "Into the airlock, everyone!"

As if to speed the response to his order, the radiation warning blared out again. With Sarrhezz leading the way, the students headed into the airlock and the first group cycled through.

Serge turned back to Hing and clicked back to their private frequency. "The Professor and I scanned that crevasse when we first explored this cavern, and it is at least thirty meters to the bottom. In all probability, we cannot recover him, but at the least we must look. Would you rather I check the crevasse, while you search the cavern for Khuharkk'?"

"No, I'll go with you," Hing said, bracing herself for what she was certain she was about to see. "Let's hang on to each other, okay? No sense in someone else falling over the edge." Linking hands, they began shuffling toward the drop-off.

"Radiation warning! Radonium-2 levels dangerous to most life-forms detected in this area! Evacuate immediately!"

"*Silence!*" Serge snapped, his voice for the first time betraying the strain he was under. "I wish I could turn that warning off," he added.

"Well, we can't, so we'll just have to live with it," Hing said, wishing her suit had a clear chin-plate so she could see where she was stepping. It was unnerving to approach a precipice and not be able to watch one's feet. "The levels can't be *too* high, yet, or our suits would be warning us, too."

"That's true . . . which is odd," Serge allowed, but by now they were almost at the edge of the crevasse—there was no time to think of anything but the danger they faced.

When they were within a meter of the drop-off, both humans awkwardly knelt. Bracing their gloved hands carefully on the rocky lip, they peered over. Hing heard Serge gasp, then a moment later she was barely able to hold back a yelp of mingled terror and jubilation.

Professor Greyshine's still form lay about five meters below them, precariously resting on the narrow ledge where the Mizari field generator was installed! If the fall hadn't killed him, he was still alive, because he was still within the pressurized portion of the cavern!

"Serge, if he moves—" Hing began.

Her companion was already wrenching off his helmet. "Professor Greyshine! If you can hear me, *stay still*!" he yelled, using the alien's native tongue. The Mizari voder Hing had placed on her ear before coming on the field trip (standard procedure when dealing with large groups at StarBridge Academy) automatically translated his warning. "Greyshine! Can you hear me?"

The Professor did not reply, but a moment later his left leg twitched, inching a perilous few centimeters closer to the edge. Hing's heart contracted painfully. If the Heeyoon thrashed with pain, or turned over, he'd fall again, only to die the moment he plunged through the pressure-containment field into hard vacuum!

"We must bring him up before he falls," Serge yelled to Hing, and she nodded. Quickly he snapped his helmet back on so they could speak without screaming at each other. "There is a powered winch over in that corner—we used it to move rubble and fallen boulders out of the way. We can use that to lower a rescuer. We will need to make a climbing harness, and fashion a sling to wrap around the Professor so he can be lifted as safely as possible."

Hing nodded as she gauged the distance between the stony walls of the crevasse, biting her lip as she noted the sharp edges of protruding rocks. "It's awfully narrow down there . . ." she muttered. Below the shimmer of the Mizari field, the crevice continued down into utter blackness. Hing sucked in a deep breath. "I'll go down," she announced, and was proud that her voice emerged without a quaver.

Serge gave her a long look. "I am afraid that you will have to," he said quietly. "I mass nearly twice what you do, and the line on the winch is only four meters long. We will have to extend it by some means, and do some of the lowering and raising manually. You wouldn't have a hope of lowering me, much less pulling the Professor up."

"Are *you* strong enough?" she asked, remembering the alien's bulk.

"I will have to be," Serge said simply, scanning the supplies stacked in a corner. A moment later he pointed excitedly. "Voilà! We can use that spool of grid-marker cord to extend the cable!"

Hing eyed the thin, colorful strands doubtfully. "Will it be strong enough?"

"It is made of plas-steel. If we double it—"

"Better yet, we'll braid it!" she broke in, inspired by the feel of her own braid touching the back of her neck.

Serge nodded approval. "That will work! Let's get—"

He broke off as Hing gasped sharply and jumped. Something had grabbed her ankle! Turning as quickly as possible while encumbered by her suit, she let out a glad cry as she saw the four-legged form crouched behind her. "Khuharkk'! We thought you'd gone over the edge, too!"

The Simiu braced himself against the wall of the cavern before he put on his suit helmet. A moment later they heard him over the radio. "I fell behind those rocks over there," he said, pointing. He sounded clearheaded, but pain roughened his voice. "I only just regained consciousness."

"Are you injured?" Serge asked, and Hing noticed that the Simiu held his hind leg at an awkward angle.

"My head aches, and my foot is either broken or sprained, but otherwise I am unhurt." A touch of typical Simiu arrogance reentered his tone as he added, "My strength is unimpaired. I will assist you in pulling the Professor up."

"I believe I can manage alone," Serge said. "It could be dangerous to stay here with the radiation alert." As if on cue, the warning blared forth again. "The other students have—"

The human broke off as Khuharkk' drew himself up with an affronted air. "Honor demands that I stay and aid you in the rescue," Khuharkk' stated in a tone that brooked no argument.

Hing was ready to nudge Serge if he'd continued to argue, but the instructor knew better than to dispute with a Simiu over what constituted honorable behavior. "Thank you, Honored Khuharkk'. I will be grateful for your assistance."

Under Serge's direction, Hing and Khuharkk' worked together

to braid long strands of the plas-steel cord together into a five-meter length, while the instructor dragged the winch over to the lip of the chasm and tested it. "It is working fine," he said, scant minutes later. "Have you finished?"

"Just a second . . ." muttered Hing, braiding furiously while Khuharkk' held the ends to keep them from tangling. Quickly she made the final crossovers, then tied both ends tightly. "Got it!"

Serge pulled off his helmet, then leaned over to shout, "Professor Greyshine! We are coming for you! Do not move!"

He listened intently for a reply, then bleakly shook his head and redonned his helmet. Khuharkk' was busily rigging a sling out of a sheet of solar-reflecting material Hing had retrieved from the emergency first-aid kit that was stored inside every airlock. It wasn't large enough to cradle the Professor's entire body, so Hing would have to tie him into it.

Hampered by her suit gloves, the student clumsily looped the end of the braided cable beneath her armpits. "No, that's not it. Like so," Serge said, taking the cord away from her. Quickly, deftly, he rigged a climbing harness, running the cord behind her, passing it between her legs, over her left thigh, then behind her so it cupped her buttocks. Winding a loop around her waist, he finished up by passing a last length beneath her arms and cutting the cord, so she could keep the climbing harness on while the Professor was being hauled up and not have to retie the entire thing.

Serge carefully tied the braided end in a knot, then fastened it onto a snap. He hooked it onto the front loop of the climbing harness. "Lean back, bend your knees, and 'sit' down. Like this," he instructed, miming a demonstration. "That way, you can make use of handholds or footholds."

"Thanks," Hing said. "I'm glad one of us knows what he's doing."

"I went rock climbing in the Alps when I was younger," he said abstractedly, giving each of the knots a final check. "Naturally, *Maman* hated the idea. She was always concerned that I would hurt my hands . . ." Behind the transparent faceplate, his mouth quirked sardonically. "There," he added, all business once more, "you are ready."

Hing stepped toward the edge, prepared to swing over, but Serge stopped her. "One moment. I want to check in with the students." He clicked over to the common frequency. "Susan . . . Howard. Serge here. Do you read me?"

"We read you!" Howie answered. "We're here in Cavern One. We called the school. An emergency team is on the way."

"Good," the instructor said tersely. "Khuharkk' is okay, and the Professor is still alive . . . but he is injured—how badly, we do not know yet. When will the rescue shuttle arrive?"

"ETA is ten minutes," Howie reported.

"That fast?" Hing broke in, amazed.

"When we called in, they already knew we had a crisis. Don't ask me how. Janet had just left."

"Good," Serge said. "When the team arrives, I would like you, Howard, to escort them to the Cavern Two airlock—but do not enter yourself, understand?"

"Roger," the young man said. "I read you."

"Good. Cavern Two, over and out."

Hing regarded Serge and Khuharkk'. "Do you think we ought to wait, since they'll be here so soon?" she asked. The yawning blackness before her seemed deeper and darker than ever, now that she knew help was so close. "We might hurt the Professor worse by moving him."

Her answer came, not from either of her companions, but from the injured Heeyoon himself. Below them, Professor Greyshine shuddered, then his hands and feet began scrabbling feebly at the ledge, as though he were groggily trying to lever himself up. Rock dust cascaded over the lip of the ledge.

"*Greyshine,*" Serge yelled, after hastily snatching off his helmet, "*do not move! Remain still!*"

But the alien continued to twitch restlessly.

Hing wordlessly stuffed the silvery material of their jury-rigged sling into her front suit pocket. "Here," Serge said, picking up the Heeyoon's helmet. "Fasten this to your belt and put it on him as soon as you reach him."

She nodded, and a moment later signaled that she was ready. As Serge and Khuharkk' held the end of the makeshift line, she swung herself over the edge.

Jerkily, they lowered her, hand over hand. Concentrating on steadying herself with her hands and feet, Hing tuned out the monotonous radiation alert, the comments Serge and Khuharkk' exchanged, everything but the rocky wall before her. She could no longer see the edge . . .

At first the descent was easy, and Hing had plenty of time to fend herself off from the jagged walls as she went down. But all too soon the crevasse narrowed, and the sharp-pointed rocks were everywhere.

"I am activating the winch now," Serge said, and she could hear the strain in his voice. "Are you okay?"

"Fine," she replied. "It's getting pretty dark down here. I'm going to have to turn on my—"

Her left hand halfway to her helmet, Hing broke off as her right hand slipped from its handhold. The force of her grab sent her spinning out, away from the face of the cliff, and suddenly there was only black emptiness beneath her. She gasped, trying not to panic as she dangled helplessly, then swung back toward the rocky face. She put out a foot, trying to brake herself, missed, and slammed against the wall hard enough to momentarily drive the breath from her lungs.

"Hing!" Serge shouted. "What happened?"

For a moment she scrabbled in mindless terror at the rocks, then the vertigo faded as she found handholds. It was only then that she took in the mechanical tones sounding in her earphones.

"Warning. Suit material has been breached. Warning. Repairs commencing."

"Damn!" she muttered, afraid to move. While she was here in the pressurized area, all she had to fear from a ripped suit was radonium-2 poisoning—hardly a reassuring idea, but not immediately threatening. But if she moved below the level of the Mizari field, it would be an entirely different story. Explosive decompression was a particularly nasty way to die.

"What happened?" Serge shouted. "Are you hurt?" His voice rasped harshly with fear.

"Ripped my suit," Hing replied tersely. "Hang on a second while I check my diagnostics . . ." Moments later she gave a sigh of relief. "The emergency sealant is holding!"

"Perhaps I ought to take over. There is no way to tell how strong that sealant is," he said tightly. "If the tear is too large, the patch might not hold in vacuum."

"Don't be silly," Hing said, trying to sound more confident than she felt as she flicked on the spotlight built into the top of her helmet and stole a cautious glance at her destination. The Professor was still resting on the ledge, though one foot now dangled over nothingness. "I'm three quarters of the way down by now. Just lower me slowly, okay?"

They did so, letting her down only a few handspans at a time, as Hing used her climbing harness to brace against the cliff and search for handholds and footholds.

"You are getting very close," Serge said. "Only another meter or so. Can you land on the ledge?"

She groped, then managed to grasp a jagged rock and draw herself toward the Heeyoon. Greyshine took up almost all of the narrow ledge, and Hing's boots barely had room to rest. She dared to push one of his arms aside with her toe so she could step over him, then she squatted down at his head. "I'm down," she declared, feeling a little light-headed with relief. "The chicken has landed."

"I beg your pardon?" Khuharkk' sounded puzzled.

"Très drôle," Serge growled, not at all amused. "How is the Professor?"

Hing bent over the alien and shouted, "Professor? Can you hear me?"

Faintly, she heard him groan.

First the helmet, she reminded herself, lifting the shaggy head and sliding the transparent egg shape over the limp gray ears. It took her several anxious moments to lock the unfamiliar seals into place, but finally she managed. "I've got his helmet on," she reported. "I can't tell how badly he may be hurt . . . but his leg's at a funny angle. It's probably broken. I'm going to tie him into the sling now. Give me some slack."

Coils of the braided cord rippled down beside her, then Khuharkk's voice reached her, speaking in rapid Simiu. "May I suggest something, Honored HingOun?"

"Of course, Honored Khuharkk'."

"Before you move the Professor to place him in the sling, I believe it would be wise to increase the air pressure inside his suit, thus splinting any possible injuries Honored Greyshine may have."

"You mean . . . deliberately overinflate his suit?" Hing had been cautioned against that very thing so many times that it had become second nature never to overpressurize a spacesuit.

"Exactly! That is a recommended first-aid technique I recall from pilot training."

Hing peered down at the Heeyoon's suit, trying to figure out the unfamiliar controls. They were labeled in Heeyoon, obviously, but as CLS regulations decreed, they were also labeled in Mizari script—but in such small letters that she had to strain her eyes to read them in the light of her headlamp. Finally she found the correct control, then carefully activated it. She watched anxiously as the Heeyoon's suit began filling up like a balloon.

The cool rush of air over his limbs must have partially roused the unconscious Heeyoon, for he suddenly thrashed as hard as the rapidly stiffening suit would allow. His arm slammed against Hing's knee, catching her off-balance. She teetered on the narrow ledge, grabbing at air, then with a shrill, breathless scream, she was falling!

The glow of the Mizari field flashed past her helmet as she plummeted downward. If it hadn't been for the change in the gravity, she might have been badly whiplashed when the cable ended and her climbing harness caught her, but the jerk was softened by the one-tenth gee. She hung there, feeling her stomach bouncing in the low gravity, struggling not to throw up. *If you barf, you'll have to live with it all the way back to the school,* she warned herself, biting her lip until the pain distracted her from the wave of nausea.

It was only then that it occurred to her to wonder whether the sealant would hold. Hing tensed, her queasiness forgotten. *If that emergency patch doesn't hold,* she thought, her mouth dry with fear, *I've got about thirty seconds to live . . .*

But the sealant held.

Hing drew a deep breath, hearing once again the ubiquitous radiation warning booming through the cavern. Serge was shouting over it, his voice rasping with fear. "Hing! Hing, answer me! Are you okay? What is happening? Hing? *Hing!?! Répondez-moi!*"

"I will, if you'll shut up and give me a chance!" Hing snapped, then immediately regretted her lapse. "Sorry," she said stiffly. "I'm sorry, Serge. Don't worry, I'm okay."

"What happened?"

"The Professor started thrashing around and knocked me off the ledge, but I hadn't unfastened my harness. I'm fine. Pull me back up."

Within moments she was back on the ledge. Feeling sweat coursing down her face, Hing tucked the silvery sheet as far beneath the injured alien as she could, then she alternated tugging at him and tucking it farther until he was lying in the middle of it. She was panting by the time she had finished, and began wrapping the impromptu sling around his torso.

Now don't move, Professor, she cautioned the alien silently, her heard pounding with fear as she fumbled with the line snapped to her climbing harness. *Don't move, for the love of all that's holy, please don't move!*

Trying to keep her back safely against the cliff face, she wound the line around the Heeyoon's body, through the belt on his suit, then wove it through the grommets studding the sides of the improvised sling. The Professor's arms and legs stuck out stiffly, sausagelike. "Just like a big hot dog wrapped in foil," she mumbled, then realizing that the alien's lupine image made that into a very bad pun, Hing struggled against a series of hysterical giggles.

"Excuse me?" Serge demanded suspiciously. "I didn't catch that. Did you say something?"

"Nothing," she said. "Just checking these knots." *Just keep it together for another few minutes,* she admonished herself. "Okay," she said briskly. "He's ready to come up. Haul away!"

Slowly, the Professor's still form ascended as Khuharkk' and Serge pulled together. She heard the two of them panting in her headphones. "He's a lot heavier than I am," she said. "Especially unconscious."

The only reply was a grunt.

There was one heart-stopping moment where it seemed as though the alien's overinflated form wouldn't make it between two jaggedly protruding points of rock, but by skillful use of the winch controls, timing his moment to coincide with the slight swing of the alien's body at the end of the cable, Serge was able to bring Greyshine up the rest of the way. Together, human and Simiu hoisted him over the edge.

"Your turn," Serge called, dropping the cable back down.

Hing had just snapped the line back onto her harness when a voice erupted in their earphones. "Serge! Hing! Are you okay?"

"Janet!" Hing said, recognizing the Chief Engineer's voice.

"Where are you?" Serge demanded.

"We've just reached Cavern One. We'll be there in a few minutes."

Rescue was here—soon they'd all be safe! Reaction made Hing's hands begin to shake, but she resolutely forced herself to pay attention to checking that her line was snapped securely. It would be just her luck to fall down the bottomless pit at the precise moment the cavalry came charging over the hill. "Okay, Serge, bring me up!" she called, giving a tug on the cord to indicate her readiness.

As she rose toward the edge, Hing found herself wondering how much radiation she'd taken. It couldn't be too bad—her suit hadn't warned her, after all. But did the sealant block radiation? Would she be burned on her leg? Or had the exposure been enough to damage her genes? Marriage and children seemed a far-off thing, but she'd always thought that someday she *would* marry, would have a baby. What if—

She was jerked out of frightening speculation a moment later as her suit nearly hooked on the same jagged projection that had almost trapped the Professor. Grateful for the interruption, Hing fended herself off from the protrusion. Moments later she was grabbed and hoisted bodily over the edge by Khuharkk' and Serge.

"The Professor?" she gasped, feeling her legs ready to buckle; she was trembling like an adolescent on a first date. Serge put a steadying arm around her as they moved away from the crevasse. "Where's Janet?"

"Right here!" came the reply, and they both turned to see the airlock door slide open. Janet Rodriguez and three of her engineering staff were crammed in along with a huge first-aid kit and an anti-grav stretcher. The woman stepped forward, taking in the Professor's bloated form, the winch with its jury-rigged cable, and the three rescuers. "Well done, all of you," she said, motioning to her crew to pick up the Professor. "But let's save the congratulations for later. Right now I've got to get you all back to the hospital."

"Hhh . . . hospital?" Hing tried to swallow, but her mouth was too dry. "Khuharkk' and the Professor are hurt, but Serge and I aren't—"

Janet shook her head, and behind her faceplate, Hing could see her frown. "You can't mess around with radiation, Hing," she said curtly. "There's no time to spare. We've got to get you to Decontamination."

CHAPTER 7

♦

Contingency Plans

Coiled sinuously before Rob Gable's desk, Ssoriszs listened to his friend and felt his fangs unfold—an involuntary response to shock. As his bright dreams crumbled to dust, he tasted the bitterness of his own venom like a physical echo of his emotions. It seemed that Professor Greyshine had discovered the missing piece of the Lost Colony puzzle, the star-shrine, only to have the discovery snatched away and rendered inaccessible. Even now the caverns must be filling with lethal radonium-2 radiation—would that mean that the search for the Lost Colony's relics would have to be abandoned?

"If it hadn't been for Hing, Serge, and Khuharkk', I'm afraid Professor Greyshine would have died," Rob finished. "If those kids hadn't had the nerve to look down that crevasse, fully expecting to see a friend spattered all over the sides of the thing . . ." The psychologist spread his hands and shrugged eloquently.

Ssoriszs' tentacles, usually so graceful, kinked stiffly as he struggled to regain his composure. Baring one's fangs in the presence of a friend was considered very rude on Shassiszss, so the Mizari waited to speak until they were once more folded back against the paleness of his gums, no longer visible. "This is shocking, Rob. Thank the Spirits of the Stars and the Sands that they were able to rescue Greyshine! Where are they now?"

"Janet just called in. The shuttle will be here in just a few minutes."

"Professor Greyshine?"

"Still unconscious. The medic said one leg was broken, and a couple of ribs. But the head injuries are the most dangerous."

"What about Serge, Hing, and the Simiu student?"

"We won't know for sure until Dr. Mysuki and Dr. Zemez finish their examinations, but the rescue team didn't report any outward sign of radiation poisoning or burns. When I spoke to Serge, he said their suit detectors never activated, so the levels must have remained fairly low—at least while they were there, which is a major blessing." The psychologist frowned. "Physics isn't my strong suit, but I think I remember that radonium-2 reactions start slow and build until they're extremely volatile . . . right?"

Lost in thought, Ssoriszs didn't answer. *Further excavations may prove impossible,* he was thinking. *Now I may never learn the fate of the Lost Colony . . . and of my missing kin.* He felt suddenly very old, very insignificant, very alone in the vastness of this huge, indifferent universe. A moment later he realized that Rob was still staring at him, obviously waiting for a response, and the Mizari struggled to recall what his friend had been saying. "Ssoriszs, are you all right?" Rob asked worriedly.

"Yes, of course, I am fine," the Liaison managed. "This is a shock, of course. I am afraid that I lost the thread of what you were saying?"

"Radonium-2 reactions," the human prompted. "Fast or slow?"

"They are slow at the beginning," Ssoriszs confirmed. "However, if memory serves me accurately—and I am not a physicist either, remember—when the crystalline structure of normal radonium destabilizes to form radonium-2, the reaction builds almost exponentially. The cavern and the artifacts might then be in danger—and soon."

Rob gave the Liaison a glance that mingled surprise and— Ssoriszs couldn't be sure—was it reproach? "Frankly, I'm more concerned about the school," the human said after a moment. "It's been over six years since I saw the radonium vein schematics of this asteroid, but I think the stuff crisscrosses this hunk of rock like a ball of yarn after Bast has played with it for a while. If any veins are near the school, and they destabilize into radonium-2, we're all apt to be history, right?"

Ssoriszs felt a wave of guilt. *How could I have been so self-centered?* he wondered. "I am abashed, Rob," he said quietly. "It never occurred to me that the school itself might be in danger, but you are correct. There are several veins of radonium near the school. One of them lies approximately fifty meters below us, and that one is the closest."

Rob glanced down at his feet as though half expecting the floor to disintegrate any moment. "Oh, shit," he muttered. *"That close?"*

"Twenty-five or -six meters of solid rock constitutes a fairly substantial buffer," Ssoriszs pointed out mildly. "But still, the problem must be checked into immediately."

"Horizons Unlimited is the contractor charged with keeping tabs on the radonium," Rob said. "So I called them immediately. We're lucky that Jeff Morrow has been handling several projects out of StarBridge Station, so his secretary promised me that he'll call me as soon as he returns from his site inspection tour."

"When will that be? I do not believe we can afford to wait very long."

"Tomorrow, early. Janet wanted to go out to the Cliffs and start running tests, but I persuaded her to wait. H.U. will have state-of-the-art shielding and equipment."

"Of course," the Mizari agreed. "We are indeed fortunate that Jeffrey will be able to give this problem his personal attention. We *are* speaking of the same Jeffrey Morrow who was a student here, correct?"

"Yes. Jeff's a vice president and multisector foreman in his dad's space-construction and mining company now," Rob said. "He's very concerned for the school's welfare . . . I know he'll give this his full attention. I'm sure the problem will be solved quickly." Ssoriszs, accustomed to reading human intonations and inflections after all these years, clearly heard the note of determined hope in his voice.

The alien shifted his coils restlessly as he selected his next words. "Still, I am disturbed about all of this, Rob. Horizons Unlimited performed a routine inspection here at the school and out at the Lamont Cliffs only a few of your Terran months ago. Why did they not detect signs of instability in the radonium deposits at that time?"

"Radonium can mutate into radonium-2 very rapidly," Rob pointed out. "That's why Jeff's teams check it twice a year."

Ssoriszs thought about Jeff Morrow, remembering the youngster who had been so reserved, so stoically controlled, as he climbed aboard the ship that would take him back to Earth. *Never have I seen anyone face such a profound failure with such courage,* he thought sadly. *I wish I could summon some of that courage for myself. Perhaps then I would not feel so . . . defeated.*

Rob's dark eyes regarded him intently, and now they held no impatience, only sympathy. "I realize how you must feel," he said quietly. "I understand how important this discovery was to your people. Perhaps Jeff can get this thing cleared up with no problem, and then the team of experts can come out anyway."

"With a newly discovered star-shrine to entice the Mizari Archaeological Society, I should think they would," Ssoriszs said, trying to summon up some of Rob's optimism. "I will certainly speak to Rizzshor, the team leader, about this. I shall also," he went on, thinking swiftly, "contact Dr. Andreiovitch about this development."

"Andreiovitch?"

"Mikhail Andreiovitch is one of the foremost experts on asteroid mining and small-body excavation in the CLS," Ssoriszs said. "He holds degrees from several Terran universities in geology, physics, and archaeology. He worked on the prototype of the first neutron emitter."

"Sounds like quite a guy," Rob murmured, suitably impressed. "And if he's a physicist, he'd know about radonium and radonium-2."

"Precisely. I have known Mikhail for years, since he was nominated to the intercultural exchange program on Shassiszss. He will certainly be able to assess our situation here and offer valuable advice concerning the preservation of the site."

"As a doctor, I can certainly appreciate the merit in getting a second opinion," Rob said, leaning back with a tired sigh. "God, I'm bushed. It seems like it's just one thing after another these days. Why can't anything ever be simple?"

Now it was Ssoriszs' turn to look at his friend sympathetically. "You still have not heard from Shrys, have you?" he asked gently.

Rob ran a hand through his curls, wincing as he snagged several locks. "I've got to get a haircut," he muttered distractedly, then he sighed and shook his head. "No, I haven't heard from Shrys. And if he were coming back, I should have heard something by now. I know I shouldn't judge other cultures, traditions, or belief systems, but . . . Shrys had so much enthusiasm . . . so much to offer! But I'm afraid that he's already dead."

Ssoriszs gazed at his friend, noticing, for the first time, that gray hairs mingled with the dark ones on his head. The sight distressed him. "Do not give up hope," he said automatically, trying to sound encouraging—though without much success. Privately, he thought the human was probably correct.

"What is it?" Rob had noticed the alien's fixed stare. "What's wrong?"

"Robert, your hair . . ." the Mizari hesitated. "I see light strands mixed with the others. I never noticed them before. Is that not a sign of . . ." He stopped, trying to think of a way to phrase the question gently. "Human maturity?" he finished.

Rob began to chuckle, genuinely amused. "Always the diplomat, Esteemed Liaison," he teased. "You mean you never noticed my gray before? You need your eyes checked, old friend. Hey, at least I've still *got* hair. A lot of men my age don't have enough left to comb, if they let nature take its course—which most of them don't, they're too vain."

But after a moment the psychologist's expression sobered. "Let me tell you, Heather Farley is personally responsible for at least fifty of these silver threads—first that stunt with Khuharkk's toilet, then calling me today with her instructor, insisting that the students were in danger out at the site."

"She was correct," the Mizari said neutrally.

"She sure was." Rob shook his head. "That kid scares me, Ssoriszs. You know how far it is out to that dig! I never heard of a human receiving from that far away before! Heather is a much stronger telepath than anyone ever expected. I feel like I've got a tiger by the tail. I'm tempted to ship her back to Earth on the next ship."

"Today, we all have cause to praise her abilities," the alien reminded him.

"Yes, but what if tomorrow she decides to play jokes again . . . dangerous ones? She could be as lethal as the radonium-2," Rob finished bleakly. "I'm getting too old for this job, Ssoriszs."

"I was old before your father's father was born, Rob," the elderly Liaison said quietly. "If anyone on this asteroid has the right to complain about being too old, it is I."

"Please remove all clothing and all jewelry, placing your items in the chute to your left," the computer voice instructed.

Serge shivered convulsively as he began stripping off his one-piece garment. It wasn't that the nearly featureless cubicle was cold—like all of StarBridge, the infirmary was maintained at a constant temperature, unless otherwise dictated by the needs of the occupant. The chill came from inside him, and it had a name—fear. He was scared, and he had to grit his teeth to keep from crying out or, worse yet, whimpering.

All the way back in the shuttle he'd been so composed, so calm—Hing had been the one shivering with reaction. She'd leaned against him, and Serge had put a comforting arm around her, reminding himself all the while not to take it for more than a simple comfort-seeking response; any fellow human would have served.

Now, in the cramped safety of the decontamination cubicle, Serge watched gooseflesh spring out on his arms and belly, felt his genitals draw up against his groin. His heart pounded painfully, and he began to shake. *Calm yourself,* he commanded himself sternly. *This is nothing but a delayed "fight or flight" reaction. It will pass.*

Forcing himself to take deep, slow breaths, in through his nose and out through his mouth, he fought the panic that wanted to consume him, and gradually it faded.

"Sensors indicate you have not removed all clothing or jewelry," the computer said. "Please comply with instructions. These procedures are essential for maximum safety and effectiveness."

"Tais-toi!" he snapped. This was the second time today that a machine had given him orders, and he wished *this* one would shut up almost as much as the warning system out at the dig.

Fingering his school ring, he was tempted to disobey the command. What difference did it make if he kept it on, he wondered blackly. It wasn't as though his hands could be hurt by radiation—unless radonium-2 contamination might overload the microsensors, the artificial neurons and ganglia, or the power pak. Staring down at the ring's yellow-orange flame gem set into a golden-red Mizari alloy, he thought of the day he'd first slid it on—and of how he had failed at the mission it symbolized. Scowling, Serge wriggled it off, dropping it on top of his clothing.

"Sensors indicate that you have not removed . . ." the computer said again, and Serge realized that he'd forgotten the earring, Hing's gift. For a moment he was tempted to refuse, then he remembered that metal could become radioactive—and that his earlobe was flesh and blood. He had a sudden vision of half his ear oozing and finally falling off. *"Merde!"* he muttered, startling himself. He rarely swore—and almost never aloud.

Quickly he began tugging at the gem, wincing as he tried to twist the post free of the backing. He'd never taken the earring out since the day she'd given it to him, and the post seemed permanently welded into the back. But finally it gave, and the sapphire came free. Gently, Serge laid it down inside the circle of the ring, wondering if he'd ever see it again.

Don't be paranoid, he thought. *Remember, our suits never warned us. Our exposure levels couldn't have been that high.* But he knew that the sensors in the caverns were far more sensitive than the ones built into pressure suits. How much radonium-2 did it take to damage human tissue or chromosomes? He didn't know.

And Hing . . . she had ripped her suit; her exposure had to be more than his. Fear gnawed at him again, but this time it was fear for her, not for himself. Radiation sickness was a terrible way to die. He thought of her silky black hair falling out, and felt his stomach lurch queasily. And what about the Professor, who had received the most exposure of any of them? Would he live?

"Thank you for your compliance. Decontamination procedures will begin now. Please remain still throughout each treatment."

Taking a deep breath, Serge braced himself.

"Please close your eyes, as initial decontamination procedures begin," the computer instructed. "First step is a chemical shower. It will last ten seconds and will feel cold."

Serge shut his eyes, grateful for the distraction as he willed the images out of his mind. The cubicle, barely two meters square and infused with dim red lighting, made him feel as though he were standing in an upright coffin.

He heard a hissing above his head, then an instant later, a stinging shower drenched his hair and skin. He wanted to gasp, but he didn't want to taste or inhale the stuff, so instead he clamped his jaw tight and counted the seconds . . . mercifully, only ten or so, as the computer had said.

"Please keep your eyes closed, and wait for the sensor scan," the computer said. "This will feel warm. We apologize for any temporary discomfort you may be experiencing."

It was suddenly as though he were standing in the naked glare of a too-bright sun. Squinching his eyes shut as tightly as he could, Serge counted seconds and tried to make his mind a blank otherwise. But thoughts of Hing and Greyshine kept intruding. Were his friends all right?

The last two procedures were not unpleasant, and then he was allowed to take a normal shower and dress in a fresh coverall and soft shoes. Dr. Rachel Mysuki, one of StarBridge's physicians, appeared briefly to tell him that his tests results were being evaluated, and would he please wait. When he tried to ask about Hing and the Professor, she told him that they were undergoing much the same decontamination procedures, and that he'd be able to see them later.

The waiting room of the school's infirmary was as neutral and sterile as any other he'd ever been in, despite the holos that hung on the walls. At the moment, probably for his benefit, they'd been programmed to show scenes of Earth, but the views of the Taj Mahal, the Grand Canyon, the Himalayas, and a wildflower-speckled meadow in the Alps failed to distract him as he paced restlessly, then finally sank into a seat, arms crossed on his chest.

For the first time in years he wanted to bite his nails, as he had when he was a kid, much to his parents' dismay. *I'd probably break a tooth,* he thought grimly, staring down at the ends of his fingers.

Where was Hing? It had been nearly ten minutes by now; why wasn't she out here with him, waiting for her test results? The medics Janet Rodriguez had brought to the dig had confirmed immediately that the Heeyoon's leg was broken, so Serge could understand his treatment taking longer. But *Hing* shouldn't still be under treatment . . . should she?

Unless something was wrong . . .

Closing his eyes, Serge found himself praying for her safety, then felt ashamed of himself. When he'd lost his hands he'd decided that there was no God, and nothing in the intervening years had ever changed that conviction. So what was he doing now, resorting to superstition?

Moments later, staring distractedly at one of the holo-images that now showed the temple of the Diving God in Tulum, Serge realized that he was praying again. *Stop it, you idiot,* he thought disgustedly.

Moments later his breath jolted painfully from his lungs when a silent voice filled his head. *Serge . . . Serge . . . I'm here.*

Mon Dieu! he thought wildly; for one heart-stopping instant he was on the verge of looking for a burning bush or some other divine manifestation—then he realized who it had to be.

"Heather?" he said softly, out loud. His voice cracked in the empty room.

Yes, Serge, it's me, the voiceless reply filled his mind. *I'm sorry for butting in like this, but I couldn't think of any other way!*

It was exactly as though she were standing beside him and speaking aloud—except that Serge was conscious of no sound. For a moment he was surprised that he should "hear" her mental communication as individual words spoken in Heather's voice, but then he remembered that other people said that was a fairly common occurrence when dealing with telepaths. Apparently the human mind often chose to perceive mental communication in familiar terms.

"Where are you?" he asked softly. He didn't seem to be able to formulate his thoughts very well unless he vocalized.

I'm in my room. Oh, Serge! it was a mental wail. *Is Hing okay? She was so scared—I could feel it all the way from the dig!*

"You mean you sensed her?" He could hardly believe it.

Yes. I told my instructor, and he—or they—whatever—called and notified Janet Rodriguez that there was an emergency.

"Then we have you to thank for the rescue ship already being en route!" he exclaimed, feeling a rush of gratitude. Those five or ten minutes saved might well mean the difference between life and death for Greyshine.

Warmth filled her communication as she "read" his silent appreciation, then concern soon was uppermost again. *Serge, is Hing hurt? I can't sense her at all!*

"When I last saw her, she was fine. Tired, of course, but she was the one who rescued Greyshine—anyone would have been exhausted after that."

She's so brave! The mental communication was accompanied by a glow of admiration. *First she faced Khuharkk' to save me, then she saved the Professor! I wish—I wish I could be like her . . .* Heather finished wistfully.

"Hing has great courage," Serge agreed, feeling his throat tighten. She had to be all right, he told himself. She *had* to be . . .

You have great courage, too, Serge, the mental "voice" came again. *Anyone who could go through what you did, losing your hands and your music, and then have to start a whole new life is really brave, too.*

Serge felt as though his insides had turned to ice for a moment, then fury blazed within him, and his fists clenched in the empty room. "What do you know about my music?" he said, his voice very soft and cold. "Heather, you have been reading my mind, haven't you? Don't deny it. How could you? That's—that's—I—" He choked on rage and a feeling of violation. Paranoia flowed over him in a wave. She knew everything, all of his thoughts, his feelings. Had she told Hing? Ruined things for him?

Oh, Serge, I'm sorry! Her "voice" was a silent sob. For a moment her guilt filled his mind. *I didn't mean to! I haven't done it since that first day, honest! I'm sorry—*

"*Catin!*" he snarled, then, in case she hadn't understood, translated, "Little bitch! Stay out of my mind, do you hear? *Stay out!*"

The mental contact was gone, as swiftly as a thread snapping. Serge was alone in his own mind. He sat back, breathing hard, still so furious that he was shaking. How dared she? How *dared* she?

"Serge?" the buzzing resonance of a voder filled the silence. The human jumped, startled, then leaped to his feet and rushed over to the being who hovered in the doorway. "Dr. Zemez! How is Hing? And Greyshine?"

The Apis physician drew back as he barreled at her, then hovered just out of reach, her furry, striped body hanging almost at his eye level. "They are resting comfortably," she replied. "Hing has some bruises, and she is very tired, so we are letting her sleep while Rachel and I keep an eye on her."

Serge let out a sigh of relief that seemed to come all the way from his toenails. *"Grace à Dieu . . ."* he muttered, scarcely aware of what he was saying. "And the Professor?"

"The Heeyoon has what in humans would be called a concussion, in addition to his other injuries, but he will heal, given time," she answered. Moving closer to Serge, she fixed her huge, faceted eyes on him. He could see himself mirrored, over and over, pale and anxious. "But are you not concerned for yourself, young Serge?" she demanded, gently chiding.

"Not particularly," Serge replied honestly. All at once he was tired . . . so tired that he could have collapsed on the floor and gone instantly to sleep. "I suppose I . . ." he trailed off, then asked, "how much radiation did I take?"

"None," she said flatly.

Serge's jaw dropped. "None?"

"Only the normal traces of background cosmic radiation were present in any of the four of you—or of any of the students on the field trip," the Apis said. "Under the circumstances, we were puzzled by this, but a consultation with Janet Rodriguez helped to explain it. The radiation alarms installed by the engineers are far more sensitive than they have to be, in order to allow the greatest possible safety margin. Your suits protected you, and your exposure was, fortunately, quite brief."

"Our suits protected us," Serge repeated, scarcely believing the good news.

"Yes. The shielding built into them to handle normal cosmic radiation was more than adequate to deal with the minimal amount of radonium-2."

Serge felt another wave of relief as a new thought occurred to him. "Then that means the artifacts won't be affected!" he blurted. "I can recover them!" For the first time in over an hour he remembered *why* the Professor had fallen in the first place. "I will be able to retrieve the star-shrine!"

"Perhaps," the alien doctor said. "However, Janet has also cautioned us that no one must return to the site until the engineers have inspected it thoroughly. Radonium-2 proliferates extremely quickly. All of you were very fortunate, young Serge. And by the way, I believe these are yours." She extended one of her forelimbs, with its long, spiky "hairs" that were actually sensory receptors. Clasped in her chitinous "fingers" were his ring and a tiny, winking spark of brilliant blue. "You may wear them without fear."

"Thank you," Serge said, taking them and slipping the ring back on, then inserting the stud back into his earlobe. "I am relieved that I didn't have to give these up."

"All of you were most fortunate," Dr. Zemez said, tilting her head so that the light from the overhead panels caught in the facets of her eyes, turning them to onyx jewels.

"We certainly were," Serge agreed automatically, his mind full of plans for retrieving their finds. Wait until Esteemed Rizzshor found out there was a star-shrine—they'd have a full team aboard the next ship—priority transport! There would be no question of not funding the site now!

"Serge, *Serge!*" Dr. Zemez had to speak sharply to get his attention. "Open your mouth."

Dr. Zemez had conducted the young man's last physical, so he knew what she wanted. Obediently, he opened his mouth and extended his tongue so she could taste-sample his saliva. The first time she'd done it, he'd had to brace himself to hold still as her long, tubular tongue brushed his, but this time the procedure seemed almost as normal (not to mention much briefer and less undignified) as a human physician's pokes, prods, and command to: "Turn your head and cough!"

"I taste great fatigue poisoning your tissues, young Serge," she said sternly. "Perhaps we should confine you in the infirmary so we will be certain that you rest."

"That is not necessary," Serge said. Like most healthy young people, he disliked hospitals. "I swear that I will go directly to my quarters and lie down. But first . . . could I see Hing?"

"She is asleep," the doctor reminded him.

"Then what about Greyshine? Is he conscious yet?"

"He was when I left," she admitted. "And he was demanding to speak to you." Her voder's flat voice seemed to take on a stern overtone. "I will allow you sixty seconds—no more."

"Fine," Serge agreed meekly.

In the corridor they met Khuharkk'. The Simiu's hindquarters were strapped into a rolling brace that would support his injured leg. "Khuharkk'! Are you okay?"

The Simiu nodded, a gesture his people had picked up from humans long ago. "I am well, FriendSerge," he said, using the familiar form of address. Serge felt a warm glow at this unusual honor. "The injury is not serious. How are you?"

"I am fine," he reassured the alien. "Thank you very much for your help. We could never have managed without it today, FriendKhuharkk'."

Dr. Zemez buzzed at him, reminding him that the Professor was waiting, so Serge hurried after her. It still felt rude to Serge to simply walk away, but he knew from experience that was what Simiu expected.

Standing in the doorway of the Heeyoon's room, Serge regarded his friend anxiously. Professor Greyshine lay curled up on a pallet, with various scans and diagnostic equipment humming unobtrusively in the background. Dr. Strongheart, the Heeyoon's mate, lay beside him, her nose almost touching his. At first Serge thought the Heeyoon might be sleeping, and he prepared to tiptoe away, but then the yellow eyes opened, fixed on him. The Professor raised his head. "Serge!" he yipped.

"I can only stay a moment, Professor," the human said, stepping into the room. "But you will be fine, they told me your injuries are not serious."

"Hing? Khuharkk'?" the alien's voice was faint, but he plainly wanted an answer.

"They are well," Serge replied reassuringly.

"Tell them . . . tell them their courage is beyond measure, and that I owe them my life," the alien said. "Tell them . . ." His voice faded and his eyes began to close.

"I will, Professor Greyshine," Serge said, knowing that Dr. Zemez would order him out of the room at any moment. "I will tell them."

He started to step back, but halted as the Heeyoon's eyes opened again. The alien was making a palpable effort to cling to consciousness. "My star-shrine, Serge . . ." he whispered. "The engineers . . . they will disturb it. Perhaps . . . steal it. It is . . . a great treasure . . ."

"I know," Serge said.

"You must take it, lad . . ." the Heeyoon said. "Don't let them have it . . ." The gray head dropped onto the pallet, the soft ears drooped limply. The yellow eyes closed.

"Time to go," the Apis physician commanded.

Knowing the alien was either unconscious or asleep, Serge hesitated. But even if Greyshine couldn't hear him, Dr. Strongheart could. She would tell her mate as soon as he awoke. Drawing himself up to his full height, Serge's voice rang out with the strength of one taking a solemn oath. "I will retrieve the star-shrine, Professor, I promise. Don't worry."

Turning, he left the infirmary with dragging steps.

Heather clutched the edge of her terminal desk with both hands, fighting back the sobs threatening to surge past her clenched teeth. She would *not* cry. She hadn't cried in years, not even when Uncle Fred had slapped her silly, and nobody, nothing, was going to change that. Not even Serge LaRoche.

Especially not Serge LaRoche.

*Little bitch, little bitch, littlebitch, bitch,bitchbitch**bitch** . . .* His mental "voice" rang in her mind, and her fingers tightened until the edge of the desk scored her fingers. "I hate you," Heather whispered, her voice harsh in the silence. "I *do*. Damn you! Damn you to Hell, Serge LaRoche! You *bastard!*"

After a long time her trembling and gasping eased, and she was able to straighten up, trying to ignore the pain she felt inside. The girl was surprised to realize that the hurt actually felt *real*—physical, as though someone had taken her heart and wrung it viciously, leaving it twisted into some agonized shape within her chest.

Heartache, she thought dazedly. *It's real. I thought they made that up to put in sappy love songs . . .*

"I hate you . . ."

But that was the worst of it . . . she didn't. Instead she was guilty and ashamed of herself, and the memory of how *violated* Serge had felt made her bite her lip as tears threatened again.

Of all the people in the universe that she didn't want to hurt, Serge was the one—but she *had* hurt him. She'd hurt him badly. If only she could talk to him, apologize . . .

No! He's pissed off, and he'll never forgive you, her survivor-self insisted. *All you can do now is get out of here. That will show him. That will show **all** of them . . .*

Straightening her shoulders, Heather began willing herself into a calm, analytical state of mind. There was nothing she could do about Serge. He'd never accept her apology, and she didn't want to remain at StarBridge if the person she cared about most really hated her. Serge might even report her mental snooping to Rob Gable, and the psychologist had warned her that she was here on probation. Rob was already suspicious about her role in Khuharkk's "accident"—Serge's complaint might very well convince Gable that he should ship her back to Earth.

But she wasn't going back—*ever*.

Forcing herself to take deep, steadying breaths, the girl opened her eyes and ordered on the computer. What was done was done. All she could do now was continue the work on Phase Two of her contingency plan—the plan to gain her enough wealth to get off this rock, and go wherever she wanted . . . in style.

Her fingers moving rapidly over the keyboard (she didn't want to speak aloud in case Hing came in quietly and heard her commands), Heather called up the secret account file she'd set up several days ago, skipping over the multitude of entries to examine the total. Excellent! The balance was growing nicely. It was time to open an interest-bearing account up at one of the StarBridge Station banks, so the money would grow even faster.

Heather had written her money-garnering program almost a week ago, then had turned it loose on StarBridge Academy's accounts. After a day to test it for possible bugs, she'd then duplicated her baby within the fiscal programs on StarBridge Station. It was an old idea, and for anyone else, it would have been impossible to implement, given the intricate safeguards programmed into modern computers. Even the simplest fiscal system now boasted a veritable maze of trips and traps to catch a would-be thief. For hundreds of years computer programs had been designed to avert any such tampering—but the systems engineers and programmers had never reckoned with Heather and her unique skills.

Simple, so simple . . . and foolproof. And it wasn't even stealing—not really. Heather frowned. She supposed the damned authorities *would* deem it illegal. But, practically speaking, if nobody knew about it, and nobody missed the money, you couldn't call that stealing, could you?

Every day, hundreds—in the case of StarBridge Station, it was *thousands*—of financial transactions occurred. Heather's program intercepted these figures before they could be entered, then skimmed rounded-off credit fractions randomly from the totals, depositing the fractions into a secret account. The skimming wasn't enough to change totals, and would probably never be noticed short of a comprehensive audit and systems overhaul. Heather planned to be long gone before that possibility threatened.

Now, working busily, she opened an ordinary savings account under the name Helen Benson (she'd seen several of Rob's treasured antique "movies" since her arrival) and channeled her new funds into it. As her skimming programs continued to swell the total balance, the account would grow by leaps and bounds. Heather realized that a mere savings account wouldn't bring her the best interest rate, but this would do until she was ready to implement Phase Two.

At this rate, she'd have a lot of money in a surprisingly short time. Possibly enough for a ticket out of here by the end of next week. *Where should I go?* she wondered, repressing a pang as she thought of Serge and Hing. She could try one of the Terran colonies . . . Jolie, Novaya Rossiya, NewAm, or Yamato. But a kid traveling alone would make human authorities suspicious. Scratch that.

Maybe I could go to Sorrow Sector, she thought. She knew you couldn't just buy a ticket to the legendary outlaw sector of space, where the criminal elements of many planets lived on worlds and space stations outside the bounds of CLS authority. Even the League Irenics, the peacekeeping arm of the CLS, didn't dare venture into Sorrow Sector—at least, not if they wanted to return. But there were worlds on the fringes where it was rumored that you could buy a ticket— if you had the money to grease the right palms. Or paws. Or tentacles.

They even said that the entire criminal underworld of Sorrow Sector was controlled by a *Mizari*—a very ancient Mizari. The girl found that possibility intriguing, but difficult to credit. All the Mizari she'd ever met, both at StarBridge and at Melbourne, had been so boringly upstanding and ethical that they made her roll her eyes. Heather had a very good imagination, but even she found the notion of a *bad* Mizari almost impossible to picture.

If he actually exists, I'll bet he could use someone with my skills, she mused. *Someone like that has to worry about being bumped off, or snuffed . . . whatever they call it. I could warn him about that. And I could help him break into any system, that's bound to be worth a lot . . .*

Well, she'd decide where she was going as soon as she had the money for her ticket. At the moment, she'd better make progress on Phase Two. Phase One, the credit-skimming program, was clever, but Phase Two was Heather's pride. She'd begun the program days ago, and now, after hours of work, it was finally beginning to take shape. Sitting at the terminal, the girl called up another clandestine file. The holo-tank flickered, then a three-dimensional image coalesced, eyes closed and waiting.

"Activate," Heather said.

The red-haired woman who still bore a considerable resemblance to the real Heather Farley opened "her" eyes. They were jade-green, doubly arresting given the creamy, flawless complexion that stretched taut over aristocratic cheekbones and elegantly molded chin. Heather's freckles had been the first things she'd deleted when she'd begun working on the image. "Hello, Heathertoo," the girl said, smiling.

"Good morning, Heather," the image replied, articulating every syllable precisely—too precisely.

Have to fix that, Heather thought. *Real people slur a little when they talk, even classy people. And the voice is still too high, still too mechanical sounding* . . . For the next twenty minutes she made minute adjustments to the voice-generating program she was using to modify the computer's own speaking capabilities.

"Hello, Heathertoo," she tried again.

"Good morning, Heather. How are you?" the image responded.

Still not perfect, but better . . . much better, Heathertoo's creator thought, nodding with satisfaction. Then, after flexing her fingers, she began working again on the image, toning down the fiery red of the hair to a bright auburn and rearranging her own unruly curls into a stylish coiffure. Then she concentrated on "making up" the image, keeping it subtle, the way a successful business-woman would be likely to—putting a blush of deeper color across the cheekbones, faintly shadowing the eyelids, then darkening and lengthening the lashes. The lips . . . they were still Heather's own. Working carefully to shift the image's color and dimensions, the girl evened the slightly irregular upper lip.

The lower lip was still a bit full, but didn't adults regard a full lower lip as sensuous or seductive or some such? After a moment of cogitation, Heather decided to leave the lower lip the way it was. Then she made the nose turn up a hair, the way her own did. She didn't want her altered image to be *too* perfect. Humming off-key, she rouged both lips, but not much—Aunt Natalie had used lots of lip color, and the girl had always thought she looked like a vampire with her pale features and too-bright mouth.

After some consideration of the "completed" image, Heather went on to suggest lines-yet-to-come at the corners of the eyes and mouth.

"Much better," she mumbled, studying her "aged" image. "Now you look mature, but not really *old.* Or should you actually be *old*? Thirty, maybe?"

She ruminated, but in the end decided that the same effect could be achieved without crow's-feet or furrows. She'd work on the clothes and the body. Heather expanded the image to a full-body one, then rolled her eyes. Heathertoo's lovely face atop the unchanged image of her own preadolescent pudgy body was ludicrous. Have to do something about that . . .

The image's body lengthened, lengthened, thinning in the middle and widening at the hips and bosom. *Breasts,* Heather thought, glancing ruefully at her own barely budding chest. *What would you like . . . small, medium, large, or humongous?* Grinning, she keyed the computer and suddenly Heathertoo's green StarBridge tunic bulged out as two monstrous mammaries extruded. *Nah,* the girl decided after a moment. *That looks cheap, and I want you to have some class . . .*

The breasts shrank until they were high and defined, but no more than average in size. *Better . . .*

After adjusting the rest of Heathertoo's figure to match, Heather called up several fashion catalogues to check current styles. She hadn't worn a dress since her mother had died, and clothes weren't normally something that interested her much. But Heathertoo had to look—and dress—just right. After some consideration, Heather chose a beautifully tailored (and extremely expensive) mauve business suit and pink blouse. After copying the image from the catalogue *sans* model, she recolored the blouse to an emerald green, and the suit to a pearl gray.

Then, her lower lip caught between her teeth as she concentrated, Heather merged the two images, keying in the minute adjustments until Heathertoo stood garbed in the clothes she had selected. The girl added accessories—a jade pin, conservative earrings, dress shoes—then sighed with pleasure as she regarded her creation. *If only I could look like that someday!*

Glancing down at herself, she grimaced. *Yeah, fat chance . . .*

Searching the catalogue entries once more, she began constructing an environment suitable to her image. She duplicated images of a handsome teakwood desk, an antique lamp, reproductions of two Monets and a Manet for the walls. Then, quickly roughing out the dimensions of an office, Heather began moving her images into place. It was fun, actually—almost as much fun as real shopping would have been.

An hour later the completed Heathertoo sat behind her beautiful desk, with just enough clutter to make the image believable. After a moment's further consideration, Heather added in an antique wall clock as the finishing touch. *Perfect!*

Now for some practice, so she could refine Heathertoo's dialogue and conversation subprogram. "Activate," she said. "Heathertoo, from this moment on, only I will call you 'Heathertoo.' When you receive or make calls from outside, you will refer to yourself as 'Helen Benson,' understand?"

"Yes, Heather," the image replied obediently.

"Good. Now prepare to receive an incoming call—audio only. Access all financial programs and open a high-yield investment account using the present balance in the 'Helen Benson' bank account. Ready?"

"Ready, Heather."

Quickly the girl changed the pitch on her audio input channel, so her voice would deepen. Then she switched off the input scanner on the screen. "Good morning," she said, consulting a script she'd prepared yesterday. "This is Dwayne Hicks of First Galactic Investment Corporation returning your call, Ms. Benson. How may I help you today?"

Heathertoo sat silent. Her creator counted seconds, then burst out impatiently, "You're supposed to respond according to program, Heathertoo!"

"The question was not addressed to me," the image said reasonably.

"Of course it was!"

"You instructed me to respond to the name 'Helen Benson.' Mr. Hicks did not address me in that way."

"Oh . . ." Computers were so damn literal. Some of the time that was an advantage, but other times, it was definitely a pain in the ass. "Uh, Heathertoo, the term 'Ms.' coupled with your new last name is an acceptable address for you, and you should respond to it. Let's try it again. Are you ready?"

"Ready," replied Heathertoo.

Quickly Heather repeated the greeting and inquiry from the fictitious Mr. Hicks, then waited tensely.

Her idealized, age-enhanced image smiled politely, showing the tips of perfect teeth. "Good morning, Mr. Hicks. I wish to open an account with your investment company."

"What kind of account were you thinking of, Ms. Benson?" "Dwayne Hicks" inquired. "We have several kinds."

"List types of accounts," Heathertoo ordered.

"Pause program," Heather snapped. *Damn! She still sounds so mechanical! How can I get her to sound real?*

She sat staring at Heathertoo's frozen image for several minutes, slowly realizing that in order to make Heathertoo sound *real*, she would have to merge her mind into the computer's while the program was activated. Then she could direct Heathertoo's speech and movements from within the program itself, pull Heathertoo's strings from *inside* the image, as it were.

That would require going deeper into the machine's short- and long-term memory and "thinking" processes than the girl ever had before. Heather felt goose bumps pop out on her arms, and she shivered slightly. Before this she'd only merged her consciousness with the computer for scant moments while she'd altered programming, accessed guarded storage for passwords, or tampered with memory. But this linkage would require deep, almost total immersion, for many realtime minutes.

For a moment she was tempted to forget the whole thing, trust that the programmed responses she'd given Heathertoo would do the job, but then the girl's jaw tightened stubbornly. She could do it—and the results would be worth it.

Little bitch . . . she could hear Serge's words echo in her memory. Uncle Fred had called her that, too.

I'll show you . . . all of you! Taking a deep breath, Heather closed her eyes and launched her mind . . .

CHAPTER 8

◆

Images, Past and Present . . .

The intercom on Rob Gable's desk had barely begun to beep before the psychologist reached it and silenced it. "Rob here," he said tersely. "Janet?"

"I'm here at the airlock with Jeff and his assistant. I'll bring them down immediately," she said.

"We'll be waiting," he promised.

Glancing up, he regarded the other two occupants of his office steadily. "Janet's bringing them down," he told Esteemed Ssoriszs and StarBridge's Chhhh-kk-tu Administrator, Kkintha ch'aait. "They'll meet us in my conference room."

"Have they already been out to the site?" Kkintha asked. The little furred alien appeared doubly small and compact next to the Mizari's sleek, elongated length. Her bright blue eyes studied Rob anxiously from a bandit mask of dark seal-brown, though most of her body was a pale fawn in color. Her whiskers quivered as she nervously groomed her thick chest ruff with her tiny clawed fingers.

"I believe they were planning to do a quick site inspection before they met with us today," Rob said. "When Jeff got back, and whether he had time to go over the site, I don't know."

Rising, he headed into the room next to his office. He could hear the quick patter of Kkintha's feet behind him, as well as the sinuous whisper as Ssoriszs uncoiled his massive body and slithered after them.

The neutral-colored, burgundy-carpeted conference room was fitted with a variety of seats and resting places that could accommodate most life-forms from the Fifteen Known Worlds. Each place was also equipped with a computer terminal and small holo-tank. Quickly Rob programmed the room's controls for three human-style chairs, plus seating for one Mizari and one Chhhh-kk-tu. Moments later Kkintha scrambled nimbly up onto a high, padded stoollike seat that would bring her up to the same eye level as the humans, while Ssoriszs coiled himself into one of the boxlike Mizari compartments.

Rob himself was too keyed up to sit; he paced restlessly, then, remembering that Jeff was a coffee drinker, keyed the servo for a pot.

Before the coffee could arrive, the door slid open and Morrow entered. Despite the smile he flashed, he looked haggard, as though he hadn't been sleeping well.

"Hello, Jeff," Rob said, noting the dark shadows beneath the engineer's eyes. "How are you?"

Morrow shrugged, giving his friend a "don't ask" look, then turned his attention to the Chhhh-kk-tu and the elderly Mizari. "Greetings, Administrator," he said, then bowed formally to Kkintha. Then, raising his hands over his head, Morrow addressed Ssoriszs in halting Mizari. "The stars shine upon you, Esteemed One." He bowed deeply.

"We are glad to see you again, Jeffrey," Kkintha said formally, "and we thank you for coming so quickly."

"You have been often in our hearts," Ssoriszs said, inclining his head in the Mizari greeting bow. "Greetings, Jeff . . . and to your colleague, greetings."

"I'm forgetting my manners," Jeff said, turning to present the tall, angular black woman who waited a step behind him. "I'd like all of you to meet Andrea Lynch, my assistant and crew boss. Andrea, this is Rob Gable, Esteemed Ssoriszs, and StarBridge's Administrator, Kkintha ch'aait. And, of course, you've already met Janet Rodriguez."

"Hi," Lynch murmured. No smile brightened her narrow, dark features. The woman wore a baggy tan coverall with the sleeves rolled up above her elbows. Her hair was cropped close to her skull, and that, coupled with her height and wiry thinness, might almost have caused her to be mistaken for a man . . . except for her eyes, which were large, the color of onyx and fringed with beautifully curled (and completely natural) lashes. Rob could tell from her body language that Andrea Lynch was tense, though she was trying to convey a bored aloofness.

She's wound like a spring, he thought. *Why?* There were a number of possibilities, but he decided to reserve judgment for the moment. All question of blame or culpability over the radonium-2 monitoring aside, Lynch might simply be one of those humans who was uneasy around aliens. Or telepaths. The woman sported a teledistort cuff on her ear, one of the expensive Mizari models like Rob's own.

"Coffee?" the psychologist asked, taking the pot out of the servo. "Forgive me for saying so, but you look like you could use some, Jeff."

" 'No rest for the wicked,' " Morrow quoted with a wry grin, accepting a mug. Lynch merely shook her head impatiently as the group gathered around the table. "First of all," Morrow began, "let me assure you that we're going to clear up this problem as quickly as possible. We've just been out to take a fast look at the site. The bad news is that our preliminary analysis indicates that there is some radonium-2 activity in that smaller cavern. But the good news is that there are ways to contain and control radonium breakdown, and we have the people and the equipment to handle that. It shouldn't take more than a few days."

Rob sighed with relief. "That's good to hear."

"Will the artifacts be contaminated by radiation?" Ssoriszs asked suddenly. His question, harmless enough in itself, was so abrupt that it sounded accusing. Rob, accustomed to the Mizari Liaison's unfailing politeness, regarded his scaled friend with consternation. *He's really obsessed with this Lost Colony quest . . .*

"Yes," said Lynch firmly, in reply to the Liaison's query.

"No," Jeff Morrow declared simultaneously, speaking with equal certainty.

A brief, awkward silence ensued. Rob broke it. "Well, which is it?" he asked curiously, glancing from Jeff's handsome features to Lynch's rather predatory ones. "Are the artifacts contaminated, or aren't they?"

"Well, actually we're both right," said Morrow with a self-deprecatory smile. "I was referring to the artifacts that are resting in the stasis fields in the main cavern. Nothing in the main cavern shows any sign of contamination, as of this morning. But I believe that Andrea was thinking of the object in the smaller cavern." He glanced at his assistant for confirmation and she nodded. "The religious object . . . what's it called?"

"Star-shrine," Ssoriszs supplied.

"Right. That item, I'm afraid, is contaminated, and will need to be neutralized before it can be removed."

"Is that difficult?" Ssoriszs asked.

"Not really. It will just take us a little time, since we'd have to order in a neutralizer to generate the necessary field. That would take several days to a week, probably. We'll let you know when your star-shrine is accessible again."

Janet Rodriguez leaned forward, brushing a lock of bronze hair back off her forehead. "I have a portable neutralizer here at the school, if you want to use that. However, even more important than those artifacts—if you'll excuse me for saying so, Ssoriszs—is the school itself. Can you tell how much of the radonium beneath the Lamont Cliffs is now changing into radonium-2? How quickly is the reaction spreading?"

"And, most importantly, could the school be in any danger from this radonium-2?" Kkintha ch'aait's whiskers twitched with concern. She was still absently grooming herself, Rob noted, and small tufts of pale fur clung to her clawed fingers.

Jeff raised a hand, his fingers tucked into a fist. "One," he said, counting off his forefinger, "no, we don't know the percentage of radonium that is breaking down into radonium-2. We'll know that in a day or two . . . certainly by the end of the week. Two"—he counted off his middle finger—"the radonium into radonium-2 reaction appears at the moment to be spreading slowly—which is lucky for us."

Morrow gave the Administrator a reassuring smile as he ticked off his ring finger. "And, finally, three: no, at the moment, and unless the situation were to change dramatically, the school is in no danger whatsoever. We should be able to contain this problem before there's even a hint of a threat to the Academy."

"Threat?" Kkintha was determined to hear the worst. "Then there is some danger, is there not?"

"Hell yes, it's dangerous," Andrea Lynch said bluntly. Her manner was patronizing as she spoke slowly, as though to a child. "Radonium-2 is nothing to, uh . . . mess around with. It's very nasty stuff, Administrator ch'aait."

"Before we continue, Jeff," Rob broke in hastily as he saw the Chhhh-kk-tu's small round ears flatten in anger. "Forgive me for making you go back to basics, but could you or Ms. Lynch possibly brief us nontechnical types on just how this radonium into radonium-2 reaction works? Ssoriszs and I were trying to remember our elementary physics courses, but we're still foggy on just what's going on out at the Cliffs."

"Sure, Rob," Morrow said. He keyed his terminal link for a moment in silence, then waved at it. "If you'll all glance at your holo-tanks . . ."

Rob did so, seeing an atomic representation of a three-dimensional molecular structure, showing individual atoms in a rainbow of hues, with the whole molecule outlined in glowing green. "This is stable radonium," Jeff said. "It's a compound, not an element. Normal radonium is a crystalline lattice made up of the indicated elements, which includes one transuranic"—a vivid blue atomic structure brightened—"and a couple of superheavies that are—potentially—extremely unstable." The two atoms that glowed different shades of red brightened to highlight them. "You can see how, in this configuration, the lattice structure is delicately poised. The transuranic atom keeps those two superheavies balanced. Under normal circumstances, radonium is safe and stable. You could pick it up with your hand if you wanted to."

He keyed another command into the terminal, and Rob saw several small particles dive-bomb the lattice. One particle struck one of the delicate linkages near the superheavy atoms, knocking it away, and suddenly the entire structure lurched, slipped, then altered into something that was no longer symmetrical. A violet glow began emanating from the lopsided representation, pulsing brightly. "But . . ." Jeff continued his explanation, "if you bombard basic radonium with neutrons, it becomes unstable, and that's what we call radonium-2."

The image of the radonium-2 mutated back into the stable molecule, then it shrank and was joined by others, until its distinctive crystalline shape appeared solid. A gentle, golden glow surrounded the radonium. "Normal radonium is the good guy of modern technology," the engineer continued. "We power starships with it. Without radonium we'd never have the properties or the power to generate the field that allows us to make the transition to metaspace. A little radonium goes a very long way."

"I was told that the veins of radonium running through this asteroid could power the school for ten thousand years—at a minimum," Rob said. "That's why the Mizari gift of this asteroid for the site of StarBridge Academy was so incredibly generous," he said, smiling and nodding at Ssoriszs.

"This school is vital to the preservation of interstellar peace," the Mizari said slowly, his appendages trembling with deep emotion, "therefore our gift was not *generous,* it was *necessary.*"

"StarBridge means a great deal to all of us, Esteemed One," Jeff said, and for a moment Rob glimpsed something haunted behind his eyes. Without being told, he knew his friend was remembering how hard he'd tried to become part of StarBridge and its mission—and how devastating his failure had been.

After a bare second, Jeff was all business again. "Now watch what happens when radonium-2 begins to spread," he said. He keyed in a command and the radonium on the screen abruptly lurched, tilted, altering into radonium-2. Then the individual molecule shrank until it was only one of many unbalanced molecules. A lurid violet light began pulsing hypnotically as it surrounded the unstable mass, which continued to grow like something living. "When radonium-2 forms, it sets up a domino effect, 'infecting' normal radonium, changing it . . . decrystallizing it. The instability grows quickly, almost geometrically. We call this 'breeding.' "

Morrow licked his lips, staring down into his holo-tank as if mesmerized, then he shivered and looked back up at the others. "Radonium-2 *is* nasty stuff. Volatile, extremely radioactive, it requires special techniques to contain, seal off, then remove it. If I may borrow the medical analogy again, it's like an infected limb that must be amputated, and the stump cauterized."

Now it was Rob's turn to shudder as he remembered a patient on Jolie that he'd once treated. The man had fallen while rock climbing, and by the time he'd been missed, located, and rescued, gangrene had been far advanced. Despite all the advances of modern medicine, his leg had been beyond saving. He'd nearly died.

"How do you accomplish this . . . amputation and cauterization?" Kkintha ch'aait asked.

"We generate very high heat, and use that to vaporize the radonium-2. Then we use vapor-collection tanks to remove the R-2. It's a delicate process, because if that transuranic element begins to fission, it will set up a chain reaction, and when that happens . . ." he trailed off, shaking his head silently.

Andrea Lynch smiled, a faint, derisive smile. "Boom," she said flatly.

"Boom," Rob repeated softly, his mouth dry. "As in mushroom-cloud 'boom.' "

"It wouldn't make a mushroom shape in space, without gravity or air pressure," Lynch pointed out. "It would be a sphere."

I'm so glad we have you here to tell us these things . . . the quotation ran through Rob's mind, but he bit his tongue and remained silent. Sarcasm wouldn't help. Lynch was definitely lacking in the winning personality department, but they needed her on their side.

"But after you do all of this . . . vaporizing and sealing and vapor collection"—Janet Rodriguez frowned worriedly—"will the radonium be safe again?"

"Sure," Lynch replied offhandedly, stealing a not-so-surreptitious glance at her watch. "Just as long as you keep those archaeologists of yours from playing around with their toys."

"Just a moment," Ssoriszs said slowly. "Are you saying that the archaeology dig must be *closed* after you finish your work?"

Lynch shrugged. "Who do you think caused this mess? It certainly wasn't my people! When we checked that site six months ago, it was completely stable. *Something* started the decrystallization, and it had to be them. Reactions like that don't happen spontaneously."

"No, they do not," Janet said, too evenly. "But I find it hard to believe that Serge and Professor Greyshine caused this. It seems far more likely to me that the radonium was affected by some other factor—the neutrons given off by ships entering or leaving metaspace, perhaps—and that your people missed the signs during your most recent check."

"Impossible," Lynch snapped. "I went over their results myself, and so did Jeff. It had to be those archaeologists."

"Andrea . . ." Jeff Morrow said, then he hesitated. "I know we were careful," he continued finally, "but it *is* possible that one of the crew missed something. Nobody is perfect."

"I didn't miss anything," Lynch said brusquely. "It was the archaeologists, and I can prove it. I took a look at those toys of theirs while we were checking out the site, and guess what I found? Something called a neutron emitter. I'm sure that was what triggered the reaction."

Ssoriszs' tentacles stopped waving and his sleek body froze into stillness—a sure sign of great distress among his people, Rob knew. "Serge told me last night when I spoke with him that the Professor was using the neutron emitter when the alarm sounded," the alien said finally. "But the vein of radonium . . . it lies five meters below the surface of the cavern."

"Rock is no barrier to neutrons," Lynch cried triumphantly, swooping like a vulture to seize on the Mizari's words. She favored the group with another caustic smile. "Neutrons are stopped by light-hydrogenous materials—water, oil, plastics . . . and flesh. Rock hardly fazes them."

"Oh, shit," Rob muttered under his breath, picturing Serge's face if the young man weren't permitted to continue with the excavation. Serge would be devastated . . . Rob knew how much he'd invested in this dig. In the past six years the young man had lost his hands, his career as a pianist, his career as an interrelator, and, just months ago, the first woman he'd ever cared for deeply. How many such blows could anyone take without breaking down? "You mean they won't be able to finish excavating?"

"I see no reason why they can't continue their work," Jeff said, giving Ssoriszs a reassuring glance. "But they probably wouldn't be able to use the neutron emitter again."

"The neutron emitter is a fairly recent invention, and archaeologists managed without it before," Janet pointed out. "I suspect Serge and Greyshine can make do without it." Her expression grew thoughtful. "But, really, the more I think about it, the more I can't agree with your reasoning, Ms. Lynch.

"You see, *I* helped Professor Greyshine assemble and calibrate that neutron emitter, and the intensity level simply wasn't set high enough to cause such a reaction. Believe me"—her eyes held the black woman's—"we aren't fools." Janet's unspoken "even though you obviously think we are" fairly echoed in the silence. "Both the Professor and I know what happens when radonium is bombarded with neutrons, and we checked the location of the radonium vein beneath the cavern floor. We were careful to set the emitter on the lowest intensity level."

"Maybe it got turned up by accident," Jeff suggested.

"Don't forget that crevasse," Lynch said. "My scanners showed that it was really deep. It's possible that one of your people scanned the walls of the crevasse and started the reaction breeding that way. Check with them."

"We can't ask Professor Greyshine," Janet said. "They're keeping him in hiber-heal for a couple of days. But Serge might know."

"I suspect that Dr. Andreiovitch will be able to tell us whether the neutron emitter initiated the reaction," Ssoriszs said thoughtfully.

Jeff Morrow sat bolt upright, eyes widening. "*Mikhail* Andreiovitch? You know him? You've been in touch with him about this?"

"Yes. I requested his help in this crisis. He and Esteemed Rizzshor embarked yesterday from Shassiszss. The Council arranged priority transport for them."

Andrea Lynch gasped, and when she spoke her voice was shrill. "Andreiovitch is coming *here*?" she blurted.

"Wonderful!" Jeff exclaimed. He turned to regard his assistant, his eyes sparkling with excitement. "That's the best news I've heard all week," he said, grinning. "Andreiovitch is one of the foremost authorities in the field. His advice will be invaluable."

Tight-lipped, Lynch nodded silently.

Something's going on here, Rob thought, eyeing the woman thoughtfully. *For some reason Lynch doesn't want Andreiovitch to come here. Why? Could she have made some kind of mistake six months ago, and is trying to cover it up?*

"What ship did he take?" Jeff asked. "And when is it due?"

"Andreiovitch and Rizzshor should be here in approximately ten Standard days," Ssoriszs said. "They are aboard the *Night Storm*—one of the swiftest Mizari courier vessels."

"By that time, we may have this whole thing cleared up," Lynch muttered.

"It would be an honor just to meet him," Jeff said. He glanced around the table, then at his watch. "Our crew will be assembling up at the station by now, so unless there's something else, we'd better get up there to make sure everything is in order."

"Jeffrey—" Ssoriszs extended one appendage with its tip turned up, almost like a pleading hand. "This crew of yours . . ." he hesitated, and Rob knew from long association that the Liaison was embarrassed by what he was thinking. "Are they . . . have you known them long?"

"Most of them," Jeff said, giving him a puzzled glance. "People in the mining and space construction business move around a lot, by necessity, but they're a good crew, I assure you. What's on your mind?"

Lynch stood, her mouth tight with impatience. "He's worried about his precious artifacts, Jeff," she explained bluntly. "His star-whatchamacallit and such."

"I assure you, Esteemed One"—Jeff made a placating gesture—"that I'll caution everyone that the items are valuable and not to disturb them."

"And if they should find anything new . . ." Ssoriszs still wasn't satisfied, but he was trying to get as much of a commitment out of the engineer as he could. "Please, could you notify us?"

"We'll call you," Lynch promised, surprising Rob. "And tell your Professor that I learned my lesson last time, after the fit he pitched when we moved that junk. If we find anything this time, we'll call him and ask for instructions before we move it. Okay?" She rocked back on her heels, arms crossed over her chest with a "what could possibly be fairer?" expression.

"Thank you," Ssoriszs said, somewhat reassured, though Lynch's patronizing expression made it hard to credit her sincerity.

Morrow, too, stood. "If there are no further questions—" he began, but broke off as Kkintha ch'aait waved her little forelimb. "Just one, Jeffrey," she said. "I am relieved that you are confident that this problem can be contained and eliminated, but . . . what if you are unable to halt this radonium reaction . . . this 'breeding'? What then?"

Jeff gave her a crooked smile. "Administrator, my dad has a saying, 'Don't cross that bridge till you come to it.' You want the worst-case scenario? If we can't stop the radonium-2 from breeding, the reaction will start to spread rapidly. If such a thing were to happen, it would be too dangerous for anyone to stay here."

"You mean we would have to leave? Evacuate the students?"

"Unless you'd like to wind up as part of a pint-sized cosmic dust cloud, the answer's yes," Lynch said dryly. "Just in case, maybe you'd better check out how long it would take you to ship those kids out of here, Administrator."

For the first time, Morrow seemed to react to Lynch's mordant humor. "Andrea!" He gave her a reproving glance. "That's nothing to kid about. Kkintha . . ." he hesitated. "Don't worry. At the moment all indications are favorable. But we'll report again as soon as we've done a more thorough analysis in a couple of days. If anything so . . . drastic . . . became necessary, you'd have plenty of warning."

Kkintha nodded, a gesture she'd picked up after years of association with humans. "Thank you, Jeffrey," she said. "I appreciate your frankness."

Rob stood up. "I'll walk you out," he said, and the three of them headed for the door.

Once through it, Andrea Lynch strode ahead, her long legs quickly outdistancing the two men. "She must be a real pleasure to work with every day," Rob said dryly, lowering his voice so the woman wouldn't hear.

Jeff's mouth twitched, then he gave a resigned sigh. "Andrea is a damned good crew boss and engineer," he said ruefully, "but usually I don't take her along when I talk to clients. She rubs everyone the wrong way."

"I'll say," Rob agreed fervently. "But if she's the best person for the job . . ." He shrugged.

"She is," Morrow said. "She definitely is the best." He sighed again, this time wearily. "God, I'm tired. Seems like it's been at least a month since I've had a good night's sleep."

"The insomnia's back?" Rob asked, remembering how tormented Jeff had been by sleeplessness before he'd left the Academy. At the time, he'd recognized that it was a symptom of depression, and had treated it with hypno-therapy and medication. "Or have you just been overworking?"

Morrow ran a hand through his hair. "A little of both, maybe," he admitted.

Rob caught a glimpse of something metallic glittering amid the now-tousled strands of Jeff's hair, and when he looked more closely, the psychologist was surprised to realize that Morrow was wearing a teledistort. Lynch's wearing one seemed perfectly in keeping with her personality, but seeing Jeff wearing one struck Rob as odd. "Feeling paranoid today?" he asked, trying to keep it light. "Or has she infected you?"

When Morrow looked confused, Rob tugged at his own ear. "The distort," he explained.

"Oh . . . *that.*" Jeff rolled his eyes. "I forgot I had it on. I've been wearing it night and day since I left StarBridge Station for a series of meetings with one of our subcontractors. You've been in academia too long, Rob. This is S.O.P. during business meetings nowadays," he said, touching the earcuff. "Companies have taken to hiring telepaths to 'monitor' conversations."

"That's unethical!" Rob protested. "Blackmail is a natural result of such a practice!"

Morrow shrugged. "You're right," he agreed. "But how are you going to stop it?"

I hope nobody tells Heather Farley about that, Rob thought grimly. "I suppose you can't," he said. "But it's too bad that those telepaths are making a living abusing their talent, when we have such a crying need for them here."

When they reached the airlock, they halted. Rob's gaze searched Morrow's face, finding new lines as well as the shadows beneath the younger man's eyes. "Get some sleep, okay?" he said, putting a hand on his friend's arm and giving it a little shake. "You look like hell, Jeff."

Morrow gave him a crooked grin. "You don't look so hot yourself, Doc," he said, pretending to peer at Rob's hair. "You're getting as gray as an old dog I once had. This place is sucking you dry, Rob."

The psychologist gave him a rueful grin. "That makes two of my friends in two days who have reminded me I'm getting gray," he said, shaking his head. "Maybe I ought to dye it."

Jeff's blue eyes narrowed. "Maybe you ought to get out of here," he said softly.

Startled, Rob started to laugh the remark off, then saw that Morrow was serious. "What's that supposed to mean?" he demanded. "You said you'd be able to contain the radonium—stop it from breeding!"

The engineer shrugged. "I wasn't talking about that," he said reassuringly. "The school will be fine, don't worry. I was just . . ." He shrugged. "I don't know. I'm too tired to make sense, Rob. I'm so beat I feel punchy."

"Sleep is what you need, Jeff," Rob said, relaxing. "Call me tomorrow, okay? Maybe we can meet up at the station for dinner."

"I'm going to be out at the site," Morrow said grimly. "But I'll try to get some sack time . . . if Lynch doesn't run me ragged."

"You're the boss," Rob pointed out. "Fire her if she gives you any static."

"I can't. I need her." Morrow hesitated, then said in a rush, "Rob, maybe I was stepping out of line just now, but, dammit, it seems as though you—and the other StarBridge staff—work your butts off, and all you get for it is more shit dumped on you. I read that editorial in the *Times* that pointed to your dropout rate and called for a new administration to run the Bridge. It's not fair!"

"You're right, it's not," the psychologist agreed soberly. "But the universe isn't a fair place, we both learned that long ago. I read that editorial, too. But that faction is definitely in the minority . . . at least so far."

Rob took a deep breath. "Listen, Jeff, there's something I want you to know." He hesitated, then took the plunge. "Back when you were a student here, I was going through some rough times, wondering if I'd made a terrible mistake taking on this job. I suspect that you were more observant than you ever let on . . . that you picked up on my problems, and the self-destructive way I was dealing—or, rather, *not* dealing with them. Am I right?"

"Maybe," Jeff said, his face revealing nothing. "Why?"

Rob waited silently.

Finally Morrow shrugged, then nodded. "Yeah, okay, you're right."

"I want you to know that I've made peace with myself about all of that," Rob said earnestly. "It took a lot of soul-searching, but it was worth it. Jeff, this place . . . well, it's the best thing I've ever done. This school is worth all the hard work, all the sacrifice. It took me a while to realize that, but I know it now. StarBridge is *important*."

Morrow's blue-gray eyes were steady as they held his. "I'm glad to hear that you've come to terms with your choice," he said finally. "You're right in thinking that I observed you just about as closely as you studied me. Uh, I gather that you haven't . . . I mean, that there's been no, uh . . ." Raising his hand, he made a quick tipping gesture, as though pouring something.

"Not a drop, not in almost six years," Rob said quietly. He gave his friend a lopsided smile. "And I'm completely off medication, too." He shook his head. "Feels funny to talk about it out loud after all these years of silence, doesn't it? I knew that you knew, of course . . . I've known for years."

"How?"

"Because whenever you'd come back and we'd have dinner or an evening together, you never acted surprised when I didn't join you in a beer. That's a dead giveaway."

"I guess so," Jeff said. "Is it still hard, staying away from it?"

Now it was Rob's turn to shrug. "I've replaced the old habits with new, but there are days when the urge still hits me. You can't ever let yourself believe, 'I've beaten this, and now I don't have to be on my guard anymore.' At times, when I get stressed, it's still one day—even one hour, or one minute—at a time."

Morrow nodded gravely. "I understand. Uh, listen . . . I hope I didn't embarrass you just now. I just . . . well, you're one of my closest friends, and I want what's best for you."

Rob nodded. "I know. And I also know what's best for me, and StarBridge is it."

Jeff's eyes fell; the moment, Rob realized, was rapidly becoming too intense. "I suppose you do," Morrow muttered, then he looked back up and lightly punched his friend's bicep. "But I still think you'd be better off as President of Earth!"

Rob rolled his eyes. "Jeff, you *are* punchy," he said. "Get some sleep."

"I promise, Doc," Morrow agreed meekly. "I'll talk to you tomorrow." As the airlock door slid aside, he gave his friend a thumbs-up salute and left.

Heather existed on two levels, neither one physical.

If she allowed herself to become aware of her actual surroundings, there was only darkness, glimpses of shining straight lines and angles, all of it studded with trails of electricity, winking on-off, on-off. Existence within the computer was like nothing

she'd ever encountered before, but it had some of the same feel
as playing a complex computer game—the perception of grids,
organic crystals, multilevels . . . and endless, tiny spaces.

On the other level, the imaginary one that she'd programmed
herself, this illusional pocket of "reality," Heather existed inside
a different body, wearing a pearl-gray suit and an emerald blouse.
She sat behind an expensive desk, within a tastefully furnished
office, gazing into a computer screen at a dark-skinned man with
a formidable nose and straight, oily black hair. *That's just like the
business suit I saw in the catalogue*, she thought with one part of
her mind. *It cost a bundle.*

The broker, Mr. Shandra, glanced down at his own terminal,
then cleared his throat. "I believe I have it all clear, Ms. Benson,"
he said. "Just let me check it over one more time . . ."

Heather could tell he was racking his brain for a way to prolong
their encounter, trying to get up his nerve to turn the conversation onto a more personal level. From the moment Rajahanipur
Shandra had answered his call to find himself confronted by the
lovely image of "Helen Benson," i.e., Heathertoo, it hadn't taken
telepathy to realize what the broker had in mind.

Heather's thoughts moved Heathertoo's mouth into a smile,
then words. "I appreciate your personally taking the time on such
short notice to help me set up my account, Mr. Shandra. It was
very kind of you."

"Not at all, not at all," Shandra assured her heartily. "It is an
honor to assist you, Ms. Benson. Tell me, if you do not mind
my inquiring . . . how did you come to choose me and my firm?
StarBridge Station is a major trade hub, certainly, but, physically,
it *is* a bit out of the way."

Heather hesitated, turning over possible replies. "I heard your
name mentioned at a cocktail party last month," she said, hoping
her pause hadn't been too long. "At the Terran embassy on
Shassiszss."

"You are on Shassiszss?" Shandra was delighted. "Then on
your way back to Earth, your ship is bound to pass through
StarBridge Sector. I would be delighted if you could stop off
at the station and meet with me. Then we could discuss your
investment future in person." Now it was his turn to hesitate.
"Perhaps we might have lunch . . . or dinner?"

Oh, shit! Heather thought, but kept her consternation from
showing on her imaged face. "I'm so sorry, Mr. Shandra, but
my next assignment"—she'd given her occupation as "writer"
and had mentioned that her funds came from "royalties" when

she'd first spoken to the broker—"will take me in the opposite direction. But if I ever do get out that way"—Heathertoo flashed him a dazzling smile—"I'll be certain to let you know. Lunch or dinner would be nice. And by the way, Mr. Shandra, that's a beautiful suit. Exquisite tailoring."

"Please, call me Raj," he invited, disappointment mixing with pleasure at the compliment. "And I thank you again, Ms. Benson."

Heathertoo smiled. "And you must call me Helen," she cooed sweetly. "Thank you again . . . Raj. Good-bye."

The girl cut the connection, then relaxed with a mental sigh of relief. She'd done it! Shandra had bought the whole thing!

It was time to exit the program, but for just a moment, Heather let herself be distracted by the body she was "wearing." When she'd first slipped into it, it had seemed stiff, unwieldy, but now it seemed so real! Running her hands over her breasts, she wondered whether this was what having real tits felt like. For a moment she toyed with the idea of creating a program using an image of Serge, and having him meet Heathertoo.

She pictured him sitting beside her, holding her hand, tenderly kissing her mouth, then, greatly daring, she imagined him unbuttoning her blouse, gently stroking her breast. The thought was exciting, stimulating, but also embarrassing . . . and scary. From her telepathic snooping, Heather was well aware of what grown-ups did in bed together, but she'd never really comprehended the urge. Sex struck her as a lot of sweaty, sticky thrashing around and grunting over what boiled down to—at its best—a few seconds of pleasure *almost* as good as what she received from scarfing up a hot-fudge sundae.

Heather still giggled over what Aunt Natalie had *really* thought about while Uncle Fred had been panting and slobbering on top of her. Once, when he'd called her a "fat, unnatural little monster," she'd gotten mad enough to throw caution to the winds and tell the old son of a bitch the truth—in consequence earning herself an ass-burning from both of them. She'd been sore for two days.

I should get out, she thought lazily, looking around the office. But this was even more relaxing, more pleasant than sleeping late. *Just a few more seconds,* she promised herself. *Just—*

"Heather!" the voice spoke sharply in her ear—her real ear. She was being shaken—*who* was being shaken? Heathertoo? No . . . it was her real body, her physical body. She'd almost forgotten she had one—

"Heather, answer me! Wake up!"

With a rush that completely disoriented her, the girl found herself back in her own stocky little body. She opened her eyes to find Hing bending over her, pale and anxious. "Heather? Can you hear me?" the older girl shouted.

"Of course I can hear you," Heather said peevishly. "I just fell asleep, that's all."

"You sure did! I've been shaking you for more than a minute. Are you *sure* you're okay?" Hing peered at her suspiciously.

"I'm fine," Heather said. One of her arms and both of her feet had gone to sleep and she began flexing them cautiously, wincing. "When did you get back? I was . . . I was worried about you."

Hing sat down on Heather's bed and smiled ruefully. "For a while I was worried about myself," she admitted. "But as you can see, I'm fine. Didn't the nurse leave a message for you? I asked him to."

Heather had completely forgotten to check messages on her Mizari voder. She glanced down at the little machine strapped to her wrist, then swore softly as she saw the telltale light that indicated a message on file. "I never thought to check," she said ruefully.

"Have you seen Serge?" Hing asked. "They said he'd gone back to his quarters, but I went by there on my way back, and he wasn't there."

Memory came rushing back, and Heather was horrified to feel her eyes flood with tears. She struggled to hold them back. "I . . . didn't *see* him," she muttered. "But—but . . ."

"Heather . . ." Hing was staring at her, concerned. "What's wrong, honey?" she asked, getting up and putting an arm around the girl. "What happened?"

The sympathy nearly proved Heather's undoing. For long moments she struggled, fists pressed to her eyes, fighting back the sobs that wanted to burst out. Finally, she drew a long, ragged breath. "Serge is pissed at me," she whispered, her voice harsh with the unshed tears. "He hates me."

"Why? What happened?"

"I—I read his mind. About his music. And—and he found out," Heather gulped.

"Oh . . ." Hing shook her head. "That's the one thing that would really piss him off, you're right. C'mon out here, let's sit down and have some tea, and you can tell me the whole story, okay?"

Minutes later the roommates sat side by side in their shared living room, sipping tea from Hing's exquisite porcelain cups as Heather talked. Finishing her account, the child leaned back, feeling exhausted. Afraid to meet Hing's eyes and see Serge's anger reflected there, too, she fixed her gaze on one of the holo-posters showing views of ancient Far Eastern temples and waited.

"Wow," Hing said finally. "Serge really called you a *bitch*?"

Miserably, Heather nodded.

"I don't think I've ever heard him curse," the older student said. "Maybe once, during a fight we had, but . . ." She took a deep breath. "If I were going to be a proper example to you, I'd shake my finger and say, 'I warned you.' Telepathic snooping is very bad manners, and nobody likes an eavesdropper. But beating yourself up about what's already happened won't help. You just have to make up your mind to do better in the future."

"I will, I swear it," Heather mumbled. "But it doesn't matter . . . Serge hates me. I can't change that."

Slipping an arm around the child's shoulders, Hing gave her a hug. "No, he doesn't hate you. You owe him an apology, and you'll have to be careful to respect his privacy in the future. You'll learn from this, and go on."

Heather voiced her worst fear. "Hing, I won't be here in the future! Serge will tell Dr. Rob, and he'll send me back to Earth!"

"No, he won't," Hing said firmly. "I know Serge, and that's not his way. By now, he's probably kicking himself for losing his temper and cussing out a poor defenseless kid." She gave her roommate a wry grin. "He'll probably wind up apologizing to *you*."

"I tried to tell him I'm sorry . . ."

"I know. I'll talk to him, smooth it over. Leave it to me, okay?"

Heather gave the young woman a grateful look. "*Would* you?"

"Sure. I can't have two of my favorite people not speaking, can I?" Hing asked, giving the girl one of her wide, mischievous grins. Slowly, Heather was able to summon a wan smile in return.

"But right now, there's something you need to see," Hing said firmly. "Just wait." Moving with most of her old energy, she strode over to the wall unit and keyed in a program. "Watch. And, most importantly, *listen*."

The holo-vid screen on the opposite wall rippled, then filled with a view of a huge baroque concert hall. Crystal chandeliers hung suspended like showers of diamonds and ice, trembling slightly with the collective breath of the huge audience. An enormous grand piano stood alone on the stage. "Vienna," Hing said quietly.

As Heather watched, a shorter and much younger version of Serge LaRoche walked up to the piano and seated himself. He was dressed in an outfit similar to the one she'd seen in his mind, tight black pants and funny jacket with long tails, and a white bow tie. His hair was much shorter, and stood up in a soft brush. *He looks like he's around my age,* Heather thought.

For a long moment Serge regarded the keyboard as though it were a feast and he a starving child. Fingers poised, he took a deep breath, then his hands swooped down, descending upon the keyboard with a lover's passion. His concentration was total as music, soft at first, then building, swelling to a triumphant climax, filled the hall.

That's beautiful! Heather thought in amazement as the prodigy's hands flashed up and down the keyboard. She didn't recognize the piece—the girl knew next to nothing about classical music—but the beauty of it awed her. It was so flowing, so pure, so deceptively simple.

"That's Mozart," Hing said softly.

As the piece ended, the view rippled, and there he was again, this time in all-white tails, accompanied by a full orchestra. The music was different, more syncopated, with jazzy overtones that made the girl nod her head in time to the music. "Gershwin," Hing whispered.

The concerts continued in a pastiche of settings, outfits, and composers. Softly, Hing identified each composer as the program continued, and Heather watched, rapt.

Beethoven . . . Schubert . . . Satie . . . Rachmaninoff . . .Tchaikovsky . . . Liszt . . . Chopin . . . Brahms . . .

Serge played them all, and more.

The last two compositions Hing did not identify, but Heather recognized one. StarBridge Academy's anthem, a stirring piece that she'd heard many times at school functions in Melbourne. Then the last piece, an étude (as identified by Hing) had Serge's fingers flashing up and down the keys like dancers, with a melody so unexpectedly lyrical that she closed her eyes to savor its beauty . . .

"Oh, Serge," Heather whispered reverently, when the program ended. "Oh, God, Serge," she repeated, her throat tight. The girl was embarrassed by her emotion until she noticed the tears sparkling on Hing's cheeks. "That was . . . beautiful. I see now why he can't bear to have his music mentioned. Hing . . ." Heather whispered, "who wrote those last two pieces? The Academy's anthem and the étude?"

"Who do you think?" Hing asked simply.

"Serge?"

The Cambodian girl nodded. "He wrote the anthem long before the school was built, so it could be played at all the fund-raisers."

"And now, because of the accident, it's all gone," Heather whispered, shifting restlessly. She was stiff with sitting still for so long. "What must it be like, to be able to play like that, then to know you can never play again?"

Hing's mouth twisted. "That's the hell of it, really. He *could* play, if he wanted to," she said bitterly. "If Serge wanted to, he could play anything he used to."

"But his hands—"

"Work even better than the originals. The Mizari designed them very well. Too well, maybe."

"What do you mean?"

"More than a year after he lost his hands, Serge entered a competition. He'd worked hard in therapy, trying to regain what he'd lost. So he took part in the Inter-Colonial piano competition and he played very well—matter of fact, he was declared the winner. But one contestant lodged a protest, saying that Serge had an unfair advantage because his artificial hands could move faster and had slightly longer fingers than his real ones. That girl gave a press interview, during which she implied that Serge had trumped up the story about the aircar accident and had his hands *intentionally amputated* so he could receive artificial ones. Can you believe that?"

Despite her shock, Heather could. She'd known a lot of twisted people. "What happened then?" she whispered.

"Serge didn't even wait for the ruling. He withdrew from the competition, announcing that he *had* cheated and that he would never play again. And so far as I know, he hasn't. The one time I was able to get him to talk about it, even for a couple of minutes, he told me that the girl who protested was correct—oh, not about the amputation, or the reason for it, but that she'd been right to protest. He said that fake hands might be physically superior, but that they could never convey the genuine emotion an artist must feel, and thus he had no right to play anymore."

"But to give up a gift like that . . ." Heather trailed off.

"I know. I think that in some way Serge is still punishing himself for being stupid and messing with that aircar. I think his decision is stupid and perverse, but it *was* his decision to make," Hing said, scowling. "You have to respect his right to decide, even if you don't agree with him. But it's awfully hard for me to remember that, when I hear him play."

"I guess I can understand how he could feel that it was unfair of him to play with his artificial hands," Heather said slowly, thinking hard, "though I don't agree. That's like saying that a photographer or a holo-vid producer can't create art because he or she uses technology to achieve the final product. But even if he doesn't want to play again, what about composing? There's nothing artificial about Serge's brain—or his heart!" She was surprised to hear the passion that tinged her own voice.

Hing gave her a sympathetic look. "I said the same thing to him," she murmured. "More than once."

"I guess he didn't listen."

Hing sighed. "No, he's not ready to hear that," she said sadly. "Maybe he never will be."

"That would be the real tragedy," Heather remarked quietly.

Hing nodded.

"Esteemed Ssoriszs?" Serge peered into the dimness in the Observatory Lounge, barely making out a massive shape coiled between two Terran sofas. The faint starlight shone through the transparent plas-steel dome, awakening a gleam from a lidless golden eye. "Is that you?"

The shape moved, flowed, resolved itself into the Mizari as he made his sinuous way toward the young man. "Serge! I see you received my message," the alien exclaimed. "I am so relieved to know that you were not harmed. I assure you that as soon as things at the Academy return to normal, the school will recognize your courage—and that of Hing and Khuharkk', also, of course."

"We were definitely a team," Serge said absently. Stepping into the Observatory, he walked over and plopped down into a chair beside the Mizari. Silently, both of them looked up at the profusion of stars, seemingly close with no atmosphere to distance or distort their glory.

"They are out there, Serge," Ssoriszs said softly. "My lost kinspeople are out there. I feel in my spirit that that is the truth."

"I hope someday we can find where they went," the human said, his voice as quiet as the alien's. *Was it the Lost Colony that we found? Perhaps we will never know, now . . .*

"Someday, we will know what happened to them," Ssoriszs said. "I only hope that I live to see that day." After a moment he turned his eyes away from the heavens and fixed Serge with a (naturally) unblinking stare. "How is Professor Greyshine?"

"The doctors are keeping him sedated, in hiber-heal," Serge said. "They say it will be at least four or five days before he will be ready to be released."

"May the stars shed their healing light upon him," Ssoriszs said, giving the words the cadence of a formal invocation.

"Ainsi soit-il," Serge whispered, and they didn't speak for almost a minute. The human finally stirred, turning to regard the elderly alien. "You were at the meeting today. How did it go?"

"The Horizons Unlimited people believe that they will be able to contain the radonium-2 outbreak," the Mizari replied. "And, Serge, they are saying that you and the Professor started the radonium breeding when you used the neutron emitter in the cavern."

Serge gaped at him, then began sputtering indignantly. *"Mais, c'est ridicule!"* he cried, then hastily reverted to Mizari. "That's an outrageous accusation! We made only one brief scan in there, and we double-checked the intensity calibration before we ever turned the instrument on! They are wrong!"

"So Janet Rodriguez and I attempted to tell the Horizons Unlimited crew boss," Ssoriszs said dryly. "Morrow was willing to entertain our argument, but her mind was closed to any opinion but her own."

"I am concerned about what those people will do to the dig," Serge said, his hands tightening involuntarily into fists. He could feel the neuron-connected components begin to strain, and forced himself to loosen his fingers. "If they find any other artifacts, they will probably do worse than move them this time. And the star-shrine! That is the most valuable piece, and it is covered with semiprecious gems! What if one of those workers were to steal it?"

"That thought occurred to me also," Ssoriszs said heavily. "However, the shrine must first be neutralized before it can be removed and transported. That will ensure that it is not tampered with until Mr. Morrow can order in a neutralizer."

"Janet has one, I believe," Serge said. "As part of her emergency equipment. Frankly, neutralizers aren't that difficult to procure or set up, Esteemed One. Someone bent on theft could neutralize the star-shrine, then steal it while no one was looking."

"That would be a very risky proposition, would it not?"

"Esteemed One," Serge said earnestly, "if that shrine proves to be the work of one of the Lost Colony masters, it would be *priceless*. Even a trustworthy person has been known to be corrupted by the promise of great wealth. That star-shrine would be worth risking one's life."

"But surely no dealer would purchase such a distinctive piece," Ssoriszs protested. "It would be instantly recognizable as having been stolen!"

The human gave a harsh, humorless chuckle. "There are so-called reputable dealers in antiquities who purchase black-market items and then sell them to collectors who understand that they can never exhibit them, but who only wish to possess them for their private hoards." Serge shook his head. "The black market in stolen antiquities is flourishing and has been for centuries."

Like most Mizari, Ssoriszs was profoundly shocked by unethical or illegal acts. Crime on his world was virtually unknown, and considered evidence of a severe mental impairment or disorder. His appendages rippling with strong emotion, the elderly Liaison struggled to find words. "I had known that a black market exists," he said finally. "But it is extremely distressing to know that it is so old—and so universal."

"Hasn't Rob ever shown you *Raiders*?" Serge asked in surprise. "I would have thought . . ." He trailed off as he recalled the scene in which Indiana Jones dispatched the scaled denizens of the ancient Egyptian tomb, and decided that Rob had exercised discretion in sparing the Mizari *that* opus. Ssoriszs was gazing at him, politely waiting for him to continue. The young man cleared his throat. "Ummm . . . never mind. The important question is, what can we do to protect the artifacts, especially the star-shrine?"

"Morrow said that Cavern Two is already contaminated by radiation," Ssoriszs said. "But Cavern One is still safe."

Serge rose to his feet, sudden decision brightening his eyes. "Then I believe we should go out there right now and collect the artifacts in the stasis fields," he said. "Perhaps we can persuade Mr. Morrow to let us set up Janet's portable neutralizer, so we can remove the star-shrine tomorrow."

"But the radiation danger—" Ssoriszs began doubtfully.

"I can borrow one of Janet's heavy-duty pressure suits. They've got twice the normal shielding," Serge said. "She's a tall woman, I'm sure I can adjust it to fit me. And you could wear one of the extra-dense fields. That ought to be plenty of protection for Cavern One, at least."

The Mizari's slender tongue flicked out of his mouth as he hissed with approval. "Yes! Surely once we are there, they will not deny us admittance, especially if we are wearing suitable shielding. Let us go immediately!"

Thirty minutes later the odd duo entered the airlock leading to the shuttle hangar. Serge was wearing one of Janet's bulky suits, which proved a tight fit, but he reassured himself that he'd only have to be in it for an hour or so. Ssoriszs was surrounded by a greenish-golden glow as he slithered beside the human.

The airlock door slid aside and they were facing the un-pressurized portion of the hangar dome—though the gravity was still CLS standard, slightly less than one gee. Several small scooters were lined up against the wall; Serge chose one that had a large cargo compartment. Carefully, grunting with effort, he hefted the portable neutralizer into place behind the pilot's seat, then strapped it on securely. When he'd finished, the Mizari draped himself into the cargo section, adjusting his massive coils in the confined space with some difficulty.

Then it was Serge's turn to squeeze into the pilot's seat of the scooter; the bulkier suit with its extra shielding made it a tight fit, but he managed. As he activated the controls, the spidery little scooter rose up on its anti-grav jets, then glided forward as LaRoche applied thrust.

The scooter had no cabin, and Ssoriszs had not gone back to his quarters for his voder, so they perforce rode in silence. Beneath them the grim and torturously beautiful rockscape flashed by, the slagged rocks rising and falling below Serge's feet like the cindery ghost of a long-dead sea. Memories of his last ride out to the dig—could it be only yesterday?—filled the young man's mind.

He hadn't seen Hing today. What was she doing? Did she remember how she'd huddled in the shelter of his arms on the trip back from the dig?

And had she seen Heather? Remembering how he'd sworn at the child, Serge grimaced inwardly. He'd had every right to be angry, but he knew he'd overreacted. The poor kid had been scared, worried for Hing, and he'd been a selfish *bête*. He'd have to talk to her, explain why he'd been so angry, beg her pardon for what he'd said.

Lost in his musings, the trip seemed to take only a few minutes. As he circled the scooter over the flat plain that led up to the cliff face leading into the caverns, Serge groaned aloud, though there was no one to hear him. He'd had a faint hope that they'd beaten the Horizons Unlimited crew to the site . . . after all, it had been less than thirty-six hours since the radonium-2 alarm had first sounded. But Morrow's crew had been busy.

Five bubbletents of varying sizes had been erected on the glassy rock plain leading up to the mountains, and brilliant floodlights illuminated the entire camp. In their harsh, knifelike glare, the slag gleamed, black streaked with red, brown, and greenish-gray.

Serge landed the scooter fifty meters from the cliff face, then he and the old Mizari dismounted and started toward the airlock. When they reached it, Serge quickly keyed in his ID code, signaling the lock to open.

It didn't.

Biting his lip with frustration, Serge keyed in the code again. He was angry—but not particularly surprised—to discover that the code had been changed.

Suddenly a voice spoke over his radio, almost deafening after the long silence. "May I help you?" The words were polite, but the tone was surly.

Turning to look for the newcomer's whereabouts, Serge started violently to find a tall figure wearing a heavy-duty suit standing behind him—so close they were almost touching. Peering into a face shadowed by the helmet and the floodlights, he glimpsed enough of the features to realize that the newcomer was black, but could tell little else. "Uh, hello," he stammered. "I am Serge LaRoche, one of the Academy instructors, and this is Esteemed Ssoriszs—"

"I know who he is," the newcomer interrupted. "I was in a meeting with him for about an hour today." Serge could still not guess the sex of the speaker. Wishing that he could talk to the Mizari, Serge glanced uneasily at the alien.

"I am one of the archaeologists who has been working here at the Lamont Cliffs dig," he tried again. "May I ask who you are?"

"Andrea Lynch, crew boss," she identified herself brusquely. "Can't he"—she jerked her helmet at the Mizari—"talk to us?"

"Not unless we step into the airlock," Serge said. "The Esteemed One is not wearing a voder at the moment."

"Come on then," she said shortly, then keyed them into the airlock. Serge was careful to keep his helmet pointed toward her face, but his peripheral vision was excellent—he saw and memorized the code Lynch used.

Once in the airlock, the two humans removed their helmets and Ssoriszs turned off his field. Quickly Serge explained that they wished to attach the portable neutralizer to the star-shrine, then collect the other artifacts and their equipment before everything was contaminated. Lynch began shaking her head before he was halfway through his plea, and she continued to shake it even after he was silent again.

"No," she said, biting the word off as though she had a bad taste in her mouth. "I can't allow that. It's too dangerous."

"But I am wearing a heavy-duty suit of the same type as you are, and Ssoriszs has on a field that provides maximum radiation protection," Serge pointed out, his heart sinking. "We will only be here for perhaps thirty minutes. Even with regular pressure gear, our exposure in that time would be negligible."

Lynch shook her cropped head. "No," she said flatly, then, as though remembering that she was actually employed by StarBridge Academy, she amended her refusal to, "I'm sorry, but that is impossible."

"But—"

The crew boss's mouth tightened. "I'm very busy, and must get back to work now. We'll let you know when the site is safe again."

"Ms. Lynch," Ssoriszs said, "only today I heard Mr. Morrow say that there was no danger in Cavern One. May we not at least remove the artifacts in their stasis fields and the archaeological equipment? Some of it is extremely delicate, and we fear that it will be in the way of your workers and become damaged."

"I'm sorry, uh, Esteemed Liaison"—she'd obviously had to think to recall Ssoriszs' title—"but I have my orders. Our insurance carrier will not permit anyone but a Horizons Unlimited employee access to a contaminated worksite."

"We would be entirely willing to sign any type of waiver that you wish," Serge said hastily. "I'm sure Mr. Morrow would allow us on the site—he's supported our project since the beginning. May we speak to him?"

"He's up at the station."

"Well, can you call him?"

"Mr. Morrow is asleep," Lynch said curtly, "and I'm not going to disturb him over something like this. I will tell him that you were here when he checks in."

Serge stood his ground. "We'll wait, if we may, until we may speak with Mr. Morrow. I saw an empty bubbletent as we landed . . . we can stay there."

Lynch's skin was too dark to betray an angry flush, but her eyes flashed and she took a slow, deep breath. "Listen, Mr. LaRoche, I don't have time to argue about this. I have to oversee my crew."

"*You* listen—" Serge began, then he broke off, aware that if he said any more, he'd say too much. He kept his temper in control only by clenching his teeth until his jaw ached. Silently, he and Lynch eyed each other.

Finally, after what had to be more than a full minute of silence, Lynch glanced away, and Serge heard her mutter an obscenity under her breath. "Look," she snarled. "I can't let you into the caverns, and that's that. But since you insist, I'll bring the damned artifacts in the stasis fields and all the equipment out to you, and you can take 'em back to the Academy. That's the best I can do." She fell silent, but Serge could almost hear her unspoken final thought. *Take it or leave it*.

He glanced at Ssoriszs, saw the Mizari's tentacles dip downward in unison, then up again. Serge's mouth twitched. *Not quite a nod, but I get the message, Esteemed One*. He nodded at Andrea Lynch. "Thank you," he said coldly. "And when you are moving the stasis containers, please, I implore you, be careful."

"Wait out by your scooter and we'll bring them out," Lynch said impatiently, helmet raised, poised to go.

"We will need plas-steel cord to tie the items safely in place," Serge reminded her.

"Right." The helmet was already past her nose. Serge quickly donned his own, locking it into place.

Back at the scooter, Serge stood looking at the little vehicle, trying to figure out how in the universe he was going to cram all the equipment and artifacts onto it. Motioning Ssoriszs up into the cargo compartment, he waited impatiently for Lynch.

Scant minutes later she appeared, arms full, with another spacesuited figure behind her. Serge piled the artifacts around Ssoriszs, wedging the stasis containers securely into place. Then he began trying the instruments onto the scooter, using every projection available. Lynch stood by silently as he worked.

Serge finished, then put a hand on the back of the pilot's seat, preparatory to climbing aboard. But before he did, the young man turned back again, knowing that although the crew boss could not see his expression, she would be able to hear the tone of his voice. "Thank you so very much for your gracious assistance, Ms. Lynch," he said, letting the sarcasm drip. "And be assured . . . we will be contacting Mr. Morrow about the star-shrine."

"You do that," Lynch retorted, turning to leave. As she did, her foot struck a small forked object that Serge had overlooked because it was lying in the absolute blackness of the scooter's shadow. "Shit!" she muttered, catching herself, then scooping it up. "Here, Mr. LaRoche. You almost forgot your damned dowser."

My what? Serge wanted to demand, but she had already thrust the moisture finder into his hands and was skip-bouncing away, knees bent and flexed, moving with the grace and assurance of one who has spent hours in a pressure suit in extremely low gravity.

His fingers hampered by his space suit gloves, Serge managed to fasten the small Y-shaped device to his belt. *Good thing I didn't lose this*, he thought. The moisture finder was designed to analyze rock and soil and indicate where water had once run or stood. Archaeologists used it to trace the paths of vanished rivers, or to find the locations of wells that had been dry for centuries or millennia.

Finally, after a considerable struggle, Serge managed to squeeze himself into the pilot's seat without snagging his suit on any of the equipment tied behind it. As he fastened his seat restraints, he felt fatigue wash over him like an ocean.

Moving like an automaton, he powered up the scooter and took off, fighting the fog of exhaustion that threatened to engulf him. *To the victor, the spoils*, he thought grimly. *And Andrea Lynch was certainly victorious today. She remains in possession of the star-shrine . . . the real treasure. I fear that it is lost to us, lost forever . . .*

Sick with despair, Serge wondered how he'd ever face Professor Greyshine again.

CHAPTER 9

♦

Collision Course

Four days after their first meeting, Rob, Ssoriszs, Kkintha ch'aait, and Janet Rodriguez gathered to meet with Jeff Morrow and his crew boss at Horizons Unlimited's office at StarBridge Station. Rob arrived late; he'd been delayed by an incident between a Vardi senior and a Heeyoon freshman. After helping to defuse the potentially explosive confrontation, and soothing ruffled fur and fronds, he'd left the two safely in the care of the guidance counselors for their respective species.

The meeting was under way when he walked in. Muttering a quick apology, Rob took his seat. Jeff nodded, continuing with what he'd been saying. " . . . unsure of what could have triggered it, but it's a disturbing finding. I wanted to let you know as soon as possible."

Rob was sitting next to Janet Rodriguez. He leaned over and breathed, "What's up?"

"The radonium-2 is breeding in more than one location under the Lamont Cliffs," the engineer whispered back. "It's now in several veins, instead of just one."

Damn! Rob thought. *I should have figured—nothing is ever simple around here!*

Kkintha ch'aait was the first to speak after Morrow's announcement. "How do you propose to remedy this, Jeffrey?" she asked in her high-pitched, chittering voice.

"Expediently, I hope," Morrow said. "The first thing on the

docket is a thorough survey of *all* the radonium veins running through the asteroid. If they are as they should be, then we'll concentrate on sealing off the contaminated deposits beneath the mountains, isolating them. Then we'll remove the R-2 by the vaporization technique I described to you during our initial meeting."

"Sounds like a big job," Janet said, looking at Andrea Lynch.

The crew boss nodded. "Yes. I'm going to need a larger crew, and I've already taken steps to hire more people."

"When will your survey be complete?" Kkintha asked.

"Five days . . . six at the outside," Andrea Lynch replied. The woman seemed greatly subdued this meeting—much of her smug condescension had evaporated. Maybe Jeff had spoken to her about her attitude, Rob thought, or—he took a closer look at her—maybe Lynch was too tired to cause trouble. Today it was the crew boss's turn to look as though she hadn't been sleeping. Her features were pinched, as though she'd lost weight these last couple of days.

Jeff looked slightly better—at least the shadows beneath his eyes had faded. But the normally impeccably groomed engineer was a mess. His clothes appeared slept-in, and his hair was tousled, as though it hadn't been combed since he first got up. The distort cuff he still wore (as did Lynch) was slightly askew. Knowing that the younger man had been working 'round the clock to try and save the Academy touched Rob.

Jeff's busting his ass, he thought. *I just hope his best will be good enough . . .*

"We'll be sending a team over to do extensive testing here in the school," Morrow was saying. "There are a couple of veins that run right below it—one big one in particular that we'll have to keep an eye on."

"I've been running checks myself every twelve hours," Janet said. "No indication of any change."

"Your equipment isn't as powerful as ours," Lynch said. "We've got a new radiation sensing device that's state-of-the-art."

"I believe we should plan for an evacuation," Kkintha said quietly. The little Chhhh-kk-tu's formerly luxuriant chest ruff looked thin and patchy as she absently groomed herself. "As soon as I leave here, I shall begin drawing up a comprehensive strategy for removing our students to a safe location—most likely, here on StarBridge Station, at least as a temporary refuge."

"Evacuate?" Rob stared at her. "Don't you think that's a bit premature, Kkintha?"

"I agree with Rob, Administrator," Jeff said earnestly. "Hold on until we finish our survey, and then you'll know for sure whether there's genuine cause for alarm."

"I would rather have something active to do, rather than simply wait and worry," the little alien said, puffing out her cheeks, whiskers quivering. "If no evacuation is necessary, that will be wonderful, and I will gladly discard my plan." She glanced around the table, her round blue eyes anxious in her dark face. "But in the event one is needed, I will be prepared to implement my plan as soon as you give me the word. Frankly, from what I have heard today, I am beginning to fear the worst."

No one spoke for nearly a minute following the Administrator's speech. Rob swallowed and glanced around at the other faces, seeing his own apprehension mirrored there. It was as though Kkintha ch'aait had put into words all their worst fears—and by doing so had made them concrete, real.

"Administrator ch'aait," Jeff finally said, "I can't argue that forewarned is forearmed. That's why I asked you to meet with me today. But you've got to remember that we have teams working around the clock to deal with this crisis. The initial outbreak is now contained and sealed off. Even as we speak, our engineers and technicians are vaporizing the radonium-2 beneath the floor of Cavern Two, and will be collecting it for disposal."

"How do you get rid of it?" Janet asked curiously.

"It's so volatile that we suction the vapor into self-propelled tanks. Each tank is equipped with a rudimentary guidance system that we'll program to soft-land on a worthless hunk of rock several million kilometers away from here on the edge of StarBridge Sector—well out of the space lanes."

"But suppose someone finds the tanks?"

"They're equipped with a warning beacon, so no one finding one before it reaches its destination will be tempted to mess with it. Then, after all the tanks are collected, we detonate the whole thing by remote control. You ought to be able to see the flash from here," Morrow replied.

Boom, thought Rob, glancing over at Andrea Lynch. When his eyes met hers, she looked down at her holo-tank.

"While you investigate the logistics of moving our students," Ssoriszs said to Kkintha, "I will contact the CLS Council about funding for such an endeavor. Our budget will not stretch to cover such an expense—we must have emergency funds allocated to us."

"Do you think the Council will okay that?" Rob asked doubtfully. StarBridge was an expensive proposition as it was. The CLS was no different from any human bureaucracy in its distaste for bailing out agencies that had run over budget.

"That remains to be seen," Ssoriszs said. "We have our detractors on the Council. One of the new representatives from Hurrreeah is extremely conservative, and reportedly, her clan owes honor-debts to the Harkk'ett clan."

Rob nearly groaned aloud. The Mizari was referring to the Simiu clan that had, nearly sixteen years ago, pledged themselves to an undying honor-debt against all the human worlds. The Harkk'etts were a relatively small minority on their planet, but they were also among the most vocal. They regarded StarBridge Academy as a human-tainted institution, and seldom missed a chance to criticize—or, on occasion, denounce—the way the school was run.

"Great," Janet said bitterly. "She ought to find plenty of support from the Heeyoon centrists and the Drnian anti-expansionists. We'd better start filling out grant applications—it looks like we may need them!"

Frustrated, Morrow waved for their attention. "Let's not forget, there's a very good chance that none of this will be necessary!"

"It never hurts to be prepared, Jeff," Lynch said unexpectedly. She glanced at her watch, then stood. "I've got to get back to assign the second shift." With a halfhearted wave, she hurried out.

Morrow nodded. "I'd better go, too. Try not to worry, everyone. I promise I'll keep in touch, and you'll know the instant we have news, either positive or negative."

Amid subdued farewells from the StarBridge contingent, Jeff departed.

Rob took a deep breath. "I keep hoping that if I just pinch myself hard enough, I'll wake up," he said slowly. "This doesn't look good, my friends."

"No, it doesn't," Janet said. "I can hardly wait for Andreiovitch to get here so we can get a second opinion. I don't like that Lynch woman, and I don't trust her, either."

"Just because she has all the charisma and personal charm of a Drnian spike-roach doesn't make her incompetent," Rob pointed out. "She's obviously intelligent, and Jeff sets great store by her opinions. Says she's 'the best' at her job."

"I'm not saying she's dumb or incompetent," Janet replied tartly. "I'm saying I don't trust her. I'm going to want to examine H.U.'s findings for myself."

"Under the terms of our contact with them, you have every right to do so," Kkintha said.

"What do you think might be wrong?" Rob asked curiously. Personally, he'd speculated that Lynch might be trying to cover up errors her team had made during H.U.'s last radonium check. "Insofar as Lynch is concerned?"

The engineer sighed with frustration. "I don't know! There's nothing concrete! I don't have a single shred of hard evidence . . . just my gut feeling that she's covering something up."

"I've thought the same thing," Rob admitted, and then continued, in response to Janet's surprised glance, "I've wondered whether she or her crew screwed up during the last monitoring session, and she's trying to cover it up—hide her mistake from Jeff, as well as from the Academy."

"That could be it," Janet said slowly. "People will go to great length to protect their jobs. Of course, it's entirely possible that she's just naturally defensive and surly, and we're jumping to conclusions because we don't like her."

"Serge believes that she may be plotting to steal the star-shrine," Ssoriszs spoke up, taking all of them aback. "After all, if it indeed came from my people's Lost Colony, it would be a priceless treasure."

"A good point," Kkintha said. "There is a thriving trade in uncoded, unregistered antiquities, is there not?"

"The humans call it 'the black market,' " the elderly Liaison told her.

"A good name for it," Kkintha said. "And I must say, I share your dislike for Ms. Lynch."

After a long moment of silence, Rob straightened. "We can't condemn someone just because she's rude," he said finally. "But we *can* keep a close eye on her. There's nothing to prevent us from doing that."

A silent glance of agreement flashed around the conference room, then they all rose to leave.

"Excuse me, Mr. Morrow . . ." Serge said, stepping away from the wall where he'd been leaning. He'd been here, loitering outside the conference room in Horizons Unlimited's suite of offices, ever since Janet Rodriguez had tipped him off about the meeting. He'd stayed out of sight until Andrea Lynch had gone into her cubicle because he didn't want to speak to Jeffrey Morrow with her present.

"Yes?" Morrow said, slowing but not halting.

"May I speak to you for a moment? My name is Serge LaRoche."

Morrow stopped. "The archaeologist, right?" He glanced at his watch. "I'm really busy . . ."

"Please, it is important," Serge said. "I was out at the site several days ago and spoke to Ms. Lynch there. She told me she'd tell you that I was there, but when I didn't hear from you, I wondered whether she might have forgotten. I have been waiting to hear from you . . ."

"Andrea didn't mention having spoken to you," Morrow said. "I'm sorry to have kept you waiting."

Serge wasn't surprised to discover that Lynch had said nothing—he hadn't expected her to keep her word. "That is quite all right," he told the older man. "Is there somewhere we could talk for just a moment? There is something I must ask you, Mr. Morrow."

"Please, make it Jeff," Morrow said. " 'Mr. Morrow' is my father."

Serge extended his hand, something he rarely did upon meeting someone for the first time, but he wanted to gauge Jeff's reaction to his artificial hand . . . find out what kind of man the Horizons Unlimited engineer was. "Serge, please," he said.

As Morrow's fingers gripped Serge's, his eyes widened slightly, but he showed no repugnance and his grasp was firm. The instructor's opinion of the engineer rose considerably. He was certain that Lynch would have had a very different—and unpleasant—reaction.

"Listen, it's lunchtime," Jeff said. "How about if you join me?"

"Thank you, I would appreciate that," Serge said.

After a short walk through the station, Morrow waved the younger man through the open door into a small Mexican restaurant. As soon as they had ordered—fajitas and tequila for Serge, chicken enchiladas and a beer for Jeff—Morrow sat back, stretching, then folded his arms on the table and regarded Serge expectantly. "What can I do for you?"

"I'm concerned about the star-shrine at the dig," Serge said. "I promised Professor Greyshine that I'd keep it safe for him, but Ms. Lynch told me I wouldn't be permitted on the worksite because of insurance regulations."

"She's right about that," Morrow said. "Our carrier would drop us if we allowed non-H.U. personnel onto a contaminated site."

"How much longer will Cavern Two be contaminated?" Serge

asked. "I know from Janet Rodriguez that your crew is removing the radonium-2 very quickly."

"They are," Jeff said. "But I'd say it will be at least another week—maybe two."

"What if I signed a waiver for your insurance company?"

The older man shook his head. "If you signed over your firstborn *child,* they wouldn't agree to anyone but one of our employees coming on-site."

Drinks arrived at that moment, and Serge stalled, thinking fast, while he busied himself with the lime, salt, and tequila. The liquor burned his throat and a warm glow spread through him. With it came an idea.

"Your insurance company will not permit anyone except a Horizons Unlimited employee access to a contaminated site, correct?" he asked.

Eyeing him curiously, Morrow nodded as he sipped his beer.

"Then hire me," Serge said. "As a temporary—I don't know—consultant on the archaeology site. I could come and go for as long as necessary to permit me to set up the neutralizer, then remove the shrine and place it in a stasis container." He took a deep breath, his eyes holding the engineer's. "Hire me, issue me a check if you need to, to make it official. It will become lost off my credit balance, I assure you. I shall never touch it, I swear. If we did it that way, your insurance carrier would be satisfied, and the star-shrine would be safe."

Morrow smiled slowly as he took a bite of his enchiladas. "That's quick thinking, Serge," he said. "And it might work. But tell me, what makes you think the star-shrine isn't safe right where it is? Contamination by radonium-2 may make it radioactive, but it won't harm the appearance or the structure of the object. And the radonium-2 can be neutralized, you already know that."

Careful now, Serge cautioned himself, spearing a piece of pepper. *Rob told you that Morrow considers Lynch one of his most trusted employees* . . . "The radonium-2 contamination could conceivably alter some of our instrument readings," he began, choosing his words as though he were treading on glass shards. Morrow was watching him intently, and he knew the man must be perceptive. So he didn't lie . . . quite. "Which could make it even more difficult to determine the origin of the star-shrine. The longer the shrine rests in a contaminated area, the worse the potential for that damage becomes."

"I see," Jeff said. "And I appreciate your diplomacy in not pointing out that the star-shrine is covered with semiprecious gems and potentially extremely valuable—that is, it's eminently worth stealing!" He smiled, his eyes crinkling with amusement. "Trust a StarBridge graduate to exercise the greatest of tact."

"I'm not a StarBridge graduate," Serge said, staring fixedly at his food as he pushed it around his plate. Any appetite he'd developed from relief at Morrow's quick understanding was quenched in a rush of shame at having to admit his failure. Morrow had been honest with him—he owed honesty in return.

"I studied to be an interrelator, but I never graduated," Serge said stiffly. "Rob Gable and the others let me stay on because I was useful—a good Orientation Guide, and I teach Intro to Archaeology, but . . ." He took a deep breath. "Please don't confuse me with someone who has—what is the English expression?—made the grade at the Academy."

Jeff was staring at him, and Serge saw him swallow. "I never graduated either," he said in a voice barely above a whisper. "I couldn't even learn Mizari."

Serge was surprised, then touched, by the older man's admission. Morrow's words forged a bond between them. "Yes, but weren't you nearly my age when you came to the Academy?" he asked.

"Depends," Jeff said with a rueful smile. "How old are you?" He glanced at the empty glass of tequila. "Or do I want to know? Corrupting minors isn't my usual custom."

The archaeologist grinned. "I am twenty-two," he said. "And any corruption took place long ago. But, Jeff"—Serge leaned forward earnestly—"do not reproach yourself for not being able to master an alien tongue, having started so late. It is a well-known fact that languages are best learned by the young, and the older one grows, the less chance that a language will become, as it must be for diplomatic work, second nature."

Morrow nodded. "I know that," he said. "Rob warned me before he ever let me come here that I was, in all likelihood, too old to succeed. But I had to try," he finished, his voice roughening. Quickly he polished off the last of his beer.

"I have a feeling you and I have a great deal in common, Serge," he said, flashing the younger man a lopsided grin. "How about another round?"

"Okay," the archaeologist said, "but before we do—what about my proposition? Will you hire me so I can retrieve the star-shrine and keep my promise to Greyshine?"

Jeff thought for a moment, then said, "How about if we do it this way: let me finish the radonium survey of the Academy's asteroid. That'll require my full attention, believe me. By the time that's completed, the radonium-2 level in Cavern Two ought to be negligible anyway. *Then* I'll put you on the payroll and you can get the star-shrine. But while you're waiting for it to be neutralized, you can help out my crew and earn that paycheck. What do you say? Do we have a deal?"

Serge still chafed at the delay, but he recognized that Morrow was bending over backward to accommodate him. What could he say? "Thank you, Jeff," he said, putting out his hand. "We have a deal."

"Good!" the engineer said, and beckoned to the hovering waiter. "Another round, please!"

"Your call is going through now, Esteemed One," Ssoriszs' Chhhh-kk-tu assistant's voice came over the intercom. Alone in his quarters, the old Mizari quickly straightened himself to his full height. Hundreds of years of experience had taught him that the ability to project a positive attitude and complete self-confidence were among the most formidable weapons in a diplomat's arsenal.

Expressing his thoughts through the use of such a warlike metaphor brought him up short. Ssoriszs' appendages twitched in the Mizari equivalent of a shudder. *I am beginning to sound like the humans,* he thought. *It comes from spending so much time with them, speaking their language, I suppose.*

Even as he strove for inner serenity, the air before him shimmered, then seemingly solidified, presenting him with a three-dimensional view of the CLS Council chamber, an enormous, domed expanse that would have dwarfed StarBridge's Observatory. Stars spattered the view through the vast dome, for the CLS Council was quartered on a space station orbiting Ssoriszs' homeworld, Shassiszss.

Seeing and recognizing him, the current Secretary-General, a Heeyoon named Moondancer, bowed deeply. "Esteemed Liaison, we are honored with your presence today. Please, may we know the reason for your request to address the Councillors?"

Speaking briefly but eloquently, Ssoriszs summarized the current situation at StarBridge, ending with a plea for emergency funding to cover the costs of Horizons Unlimited's services, plus the promise of additional funding should an evacuation and temporary relocation prove necessary.

Despite the confident air he'd summoned, Ssoriszs knew that his request could hardly have come at a worse time. The Vardi and the Apisians were having economic problems, and two Simiu clans were feuding. The Rigellians had gone on record last year with their disappointment that the Academy hadn't made enough environmental adaptations quickly enough to host a fair proportion of students from their world.

Worst of all, the Heeyoons were experiencing terrible economic difficulties, the worst in their history since joining the CLS hundreds of years ago. Their first colony world had just experienced a truly devastating winter, the worst in their recorded history. Thousands of colonists had perished, while many others had to be evacuated or relocated. The cost to the mother world was staggering. The Heeyoons had already requested this year to be relieved of their CLS dues until they could stabilize their own economy in the wake of such disaster.

And the Heeyoons were among the Academy's staunchest supporters.

Having stated his case, Ssoriszs took a moment to scan those present. The Arena's tiers were filled with every type of seating arrangement imaginable—couches, slings, perches, chairs, compartments . . . and more. A number of cubicles were surrounded by the glowing protective fields, where extreme environmental needs could be met for people such as the Rigellians.

Many of the tiers were dark, however. Ssoriszs felt disappointment rise in his throat like venom as he realized that almost half of the various seats and cubicles were empty today. There were only a few Apis and Heeyoon Councillors visible.

Glancing at the section reserved for the Simiu contingent, he was even more disturbed to see that Duquukk', the new member he had mentioned to Rob, was sitting next to the First Councillor.

If she gains Ankk'aarrr's ear, the Academy will be in terrible trouble, he thought bleakly. *Not only will we be refused emergency funding, but we are likely to find our present budget in shreds!*

The Secretary-General raised a paw. "Discussion from the floor?" Moondancer asked.

One of the Mizari, Zarshezz, signaled that he wished to speak. Ssoriszs braced himself; Zarshezz was his only surviving grandchild, but they had been estranged for years. The Liaison knew that his grandson would have little good to say about where the Academy was located and how it was administered. Zarshezz believed that the school should be brought into the mainstream of the CLS's sphere of influence, and from the beginning he'd argued that the school should be located near Shassiszss, instead of in space, close to no world.

"Most Esteemed Secretary-General and Councillors," the Mizari began, "I feel it is my duty to point out that the Academy at StarBridge is now more than six years old. It is true that the school has produced a number of impressive students, but if we honestly weigh its successes in comparison to its many failures— I speak of the high dropout rate, of course—one begins to wonder whether this school is worth its tremendous cost. And now we are told that there will be even greater costs—and that our gift, the asteroid itself, has been contaminated!"

Ssoriszs had meant to keep silent, but Zarshezz's words made his temper flare. "Six years is but a fleeting breath in the winds of Time!" he retorted. "And the contamination was not—" he broke off, then subsided, seeing Moondancer's warning glance.

"Perhaps now is the time for the CLS and the Council to take a more active role in overseeing the day-to-day administration of the Academy," Zarshezz said. "To do that would require the school to be relocated, but that seems to be the next step, given the current situation." Ssoriszs' grandson gracefully dipped his head to indicate that he was finished, then sank back down.

Moondancer glanced at her podium to see which Councillor should be recognized next. She signaled to the Simiu contingent.

"I share the fears of my associates here." Duquukk's crest rose slightly as she stood. "I feel we have been pouring funds into a dream that has little reality now, and will have none if it must be relocated. They say this move will be temporary. How do we know this? What assurance do we have?"

Ssoriszs signaled that he wished to respond. "Dr. Mikhail Andreiovitch is on his way to StarBridge to evaluate the situation," he countered. "He will surely be able to render a definitive opinion."

"Andreiovitch is a human!" the Simiu said scornfully. "And the humans are the ones who have tried to take over the Academy for their own glory!"

The senior Councillor for the Drnians signaled to be allowed to speak. "I believe the Academy merits every support we can give it. One of the first graduates of the Academy has just been appointed our new Ambassador to Shassiszss. Although still quite young, he has remarkable maturity and insight into other cultures. StarBridge also gave him an impressive skill in languages. We are convinced he is but the first of many outstanding young people who will come from the Academy at StarBridge, to make all of our cultures richer through increased understanding."

The Mizari First Councillor was next. "Let us set aside the issue of the value of the Academy for the moment," Most Esteemed Rezantz began. His scales gleamed reddish-orange and silver-white beneath the starlight. "I do not believe that the Academy's worth is in serious question here today. Most worlds agree that the Academy is important. However, should the Academy's asteroid become poisoned or destroyed by this radonium-2 contamination, my people could never afford to sacrifice another of our radonium-rich asteroids."

A Heeyoon delegate was next. "My people have a moon that would be suitable," he said. "There is a large university facility there, plus an observatory. We would be honored to have the Academy in orbit around Arrooouhl."

Now it was Duquukk's turn again for a biting retort: "And honored, no doubt, to have undue influence over the way the school is run, in addition to those much-needed CLS funds pouring into your economy!"

As the two delegates glared at each other, Ambassador Susan Shepherd was recognized. "Why not move it nearer to Earth?" she asked, her shoulder-length white hair sparkling in the light. "Terra is such a new member of the CLS . . . we only achieved our full membership last year. We are too new to have much influence on issues. We are also among the Academy's most ardent supporters, and we could—"

Duquukk' bolted to her feet, heedless of being recognized. "For 'new members,' you humans run too many things already!" Her muzzle curled, showing a hint of her strong white teeth. "You have already swayed otherwise clear-thinking people to give your species full membership. And it was you, if I recall correctly, who argued that students must be allowed to graduate from the Academy at their own rate, and not be limited in the time they can spend there."

"Individuals progress at their own rates," Shepherd countered. "Demanding that all students complete their program within four years is just not realistic!"

Moondancer hastily broke in to tell Duquukk' that she was out of order, and warned her not to speak without recognition again. "Other delegates are still to be heard from," she said. "No further outbursts will be permitted."

Zarshezz was recognized next. Ssoriszs knew before he opened his mouth what his grandson would say. "Perhaps the Academy should be located here, at Shassiszss. After all, this station has been the heart of the CLS for centuries."

Ssoriszs quickly signaled and was recognized to speak.

"I thoroughly disagree," he said, unable to keep his anger from showing. "The station here is officially neutral, yes. But in reality, the Mizari have too much influence because of their close proximity as hosts to the CLS Council. That influence must not extend to the Academy, which is why we chose its current location. Moving the school to Shassiszss would be contrary to the highest goals of the Academy. No one species must dominate, or StarBridge may become a political pawn!"

"Keeping the Academy so far away from the hub of interstellar and CLS commerce makes it much more expensive than originally planned for," Duquukk' said, having been officially recognized this time. "Not to mention the special purchase we authorized last year—"

"We needed a new shuttle," Ssoriszs broke in, and knew that Moondancer would warn *him* next. "We only had one, and it was too small for our needs. Our costs have been . . ."

The debate continued, growing ever more emotional and volatile. Finally a breath of reason, in the person of the Vardi First Councillor, moved that the Academy's request be separated into two parts, to be voted on separately. Part One would provide funding for Horizons Unlimited to keep working on the radonium-2 threat, provided Dr. Andreiovitch agreed with their assessment and methodology. Part Two would provide emergency funding for moving the Academy to temporary quarters on Shassiszss, should that prove necessary.

After the Vardi had finished, Moondancer signaled for quiet one final time. "Esteemed and honored colleagues, this debate has gone on, and I believe all views have been heard at least once. Discussion is becoming redundant. Our time today grows short. We must either table this discussion to continue tomorrow, or call for a vote. What do you wish to do?"

Quickly members flashed their decision to vote onto her console. "Very well," Moondancer said. "Please cast your votes at this time. Remember to vote on both Part One and Part Two of this question."

Ssoriszs held his breath as the votes were cast and compiled. Finally, Moondancer raised her head, obviously not pleased, but bound by the will of the majority. "Esteemed Liaison," she said, "the Councillors have decided. Funding is approved to allow Horizons Unlimited to continue with its work for the moment, until Dr. Andreiovitch can give a second opinion on the feasibility of their planned course of action. As for relocation, temporary or otherwise, the vote is no."

Ssoriszs bowed one final time, then terminated the connection. *I have lived too long,* he thought, feeling his strength drain away until he could scarcely summon the energy to coil himself in his sleeping compartment. He knew he should call Rob and Kkintha, but he was too heartsick. News as bad as this could wait until he felt stronger.

He stared at his meditation disk, and wondered if there was anything he could have done to have changed the Council's decision. *Perhaps a younger person could have been more vital, more convincing,* he thought dully. The memory of Zarshezz's words stabbed him, until he writhed in the solitude of his quarters.

Zarshezz was his third grandchild. Handsome, with pale gold diamonds patterning his dark green back, he had followed his grandfather's path into public service. Unlike Ssoriszs, Zarshezz liked politics and had always argued for more Mizari influence in the CLS, rather than less.

His grandson had always been openly scornful of Ssoriszs' yearning to discover the fate of the Lost Colony. "It is the future that is of importance now, not the past," he'd told his aged relative on many occasions. "Your vision is shadowed by your years, Grandfather."

The intercom chimed again, and in a voice barely above a whisper, Ssoriszs acknowledged it. "It is your grandson, Zarshezz," his assistant said. "Will you take the call? He sounds most anxious to speak with you, Esteemed One."

"Tell him—tell him I am not well," Ssoriszs said. He knew he was being a coward in not facing Zarshezz, but at the moment he felt he could endure no more. "Tell him I will call him in a few days."

"Yes, Esteemed One," she said, and then he was alone again, with the quiet. Slowly, Ssoriszs stretched his head out, resting his lower jaw on the padded riser of his sleep-cubicle, all the while wishing dully that he could fall asleep and never wake up. *Truly, by the Spirits of all the Stars, I have lived far too long . . .*

Serge paced nervously in the waiting area outside Docking Tube Five at StarBridge Station. Scowling, he glanced at his watch for the twelfth time in as many minutes. *There must be a cosmic rule that says shuttles and Hing Oun are never on time,* he thought ruefully.

The *Night Storm* was a few minutes overdue . . . Hing was considerably more. They'd come up together several hours ago, had a quick bite of lunch, then she'd gone "to pick up a few things, and be right back." Knowing her as he did, Serge had repressed a knowing smile as he watched her stride away.

Things were growing easier between them, and the stiffness was nearly gone. If nothing else, Serge's efforts at reconciliation had resulted in a renewed friendship. *Which is nothing to denigrate,* he thought with a sigh. But he knew that he wanted more. But how to make the first step? Hing had always taken the lead in advancing their physical relationship. Serge had never fancied himself the caveman type.

Glancing at his watch again, he frowned. *That ship will be here any—*

"Your attention, please," he heard the announcement in Mizari. "StarBridge Station has the Mizari cruiser *Night Storm* on our sensors. The ship will be docking in five minutes. Passengers will be disembarking immediately following docking."

Serge straightened his StarBridge jacket, then tugged at his best jumpsuit, feeling suddenly nervous. Most Esteemed Rizzshor was one of the greatest archaeologists who had ever lived. His work had set the foundations for most of what the Mizari now knew about their own prehistory. He was also the foremost expert on the Lost Colony.

Calm down! he scolded himself as he squared his shoulders. *You've met hundreds of celebrities before, remember?*

He had, too—monarchs, emperors, planetary rulers, presidents, holo-vid stars, athletes—all had come to hear him play and expressed admiration for his talents.

Serge's mouth quirked slightly as he recalled one particular time, meeting the Queen of England, Victoria III. Ten years old, feeling giddy and full of himself after a superb rendition of Mozart's Piano Concerto No. 1, he'd forgotten that he was not to speak unless spoken to, and had asked "Mrs. Windsor" how she had liked his playing. His parents had been mortified by this breach of etiquette; he'd been grounded for a week and required to view endless holos on the subject.

"Am I too late?" a breathless voice called. He turned to see Hing racing down the hallway. She'd dressed up for the occasion in her best uniform jumpsuit, and her hair tossed behind her as she ran, billowing like a black wave. "Did I miss them?"

"No, they will be docking in a few minutes," Serge said, eyeing her armful of packages. "Here, we had best stow these in a locker," he advised, keying one open with his thumbprint. "I would prefer to meet our guests down at the end of the tube, if that is okay with you."

"Sure," she said agreeably, obediently filling the locker, then snapping it shut. "Where is Ssoriszs?" The Mizari had accompanied them up in the Academy's smaller shuttle, the *Fys,* which Serge had piloted.

"The Esteemed Liaison is waiting in the lounge," he replied. "He was too keyed up to wait in public, he said."

"Don't worry," Hing told him, slipping her arm through his companionably, "I'll be your moral support, and, if necessary, prop you up physically!"

Serge gave her a wan smile. "I *am* rather nervous," he admitted. "Does it show that badly?"

She squeezed his arm against her. "Only to someone who knows you well," she said, flashing him one of her irrepressible grins.

He laughed, feeling his anxiety slip away. Hing was with him and suddenly he felt wonderful. "By the way, I want to thank you for helping me make up with Heather," he said. "I acted like a . . ." He cast about for a suitable idiom.

"Creep? Heel? Sumbitch?" Hing suggested helpfully.

"One or all of them," he said. "I'm the adult, but I let her prying make me lose my temper."

"Welcome to the human race," she said, and the expression in her dark eyes made his breath catch in his throat.

Slightly flustered, he added, "It is too bad that Heather had so much studying to do that she couldn't accompany us today." He mentally crossed his fingers as he spoke, because, truth be told, he was delighted to have these moments alone with Hing.

She nodded. "Either Heather's really decided to apply herself after the pep talks I've given her . . ." she paused, then added cynically, "or she's up to something. Come to think of it, she's been spending an awful lot of time in front of her terminal lately."

By this time they were through the backup airlock, which stood with both doors open, because the primary airlock was at the docking area at the end of the long tubelike structure that was Dock Five.

The entire docking tube was made of transparent plas-steel, affording a magnificent view to those accustomed to the vastness of space. (Newcomers usually docked at Docks Six or Seven, which had opaque walls, to coddle their delicate stomachs.)

Above Serge's head, a ship winked out of realspace existence in a splash of color.

Serge glanced around them for the *Night Storm,* thinking that he ought to be able to see it heading in past Dock Six, where the *Fys* was berthed. He glanced down, staring past his feet, his attention momentarily diverted by the sight of a Drnian freighter popping out of metaspace. "They ought to be in sight any moment," he said. "Dr. Andreiovitch will be—"

He broke off as Hing gasped, eyes widening in horror. She was staring over his shoulder, then pointing. "Ohmigod, Serge! That ship's coming in too fast! It's going to crash into the tube!"

CHAPTER 10

◆

Trapped

Hing stood frozen as she watched the *Night Storm* hurtle toward them, feeling a scream caught in her throat and trying to claw its way out. *This can't be happening!* she thought. Her worst fear, coming true!

A hand seized her wrist in an inhumanly strong grip, nearly yanking her off her feet. *"Run!"* Serge shouted, dragging her toward the backup airlock. Hing tripped, would have fallen if not for his grasp, then she was pounding after him. Inside the airlock they had a small chance. Outside it, none at all.

Twenty meters . . . ten . . . five . . . She caught a glimpse of the ship out of the corner of her eye—it was almost upon them!

Two meters . . . one—

As they reached the airlock, Serge shoved her in ahead of him, then jabbed frantically at the controls. Hing staggered, fell in a heap. The doors began sliding shut. Watching them glide in seeming slow-motion, she sobbed with terror, willing them to close faster—*faster!*

Just as the doors sealed shut with a faint sigh, they heard the screech of bending plas-steel, then a gigantic ripping *crash*. Hing screamed as the floor bucked beneath them like an enraged bronco, side to side, then up and down. Then the crashing, ripping sounds were drowned out by a massive *whoosh* as all the air in the dock-side of the tube exploded into space, trying and utterly failing to fill that endless void.

Then, abruptly, all sound was gone. Hing knew there was no longer any air outside the dock-side airlock door to carry sound waves. Their refuge was still shuddering, but the little cubicle was intact—

—almost.

Hing heard a rapid popping sound as the automatic sealer released from its case in the wall above her head, even as she heard the shrill hiss of escaping air. Down in the corner beside the door, the plas-steel must have been struck by debris, for it was now buckled inward. There was a thin rip at the juncture of floor and wall.

Suddenly, painfully, Hing's ears popped, even as the automatically released sealant splatted against the leak. The hissing whine lessened, lessened . . .

But it didn't stop. The sealer hadn't been enough to cover the entire crack. "Serge!" Hing gasped, pointing, but he was already moving, ripping off his StarBridge jacket, then dropping to his knees to jam the wadded fabric against the tiny lethal fissure.

"Get the emergency kit!" he ordered. "We are still losing pressure! *Vite, vite!*" His voice sounded funny, higher-pitched, whether from fear or the sudden drop in pressure, she didn't know.

Hing scrambled to her feet and lunged for the emergency kit that every airlock held by law. Her movement caused the cubicle to sway, and she wondered for a horrifying instant whether the lock had broken clean away from the station, and they were now drifting in space. But even as she thought that, logic told her that they were still attached; the artificial gravity was still functioning.

Grabbing the kit, she opened it, tossing aside the first-aid supplies, scrabbling for the tube of sealant. Yes, it was here— *thank God, thank God!*—and she thrust it at Serge. "Here!"

"*Bien,*" he said. "Now I am going to stand up for a moment, and I want you to put your foot down to hold this jacket in place, *comprenez?*"

"My foot?" she said, staring down at the soft boots that went with her uniform. "I can hold it better with my hands . . ."

"No," he said firmly. "It is very cold. Use your foot."

Carefully, he eased his fingers up, one at a time, as she placed her foot down to hold the jacket in place. They were still gradually losing pressure; Hing's ears popped again.

Serge frantically unsealed the front of his StarBridge jumpsuit. "The sealant patches may not hold. I will double-seal it with sealant spread over this." Yanking the uniform down over his waist, he paused to pull off his boots. A moment more, and Serge stood clad only in his low-cut briefs, briskly rolling his jumpsuit up.

Hing eyed him worriedly. With the lost air had gone much of the warmth, and the temperature inside the airlock was now as chilly as a brisk autumn day back on Earth. "You'll freeze!" she protested. "Can't you use the jacket?"

"The material of the jacket is too stiff and porous. This fabric is better."

Cold was creeping up Hing's foot from where it rested on the jacket. She watched Serge spread the sealant along one side of the rolled-up jumpsuit, unable to halt the shivering that wracked her. He caught her motion out of the corner of his eye, and said reassuringly, "Almost finished . . ."

Within a second he was through, dropping down to cautiously tug the jacket away, millimeter by millimeter, as he did so pressing the sealant-coated fabric of the jumpsuit into the narrow fissure.

The faint hissing grew still fainter, then stopped altogether.

"You did it!" Hing whispered, huddled beside him. Serge was still pressing the jumpsuit against the crack, holding it grimly in place. "Can't you let go now?"

"No, I think I had better hold it," he said. "If the crack were to widen even a little as the airlock moves, the jumpsuit might be sucked out, which would widen the leak still more—and that would mean the end of us."

Picturing that, Hing swallowed, then nodded. "Let's put your jacket under you," she suggested. "The floor is freezing!"

"It is," he agreed. "My legs are tingling."

"I don't know whether that's from the pressure drop or the cold," she said. "So are mine." She rubbed her palms together. "And my hands, too."

He smiled thinly. "Mine are fine."

Remembering the cold that had seeped up into her feet, Hing knew that if she'd tried to hold the jacket against the crack with her bare hands, they'd probably have been frostbitten by now. Would the cold hurt Serge's hands, she wondered, as she took his jacket and unfolded it, wincing at the icy feel. Spreading it beneath his legs as he knelt there, she used the sleeves to wrap the garment around them, anchoring it as well as she could. He was shivering now; she could feel the trembling of his entire body as she leaned against him to pull his socks and boots back on.

"Activate the emergency alarm, then try the intercom," he said, through teeth that he had to fight to keep from chattering. "They may not know we are here."

Nodding, Hing went over to the control panel, feeling the cubicle shift again beneath her weight. She had a sudden vision of it tilting, ripping free, then drifting off into space. No one would ever know what had happened to them . . . no one would come looking. They'd assume that she and Serge had been sucked into space when the *Night Storm* ripped the tube open.

Her fingers were growing numb at the tips as she pushed the button for the emergency alarm. The alarm was designed to register in the station's security offices—she had no way of knowing whether it was working or not. Or, for that matter, whether the security offices were still intact.

Swallowing the dryness in her mouth, repressing the way her teeth wanted to chatter, she keyed the intercom. "This is Hing Oun in the backup airlock leading to Dock Five," she said, her voice cracking with mingled fear and hope. "Is anyone reading me? Serge LaRoche and I are trapped in here, and we don't have much air!"

No response.

Hing tried the channel several times, then turned back to Serge with a shrug. "Nobody there," she said. "Or it's broken and there's no way to tell."

"Wait and try again in a minute," he advised. "The security area is undoubtedly in chaos, red lights and alarms going off everywhere, because of the crash. No doubt official emergency transmissions have been granted automatic priority over all communications channels—including the intercom system."

"Well, I hope they notice that alarm eventually," Hing said. "We're safe for the moment, but our air won't last long."

Serge nodded agreement; he was shivering all over as he held the jumpsuit in place. Hing stole covert glances at him as she paced nervously in a tiny circle, rubbing her arms for warmth. *I forgot how well built he is,* she thought, eyeing his broad shoulders, long legs, and flat stomach. He swam every day, and his muscles, though well defined, were long and lean, like a dancer's. *He's so damn beautiful,* she thought suddenly, feeling her throat tighten.

Turning away abruptly, Hing tried the intercom again. Nothing. Glancing at her watch, she was thunderstruck to see that less than ten minutes had passed since she'd come hurrying up to him, her arms filled with packages. *My watch must be broken!*

But no, it was running fine. They'd been trapped in this airlock for perhaps five minutes, tops. "I'll try again in a couple of minutes," she promised, abandoning the intercom. "Let's try and get you warm." Dropping down beside Serge, Hing began rubbing his shoulders and arms hard, trying to restore the circulation. His skin felt chill and clammy. "Let me hold the jumpsuit," she urged. "I can take over for a while!"

He shook his head doggedly. "I am fine."

"Sure you are," she said, rubbing his back, digging her palms in hard. "You're turning into an icicle."

"Hardly that," he said softly, giving her a sidelong glance.

Hearing the warmth in the tone of his voice, Hing felt herself coloring. She ducked her head, her hair hanging around her face, hiding her from his eyes. "Serge . . ." she began, suddenly breathless, whether from the thin air or the exertion, she didn't know. "You—you saved my life. If it hadn't been for you, I'd have been rooted to the spot when the ship hit. I froze."

He didn't answer until she had pushed back her hair and looked at him. The artificial glare lightened his eyes, turning them silver-blue. "I deserve no accolades for courage," he said quietly. "I acted strictly on instinct. I never thought about what I was doing."

"And I suppose it was your instinct for self-preservation that made you shove me in here first?" Hing asked tartly. She glared at him, suddenly angry—though she wasn't sure exactly why. "Dammit, Serge, I'm trying to thank you, and you're just shrugging it off! You were brave—a real hero, and I—I—" she stammered to a halt, realizing suddenly that their faces were only a handbreadth apart. She sucked in a breath of cold air, feeling her heart race.

He was smiling faintly. "In Rob's old movies, the heroine does not rely solely on *words* to thank the hero for saving her life," he told her softly. "If you are truly grateful, you might consider reviving that trad—"

Hing leaned forward and stopped him in midword.

It had been so long since they'd kissed! The feel of his mouth was both familiar and strange, comforting and exciting—like taking a bow before a cheering audience, or sipping fine champagne on opening night. It was like coming home after a long and unhappy exile.

Hampered by their awkward positions—*I'm glad no one can see us, necking in a leaky airlock, they'd die laughing*—Hing pulled back after the first moment, running her fingers through his hair, stroking it back as she murmured endearments. "I've got to figure out another way to go about this," she muttered, kissing his left earlobe, her lips brushing the sapphire, her gift. "If I don't, I'm going to end up with a serious crick in my neck. Maybe I could slide underneath you," she said, half-serious.

"If you do, we will both get warm," he warned, smiling, then he turned his head to nuzzle her fingers as they caressed his jaw. His tongue felt hot in the chill air as he ran it along the underside of her wrist, where the pulse was. "Very warm, that I promise you."

In the end she compromised by ducking beneath his arm and leaning back against the wall. Serge could not hold her, for obvious reasons, but she held him tightly enough for both of them. The feel of his skin, and the muscles beneath it made Hing's head spin. Or was it the thin air? She couldn't tell, and at the moment she didn't care.

Finally, it was Serge who pulled away, gasping. "Hing—Hing, *stop!*"

She tilted her head, giving him a lascivious smile. "Too much for you, eh?" she murmured. "Just wait, you haven't seen—"

"*Listen!*" he commanded.

She obeyed, then immediately began wriggling out from under him. *The intercom!*

"Attention, Dock Five airlock," a female voice was repeating. "Is anyone there? Answer me, please! Dammit"—the voice grew fainter, as though the speaker had turned her head—"I've got an alarm from that lock here on my board, but there's no one there."

Hing slammed her hand against the switch. "Oh, yes there is!" she cried. "We're here! We're alive! Get us out of here, please!"

"Thank God!" the woman exclaimed. "Who are you? Please identify yourself."

"I'm Hing Oun, and I'm trapped here with Serge LaRoche. We're both from the Academy," Hing said in a rush. "Can you get us out of here?"

"We're working on it. I'll alert the emergency crew in your sector," she promised. "It shouldn't be too long. Just hang on."

"We will," Hing vowed, "but, listen, if you can't get us out right at this moment, can you at least repressurize this lock? We lost partial pressure following the crash. We're freezing and our air isn't too good!"

"We'll work on it," the security tech said. "But systems in that area are pretty scrambled."

Hing grimaced and swore under her breath. "I understand," she said aloud. "Can you tell me whether the pressure is normal on the station side of the lock? Because if it is, we can just open the station-side door." *If it's not jammed,* she thought, remembering the way they'd been bounced around.

"Negative on that!" the woman ordered sharply. "It may be okay, but we can't be sure. There are minor leaks all over. We have crews out in pressure suits checking, so we'll soon know. There is debris blocking the main entrance to Dock Five, but security is working on clearing it. Are you still losing pressure?"

"No, at least we don't think so. If we are, it's so slight we can't notice it."

"How bad is your air?"

"We're breathing okay, but it's getting pretty stuffy," Hing allowed.

"Do you have a first-aid kit?"

Hing glanced down at the medical supplies scattered all over the floor. "Yes."

"Good. You should have a temporary oxy-mask in the first-aid kit. Do you see it?"

Hing looked, then pounced. "Yes!"

"Trigger it. It has a fifteen-minute supply of pure oxygen. Hopefully, by the time it's exhausted, we'll be able to give you the all-clear to open the door."

Gingerly, Hing triggered the oxygen mask, heard the faint sigh of the gas as it was slowly released. "It's working!" she announced, immensely relieved. "Now if it just w-wasn't so c-cold," she said, her teeth beginning to chatter despite all her efforts at control.

"Check the aid kit again," the woman said. "There should be a thermal sheet in it."

"Eureka!" Hing exclaimed a moment later as she unwrapped the small packet that unfolded into a gauzy sheet large enough to cover an adult. Quickly she draped it over Serge, then pressed the corner to activate the heat. "Whoever you are," she told her unknown savior on the other side of the intercom, "thanks a million. That'll help a lot."

"Think nothing of it," the woman said. "By the way, my name is Ruth, and Esteemed Ssoriszs from your school is here with me. He was the one who insisted that we look for you, because he was sure you'd managed to make it to safety before the crash."

"Tell him thanks," Hing said, using the Mizari word that meant the highest degree of gratitude. "Uh, speaking of the crash, how bad was it?" she asked, feeling a pang of guilt. She'd been so busy worrying about herself and Serge that she hadn't spared a thought for Ssoriszs, the station, or the *Night Storm*.

"Not good," the woman said grimly. "But I guess it could have been worse. Only one confirmed death here on the station, plus fourteen injured—but everyone aboard the Mizari ship is now confirmed dead."

"Dr. Andreiovitch and Esteemed Rizzshor . . ." Serge murmured sadly, his expression bleak. "What a terrible loss!"

"Thanks for giving me the news, Ruth," Hing said, feeling tears well up. "You're right, it could have been worse. Serge and I could have been killed, too."

"You're very lucky to be alive," the tech agreed. "Count your blessings."

Hing flashed Serge a watery smile. "Oh, I am," she said softly. "I am . . ."

"Listen, Hing, I've got some more alarms to attend to. I'll call you the moment the security team signals that you can open your door," Ruth said. "Call me if you need me, okay?"

After the technician switched off, Hing went back over to Serge, knelt, then lifted the thermal sheeting and crawled under it. Sliding her arms around him, she pressed herself against his back, exulting in the warmth that began creeping over her. Recalling survival training that advised skin-to-skin contact to combat hypothermia, she unsealed the front of her uniform, telling herself that it was standard procedure under the circumstances . . . but as she settled against him again, there was no doubt that his skin felt very good against her own.

"Are you all right?" she asked quietly after a few minutes. "You must be getting awfully stiff." A moment later she realized her double entendre, and hastily amended, "I mean, are you sure you don't want me to take over holding on to that seal? I could wrap a fold of the sheet around me to protect my hands."

"I am fine," he replied slowly, his accent suddenly very noticeable as he searched for words. "More than fine. Hing . . . *chérie* . . . it is a terrible thing to say, under the circumstances, but I truthfully cannot remember having been this happy for a very long time. You know how long."

"Serge . . ." She bit her lip, searching for words. "We can't afford to rush this. It may be just a fluke because of shared danger and almost dying. You know—love in the trenches." She took a deep breath. "On one hand it feels so good to be near you again . . . but . . . I can't forget the way we hurt each other. I'm scared."

"I bear much of the responsibility for that hurt," he said. Hing wondered what his expression was, what his eyes held. But she didn't have the strength to raise her head and look. All her energy seemed to have vanished now that rescue was on the way. She could only lean her forehead against Serge's shoulder and wait. "And . . . *chérie* . . . I have regretted the things I said every day— sometimes many times a day. I am sorry, a million times over."

"I pushed you too hard, Serge." It was the truth, she knew that now. "That's one of my biggest faults; I start thinking I can direct the people in my life the way I do my actors on the stage, then I get mad if they won't let me push them around."

"I will not let you push me around," Serge promised. "But much of what you said to me that night was true, I know that now. I held you away from me, kept you out of my heart, the way I did everyone else, because I am angry inside. With Rob's help, I am learning to change that."

"I know. I can tell."

"Hing . . . you do not want to rush, either physically or emotionally, *je comprends,* and that is okay. I am learning also to be patient. But—is it possible—would you be willing to try again? Perhaps . . . someday . . . wear that ring I gave you again?" He spoke hoarsely, with many pauses, as though his throat were tight.

The silence between them lasted for seven heartbeats—Hing knew, because she could feel his heart thudding against her palm. Then, tenderly, she kissed the top of his shoulder. "No promises, no rush," she said quietly, earnestly. "But yes . . . I want to try again."

"*Bien,*" he said quietly, then they lapsed again into silence, and in silence waited.

As the minutes went by, Hing was vaguely surprised to find herself growing drowsy, and for a moment she worried that it might be hypoxia setting in, but if it was, there was nothing she could do about it. Her eyelids drooped, then closed completely, and her breathing grew regular as she drifted . . . drifted . . .

An unmistakable knock thudded against the airlock door! Two more followed.

Hing sat bolt upright, then leaped to her feet. "Oh, God, they're here! They've found us!" she cried. It was only now, on the verge of rescue, that she realized how very frightened she'd been. Quickly she rapped back on the door, knowing that the rescue team was probably wearing pressure suits and wouldn't be able to hear her voice even if she yelled. But they'd be able to feel the vibrations.

"Hing!" Serge had to shout to get her attention.

She turned back to him. "What?"

"Perhaps you should fasten your uniform," he said, eyeing her with a smile. "Before you unseal the door. Not that you don't look lovely, but . . ."

"Smartass," Hing said, hastily resealing her garment. Then, seeing that he hadn't moved, she reached out her hand to him. "Come on, as soon as they signal it's safe, we can get out of here."

Serge's grin vanished; he looked away. "I am afraid that I can't move my fingers to let go," he said tonelessly. "I have not been able to move them for some time now."

"Oh, no!" She stared in distress at his fingers as they gripped the jumpsuit smeared with the sealant. "Are they just stuck, like with glue?" she asked, knowing they weren't.

He shook his head. "No. The artificial neural relays must be frozen. The wrists and fingers will not move, and I dare not pull the jumpsuit away—that might widen the crack in the wall. Tell them they will have to cut me free."

Hing hammered on the door in sudden frustration, angry and worried. *What if Serge's hands are ruined? It took him a year to learn to use the new ones!* "Hey, is it safe?" she yelled. "My friend is hurt! Can I open the door?"

She pressed her ear to the other side, and heard three knocks, then suddenly Ruth's voice erupted over the intercom. "They're giving me the all-clear, Hing! You can open the door!"

Trembling, Hing pressed the control to equalize pressure, then open the door. Slowly the portal slid aside, revealing three people in pressure suits. Hing stumbled out, feeling hot tears against her cold face, wondering why she was crying *now,* but too relieved to be embarrassed. One of the rescuers slung a blanket around her shoulders, then half supported her as she haltingly explained Serge's problem.

Minutes later they half carried Serge out. He was swaying, plainly too weak to stand by himself, and both hands were raised stiffly before him, fingers crooked, still clenched on the rags of his cut-away jumpsuit. As he saw Hing, he gave her what was meant to be a reassuring grin, but looked more like a grimace of pain. His rescuers quickly made him lie down on an anti-grav stretcher, then covered him with a blanket.

Hing insisted that she could walk, so she clutched her blanket around herself and stumbled in the stretcher's wake. The student stared, horrified, as they passed a huge plas-steel viewport that looked out onto Docks Five and Six. StarBridge Station appeared to have been bombarded—rips and holes marred its shining exterior, and naked girders and tangles of debris clustered where the two docking tubes had extended.

"God, this is terrible!" she muttered.

"It sure is," the man who kept one hand beneath her elbow said. He still wore his pressure suit, but it was equipped with special pickups and speakers so he could hear and converse with those not wearing a suit. "Damage will run to the millions, I'm betting. We're lucky more people didn't die."

"But what could have caused it?" Hing asked dazedly. "How did it happen?"

"They're saying the guidance beam cut in too soon, and brought the Mizari ship in too fast," he said.

"But—but those beams are automatic!" Hing protested. "They're controlled by the computer!"

"Yeah, that's what makes it so weird," the rescuer said. "The computers are supposed to be fail-safe."

"How could it happen?" Hing wondered again, speaking more to herself than to him. "How?"

"They don't know, Ms. Oun," the man said wearily. "But I can tell you one thing, you can bet they're not going to quit until they find out."

Look at you, you're turning into a real chicken, Heather fumed to herself, glaring at the computer screen. *That's what you get for being around all these namby-pure StarBridge students. You start thinking like them! It's like a damned contagious disease!*

Ever since she'd begun working on Heathertoo today, she hadn't been able to shake the growing feeling that she was doing something really *wrong.*

Scowling, she manipulated one of her computerpens, tapped an accompanying command on the keyboard, and watched Heathertoo begin an imaginary discussion. The young programmer stared at the make-believe office, the furniture, the perfect setting. All fine. She checked Heathertoo's clothing, her hairstyle—that was okay, too.

So why couldn't Heathertoo function on her own yet? The body stance, the facial features, the slow uptake . . . they still weren't right. Heather gnawed her lip in frustration. In a moment of brutal honesty, she had to admit that her creation was about as lifelike as a cheap Heeyoon animation.

So what? she argued. *You can just go inside, become her, make her talk, walk right, make her say the right things, act the right way* . . . She couldn't even convince herself.

Sure, she could just go into the machine, manipulate the program with her mind, nudge the organically based artificial intelligence gently a little here, a little there, make it do what she wanted it to do. Doing it again would be so *easy*—the way it had been when she'd "fixed" Khuharkk's toilet . . .

So easy. Heather swallowed. Easy, all right. Easy to get caught. That day that Hing had come in and found her while she was inside Heathertoo—that could have been it, right there, if she hadn't managed to convince her roommate that she'd fallen asleep while studying. Then, of course, they'd begun listening to Serge's music and that had occupied all of their attention.

So it hadn't been until much later that it finally dawned on the girl exactly how close she'd come to disaster. Luckily, she'd been "out" long enough that the holo-tank had automatically dimmed to save power, so Hing hadn't seen Heathertoo's image. But she could have, if the older girl had come in only a few minutes earlier.

Uneasily, she remembered Rob's veiled threats after the toilet incident. What he would do to her if he even suspected Heather of being able to manipulate the computer from *inside* didn't bear thinking about.

Would Hing stick up for her? Heather's mouth tightened. Probably not. She liked Hing, true, but she had no illusions. Hing's job was to be a "good influence," to be a friend to the lonely little telepath—and, along with it, convince Heather to toe the line and become just another StarBridge student, upright and lily-white and oh-so-good and moral.

Face it, if Hing had any idea what Heather was up to inside the AI, she'd burn a path to Rob's door and there'd be one less telepath complicating things at StarBridge.

So, that means the game can go on . . . she decided, manipulating Heathertoo, adding fine details. *But from now on, the main rule will be—don't get caught.*

And her best chance at accomplishing that was to stay out of the damned AI. It was just safer that way. Besides, she was a good programmer. With a little diligence, she could do this. It was slower, sure . . . but it would work. She tapped in a new code, overlaid a new intelligence/initiative matrix with her pen.

Heathertoo walked smoothly around the office, tapped a code on the keypad on her desk, moved the hair back away from her face. *Better,* Heather thought, *but not perfect.* She felt her frustration surge. Dammit, why did this have to be so hard?

"Helen," Heather said to the image, "how old are you?"

"Twenty-six," the woman said flatly. "How old are you?"

Heather frowned. She couldn't remember too many adults firing back such a blunt question. "Why'd you ask me that?"

"My interpersonal relationship matrix suggested it as part of a conversational give-and-take," the woman said calmly. The inflection in her voice was still wrong. It was more modulated than before, but still preternaturally calm, like someone who'd been through too much therapy.

Quit all this crap! she ordered herself. *You could do this in ten minutes if you just went in there. This is taking forever!*

Heather closed her eyes, tried to ignore the impatient side of herself that was always getting her into trouble. She remembered Rob's warning that messing with even a simple toilet meant you were messing with the entire environmental system.

Messing with the AI is too risky, and you know it, she told her impatient, pushy self. It was her survivor-self speaking, that canny side of her that always allowed her to come out on her two feet, if not on top. *There's no way to know everything I might be affecting when I'm zipping around in there. Remember, nobody's ever done it before. It's not like there's a tutorial to help me do it correctly!*

Not to mention that it was scary being inside the machine. Seductive. Like you could just stay in there and do stuff forever. Computers were cooperative like that. Totally nonjudgmental.

Grimly, she set back to work on Heathertoo. If she could make her appear *real* enough, Heathertoo could be independent, able to run all of Heather's financial dealings, even while her creator was off doing other things—like going to class, or having a sundae at the Spiral Arm with Hing, or even Serge and Hing. If she could perfect Heathertoo, she, Heather, wouldn't have to be tied down in front of this holo-tank, endlessly supervising her image in all the business transactions adults found so engrossing. Heather shook her head with a sigh. Talk about terminal boredom—and then, realizing her pun, she giggled.

I'll just have to keep at it until the program works perfectly, she thought, then sighed again as she fine-tuned Heathertoo's logic capabilities. *That's a big order,* she mused, dismayed at the enormity of the task she'd set herself, feeling her determination and confidence waver. *You're just tired,* she assured herself. *You've been at this too long.*

And she was grumpy, too. She'd really wanted to go with Hing and Serge up to StarBridge Station to see the *Night Storm* come in, and maybe get introduced to those hotshots Serge was so excited about meeting. She'd been tempted to take Serge and Hing up on their invitation, but she'd finally declined, knowing this would be one of her best opportunities to work on Heathertoo in undisturbed privacy—and safety. She wondered whether Hing had believed her when she'd said she was going to study.

Got to get this done while Hing's gone, the girl reminded herself. *Who knows when I'll get another chance?*

She keyed in another succession of commands, but that only made the expression on Heathertoo's face positively *dopey.* "Dammit!" she snarled, thumping her fist beside the keyboard.

Suddenly the computer blinked off, then on, as if the violence of her reaction had loosened something. The girl gasped, blinked herself, and stared. Her computer, like every other one on StarBridge, was tied into the main AI. It just didn't *blink* off! But it had. For just a half second. Heather felt uneasy, thinking about backward toilets and environmental systems—things she was fond of like gravity and air—all linked into the same computer. And was it her imagination, or did Heathertoo now look kind of dazed?

Got to be something wrong with this terminal, she told herself, trying to believe it. *A hardware problem.*

Then Heathertoo spoke. "The guidance beam setting is all wrong!" the image said clearly, with more emotion than Heather had ever been able to successfully program into her. "Guidance beam error—error, error—too soon—too fast! Evacuate Docks Five and Six! Emergency override on that guidance beam!" The image was flushed, the eyes wide with terror. For a moment her image crawled, as though another's features were struggling to surface, then Heathertoo's countenance steadied, was normal again.

What the hell . . . ? Heather stared at the image, but her creation's expression was calm, almost vapid—as usual. "Heathertoo, what's the matter? What's happening?"

The woman's image blinked calmly. "Nothing's the matter. Nothing's happening. What's happening with you?"

Heather nearly went into a rage at the stupid machine. *Docks Five and Six . . .* she thought, *we only have two docks down here at the Academy.* So that message had to be referring to the station. Could there have been some kind of bleedover or swapout that had cross-routed messages from the station?

Exiting the Heathertoo program, Heather set to work and soon tapped into the Academy's Traffic Control console. The security at the school was pretty good, but she was only eavesdropping, which wasn't hard to do.

The moment she made the connection, Heather could see and hear the school's traffic controller, a woman with a long, thin face and curly brown hair, plus a young black man who, from what she picked up, had been hastily drafted from Janet Rodriguez's staff to assist her. She watched and listened as the two of them worked frantically, contacting ships in metaspace, rerouting them if possible, instructing them to assume a long orbit if they were too close to change course, and moving all those now waiting to dock over to the space on the other side of the station, where they were instructed to wait.

"How long?" one of the frustrated captains demanded. Heather could faintly hear his voice as it came over the controller's screen, but he was too far away for her to pick up his transmission directly. "We can't just hang by our toes until further notice! What the hell is wrong over at the station?"

"We don't *know* what's wrong," the Head Controller said calmly and firmly. A patch on her uniform identified her as T. Phillips. "And until we do know, *no one* is to dock at the station. There's something wrong with the docking guidance beams. We can't risk allowing you—or anyone—to dock."

There was a garbled communication from another vessel; this one must have been even farther away, because Heather couldn't make it out. She had no way to enhance external communications.

"Yes, we've confirmed that the guidance beam brought a ship in too fast," Phillips said. "That's what all this is about, why the Academy is handling docking and traffic control communications while the station deals with the emergency. StarBridge Station has lost pressure in several areas, and sustained damage, we don't know how much yet."

Damage? thought Heather. *Lost pressure? Shit, this sounds serious!*

Yet a third ship demanded to know how long it would be before they could dock. "It shouldn't be too long," Phillips said, trying to project reassurance. "We've got everyone available working on the problem. We're going to bring up the old manual routing system."

Squawks of protest resounded from her listeners. "I can't help it if your pilot is out of practice," she said, a touch of exasperation emerging. "I repeat, *all* dockings will be manual until further notice, but there will be *no* dockings until the emergency with the *Night Storm* collision is dealt with."

Heather froze in her seat. The *Night Storm*. The ship Hing and Serge had gone to meet. Was that the one that had crashed?

"No"—Phillips shook her head—"we don't know the extent of the damage. All we know is that the ship was pulled in too fast, and crashed into the dock. All reports indicate that the *Night Storm* exploded during the crash. That station lost pressure in several of the docks, and in adjoining areas. The observation deck, for example—complete decompression there. We have no confirmed casualty count, but at least one person on the observation deck was killed. We have no idea what the total body count will be."

Hearing this, the child struggled for breath. *It couldn't have been Hing. Or Serge! I'd know if either one of them died! I'd know!* But would she? The station was so far away. It was one thing to hear Hing's cry for help from the Lamont Cliffs, but all the way from the station? That was way too far! Besides, if Hing and Serge had been sucked out into space would they even have the time to feel panic, or anything, before their bodies literally exploded from the inside out?

Heather bit her lip hard, trying to pull herself together. *Don't assume the worst,* she thought. *They might not've been at the gate yet. They're probably fine.*

But another part of her mind whispered, brutally, *Just like your mother and father, kiddo. Anyone who gets close to you has the worst luck, don't they? Your mother, dead. Your father . . . insane, and despite your brave hopes that someday he might get better, you know he never will. Never, never . . .*

Shuddering, she clenched the edge of her terminal desk, clenching her teeth to stop herself from whimpering like a damned baby.

Stop that! her survivor-self ordered brutally. *You're acting like an idiot. What do you care what happens to them? Ten minutes ago you were thinking that they'd corrupted you with their namby-pure attitudes and oh-so-moral crap, and now you're sniveling like a major asshole. You've got to look out for yourself, sweetcheeks, because you can bet all of "Helen Benson's" bankroll that if Serge and Hing knew what you were doing, they'd turn you in in a second and your ass would be out of here. Think they'd ever give you a second thought once you were gone?*

The concentrated burst of anger calmed her down, made her think more clearly.

Phillips was still talking, setting up tentative timetables for manual docking at Docks Eleven through Twenty, on the other side of the station, the uninjured side. "And by the way," she said, "we've just received a communication from StarBridge Station's security chief. Just prior to, or during the crash, which occurred at 13:24 station time, did anyone notice anything funny glitching up your computer?"

All of the ships must have replied in the negative, because she continued, "Well, I guess that confirms that it was strictly some local glitch—whatever it was. What happened here at the Academy *and* at the station was that at 13:23, a full minute prior to the crash, the entire system blipped out for a fraction of a second. It just blipped off, then back on. Then for a moment when it came up again, we saw . . . well, let me show you."

She must have pressed a control, because a window suddenly showed to her right, taking up about a quarter of the image. It was filled with ship and vessel coordinates and schedules, plus docking times. Heather watched as the playback suddenly blinked, as the computer hiccuped . . . and then data vanished and was replaced with—

—Heathertoo.

The image was exactly as the girl had seen her, wearing that terrified expression, then it tried to melt and meld into some underlying image but never quite made it. The image spoke: "The guidance beam setting is all wrong! Guidance beam error—error, error—too soon—too fast! Evacuate Docks Five and Six! Emergency override on that guidance beam!"

Then the window blinked again, and the normal shipping and docking data returned to the playback.

"Ever see anything like that?" Phillips asked, then cocked her head as she listened. "No, me neither. Totally illegal swapout or something. No, I've never seen her before, and from what the head of Security said, no one else has, either. She's certainly not one of the controllers, though one of the controllers remembers saying part of that as soon as she realized what was happening with *Night Storm*. But that part about 'error, error' sounds like it was the *computer* talking. Doesn't make a damned bit of sense."

Phillips paused for a moment, listened, then said, "It's got to be connected with the crash, it can't just be random garbage. The communication was local, we know that much—and it won't take long to track it down and identify whoever that was. The Security Chief is saying it has to be sabotage, so that redhead's going to have a lot of explaining to do, whoever she is."

Heather gasped and, unable to take any more, switched off the terminal. She felt the room spin around her, heard her blood roaring in her ears. *I'm gonna faint,* she thought dispassionately as her palms went clammy and her eyelids fluttered.

*You don't have **time** to faint!* her survivor-self barked. *Put your head down, asshole!* Immediately, Heather dropped her head between her knees, gulping air desperately. Her eyes watered, and her stomach heaved. She forced herself to slow down her breathing, easy . . . easy. Cautiously, she raised her head, saw that everything was stable again. She swallowed hard.

They'd seen Heathertoo. They'd be looking for her. With really sophisticated search programs, tracer programs. And when they found "Helen Benson," they'd trace her to Heathertoo—and then to Heathertoo's creator. This was no longer just a case of computer tampering. People were *dead.*

She kept hearing Rob's warnings about messing with the computers, the environmental systems, how everything was tied in together.

That's impossible! I only messed around with the school's AI. I never tapped into anything at the station except those financial programs! Nothing I did could've affected the guidance beams . . .

You called the station while you were inside the AI, a brutal voice inside her warned. *You stayed inside, pushing and prodding, moving things, making sure Heathertoo did what you wanted. How would you know what else you might have affected? **You never paid any attention to anything else!***

Heather shuddered convulsively. Computers were so weird the way they consolidated data, the way systems handled programs. And the AI was the weirdest part of the computer. It was organic. Made its own rules. Wrote its own programs. It *thought,* not quite like a human thought, but it thought. Fast. Really fast. And this one had Mizari origins, so it'd be less humanlike than a human-originated AI. She'd been bouncing around in there, pulling strings, making sure Heathertoo the puppet danced just right. *Oh, shit. Oh, shitshit**shit!***

She suddenly felt very small, very helpless, very young. Shivering, she whispered to the machine, "I didn't mean to, honest!" As though apologizing to it would do any good. "I just wanted some money of my own, so I'd be safe! I didn't mean to hurt anyone! I'd never do that on purpose!"

But that didn't matter now. People were dead. Maybe Hing and Serge were dead—and it was *her* fault. Heather moaned aloud.

Don't forget that StarBridge Station Security was now looking for Heathertoo. They'd probably start by checking personnel records, which would take them a while and get them nowhere. But they'd also have programmers, systems analysts, good ones, and they'd be tracing the mystery image through the computer.

A sob of sheer panic caught in Heather's throat, making her gulp, but no tears came. That's right, she never cried, and she wouldn't let herself now—though it might have been a relief. No, she had to get busy, she had no time to snivel.

Resolutely, Heather swallowed the lump in her throat, feeling her survivor-self surge to the fore, letting it think for her, guide her. It was her survivor-self that had kept her sane and functioning during all the bad times—when her mother had died and, soon after, when her father, instead of comforting her, had dissolved into shrieking, gibbering insanity. Her survivor-self had kept Uncle Fred from killing her, helped her in all those foster homes. Her survivor-self had gotten her off Earth, into space, where Uncle Fred and Aunt Natalie could never touch her again.

Resolutely, she listened to her inner voice, then reached for her computerpen, at the same time turning her terminal back on. *You can still do something no one else can do,* it told her. *You can go in there and wipe it all out, all the evidence, all the traces. Destroy Heathertoo. Wipe the record of the call to the broker. Dissolve that money-making program back into random electrical impulses. Get rid of the money.*

She balked at that last. Destroy the money? *Her* hard-earned money? No! She couldn't. That money meant freedom. Escape.

You've got to. There's no way you could sneak off this rock now, so your only defense is to play the innocent eleven-year-old. That means scrapping everything that can tie Heathertoo to you. Everything! Now get moving!

The child sucked in a lungful of air, struggling to clear her mind. She wouldn't think about Hing. Wouldn't think about Serge. Wouldn't think about them as victims of explosive decompression, frozen hunks of red meat and organs, floating forever in space . . .

She'd only think about what she had to do. How she had to wipe out all traces of her tampering.

Just this last time, she told herself. *After this, never again. Wipe the slate clean. Start over. They'll never know. And I swear, if I get out of this, I'll **never, EVER** do this again.*

She closed her eyes and *pushed,* then it was as though her mind were falling, plunging into the computer. She submerged herself in its mechanical order, experiencing the incredible complexity that was at the same time inhumanly simple, for it had no emotions, no feelings to influence its judgment.

Nanoseconds later she was traveling the grids, the pathways of the programs, the data, heading deep into the innards, toward the organic component of the AI. But even as she sank further into the mind that was not a mind, she heard her survivor-self chuckle at her naive promise of future honesty.

Sure, the survivor purred sarcastically, *you'll never do this again. Sure.*

A mental echo of her own laughter, twisted and perverted until it sounded inhuman, evil, followed her like a ghost into the darkness.

CHAPTER 11
◆
Guardian Angels and Ministers of Grace

Rob rubbed his face tiredly as the familiar dialogue washed over him; he was only half paying attention to it. Stretched out on his couch, he wore shapeless old gray sweatpants and a sleeveless red tee-tank. The "Johns Hopkins" emblazoned across its front was so faded it was nearly indistinguishable. On the stylish coffee table in front of him rested half a piece of fudge-marble cheesecake and half a mug of tepid coffee.

He stared at the food, then desultorily took another bite, washing it down with the cooling brew. He glanced up at the wall holo showing his favorite old film.

Little early in the season for this one, isn't it, Gable? he asked himself. *Not even near Christmas.*

On the screen, Clarence, the rotund little angel, was drying the clothes he'd been buried in, in the small caretaker's shack on the bridge. Nearby, a bitter, disillusioned George Bailey fumed because he'd had to risk his life to save the angel from drowning in the icy winter river. What George had really wanted to do was kill *himself*—not save anyone else. This rescue was a *major* inconvenience.

Rob watched Jimmy Stewart handle the role of George Bailey with an uncanny verisimilitude. And wondered why he was watching this film now, tonight, for perhaps the two hundredth time.

Heal thyself, doctor, he thought. *Couldn't be because you ended up in your dad's—and mom's—business, just because you were expected to, is it? Couldn't be because you ended up running*

StarBridge because it was what was expected of you, hmmm? The less glamorous job, but the oh, so important one?

StarBridge Academy as metaphor for the Bailey Building and Loan Company, how about that one, boys and girls? He scowled at the cheesecake and shoved it away. Oh, he had the blues *bad* today!

Now George was experiencing Pottersville, the alternate-universe Bedford Falls—the town as it would have been had he never been born, the fulfillment of his depressed wish as he stood hopeless on the bridge. It was a sick town, full of greed, anarchy, corruption. An analogy for all the things good people have to fight—and lose to—on a daily basis. Boy, Capra knew how to pull the strings, didn't he?

Rob had seen pictures of Capra in his later life. It'd shocked him how much the filmmaker had come to look just like Clarence.

There was George, frantic in the graveyard, staring at the tombstone of his brother. Clarence was explaining that the reason his brother died was because George hadn't been there to save him from drowning when they were kids. And because George hadn't saved his brother, his brother wasn't alive to save the troopship filled with soldiers, and all those men had died as well.

Little pebbles, big ripples, Rob thought morosely. He glanced around his living room, trying to find comfort in his familiar things, wondering how long he—or any of them—would be here at StarBridge.

His suite consisted of four rooms, living room, den (where he was now), bedroom, and bathroom. It was his refuge, a place where he could get away from everything and everyone, and just be himself—alone.

Well, almost alone. The small black cat curled beside him slept soundly, purring softly, her rumbles of content vibrating through his body. But even stroking Bast didn't cheer him. Rob looked from her to the pictures of her mother, Isis, daughter of Sekhmet. They'd been good companions to him over the years.

His eyes moved to the left of the screen where a simple feather and grass weaving hung. He'd once had an original Peter Max hanging there, but had replaced it when this arrived. The Max had taken up residence in the bathroom, and he'd programmed the walls to match its bright psychedelic colors.

The white weaving was about a meter square, and simple in design. Over it hung an ultraviolet light, so its hidden design would glow. The design showed the stylized images of two huge cranelike avians, with a human between them. Near them was a tiny avian, a baby. The style was reminiscent of the Anasazi, he thought, yet different. Beneath it, on a piece of paper-thin beige bark was written, "From Taller, the tallest of the White Wind People, this gift presented to the See-Through Man, given through his partner, Good Eyes." At the bottom of the inked message was a large, three-toed footprint—Taller's signature.

Rob had only spoken once to the avian leader, but knew that his hologrammic projection had unnerved the proud, nontechnological alien. He was glad that he had Tesa, known to the Grus as Good Eyes, to handle future communications between them. Staring at the beautiful weaving, he thought about pebbles and ripples. Tesa was certainly a big ripple. If he hadn't given her the chance to go to Trinity, and she hadn't decided to accept that assignment, what would everything be like now?

He knew that some of those gray hairs Ssoriszs and Jeff had noticed probably resulted from Tesa's first year on Trinity. For months they'd all thought she'd been killed. What a terrible time that had been! But in the end it had all worked out, better than anyone had hoped. Tesa's work with the Grus and the Aquila had qualified Earth for full membership in the CLS.

Because he'd been there to do his job, she'd done hers. And everyone benefited.

On the screen, George Bailey screamed at Clarence, demanding to know where his wife Mary was. Clarence, pummeled and terrified, finally confessed the information, only to be tossed aside in the snow. The poor angel-in-the-making lamented, moaning that there had to be an easier way to earn his wings. Rob chuckled ruefully. *You're right, Clarence. There must be an easier way!*

If they really closed the school down, really ended it—would he ever earn *his* wings? He closed his eyes, fighting the depression that wanted to engulf him, and the tiny voice that whispered that a drink would make him feel better. It wouldn't, and he knew it, just as well as he knew that that voice might never completely die.

He thought about the early years of trying to get StarBridge growing, make his and Ssoriszs' dream a reality. Going from city to city to drum up support on Earth, then from planet to planet, begging for money, for cooperation. Wondering, doubting, every day—would it be for nothing? All the time alone, seeing the woman he loved only on holo-vid news broadcasts, rarely in person. They'd been together a few weeks here, six months there, two years after Claire had been born . . .

And then the demands of work had pulled them apart again—Mahree to her troubleshooting role as Ambassador-at-Large for the

CLS and, at one point, her two terms as Secretary-General, Rob to begin supervising the birth of the Academy.

Why, he wondered bleakly, was it so damned hard to wage peace?

Opening his eyes, Rob blinked fiercely, determined to shake off the mood. He glanced at the coffee table, at mementos scattered there. One was the kareen, an Elpind music box that Mark Kenner and Eerin had sent him. The hypnotic musical notes of the Mortenwol ran through his head. Another near disaster that had turned out for the best. Another small pebble, another big ripple.

If they shut the place down tomorrow, Gable, no one can say you didn't do your part. You've made a lasting difference in the universe. How many people get to say that?

Yeah, but at what cost? He sat up, then gently resettled the cat. She complained halfheartedly. Rob sighed. Sometimes he wished he'd just gone with Mahree, followed her as she worked, stayed with her . . . loved her. That should've been enough.

He glanced up. George had had his fill of the evil Bedford Falls. He was back on the bridge, begging for a second chance, pleading for Clarence's help. He began to sob. It started to snow.

The only snow on StarBridge was in the simulation chambers.

Snap out of it, Gable! he ordered, mentally shaking himself. *This movie is supposed to pick you up! You've changed the lives of millions of people, altered the fate of entire planets, all for the better! And that feels to you like **nothing** today? God, what an ego! What is this, midlife crisis number thirty-eight?*

With a sudden spark of hope, he remembered that Andreiovitch was supposed to arrive soon. Surely such an eminent authority would be able to figure out a strategy to stop the radonium-2 from breeding! With him advising, and Jeff Morrow's engineering expertise, they'd be bound to lick this thing!

Cheer up, Gable, he reminded himself. *There's no Mr. Potter in **this** Bedford Falls. . . .*

A second later, though, a sudden image of Andrea Lynch made him frown. *Or is there?* Then he castigated himself for suspecting the woman of wrongdoing simply because of her abrasive personality.

George was running through town, the real Bedford Falls, euphorically happy, yelling, cheering, not caring that he was facing ruin, possible imprisonment. Rob watched, feeling the old catch in his throat. Soon, they'd be there, all his friends to bail him out, with what little they could give, but all those little contributions would add up to a lot. Rob felt himself smiling. He struggled to swallow the catch. *Damn, it's working! I thought maybe this time it wouldn't, but it is!*

His intercom beeped and he jumped guiltily, hoping it wasn't Janet. If she found out he was watching *It's a Wonderful Life* again, she'd give him hell for letting all that schmaltz get to him. For an otherwise intelligent woman, Jimmy Stewart's charms were lost on her.

He leaned over the coffee table, hit the keypad. Kkintha's familiar, furry face coalesced on the table's small screen. He gazed, surprised. The Administrator appeared completely frazzled, her normally impeccable fur raked up in tufts, her ears twitching, whiskers quivering anxiously, her tiny, pawlike hands washing each other over and over.

"Kkintha, what's wrong?"

"Oh, Rob! It's so terrible! I can't . . . !" Her voice was reduced to a nearly incomprehensible chitter. She heard it herself, and stopped, took a deep breath, ceased the compulsive handwashing.

Rob braced himself. "Tell me."

"I can barely stand to say it," the Chhhh-kk-tu quavered. "It's the *Night Storm*—Andreiovitch's vessel. Something went wrong. I don't know what, no one does. Maybe the guidance beams."

"What happened?"

"It crashed into the station. The ship exploded, all hands lost. Bodies flung into space. Oh, so terrible, terrible!" She scrubbed her round cheeks rapidly with her tiny hands, looking, for just that instant, so much like a giant hamster, Rob had to blink to destroy the image.

"No . . ." he whispered, stunned into disbelief.

"They're holding all other ships out in space until they get to the bottom of it," Kkintha said as soon as she'd stopped scrubbing her face. "No traffic can leave here either. They suspect sabotage, because someone called in a warning or something . . . I'm not sure exactly what happened. A woman with red hair broke in, saying the guidance beam was malfunctioning. The computer systems both here and at the station are apparently to blame, but no one knows just how."

"At the station and *here,* too? How could that be?"

"There's so much interaction between the two, so many transactions, and the organic brains are from the same Mizari source—like twins, really. I don't really understand the technical jargon of it. But, Rob, there's more . . ."

His eyes widened and suddenly, like a flash of insight, he remembered. Serge and Hing had gone to meet that ship. "The kids . . ." he began, feeling his heart turn over. "Oh, my God!"

Kkintha blinked as though holding back tears, even though Rob knew her species didn't cry. "We don't know where they are. One report said they were alive, but trapped in an airlock, but that hasn't been confirmed officially. They *could* be dead. It could be hours before they can account for everyone! Oh, Rob, those beautiful young people, the experts who traveled so far to help us . . . I feel so sick, so desolate."

"Do you want me to come wait with you," he said, "until we know for sure?" He didn't know whether he was offering a friend's support, or a psychologist's counseling—maybe some mixture of the two.

"Thank you, Rob, but no . . . that is . . . maybe later. When we find out. If . . . it's bad . . . then yes, I'd like to be with you. It would comfort me, to have a *chaka-shin* here."

He knew the word, knew it meant that Kkintha was referring to him as though he were a member of her intimate family group. It touched him greatly. "You know where to reach me, Kkintha," he said gently. "I'll be there whenever you say the word."

"As soon as I know anything more, I'll call you." She signed off.

Rob shook his head. *And I thought things were bad before!*

The film credits were rolling. He moved to turn it off, before the cassette could restart the film over again from the beginning. He leaned over the table to stop it, call up the news from the station instead, thinking there might be reports about the crash and the rescue operations.

Between one instant and the next, something powerful struck his mind, a thought so strong, so overwhelming, that he pitched forward, slid off the couch onto his knees, grabbing his head as if to keep it from exploding.

<Rob! Rob! Hurry!>

The telepathic demand struck him like a sledgehammer between the eyes. He'd never felt anything like it. It was tinged with anxiety, fear, terrible urgency. Rob felt a sickening, disembodied urge to flee his apartment, race toward the source of the cry.

Doctor Blanket, is that you? Pain throbbed behind his eyes. He didn't bother putting his discomfort into words, just felt it, knew the telepath would quickly realize what was happening.

<Please forgive me, dear Rob,> the gentle alien projected more normally.

The psychologist tried to imagine what had upset the Avernian so much that seloz would use such force in communicating.

<Something is terribly wrong, Rob. You must hurry!>

Is it the crash at the station, Doctor Blanket? Rob asked, trying to project his thoughts calmly, in spite of the agonizing headache that still pounded with every beat of his heart. *Did you "hear" it?*

<I know nothing of any crash, my friend. It's something else. Something terrible. A call for help, so strong . . . >

Rob was shocked at the alarm radiating from the normally placid being's thoughts. He'd never "heard" Blanket like this. *What call for help? Whose? Where is it coming from?*

<From everywhere! From the school, every part of it. From the environment. No. Let me think. It's coming from . . . the Mind.>

Rob blinked, shook his head, instantly regretted it. *Whose mind?*

<It is not a "who," it is a "what." But there is a who, also. It is screaming, Rob! Cries of fear and agony coming from the Mind That Is Not A Mind.>

Either seloz isn't making any more sense than a Doctor Seuss classic, or this headache is making me hear things, Rob thought, terribly confused. "What is a who?" he muttered ungrammatically. "Who is what?" The Mind That Is Not A Mind? What could that possibly—

Oh, shit!

Rob's mouth went dry as it finally clicked. *You mean the computer, Blanket? The artificial intelligence that runs the environment here at the school, and stores all of our data? That Mind?*

There was a momentary hesitation. Doctor Blanket always had trouble with technological concepts. The Avernians had no tools, none at all. Hell, they didn't even have anything to *grasp* a tool with. When they'd first brought the fungus being to the school, the alien had complained about having to learn to "tune out" the AI's "mind," as it "thought."

<Yes. That Mind,> Blanket finally admitted. <But now there is a true mind within the artificial Mind. It is trapped, but I can sense it.>

*The AI is **calling** you?* Rob found that a little difficult to believe—though he didn't even know if Doctor Blanket was capable of lying. He suspected not.

<No! Not the Mind calling. The young one is calling, the young one with the true mind. From inside the Mind!>

Rob could tell Blanket was getting impatient with his thick-headedness. That was something in itself. In all the years they'd been friends, he'd never known the alien to show impatience about anything. <I am sorry, Rob,> Blanket apologized. <I know I am not expressing these concepts well, but this is so different from anything I have experienced before!>

Try again to tell me. You know I'll do anything I can to help, Rob vowed.

<Just "listen,"> Blanket said. <I will let you "hear" the true mind.>

The next second he was enveloped in waves of panic, suffocating terror, and raw mental anguish. *"Help! Help me! Somebody get me out of here! Oh, God, please help!"* A second later it was gone.

Rob nearly passed out from the intensity of that shared fear. But now he knew—he'd recognized who it was. *Heather, oh, my God, it's Heather! Where is she, what's happened to her?*

She hadn't gone to the station, had she? Could she be trapped in that airlock? His mind spun, teetered. He felt Blanket's serenity wash over him like a cooling breeze.

<The young one is here, Rob. She is in danger, terrible danger. She is trapped within the Mind!>

It finally meshed. He understood. But that was impossible . . . wasn't it? *In the computer? In the AI? Heather's **inside** the AI?*

<That's what I've been telling you,> Doctor Blanket insisted with more than a touch of irritation.

Understanding clicked into place like dominoes. The Simiu's toilet. The computer games back on Earth. Her smugness about her skills as a hacker. Because she could do something that no one else ever had—Heather could telepathically link with the computer!

<Hurry, Rob! You must hurry if we are to save her!>

The Avernian's command was more like a compulsion, and Rob leaped to his feet, fighting a rush of vertigo. He stopped at his door realizing he had no idea where he was going, where Heather was, physically.

<You will need to take me to her,> Blanket told him. <I will try my best to save her.>

Rob nodded dumbly, one part of him realizing the movie had started over, that he should shut it off before he left.

His intercom buzzed. He blinked at it.

"Rob!" a familiar voice called out to him, cutting through his privacy codes. "It's Janet! I know you're there!"

<Not now!> Blanket ordered. <No time!>

"Janet, I can't!" he yelled at the table.

"Rob," she shouted back at his disembodied voice, "there's something wrong with the school's computers! Someone's put something like a virus program into them! We've got a real crisis!"

"I know! I know! I'm getting Doctor Blanket. Meet me!"

"Rob, *wait!*" he heard her call, but he was already racing barefoot down the hall, just as George Bailey selected a piece of luggage he would never take anywhere.

Minutes later he was stumbling around in the darkness of Doctor Blanket's quarters, searching through the blackened cupboards, looking for the light-damper. For the life of him he couldn't remember where they normally kept it, and without that safety device, the Avernian couldn't leave seloz's quarters. White light could burn seloz's flattened, cilia-covered body, because Doctor Blanket was from a world circling a red dwarf sun.

The million-year-old fungus being stood with part of seloz's body on end in the corner of the room, cilia rippling. The Avernian glowed like a phosphorescent baby blanket.

Rob racked his brain, trying to recall where he'd last seen the light-damper, but the Avernian's anxiety was like a fog in his mind, making it hard to think. He banged his shin on a corner and cursed. The pain spurred him to action, and he methodically yanked open drawers and dumped the scanty contents until the little instrument tumbled out.

Gotcha! Rob thought triumphantly, snagging the small Mizari device. Clipping it to the right shoulder of his beat-up tee, he turned it on and checked its power. It reported that it was working fine— not that he could tell in this darkened room. *Okay, let's go,* he said, kneeling before the alien.

The being slid into his open arms and undulated over his shoulders until seloz covered his back like a glowing cape. To an onlooker, Rob would appear to be a figure walking in a shroud of darkness, surrounded by a bizarre, phosphorescent glow.

<Hurry, Rob! we have little time left. The Mind is devouring her!>

The psychologist moved to the computer, logged in his route to Heather's room. The lights along their path would be dimmed for Blanket's safety. <Let's go.>

The computer beeped at them. "Rob, are you there?" Janet's voice called out.

"I'm leaving here, Jan, no time to explain!"

"Don't you dare! I'm in your quarters. I'm trying to catch up to you!"

He rolled his eyes. "I told you to meet me at Blanket's . . ."

"You told me to meet you. You never said *where!*"

"Meet me at Heather's. She's in trouble."

"Heather! That's what I—"

"I'll see you there!" Then he and the Avernian were out the door, racing for the elevator.

By the time he skidded to a stop in front of Heather and Hing's suite, Rob was panting. He tapped in the emergency override to the door lock and it slid open obediently.

Cautiously, Rob glanced around before plunging in, just to make sure everything was darkened. As planned, everything was dim, just enough light to help him pick his way. This was the living room that the two roommates shared. Empty.

Rob crossed the room purposefully, placed a hand against the door to Heather's room. "Heather?"

<She can't hear you. Just go in.>

Rob hit the override code to the bedroom door.

The lights in Heather's room were also dimmed, but the computer screen glowed brightly in the darkness. In its light, he could see Heather, slumped in the chair before the terminal. In the eerie glow her skin was waxen. *Is she dead?*

<No. But she soon will be, if we cannot help her.>

Quickly the doctor lifted the child, carried her over to the bed, and gently laid her on it. Her skin was cold and clammy. Quickly Rob activated the bed's heating element. <Do not cover her,> the Avernian ordered, and before Rob could ask what the alien intended, seloz flowed from his shoulder onto the little girl, covering her protectively with seloz's glowing form. Rob immediately removed the damper, and clipped it to Heather's jumpsuit, to keep the alien safe.

Then he returned to the screen, moved to shut it off. That was when he first realized what was on it.

A woman. Red-haired. Upturned nose. Just as he'd seen her in Heather's records. *Heather's mother!* Rob blinked, disbelieving, his hands hovering over the keypad. Then he remembered what Kkintha had told him. Some image of a red-haired woman had warned the station just before the crash. Rob stared openmouthed at the screen, trying to assimilate what was on it. *How could that be Heather's mother?*

This was impossible, his common sense told him, unless this was some kind of bizarre home video. But even as he thought that, he knew it couldn't be. The clothes were all wrong, the setting.

Besides, the computer clock in the upper right-hand corner of the screen was giving him the same date and time as the clock he could plainly see in the fancy office.

But even more bizarre than this image of Heather's mother as the ultimate businesswoman was what the woman herself was doing. Her expression was one of sheer terror, as she pressed her hands to the inside of the computer screen like someone imprisoned behind a plate of clear plas-steel. Her hands were even flattened as though this screen were the only thing separating her and Rob, as though if he broke it, she could emerge. She pushed desperately against the screen, and he faintly heard her crying, *"Help! Help me! Get me out of here, please! Oh, help, somebody!"*

The woman stared straight at him, begging for help. It was the eeriest thing he'd ever seen, worse than the sixth remake of *The Fly*—the first holo-vid version—when they'd used a woman scientist instead of a man, and she kept begging the audience, "Help me. Help me."

Then the woman that looked like Heather's mother stared directly into his eyes and begged, "Please, Dr. Rob. Please help me!" He staggered back, stunned. The face and body were adult, but only now did he realize that the voice was purely Heather's.

<Rob!> Doctor Blanket's clear thought cut through his startlement. <Shut that thing off! It's making your thoughts too chaotic. I need you to help me with Heather.>

But, Rob thought, baffled, *isn't this Heather?*

<No, that is just the image she created to do her bidding,> Blanket told him. <Turn the thing off. We cannot afford distractions now.>

Realizing the Avernian was giving him good advice, Rob quickly saved the image for further study, then ruthlessly cut it off, shut the terminal down. But somehow he couldn't shake the feeling that he'd just turned his back on someone in dire need, like ignoring an emergency broadcast. Shaken, he went back to the bed, to Heather and the protective Avernian.

Rob quickly examined the child. She was worse than he first thought. Her pulse was thin, thready, her skin cool to the touch and clammy. Her eyes were rolled up into her head. Her extremities were icy. Quickly he wrapped her legs and feet in the bed's heated blankets, tucked her arms under the covers. That was when he realized he'd failed to bring his medical kit.

He couldn't have been more astounded if he'd left his arm behind. *Damn, Gable! And you call yourself a doctor?*

<Don't, Rob,> the Avernian admonished. <If it's anyone's

fault, it's mine. I pushed you so hard telepathically, I permitted no stray thoughts to cloud your mind.>

Before he could frame a response, Janet jogged into the room, blinking at the alien's glowing form in the dimness.

"Rob, you here?"

He moved to her quickly, grabbed her by the shoulders so fast she gasped. "Janet, thank heavens you're here!"

"I'd have been here sooner if I hadn't been chasing you all over this school! The computers are going nuts! The defense systems have caught something. A virus program, maybe, but I can't get them to tell me anything about who it is. I'm afraid it might have something to do with the crash at the station. I'm afraid . . . Heather's at the bottom of it."

"You're right, she is, but there's no time to discuss it. Her mind is trapped in the AI, and while it's there, Heather's body may die."

Janet blinked, uncomprehending. "Her *mind*? What are you talking about?" Only then did she seem to realize the youngster was flat out on the small bed.

"Later!" Rob said forcefully. "Right now, I need you. Go to the infirmary. Get me a complete medical kit, an ICU cart, and an a-grav stretcher. But before you leave here, go into the living room and tell Nurse Ch'eng Hao to get down here. Before he came to StarBridge, he worked in ICUs with coma patients, and that's the closest thing I can compare this to. Please. Do it *now*!"

For a half second she looked like she might argue, then she glanced at the child on the bed covered by an alien. Muttering a quick *"Díos!"* she left the room.

"She's freezing," Rob said to Doctor Blanket, knowing the Avernian could understand that communication just as easily. "Like her brain's not keeping her body going. What can we do to help?"

<We will have to go after her, bring her back to her body, so it can function properly again. The Mind is treating her like an invader, surrounding her, pulling her in deeper and deeper. It's trying . . . to absorb her.>

Rob thought he could feel Doctor Blanket shudder. <The Mind is locking the child away, deep inside where she can do no harm to the system. The more she struggles, the tighter it enfolds her, burying her. You must do all that you can to keep her body going, then we will have to go inside the Mind and find her.>

"Holy shit," Rob muttered. The whole idea was terrifying. "We? You and me?"

<I will take you with me. You are human, she will not fear you. She has never seen me, she does not know who I am. She might think I am part of the Mind's defenses. You must accompany me, Rob.>

"Could we get trapped, too?" What would it be like to die inside a computer?

<That is a possibility. The Mind is very fast, very strong.>

To plunge into the Mind. To go inside the AI of a computer. Rob felt sweat sheen his forehead, make his underarms feel dank.

A sound from the living room brought him out of it. It was Ch'eng. He could envision the Asian's broad, gentle smile. Nothing fazed Ch'eng. He'd seen it all.

<Rob? Are you ready?>

The doctor swallowed, and allowed his hand to rest on his Avernian friend's gently undulating cilia. "Just as soon as Ch'eng and I get her on life support, we'll go," he promised steadily. "We'll go together, old friend."

At first it had been easy. Heather had slid into the machine, just like the last time. No resistance. Once again, she was in a place that her mind perceived as physical, though in reality, she knew, most of it was just an illusion of physicality—a way for her limited senses to deal with her surroundings.

At first it was darkness and brightness, following a maze of grids in infinite space. This time, it was familiar, so there was less disorientation. It almost felt comfortable. She traveled the bright grids, her mind searching ahead, looking for markers.

The first thing she eliminated was her money-collection program. It hurt her to do it, and she stood there for a little while, watching the balance increase by fractions, quickly building up to a sum she could barely imagine. A sum that belonged to *her*. But, finally, she wiped it out, plus its backup, and any traces that it had ever existed. It seemed to take forever, following all the thin strands that ran to so many other programs. But she did it the hard way, eliminating each individual one. Creating the program had been so much easier.

Then she went after the phone call to the broker. That was harder. There were defense systems around that, waiting to trap her. Her mind perceived them as big STOP signs in all the wrong colors, heavy road barriers in eye-searing shades. *They* liked to be able to account for every call, be able to know who was talking to who. The snoops. What business was it of theirs anyway? She dodged the defenses, crawling under the barriers, around the STOP signs.

The defenses were sophisticated, but not perfect. She wiped the call. Unfortunately, that left a huge hole behind, a telltale spot of tampering. She tried to eliminate it, but could not close the gap.

It'd be easy to find such a big space, and that worried her. They'd know someone had erased something, but there was no way for them to find out what it had been. Heather turned to the next item on her list.

Now mesh fencing had sprung up under the road barriers, around the STOP signs. Fuschia pink. Boy, she hated that color! It took forever to travel the program, searching for a weak spot. She finally found one, a break in the mesh, worked at it, and eventually squeezed through.

She lay on the other side, gasping, exhausted—just as though she'd actually done it physically. That must have taken hours, getting through! Her mind accessed the computer's chronos. Three minutes. She'd only been inside three minutes. Heather couldn't accept that; her time disorientation was complete. She was starving. She had to have been here hours—no, days! Yeah, days . . . days of wandering this weird place, looking for the markers she'd put here, for markers others had put here but that she'd be familiar with.

Do Heathertoo next, something told her, but she shrugged it off. Heathertoo would be easy to eliminate, after all, she'd built her. That wouldn't take any time at all. She needed to tackle the big jobs while she still had the energy. She could wipe Heathertoo on her way out.

That thought tugged at her oddly. She realized she didn't want to eliminate her grown-up self.

You've got to! Do it now!

She stuck out her lower lip. *No. Not now. Later. Now, I'm going after the money. That'll take a long time, a lot of work. Lots harder than just a simple phone call. I'll wipe Heathertoo on my way back . . . I promise.* She felt oddly despondent about making that commitment. It seemed like murder, almost.

The girl got back on the grid and followed it a long time before she found herself in front of what her mind perceived to be a huge vault. There was still the tiny remnant of a bright glowing string leading from her money-accumulation program right into the vault. *That's where it is,* Heather thought. *All the money. My money.*

She would have to go in there and wipe it out, make it go away. Her chest felt tight, her eyes stung. She wanted to weep, but couldn't. That money would've gotten her off this rock, away to freedom. With the help of Heathertoo, she could've lived a great life, had anything she wanted, gone anywhere . . . But that was before she'd killed anybody. If she got caught now, the only place she'd be going was jail, for a long, long time.

Her lip trembled, so she bit it, and stepped up to the vault. She concentrated, and a keypad appeared at exactly her eye level. She smiled. Now she was on familiar territory. She rubbed her hands together, then wiped them on her coverall.

Biting her lip in concentration, she rested the fingertips of her right hand on the pad. *Now, be careful!* her inner voice warned. She tapped in a sequence. Heard something in the giant door click and shudder. She tapped in another. More clicks, a groan. She smiled. Slowly she tapped in another cadence.

Suddenly the keypad glowed bright red and felt burning hot. She yelped, tried to yank her hand away, found it was glued to the pad. The heat seared her. She screamed, grabbed her wrist with her left hand, pulled and tugged desperately to no avail. Suddenly police sirens wailed, just like in the movies. A thousand aircars were circling the vault, their sirens flashing, the alarms threatening to shatter her eardrums.

Remember, they're just illusions the defense system is sending you! her inner self said calmly. *Keep working. They haven't nailed you yet. You can still defeat them.*

Sweat poured down Heather's face, dripping into her eyes. She concentrated on her burning hand, telling herself it was just a computer illusion, that her fingers weren't blistering on the keypad, that she could still do whatever she wanted. The heat abated. She swallowed, tapped another sequence. The heat stopped completely, and there was a loud click from inside the vault door. She tried another combination.

The police sirens stopped, and the aircars slowed, but kept hovering. Heather felt a surge of optimism. She continued her combinations, the patterns coming from the computer itself as she tapped its mind. The aircars slowed, then disappeared. And finally, with a massive groan, the vault door slid open.

Her hand was freed from the keypad, which promptly disappeared.

The youngster stared into the vault, an endless chamber filled to bursting with stack after sky-high stack of crisp new bills. All denominations. From all over the galaxy. Her eyes widened as she stared at it all, even though she knew it wasn't real. Physical money didn't look like that anymore. Mizari credit disks were greenish, and they were the common method of physical exchange these days.

She prodded the computer's mind. Would something terrible happen if she crossed the threshold? She looked down. A wire-thin ray of blue light stretched across the doorway. She probed deeper into the alien mind. The light winked out.

Once she got inside, would the door slam shut behind her? She closed her eyes, concentrated. The vault door dissolved, leaving the chamber wide open. Someone else could worry about sealing it back up.

Cautiously, Heather stepped inside.

All the time, of course, she knew this wasn't real, that she was actually inside the computer, but the imagery her own brain constructed to help her fathom out these challenges was so real, she could feel the marble beneath her feet, smell the unique smell of real money. Just like that time Mom and Dad had taken her to that museum, the old Treasury, where they showed how money used to be made. . . .

She shook the thought away, knowing she couldn't afford the distraction. She followed the narrow aisleway that wound through the bottomless vault, searching for her account. Heather thought she must've walked ten miles before finally finding it. It sat on a shelf just at her eye level, with a little sign under it that said, "Heather's money."

She looked at it, stunned.

It was a tiny pile compared to the huge mounds of cash surrounding it. She touched it, estimated how much there was there. To her it was still a frightening amount, more than she'd ever had, more than she could ever imagine earning. Yet, compared to what was here, it was nothing.

The child suddenly felt small, tiny, insignificant in this huge place. All the work she'd done, yet the fortune she'd amassed seemed so trivial compared to all of this.

Stop worrying about that, a voice inside hissed at her. *You don't have all day. Get rid of this stuff, and get out of here!*

She nodded obediently, touched the money reverently one more time, then dipped again into the computer mind. One by one, she redistributed her tiny stacks over to surrounding ones, where their small amounts would never be noticed. It would be nothing to those accounts. Nothing. Yet, it had been so much to her.

The last stack sat there, ready to be moved, when Heather reached out impulsively and grabbed it. She couldn't let it all go, she just couldn't. She couldn't be left with nothing.

Don't! her inner voice warned. *It's just an image. It's not real! Don't do it!*

It was too late. She ignored the voice, grabbed the money, and shoved it into her pockets. Then she ran—ran as hard and as fast as she could. Through the twisting corridors of the vault, to the door, to freedom. An alarm sounded in her ears, but she ignored it. There was no door on the vault. She'd get out easy.

The yawning opening came into view. She raced for it, chest heaving, just as a gate of bars began descending from the ceiling, ready to trap her. The gate slammed to the ground seconds before she got there, and she hit the bars hard, squeezing, pushing, forcing her body through.

Then she was out, running down the grids, police sirens loud now, aircars giving chase. Panic rose in her chest.

Throw away the money, her voice said. *Then get away!*

"No!" Heather screamed. "I won't!"

She felt the stacks of bills grow heavy in her pockets, turn to solid gold, weigh her down, make her feel as if she were racing through molasses. The aircars were catching up.

"Dammit!" she screamed, trying to pull the huge, impossibly heavy bars out of her pockets, but they were too large to force out past the tight, strong material. One of the police aircars buzzed her as the weight of gold grew too heavy. She fell, expecting to land hard, but she pitched forward off the grill into endless blackness, plummeting down and down.

She screamed for just a second, then flailed her arms, trying to plunge into the computer mind, make it grant her wings, a parachute, an a-grav belt, anything. But nothing appeared and she kept falling. The gold in her pockets crumbled to dust, spilling out, swirling around her in a tornado of shining particles, blowing away. When not a speck was left, she finally hit bottom, with a rude thud, but no injuries.

"Shit!" she grumbled irritably, and tried to concentrate, bring up the grid. She'd have to go back to the vault, go back in, find that stack, get rid of it all over again. She must've been crazy to try and physically take it. She calmed her mind and concentrated, waiting for familiar signposts to appear.

But nothing happened. She concentrated harder, probed the AI, tried to force it to comply. She looked around. Nothing. Where was she now? Around her was only a black void. She shivered.

Far away, she noticed something gray, a tiny blob, floating toward her. She was relieved that the blackness was no longer total.

The speck grew larger, larger, until Heather realized it was nothing she recognized at all. It was huge, shapeless, like an amoeba, translucent . . . wet . . . sticky . . . like something alive. Like something from the organic portion of the AI? Heather felt panic building as it grew bigger and bigger, speeding toward her in the void.

Run! her brain ordered, and with a high-pitched child's scream, she did, bolting in any direction she could, as long as it was away from that *thing!*

Her legs pumped hard, her breath burned in her lungs, her blood rang in her ears—

—but it caught her anyway, slapping her hard, wrapping its gooeyness around her legs. Heather was screaming wildly as she fell again, this time with the protoplasm monster clinging to her. Then another one was there, smacking against her, holding her down while two more of the jellylike entities appeared and headed purposefully toward her.

With a terror that left her teetering on the verge of complete insanity, she realized that hundreds of them were coming, thousands, ready to encase her, entomb her alive.

As she screamed—it was all she could do, they had her arms and legs by now—one of the plasma things slapped over her face, filling her eyes and nose, her mouth, stifling the sound.

She could still breathe, somehow, still hear, still even see, though it was like looking through medical jelly. She was trapped, utterly, helplessly trapped. This was the greatest terror she'd ever known, worse than the time she'd thought Uncle Fred wasn't going to stop until he'd killed her, worse than when Khuharkk' had roared at her, worse than *anything*.

With all the strength she could summon, Heather sent her mind out, desperately seeking help, begging for help, pleading for someone, anyone, to—please!—help her.

But as the plasma imprisoned her, burying her under tons and tons of goo, she knew it was hopeless. No one would hear her here in the depths of the AI. No one would even look for her. Who would look for a telepath in the bowels of an artificial intelligence? Still, she could not quiet her mind, it was the only weapon she had.

By now the plasma things totally encased her, so many tons of them that there was no blackness anymore, just a sickly off-white fading into gray. She could no longer sense the computer. There were no images she could recognize; she was in complete sensory deprivation.

I've been here for years, she thought. *I must be old by now.* Old and shriveled, with white hair. Her mind roved the emptiness wildly, like a feral thing, touching nothing but cold barrenness. Years like this. Her whole life. However long you could live in here. Alone.

Suddenly something flickered at the edge of her vision. Heather strained toward it, searching, hoping against hope. Then she saw it again. A glimmer. Bright whiteness.

Heather trembled. That's how the attack of the plasma beasts had started, something sparkling in the void. She blinked and stared. No, this was different. The whiteness glowed bright, made motions that were somehow familiar. The figure grew larger in her vision. She recognized wings. Wings. That was something she understood, wings. She thought of huge white birds, thought of pelicans, of winged horses . . . of angels. Like the angels her mother had told her about, not the ones Uncle Fred and Aunt Natalie had described. Guardian angels with enfolding wings and gentle faces, not avenging ones with lightning bolts or swords.

She remembered the church her parents had taken her to when she was hardly more than a baby. Big statues of white-robed angels everywhere. Guardian angels. Mom said they were always around you, watching out for you. Heather had stopped believing in all that stuff when her mother had died.

But now, her heart surged. This was an angel, oh, please, make it be one! A guardian angel, come for her. "Oh, please," she cried out in a choked voice.

The figure drew near, huge, massive, gleaming wings beating back the gray plasma, the whiteness glowing so bright it hurt her eyes. She saw its face, just as its voice touched her mind, and she felt a burst of ecstatic hope. *Dr. Rob!*

"Heather!"

It *was* him! He'd come for her!

"Here!" she yelled. "Over here!"

Now she could see him fully, as glorious as an angel, giant wings waving gently, keeping him elevated, apart from the tunnel of goo. He stared at her, as though he couldn't see her clearly.

"I'm in here! Don't leave me!" she nearly screamed in her panic.

He smiled at her then, as though he'd just found her. His face had that relieved look that people wore when they just found their lost child—a child they really cared about. Her parents had looked at her like that once. "Oh, Heather. Thank heavens," he said softly. There was no anger in his voice.

He didn't know . . . couldn't know what she'd done, or he wouldn't look like that. "Oh, Dr. Rob," she stammered, "I'm sorry. I did a terrible thing! I didn't mean to be bad . . . not like that . . . I'm sorry . . ."

"I know, honey. I know. Let's not talk about that now. We can deal with it later, once we're out of here." He held his arms out invitingly to her, and the plasma-goo parted before the light emanating from him. Heather flung herself into his arms, felt him enfold her, pull her to his warm, strong body.

Burying her face against him, she closed her eyes. *"Please take me away from here,"* she whimpered, like a two-year-old. She felt something odd was covering him, like feathers, but not feathers. Something plush, cool, like cilia. Soft, downy cilia. She pressed her cheek against it.

"Your wings are so beautiful, Rob," she said, then felt silly for blurting it out.

She heard him chuckle, felt it ripple through his body, felt the happiness, the relief flow into her. "Are they, honey? Someone must have rung a bell, because I didn't think I'd earned them yet. Come on. Let's go. Hold on tight."

The powerful wings pumped hard, and they began to climb, up through the blackness. Heather dug her fingers in the cilia and held on.

"You know, this isn't just me helping you, Heather," Rob said. "I'm not a telepath. I couldn't do this by myself."

"Who's helping you?" she said suspiciously, fearing police. Authorities.

"There are friends taking care of you back at the school, making sure you don't get hurt—your body, I mean. And here, inside, there's someone with me. Someone different. Someone you've never seen. Someone kind, but not human. Don't be afraid when you see this someone, okay?"

"You'll be there?"

"Right there." He squeezed her tight, made her feel secure.

"I won't be scared."

"Good."

Then they were on grids again, bumpy ones, but familiar.

"Almost home," he said.

Home? she thought dazedly. "Do I have a home?" she muttered.

She was suddenly overwhelmed with sleepiness, felt her eyes close without her volition, felt herself drifting away, safe in Rob's arms.

• • •

"Here she comes," said Ch'eng Hao as Heather's eyelids began to flutter.

Rob nodded, watching her face, seeing the eyes move back and forth as if in REM sleep. He was only partially aware of Ch'eng, of Janet, of the small bed on which he sat, even of the physical presence of the little girl he held snugly against him, with Doctor Blanket covering them both, linking them.

"Hold her tight, Dr. Gable," the nurse had told him. "And talk to her if you can. You never know what they can sense when they're out like this."

Ch'eng had set up a brainwave scanner, attaching a small patch to Heather's forehead.

It had been hard, remembering to speak aloud even as Doctor Blanket took his mind on a dizzying descent into the depths of the computer brain. He'd seen so much, understood so little, until Blanket found Heather. A little spark of true intelligence amid all those dispassionate decision-making synapses. She'd shone like a diamond chip almost buried in coal dust.

"Heather," he said, his voice sounding more like a croak, "can you hear me, honey?"

<She hears you,> Doctor Blanket assured him.

"Heather, look at me. It's Dr. Rob."

Obediently, she opened her eyes, the lids fluttering weakly. She was still so pale that her freckles stood out in sharp relief even in the dim light. "Dr. Rob?" she whispered.

He summoned a reassuring smile, then hugged her, and weakly she smiled back. She glanced around, trying to figure out where she was, who was here. Her eyes met Ch'eng's and he grinned toothily at her. "Hey, little one! Welcome back!"

She blinked acknowledgment, looked around some more. Saw Janet leaning against the wall. The child stiffened slightly, looked back at Rob worriedly.

"Sshh," he murmured. "We'll talk about all that later, when you're feeling better. You need to sleep for a while, so I'm going to give you something so you'll sleep, peacefully."

"But what if I dream about those things?"

"Don't worry, Doctor Blanket will make sure you only have good dreams."

For the first time, she glanced at the fluffy white rectangle cloaking them both, seeing how it glowed in the darkness. Her eyes widened. Would she be terrified? Rob swallowed, ready to jump in with soothing reassurances.

The glistening cilia rippled, undulated like a miniature grainfield. The child stared in awe, reached out stubby fingers, touched the creature.

"Oh . . ." she breathed, "it was *you* . . . you and Rob . . . Oh, aren't you *beautiful*!"

Rob felt his whole body sag in relief. Her voice was the voice of a child, even a younger child than her actual age. Gone was the brittle cynicism Heather had always exhibited, of someone pushed too hard, too fast, with knowledge that she'd stolen instead of learned.

"Heather, this is my friend, a very special friend, Doctor Blanket. Doctor Blanket is an Avernian, a neuter, not a male or female. So when we speak about this person, we use the Mizari pronoun 'seloz,' because it's not very nice to call someone as special as Doctor Blanket an 'it,' is it?"

"Seloz saved me?" she murmured.

"Yes. Seloz pulled you out of the computer. I just went along for the ride."

"Can he, I mean, seloz, see me?" she asked, wonder-struck.

"Sort of. Doctor Blanket certainly knows you're here. Seloz is really worried about you, Heather, so Doctor Blanket's going to stay with you while you rest, make sure you don't have any bad dreams, okay? And when you wake up, you, and me, and seloz are going to have a few talks. Understand?"

Heather's green eyes lifted to meet Rob's. She knew exactly what he was talking about. She nodded solemnly.

"Okay." Rob nodded to Ch'eng.

The nurse looked over his readouts and made an adjustment. Within moments Heather's eyelids dropped. Rob gently eased her back onto the bed. But just before she lapsed into deep sleep, Heather reached out and gently gathered the alien to her. The Avernian flowed, until seloz lay cuddled in her arms, exactly like a real child's security blanket.

Rob smiled. It was the first really childish thing he'd ever seen her do.

"Are you okay?" he asked the Avernian, speaking aloud because his mind felt drained. "She's not squashing you, is she?"

<I am fine. I am going to work on her remaining residual fears, and give her some pleasant, but restful, dreams.>

Rob got up, stretching, feeling all his bones and muscles creak. He bowed to Ch'eng, who only grinned and waved. Then he walked over to Janet.

The engineer was leaning against the wall, arms and ankles crossed. She cocked an eyebrow at him and asked, "*You* okay, good Dr. *Clarence*?"

He started at the reference, then realized it was pure coincidence. She'd stopped in his quarters, and *It's a Wonderful Life* had been playing.

"I ain't up t'goin' ten rounds wit' you at the moment, shweethart," he warned her in his best Bogie imitation.

Janet's eyes never left the sleeping child. "Rob, do you have any idea what she *did*?" Her voice was even. Modulated. A good indicator of how tightly she was reining in her emotions.

"No one yet knows exactly *what* she did," he countered.

"Oh, come on! I know Kkintha told you about the red-headed woman that predicted the crash. That program originated from here, from Heather. You've got to know that. *I* know it. And pretty soon StarBridge Station Security's going to know it."

Rob shook his head. "I don't believe she had anything to do with the crash of the *Night Storm*." A sudden thought struck him. "Serge! Hing! Has there been any news?"

"They were trapped in an airlock for a while, but they're fine now. The hospital at the station is keeping them for observation. They asked me to transmit all the files on how Serge's hands work. Apparently they're going to have to do some repairs on them. But they have a Mizari healer with experience in microengineering up there, so she ought to be able to handle just about anything."

"That's the best news I've heard all day," Rob said, feeling relief so profound his knees sagged.

Janet was still looking at him. Rob sighed. "Janet. Not now. I can't take any more right at the moment. I told you, my gut reaction—and I was right about the toilet blowup, remember—is that *this* time, Heather is innocent."

Janet bit her lip. "I'd like to believe you, but . . ."

<Rob is correct, Janet,> Rob "heard" Blanket's communication, as did the engineer. She started, but only for a second.

"How can you be so sure?" she asked the alien.

<Today I searched the length and breadth—so to speak—of the Mind. In that vastness, I could perceive clearly what Heather had done—follow the paths she'd built before, even the erased ones. I traced everywhere she had been, as I sought her.> The Avernian paused, and Rob knew seloz was hunting for words to express seloz's thoughts. Discussing anything technical was very difficult for the alien.

<Heather's paths went only to the places the child intended them to go. None of them touched, or even came close, to that area the Mind knew as "Traffic Control," either here at the school, or at the station. Heather did not cause the disaster today.>

Blanket hesitated again, searching for words. <However, not too far from one of Heather's paths, the one that leads to her adult image, there was an area that was tightly sealed off, though that sealing was done by normal means, the way people who instruct the Mind communicate with it—the way you, Janet, would communicate. In other words, it was not Heather's form of manipulating the Mind. I could 'feel' tremendous activity there, sense the presence of many people working, but no minds intruding. The area was very secure. I believe it housed the school's guidance system. I felt the activity of many species searching for things there.>

Janet nodded. "That figures. Everyone and his brother are busy comparing the two systems, trying to find something, a difference maybe."

<That is not all I sensed, however. There was something . . . attached . . . to that location in the Mind. Something that looked new. Patched on. I did not understand it, and it was sealed even more tightly than the guidance system itself.>

"A patched-on program?" Rob suggested. He hated talking computerese with Janet. In moments he'd be in over his head.

To his surprise, she didn't immediately shoot him down. "There are always patches, changes being made to programs," she muttered, thinking.

<This one was different from all others. The seal surrounding it was impenetrable.>

She frowned. "Okay, but that's down here. The program failed at the *station*."

"Could the patch have been added on here," Rob asked, "but designed solely to affect traffic at the station, in the hopes no one would look over here?"

Janet mulled that over for a while. "Yeah. But that only makes *her* look worse." She nodded at Heather's still form. "If she was responsible, that's how she'd have to do it. From here."

<No, you are wrong. This was not Heather's type of meddling. This was different.> Blanket sounded positive. <This was done by someone other than Heather, working with the machine, not the Mind.>

Janet still looked skeptical. The Blanket was a completely nontechnological creature. Rob knew Janet would have to question seloz's judgment on this. "With all due respect, Doctor Blanket, you've said yourself the artificial intelligence is hard for you to fathom . . ."

<That's true. But this I know. I can sense the presence of what your mind would call "mental energy." Heather uses it. Whoever made this thing you call a "patch" did not.>

"Maybe Heather's adult image got transmitted for a second, because of some kind of crossover?" Rob mused aloud. "A crossover with that patch?"

"*If* there even *is* a patch," Janet said, sounding like she was at the end of her rope. "But in case there is, I'll have Security start trying to trace it. If it's as sealed as Blanket says, I'm not sanguine about them finding it, though."

She rubbed her forehead as though she could erase the troubles within. "This is making me crazy. All I know for sure is that kid is *dangerous*! She can go mind-dancing with the AI, Rob! No one's ever done that, no one! Having her here is like sitting on a bomb! What are we going to do? She's only *eleven*. What's she going to do to us when she's twelve? Fifteen?"

Rob put a hand on Janet's shoulder. "I know. It is frightening. But I was in her mind, and I saw how terrified she was. I can't believe she'd go back in the AI again voluntarily. She was scared almost literally *to death,* Janet. And with Doctor Blanket to keep tabs on her, she can't do anything without us finding out immediately! What else *can* we do?"

"Send her back to Earth," Janet said stubbornly.

"Sure . . . to a system that won't understand her, has no *concept* of what her needs are, what her capabilities are? A system that was turning her into a hardened criminal without even trying? No way, Janet. I won't do it. Heather needs to be right here, where we—especially Doctor Blanket—can watch her. Sending her back to Earth would be as immoral an act as any committed by that monstrous uncle of hers who abused her. I won't do it!" Rob's voice rose in a ringing declaration.

Janet opened her mouth to argue, studied the expression on the doctor's face, then gave in with a shrug. She nodded bleakly and stared at Heather. "Okay, okay. I hate it when you're right, *Clarence*."

"That's *George* to you, shweetheart," he shot back with a grin.

Janet watched Heather as Blanket lay silently with her, watched the rise and fall of her flat, childish chest. "*Pobrecita,*" she murmured, and left them there to care for her.

CHAPTER 12

◆

Interlude

"No, I have no further comment," Rob said, his voice too even to be genuinely patient. "As I already told you several times, Ms. Wallace, I know no more than you do about what caused the crash at StarBridge Station. I suggest you contact the Security Chief at the station and speak to him about that."

Despite the lateness of the hour, he was still in his office and had been there the entire day, except for one brief visit to check on Heather Farley where she was being kept under observation in the Academy's infirmary.

His current caller, a reporter named Joan Wallace, must have graduated from the Inquisition School of Journalism, Rob thought wearily. She seemed convinced that if she asked him the same question enough times, he'd tell her what she wanted to know. Covering his eyes with his hand, glad that he'd politely declined to activate the visual portion of the call, giving the lateness of the hour as an excuse, Rob had a brief vision of himself bound to a stake, screaming "I recant!" while robed figures—all with the faces of the succession of reporters he'd spoken with during this endless day—marched around him, chanting and waving flaming torches.

Wallace was an attractive woman in her late twenties, but she had the energy of an army ant, the determination of a kamikaze, and the tact of a rhino. Rob was two seconds from telling her what to do with herself in words of one syllable.

Now, hearing the edge in his voice, she blinked huge, doe-soft dark eyes at him from under her soft fringe of brunette hair, and hesitated for the first time in her barrage. "Dr. Gable, I know it's very late, and you must be tired, but just a few more questions, and I'll have enough for my piece." She gave him a practiced, winning smile. "Okay?"

"Depends," Rob replied warily. "Ask your few questions, then don't argue if I give you a 'no comment,' and we'll see how it goes."

"That's fair, and I do thank you for your cooperation." Rob sighed. Wallace's mother had evidently taught her little girl that old saw about catching more flies with honey than vinegar. "First question . . . I understand that the two StarBridge students who were trapped in the airlock are still in the station hospital. What is the extent of their injuries?"

"They weren't hurt, thank God," Rob said, glad to find a question he didn't have to pussyfoot around. "They're just being held for observation, and will be released soon. They're fine."

"That's wonderful," she said, though Rob would have bet a steak dinner that she'd have been happier if both Hing and Serge had been gorily dismembered. Rob had a less-than-sanguine view of the press, with good reason. He'd been misquoted enough since he'd become famous to fill an encyclopedia file.

"Speaking of those same students, my sources tell me that their names are Hing Oun and Serge LaRoche. Is that true? Aren't they the same two students who staged a rather dramatic rescue of one of your instructors almost two weeks ago?"

"I would prefer not to reveal their names until I'm sure they've had a chance to speak with their relatives," Rob said. "That isn't the kind of information I feel free to talk about without clearing it with my students first."

"But it *was* Hing Oun and Serge LaRoche who rescued their Professor from that crevasse, wasn't it?" she persisted.

The psychologist could tell that she already knew the answer, and was just letting him know that she knew. Though they'd tried to keep the radonium-2 angle on low profile, the story of the rescue was fairly well known by now.

"Actually, there was a third member of the rescue team, a Simiu named Khuharkk'," Rob replied. "I assure you that we're very proud of all of them. Our students are smart, resourceful, and capable—and we train them how to handle emergencies effectively. You can quote me on that, Ms. Wallace."

Wallace wasn't interested in the hype—though she'd no doubt use the quote. Instead she pounced. "Serge LaRoche—isn't that the name of the child prodigy who had that tragic accident and lost his hands? This isn't the same one by any chance, is he?"

Dammit! Rob thought. It was obvious that Wallace knew exactly who Serge was. "Serge's life before he came to the Academy is his own business, Ms. Wallace," he snapped. "I have no comment to make."

Wallace had already covered Ssoriszs' plea to the CLS for emergency funds, and gotten Rob's official statement several times—but she couldn't resist just one more try. "Dr. Gable, if the Academy at StarBridge *were* to close its doors, what would you, personally, do?"

Rob gave her a sarcastic grin, though he knew she couldn't see him. "As I told you before, the Academy is *not* 'closing its doors.' If the day ever comes when I leave the Academy, I'll . . ." for a moment he had an insane desire to say "run for President of Earth—I sure as hell couldn't do worse than the current administration!" then watch her reaction, but he restrained himself with an effort.

"Hmmm, I think I'll . . ." Rob paused again, dramatically. Wallace leaned forward, ears pricked. "I'll . . . go fishing," Rob finished wickedly. "I haven't done that in years. There aren't any good trout pools in outer space, Ms. Wallace. Have you ever gone fishing? It's a great way to find inner peace."

Wallace knew the interview was over, and there was nothing more to be gained from needling him. "Thank you so much for speaking with me, Dr. Gable," she said coolly.

"My pleasure," Rob said, and managed to keep most of the sarcasm out of his voice.

After he'd cut the connection, he leaned back in his chair, stretching, trying to ease the kinks out of his back. Bast, who had long ago realized that her master wasn't going to pay attention to her today, was across the room, munching desultorily at a bowl of cat food.

"What a day," Rob told her. "I'd almost rather rescue trapped little hackers stuck in the AI than fend off reporters. Every time there's a disaster, they crawl out of the woodwork, like termites. Where do they all come from?" He knew that a couple of them worked out of the station, since it was a crossroads for so much interstellar traffic. Others had not come physically—they'd conducted their inquiries via holo-vid.

"It's too bad that Cara's still en route," Rob said, still talking to the cat. "If she'd been here today, I'd have drafted her to be my press secretary and let *her* deal with them. Fight fire with fire. What do you think?"

Bast merely blinked her green eyes at him and did not answer.

When Rob hadn't been talking to reporters today, he'd given Kkintha ch'aait a hand in handling all the calls from worried parents, assuring them that the school was in no danger, and that StarBridge Station, where the crash had occurred, was forty kilometers away. A few of the parents had asked about danger from the radonium-2. Rob had replied, truthfully, that they expected to hear from the engineering firm any day now that all of the radonium left on StarBridge was completely stable.

The psychologist frowned as he realized that during the past two hectic days Jeff hadn't called at all. He should have called by yesterday, at the latest. Could he have tried to reach the school during the time when Heather had been playing hob with the computer's innards? But everything was back to normal, now, and had been for over a day. Why hadn't Jeff called?

He wondered how Ssoriszs was holding up. The Mizari had been hard hit by the halfhearted (at best) support the school had received from the CLS, and even harder hit by Mikhail Andreiovitch's and Esteemed Rizzshor's deaths. And it didn't help—though it was definitely secondary in comparison to the loss of life—that StarBridge's new shuttle, the *Fys,* had been damaged beyond repair when the *Night Storm* exploded.

Rob leaned his head back in his chair, closing his gritty eyes, promising himself that he'd get up and go back to his quarters and go to bed in just a minute . . . just a few seconds more . . .

His intercom signaled, so loud in the sleeping quietness of the school that Rob sat up with a jerk, banging his elbow against the edge of his desk. "Who the hell can that be?" he wondered, tempted to let the night staff deal with it, whatever it was. He'd put in his eighteen hours today—he deserved a rest.

Then the holo-vid tank lit up, and Rob realized that someone had overridden the lockout on his private line. It was either Janet, or . . . he watched unsurprised as Jeff Morrow's image formed.

"Jeff," he greeted his friend, his eyes narrowing in concern as he took in Morrow's bloodshot eyes, disheveled clothing, and oily, uncombed hair. "Are you okay?"

Morrow gave him a wavery grin. "Sure I am," he said, and Rob knew immediately that the engineer was drunk. He wasn't to the word-slurring stage, but he was way, way past "lit" or "mellow."

"So how're you doing, Doc?" Jeff asked, seeming not to notice Rob's scrutiny.

"Tired, but I'm managing okay," Rob said neutrally. "Uh, Jeff, do you have any idea what time it is?"

Morrow gave him an owlish stare, then grinned. "Why, it's nighttime, Rob. It's *always* night out here, you know that!"

"It's past midnight, Jeff, way past midnight. Are you having trouble sleeping again?"

The engineer laughed harshly. "Sleep? What's that?"

"Where are you?" Rob tried to see past Morrow's image to his surroundings, but the younger man was sitting too close to his pickup. "Are you up at the station? Or out at the site?"

"I'm at the site," Morrow replied.

"How is the work going?"

Jeff blinked. "What work?"

Rob restrained himself from rolling his eyes. *Be patient, Gable,* he admonished himself. "The survey," he said. "You were supposed to give us the results of the whole-asteroid survey the day before yesterday at the latest."

"That's right, I was," Jeff said, and smacked the heel of his palm against his temple. "*Bad* engineer! Bad!" He grinned amiably at Rob. "You're my favorite person in the universe, you know?" he said with a drunk's unrestrained, sloppy affection. "I wish you were my dad," he mumbled, looking down. "I hate Mike, Rob, you know?"

"I know," Rob said evenly. "Jeff, why don't you get something to eat . . . like a sandwich or something, and drink a big glass of orange juice, then get some sleep? You can call me in the morning."

"There is no morning here, Rob," Morrow said earnestly. "And no morning anywhere else, I've been thinking lately. Maybe mornings are just an illusion that's supposed to happen someday, but they never come. Doesn't it seem like that to you sometimes?"

"Yes," Rob replied honestly. "But, Jeff, listen, you really need some food, some potassium, and some sleep, in that order."

"But the survey," the engineer said. "Gotta tell you what we've found."

"You can tell me tomorrow, when we're both more awake," Rob said reasonably, hoping the logic of this would reach through into Morrow's alcohol-fogged brain.

"Meeting . . ." Jeff mumbled, as if it were a word in an alien language. "Meeting!" he repeated triumphantly. "That's why I called! 'Schedule meeting,' it says here on my list. Gotta finish my list before I can go to bed."

"Okay, then, as long as you promise to do just that," Rob said, quickly calling up his, Kkintha's, and Ssoriszs' schedules on his terminal. "Hmmm . . . how about sixteen hundred tomorrow, here at the school, since you're down here on the asteroid."

"That's fine," Jeff said. Rob watched him squint at the computer as he laboriously keyed in the information, and wondered whether Jeff would remember this conversation tomorrow, and whether he was indeed entering the time and place for their meeting correctly. He decided to call Morrow back around noon tomorrow to make sure it was still on, plus verify time and location. *He ought to have taken something for the hangover he's bound to have by then,* Rob thought cynically.

"Okay!" Jeff exclaimed a moment later. "We're all set!"

"Good," Rob said. "Thanks for calling. I'll see you tomorrow." He stared intently at the inebriated engineer. "Jeff, you *are* going to go to bed, aren't you?"

"Maybe," Morrow said coyly. "Depends . . ."

"On what?"

"If that bitch Angela will just leave me alone."

Rob stared at him, nonplussed. "Angela's with you?" he asked finally.

"The bitch is always with me. Nagging me all the time, thinking she owns me, making demands. She wants too much, Rob!"

"People have a way of doing that," the psychologist agreed sadly. "I'm afraid it's part of the human condition."

"Yeah, well . . ." Jeff obviously hadn't followed this last. He yawned suddenly, showing a mouthful of even white teeth.

Rob nodded approvingly. "Good! You're tired, you'll sleep like a baby. Good night, Jeff."

" 'Night, Doc."

After he'd terminated the connection Rob sat in silence, head bowed, now fully awake. He didn't like the way Jeff had looked. During his worst depression over not making the grade here at StarBridge, he'd never looked *this* bad. On the other hand, he reminded himself, he'd never seen Jeff really loaded before. Liquor did bad things to nice people, as he had good cause to know.

What the hell had gone on between Jeff and Angela for him to talk about her so nastily? Of course, he didn't really know her, had only met her in the flesh one time, when she'd been accompanying Jeff on a business trip and they'd come through StarBridge Station for a quick stopover, but she'd seemed a pleasant, earnest young woman, someone who had genuine caring for her new husband.

He's not your patient anymore, Rob reminded himself. *Anyone can have a momentary lapse, especially when he or she is really soused.*

But he couldn't get the incident out of his mind. *I wonder whether Jeff was drinking because of Andreiovitch's death,* he thought. *He obviously had a lot of respect for the man's reputation. Maybe he was counting on him to help solve the radonium problem here.*

As he stood up, he felt the room lurch around him, and realized that he had eaten almost nothing all day. "Time to call it a day, Bast," he said, snapping his fingers at her. Obediently, she came over to him, and he picked her up, then tucked her in the crook of his arm.

"Come on, girl. Let's go home."

The next morning, Esteemed Ssoriszs faced another holo-vid transmission of a CLS official, but this time he knew he was talking to a friend and staunch supporter, so he was relaxed instead of nervous.

"Yes, the news of the vote just reached me," Mahree Burroughs said with a sigh that was audible even across the parsecs. "I'm awfully sorry, Esteemed One. If only I had been there for that session . . ."

But the CLS Ambassador-at-Large was currently on a fact-finding and goodwill mission to Errhoun, the Heeyoon world that had suffered so badly during its past winter. Now, with the spring rains, had come floods and a new, virulent strain of illness to threaten the beleaguered planet. Mahree was there to see whether CLS emergency support was indicated—and she'd told Ssoriszs that it definitely was.

The elderly Mizari hissed softly, making a brushing-way gesture with his appendages. "How could you possibly have known this was in the offing, Mahree? Our legends of the Lost Colony tell us that they had seers, who could see the future—or futures—but neither of us is such, yes?"

Mahree smiled ruefully as she sat in the emergency hospital's bubbletent, with stacks of provisions and medical supplies behind her. She was not really a pretty woman, as humans defined ideal female beauty (a notion Ssoriszs found almost incomprehensible), her features were too severe, but her dark eyes were bright and vivacious, and the freckles across the bridge of her nose softened her, making her face one that was hard to forget.

"You're right," she admitted. "I keep having to be reminded by people these days that the weight of the whole universe isn't something I'm expected to shoulder just automatically. Shirazz tells me that I have an overactive conscience that *almost* equals my overhealthy ego!"

" 'To be a leader means that one must glide straight while others circle and backtrack, even if the path traveled leads to perdition,' " Ssoriszs quoted an ancient aphorism of his people.

Mahree laughed ruefully. "We say, 'The road to Hell is paved with good intentions,' and 'Pride goeth before a fall, and a haughty spirit before disaster,' or some such. Someone should write a book on how many ancient proverbs from different worlds tend to say much the same thing."

"Perhaps it will be a StarBridge graduate, who is also a writer," Ssoriszs said, a glint of humor in his golden eyes. "That journalist who is returning to us—Cara Hendricks—comes to mind."

"I just hope there will be a StarBridge Academy for her to come to," Mahree said, her expression sobering. "*And* a StarBridge Station for her ship to dock at! Do they have any idea, Esteemed One, of how that terrible accident happened?"

Ssoriszs' appendages drooped forlornly. "They are checking," he said. "There have been rumors that it was sabotage. Rizzshor . . . Andreiovitch . . . we are all in mourning for them. May the Stars shine forever upon their Spirits, and guide them to peace and the Oneness."

Mahree's eyes widened. "Sabotage! That's terrible! Who would do that? And *why*?"

The elderly Mizari thought of Heather, then decided it would take too long to explain the entire thing. Doctor Blanket, whom the Liaison respected greatly, stoutly maintained that Heather was innocent, as did Rob. But the child's power was so new, so frightening, that Ssoriszs didn't know what to think. It all sounded extremely dangerous to him—and to Janet, whom he'd spoken to yesterday.

"We do not know," the alien said sadly. "It makes no rational sense."

"Have there been any more incidents?"

"No. This appears to be an isolated instance."

"But *why*?" she wondered again, catching the tail end of the thick brown braid she wore over her shoulder and twirling it slowly. "If Andreiovitch and Rizzshor had been political figures, or something, I can see it. But . . . a mining engineer and physicist and an archaeologist?" Mahree frowned. "To quote another old saying, 'There's something rotten in Denmark,' Esteemed One."

"Where is Denmark?" the Mizari asked. "And why are things prone to spoilage there?"

Mahree looked up, poised to explain, then saw that the Liaison was teasing her. "Don't kid me, Rob told me about that time you two went to Copenhagen," she said accusingly. "And I know you've read Shakespeare."

"I have," Ssoriszs admitted. "He has a voice in his writing that reads almost like music sounds."

"I'm sure he'd be pleased to hear you say that." She smiled at the Liaison, then sobered. "Tell me, Esteemed One . . ."

"Yes?"

"How is Rob taking all of this?"

"I do not know. I have been so . . . unsettled in my own thoughts, I have had little energy to worry about another's," the Mizari admitted ruefully. "But Janet Rodriguez seemed to find it disturbing that Rob was watching *It's a Wonderful Life* the other day, and eating some comestible called fudge-marble cheesecake."

Mahree stared at the Liaison in dismay. "*It's a Wonderful Life*? In *July*? Oh, dear! And he only eats fudge-marble cheesecake when he's feeling lower than a sna—" she bit her lip, stopped herself, finished, "lower than low! Poor Rob!"

"This is a disturbing sign?"

She nodded. "It makes me want to climb on the next shuttle and come out there."

"Right now, we need a radonium expert, not another diplomat," Ssoriszs said practically. "Still, I am sure that you will be able to help out some way when you return to Shassiszss."

"I'll do my best, of course," she said absently.

"If you see my grandson, Zarshezz," the Liaison began, then he hesitated.

"Yes?" Mahree prodded.

"Tell him—tell him I am sorry that I have not been able to speak with him, but that I have so little energy and free time during this crisis, I must guard them jealously. Tell him I wish very much to speak with him, but not until this is over. Whatever the outcome may be."

Mahree stared at the old alien, obviously looking for shades of meaning in his message, then she nodded. "Certainly I'll tell him, Esteemed One. The next time I see him."

The Mizari bowed. "Many thanks, Esteemed Mahree."

She bowed back, hands tented above her head. "You are welcome, Esteemed Ssoriszs. Farewell . . . until we meet again."

"May it be soon," said the Mizari, giving the next phrase in the formal words of parting.

"Yes, may it be soon," she echoed solemnly.

"But, Mr. LaRoche, Ms. Oun, just one more question!" squawked Joan Wallace as Serge and Hing turned away from her and keyed open the door to Docking Bay Nineteen. "How does it make you feel to know that your ordeal was caused by an unknown saboteur?"

Serge maintained the stony silence and expression he'd assumed the moment that Wallace had asked him whether the repairs to his hands would allow him to play the piano again.

But Hing turned back to the woman. "Why don't you take a good guess?" she said viciously. Serge had never seen her so angry—her eyes flashed, and they were the color and hardness of onyx. "You don't really care what we think, or how we feel, you've made that disgustingly obvious. So just send your article in with what you wish we'd say, and we'll both be happy—you because you got your stupid article, and me because I don't have to say another word to you!"

With that, Hing turned her back on the reporter, and flounced— no other word applied—through the door and down the docking tube. Serge followed her, fighting back a reluctant smile as he noted that Wallace hadn't followed. Score—Hing Oun ten, Wallace zero.

"It feels funny to walk down one of these again," Hing said, glancing around the docking tube as Serge caught up with her. "I'm glad this one isn't transparent. I wonder if I'll ever get a kick out of the clear ones again."

"Of course you will," Serge assured her.

Moments later they boarded the small borrowed shuttle that the station had loaned the school until—and if—the *Fys* was replaced. Serge spent a few minutes familiarizing himself with the controls, then eased the little vessel—known only as 15SS—out of its cradle. "I shall have to practice my manual dockings," he murmured to Hing, who was sitting in the copilot's seat.

"I heard one of the med techs this morning say that the guidance beams had been certified for use again," Hing said. "But if you want to dock manually from now on, be my guest. I'll never cuss at Janet Rodriguez again."

The past two days since their ordeal in the airlock had been restful for Hing, stressful for Serge as the Mizari healer had worked on his hands, restoring the microcircuitry that had frozen, causing the artificial neural connections to lock up. But now they were completely back to normal, and he was infinitely relieved. As many times as he'd stared at his hands and hated them, Serge now knew that he never wanted to be without them again. *That* was to be truly crippled! He hadn't been able to feed himself, or even visit the bathroom, without someone to help him.

"That was a low blow, asking about your hands," Hing said quietly as the little ship swooped toward the Academy.

Serge, who had just finished verifying his flight plan with Traffic Control, glanced at her. "Reporters are frequently tactless," he said philosophically. "I fear it comes with the job."

"Yeah, but to hear her mention it, after we spent time yesterday really *talking* about it, for the first time . . . well, it made me mad. Somehow it cheapens what we said, what it meant . . ."

"No, it does not," Serge said firmly. "I was being honest when I told you that I felt more comfortable talking to you about music, and the piano, and my hands, than I ever have talking to anyone else—even Rob Gable."

She gave him a sidelong look. "Then, will you do me a favor, Serge?"

"Certainly," he said, knowing that whatever it was, he'd do it. He'd never been able to be that open, that trusting, with anyone before.

"Watch the holo-vid of some of your performances with me, so I can tell you to your face how much your music, your playing has meant to me!" she pleaded, eyes shining. "I never confessed this before . . . I feel silly saying it, really, but . . ."

"Yes?" he prompted when she hesitated, gnawing at her lower lip.

"I was an admirer of yours before I knew you," she admitted in a rush. "I guess you would say . . . a fan. I never told you, but I'd seen all your performances, and the day I realized it was you, in person"—she grinned, the old impudent cheeky grin—"I just about keeled over in the middle of class. You remember that class we had together, Third Millennia Mizari Poetry?"

Serge began to laugh aloud. "Is that why you stared at me so fixedly?"

"Until I noticed that you'd noticed me staring, yeah."

"I thought you were staring at me because I did so badly on that translation! Esteemed Rissaz was right in saying she'd never heard anyone deliver those lines in quite that manner before. I thought that you thought I was a fool!"

Now they both laughed, companionably.

After a moment she sobered. "Will you do that for me?"

Serge hesitated, and her face fell. "Never mind, I don't want to—"

"It is not that," he assured her. "It is simply that I have been planning a surprise for you. Shall we meet for dinner at the Spiral Arm, and then I will show it to you?" He gave her a hopeful smile. "And after seeing it, if you still wish to view my old performances, we will do that. Okay?"

"It's a deal," she said.

They spent the minutes until docking chatting about Heather, whom they planned to visit in the infirmary as soon as they reached StarBridge. Rob had explained a little of what had happened to the young telepath to them while they were in the hospital.

"Then, tomorrow, first thing," Serge said, "I must go see Professor Greyshine. He was released the day of the crash, but has been recuperating in his quarters."

"I'd like to see him, too," Hing said.

"I am sure he would wish to thank you personally for your courage in rescuing him," Serge said, then he smiled. "Actually, Professor Greyshine is quite taken with you. He never left off telling me that you are the perfect mate for me!"

Hing's mouth dropped open. "He *didn't*!"

Solemnly, Serge nodded, his eyes dancing.

"Why that old yenta!" She began to giggle, and covered her mouth with her hand automatically, a habit developed early by anyone who studied the Simiu and their language.

After Serge had docked the little vessel, the two young people visited Heather in the infirmary. Serge was shocked and worried at her pallor, but the child insisted she was all right as she sat up in bed in her darkened room, with Doctor Blanket glowing beside her. "Seloz is teaching me how to be a responsible telepath," she announced proudly to Serge. "So that I'll never again be tempted to do anything as rude as what I did to you. I'm really sorry about that!" she said softly, earnestly.

Serge smiled at her reassuringly. "I was the one who lost my temper," he said. "It is I who should apologize." Taking the stubby little fingers in his, he gave her his most courtly bow, then kissed her hand with more genuine affection and respect than he'd ever exhibited to any crowned head.

Heather flushed scarlet, so pleased that she was speechless—for once.

After leaving the infirmary, the two split up, promising to meet again at the Spiral Arm in a couple of hours.

Dinner consisted of sandwiches and french fries, with tall glasses of an exotic Drnian fruit punch. Serge raised his glass to Hing formally, then looked at it, smiling ruefully. "We should have champagne for a proper toast."

"This will do," she assured him. "Remember, Drnians can get lit off it, that ought to make it acceptable."

"Very well." Solemnly, Serge raised his glass, and Hing raised hers. "To the most pleasant life-threatening experience anyone in any of the Fifteen Known Worlds has ever had," he said, and sipped the tart, cooling beverage.

"Hear, hear," Hing said, grinning, and drank with him.

Thirty minutes later she nibbled on a french fry, then put it down. "I can't. If you don't show me your surprise, I'm going to burst with curiosity!"

Serge stood, then helped her out of her seat as though they'd been in a fine restaurant instead of the students' hangout. "Very well, then. Come along."

"Where?"

He held out his hand to her. "I told you, it is a surprise. Close your eyes," he directed as she took his hand.

"Oh, come on!"

"Please," he said, and Hing immediately obeyed, charmed in spite of herself.

Silently, Serge led her along the halls, into the elevator, then along another series of corridors, while she followed obediently, a bemused smile on her face.

Finally, they reached their destination—one of the practice rooms in the Music Department. Serge keyed the door open, led Hing inside, then locked the portal behind them. He was nervous enough doing this without worrying about anyone inadvertently disturbing them to ask directions or some such.

"Can I open my eyes yet?" Hing said, standing by the doorway.

"Soon," he promised, and led her over to the couch and seated her. He could see her sniffing the air, listening, trying to figure out where the devil she was, and he smiled. She'd *never* guess!

Then he went over to the grand piano that sat waiting for him in the center of the room and gingerly seated himself behind it, flexed his hands over the keys, not quite touching them. Serge was struck by the beauty of the instrument, and his heart felt an echo of the old thrill, the old passion as he looked at the Steinway.

"Now?" Hing said, leaning forward impatiently, eyes squeezed shut as though she had to fight with herself not to open them.

"Yes, now," Serge told her, and as she opened her eyes, he ran his fingers over the keys. Just a simple scale, but his timing was abominable, dreadful—and he actually hit a wrong note!

"*Zut!*" he muttered, afraid to look up at Hing as he tried again. Much better . . . his timing was still not what it ought to be, but perhaps it wasn't too bad for someone who hadn't done this in more than five years. His fingers worked perfectly, of course . . . no muscles to cramp, or refuse to stretch properly.

After a few more scales had convinced him that he was rusty, but capable of doing what he'd set out to do, Serge segued into an actual composition, a tone-poem that had been running through his mind for nearly a year—a cheerful little piece that nevertheless had depth, passion, and color.

His anxiety vanished as he became lost in the sheer pleasure of actually *hearing* with his ears what had, up until now, only been in his mind. Never mind that it had been in his mind for months, this was the first time he'd played it—except for times when he'd found himself moving his fingers over an imaginary keyboard as the notes ran through his head.

This is beauty! he thought, feeling the passion, the love affair with music fill him with delight. He'd missed this so much, and he hadn't even realized it. There had been a void in his life, his heart, a void so large it could only be expressed in stellar terms.

Serge was nearly weeping with emotion as he finished the last notes, then sat silent, remembering Hing, afraid to look up. By her own admission, she'd seen him so many times in his heyday. Would she be disappointed? Surely she'd noticed every hesitation, every fault in the tempo. What would she say?

It took every bit of courage Serge possessed to look up at her, but her face was glowing, and her eyes shone. Tears trembled on her lashes. "Oh, Serge!" she whispered. "That was so beautiful! I don't recognize it. Did you write it? What is its name?"

Serge got up and went over to sit beside her, his eyes searching her face for any hint that she was merely being polite, not wanting to hurt his feelings. But no, she was genuinely moved. He smiled, then gently used one finger to wipe the tears away as two of them broke free. "It has no name . . . yet, Hing. But I wrote it, and I wrote it *for* you, and I wrote it *about* you. That melody is you, the way I see you, the way you live in my heart, Hing. I am glad you like it."

"Like it!" For a moment he thought she was going to burst into tears. "Oh, God, I love it. I can't believe that you wrote it for me!"

"I had no choice," he said with a wry smile. "The music is stubborn. It persists in living in my head, and reflecting what I see around me." Gently, he slid his arms around her, then kissed her cheek. "When I kiss you, I hear music, Hing. That is an old cliché, I know, but for me it is literally true."

She turned her head so their lips met, and then Serge lost himself again, kissing her more and more deeply, feeling his head spin at her eager response. Resolutely, he kept his hands on her back, did not kiss her throat, or the skin below it, though he longed to. He had promised not to push, and he would keep his word . . . if he could. Even confining himself to kissing, he was rapidly getting in too deep to extricate himself easily.

Finally he pulled back, his heart slamming, feeling half-drunk with the sweetness of her mouth, the feel of her unbound hair as it cascaded over her shoulders. "We had better stop," he muttered roughly, holding himself back from her with an effort that was painful. "We promised to wait . . ."

Hing opened her eyes, searching his face, then she ran her fingers through his hair, then trailed them down to his open collar. With excruciating slowness, she unsealed the first fifteen centimeters of his jumpsuit. "So we did," she breathed, stroking his collarbones, then his chest. "But do you really *want* to wait?"

"No!" Serge blurted, startled into the truth. "I want to make love to you . . . passionately, for a long, long time!" He caught his breath with an effort. "That should be obvious," he added, with a weak grin. He was literally shaking with the effect her trailing finger had on him. "We had better go," he said unevenly, and began drawing away.

"No," Hing said, then slowly, deliberately, she unsealed her tunic, and, catching one of his hands, placed it on her breast, sliding it against her so he could feel her warmth with his real flesh. "Now we're even," she said, smiling.

"But—but—" Serge stammered, so aroused that even speaking was an effort, "but—"

"Serge," Hing said, grasping the front of his jumpsuit in both hands, "sometimes you're too honorable for your own good! At times like these, promises are made to be broken." Slowly, deliberately, she leaned back, pulling him over on top of her.

As the moments passed, Serge heard their passion as music, building toward a thunderous crescendo, and it shook him as nothing ever had. "I love you," he gasped, his face pressed into her hair, his body trembling as he had trembled in the airlock—except that these were shivers of pure pleasure. "*Je t'aime, chérie . . .* "

He'd never said it before, but it was the truest thing in the universe.

"I love you, too," Hing whispered, so softly that he could only hear it because her mouth was so close to his ear. "I do, Serge. Always . . . always . . ."

She'd never said it before, either.

It was fortunate, Serge thought later—much, much later—*that I decided to lock that door.*

CHAPTER 13

◆

Borrowed Time

Serge strode up the corridor toward Professor Greyshine's living quarters the next morning, smiling. He had to keep reminding himself not to grin *too* broadly, and several times he caught himself whistling, then glanced around guiltily to see whether anyone was watching. At one point, he looked down at his feet, half seriously thinking that someone must have lowered the school's gravity. But no, his feet *were* hitting the surface. He hadn't been sure.

Last night had been . . . he caught himself grinning ecstatically, and shook his head. Words failed him. Last night had been too good for words. After they'd unlocked the practice room door and tiptoed out, he and Hing had separated and gone different ways . . . for about five minutes, long enough for her to go back to her room and pick up her toothbrush and her Apis silk dressing gown.

Then they had spent the night in his quarters, talking, laughing, making love . . . and, finally, sleeping. Waking up to find Hing beside him might have been the most wonderful moment of all . . .

Thinking about what Professor Greyshine would say, how he would carry on if he knew, made Serge sternly compose his expression as he signaled the Professor's door. "It's Serge," he said at the Heeyoon's inquiring yip, and the door slid open.

"Serge, Serge!" The Professor was lying on his sleeping pallet, but his computer was on and he'd evidently been up and working. "I am so pleased to see you, lad!" Moving rather stiffly, the Professor began to rise.

"Please, don't get up," Serge said, and came forward to sit down on the pallet beside the Heeyoon. The room was furnished in typical Heeyoon fashion—pallets for sleeping and relaxing, thick, luxuriant carpets, with exotic wall hangings and suspended lamps. "So much has happened since I last saw you! How are you feeling?"

"Still stiff, and somewhat sore, but my injuries are essentially mended. You, Hing, and Khuharkk'—" The Professor waved a clawed paw-hand. "Your courage is beyond measure. I want you to know that my mate, Strongheart, has nominated all three of you to receive my planet's Medal of Honor for your bravery."

If Serge hadn't been sitting down, he would have shuffled his feet. He was so touched, so honored that all he could do was mumble, "Thank you, but really . . . Hing was the one who really did it."

"*All* of you did it," Greyshine said firmly.

They chatted for a few more minutes, comparing notes on what had been happening. Serge told the Professor about retrieving the artifacts, then Greyshine had to hear the entire saga of the airlock, and how the two humans had managed to survive. When Serge had finished telling him about it, the Professor, who had been eyeing him speculatively, said, "Again, such bravery! Frequently, shared danger is a way for a couple to become closer, lad . . . or have you already noticed that?"

Serge couldn't help it; he blushed furiously. The Professor's teeth flashed in a wide lupine grin as he noted the human's reaction, but he courteously changed the subject.

"I also hear that you have been barred from the site. Have you any idea what has happened to the star-shrine?"

The human shook his head, sobering. "None," he said. "Jeff Morrow promised me that I would be allowed to retrieve it as soon as he finishes his complete survey of all the radonium veins on the asteroid. But I have called his office several times, both from here and while I was in the hospital, and his assistant said that he was out, working with the surveying crew. I have not heard from him yet."

"I spoke to Esteemed Ssoriszs this morning, and he told me that there is a meeting scheduled for this afternoon, during which Morrow and this other person, Andrea Lynch, will be reporting on the results of the survey."

"In that case, I'll call him as soon as I know the meeting is over," Serge said eagerly. He frowned. "Andrea Lynch . . ." he muttered. "She's the one that turned me away from the site. There's something *wrong* about her, and it's more than just being curt and nasty. I'm sure she's hiding something!"

"What could she be hiding?"

"When Ssoriszs and I went out to the site to get the artifacts, she said something . . . odd. Something I do not understand, but I feel that somehow it is important."

"What did she say?"

"As I was strapping the tools on the sled, after I had loaded the artifacts in the compartment with the Esteemed Liaison, I accidentally dropped the moisture finder and did not notice. Andrea Lynch picked it up and handed it to me, saying, 'Here, don't forget your *dowser.*'" Serge used the English word. "What could she have meant by that, calling it a *dowser?*"

The Professor growled softly. "Serge, I do not like this one bit! Since you have worked with me, we normally speak my language— partly so you can practice, and partly because I am lazy—so I have taught you the Heeyoon technical terms—as well as our slang names—for the archaeological equipment we use." Greyshine growled again. "But, Serge . . . I have attended many interplanet archaeological seminars, and I recognize this word *dowser* as it applies to the moisture finder. That is the slang nickname given to the moisture finder *by human archaeologists!*"

Serge reached the obvious conclusion in a heartbeat. "Then Lynch has had some experience with archaeologists, or is even an archaeologist herself!"

"I do not see how she could have learned such an esoteric nickname unless she had been more than casually exposed to archaeological terms," Greyshine said. "As to whether she is an archaeologist . . ."

"I wager that she is! I'd wager an entire cavernful of star-shrines that Lynch is only posing as an engineer!"

"But *why?*"

Serge couldn't sit still any longer. Leaping to his feet, he began pacing, gesturing wildly. "So she can steal the star-shrine, obviously! Jeff Morrow hired her as a crew boss, but stealing our star-shrine was her aim all along! *Our* star-shrine!" He stopped, struck, and scratched his head as he thought. "But how did she know it was there?"

"Perhaps one of the workers discovered it six months ago during the radonium check, and recognized its value—but could not steal it because he or she was too closely watched while the radonium monitoring was under way." The Professor, too, was off and running now. "But then this unknown accomplice contacted Lynch, since he knew that she had the knowledge to safely remove the shrine, as well as the contacts to sell it on the black market!"

"And so she signed on with Morrow, knowing that, by the end of the year, it would be time to monitor the radonium deposits again. And then she would be in the perfect place to direct the monitoring, and steal the star-shrine!" Serge snapped his fingers. "Except that this mess with the radonium-2 came up and delayed her plans. No wonder she is so ill-mannered—her plans have been compromised. It all fits!"

"But how could the woman have the technical knowledge to pose as an engineer?" the Professor wondered.

"You were the one who told me that many archaeologists have undergradate or double degrees in other subjects," Serge replied. "Lynch could have a degree in geology, for example. Or she may have gained her experience working with a mining crew. As you know only too well, Professor, archaeologists do not make salaries commensurate with their education levels."

"Sadly, you are correct. But remember, Serge, all we have are suspicions—and we *could* be wrong. We can accuse no one without proof of wrongdoing!"

"I need to speak to Jeff Morrow—get him to give me permission to see that star-shrine today, or tomorrow at the latest!" Serge said, his eyes flashing with excitement as he planned. "If I cannot reach him, I suppose I will have to go out there secretly and see whether the star-shrine is still there. If it *is* still there, I will stand over it until it is safe to bring back here. If it is already gone . . ." he hesitated.

"Discovering a theft so early will give us a greatly improved chance at recovery," the Professor told him. "After all, 'The colder the trail, the less chance of tasting fresh meat.' " The Heeyoon thought for a moment. "But, Serge . . . how will you get into the caverns? You told me that they had changed the access code to our airlock."

Serge smiled smugly. "They did, but unless they changed it again, I memorized Lynch's code when she used it."

"Clever lad!" the Heeyoon yipped, panting slightly with excitement. "In that case, as your so-fascinating human author Arthur Conan Doyle's hero, Sherlock Holmes, would put it, the game is most definitely afoot!"

As soon as the doctors released her from the infirmary, Heather headed straight for the Simiu section of StarBridge, her chubby features set in a look of determination that made her, had she known it, greatly resemble her mother.

When she reached the Simiu section, the girl stood in the corridor for a long time, hovering, screwing up her courage.

Ha! What courage? her inner voice taunted.

She rubbed her pale, freckled forehead. *Go away,* she told the voices, especially her survivor-self. *I don't need you anymore. I can think for myself, now.* But it was hard, ignoring the voices, in some ways as hard as it was to ignore the thoughts of others.

But she was determined to succeed; after all, it was the impulsive, mean parts of her that had gotten her into trouble, nearly gotten her killed. Dr. Rob promised that if she worked with him, *really* worked with him, he'd teach her ways to control those parts. Make sure *she* was running things, not them. Make sure nothing like what had happened to her in the AI would ever happen again. She shivered, remembering.

Shutting her eyes, she reached out, searched for Doctor Blanket.

<I'm here,> the telepath responded, and she relaxed and smiled. Mom hadn't lied. There *were* guardian angels.

She'd never known another telepath as powerful as herself, never mind as powerful as the Avernian. But seloz didn't use that power against her, didn't try to beat her into submission with it, though seloz could have—with barely a thought, seloz could have reduced any being on StarBridge to a quivering mass, and Heather knew that now. But instead seloz was kind, gentle, and wanted to help others. Just like a real guardian angel.

And during the past couple of days, seloz had worked hard, showing Heather a better way to handle her skills constructively instead of to hurt, or steal. Along with Rob, seloz was teaching her how to handle her powerful talent in ways that wouldn't get her into trouble. Between the two of them, they were threatening to turn her into a respectable human being. *A regular correctoid,* she thought wryly.

Which was why she was standing here, before this door, in the Simiu living section. There was this loose end she had to tie up, and she didn't feel that she could concentrate on anything else until she took care of it.

Heather swallowed, reached a hand out to ring the buzzer, then jerked it back. *This ain't gonna work,* she thought to herself. *I'm not ready.*

Damn right you're not, said her survivor-self. *You'll never be ready to do something so stupid as this, I hope! What the hell is wrong with you? Make tracks in the other direction!*

The girl didn't move. *Doctor Blanket?* she thought.

<I'm here,> the gentle reassurance came again, steady, loving, full of strength.

She nodded. Suddenly three male Simiu came loping up the hallway, barking and coughing at each other in their own language. They looked so much like a pride of lions charging her, Heather felt her knees go weak.

<I'm here,> Blanket whispered gently in her mind.

She stood her ground, as they ran on by, manes bristling, teeth flashing, never pausing in their conversation. Each nodded at her out of courtesy, flashed a hand signal to excuse themselves as they brushed by.

Remembering what Hing had taught her, Heather kept her eyes to the ground as she exchanged the nod and returned their signal. Then they were gone. They'd treated her like anyone else. They didn't know her. They had no argument with her. She thought of their bristling manes, their huge teeth, then she looked at the door again, and her legs trembled, wanting to run.

<I'm here.>

Raising her hand, Heather touched the door signal lightly. Without hesitation, the portal slid open, startling her. She found herself almost face-to-face with Khuharkk', and hastily lowered her eyes.

Timidly, she attempted the Simiu greeting gesture that Hing had taught her this morning, touching her mouth, eyes, then chest, then extending her curled hand. It had taken her many tries to get it right, so it flowed, but now she did it almost as well as in this morning's rehearsal with Hing.

When Heather had called her, the Cambodian student had been glad to stop by the infirmary and spend some time with her, before heading to her next class and then to the inevitable play rehearsal. Hing was another one who wanted her to succeed, Heather knew. With all these people pulling for her, she felt as though they made a safety net that would catch her if she fell, like the trapeze artists she'd seen once.

It was good to have friends.

After a moment of silent regard, the Simiu slowly returned her greeting gesture, then the ball was back in Heather's court.

"Greetings, Honored Khuharkk'," she said awkwardly, her throat protesting against the Simiu syllables that Hing had so painstakingly taught her, writing them down phonetically when Heather had told her what she wanted to say. "I have something I wish to discuss with you, if you will do me the honor."

She stopped, breathing hard, her throat muscles protesting and her mouth full of spit from the strain of speaking even those few words. Heather knew her pronunciation hadn't been perfect, but she thought that the other student had understood her.

Silence. Heather's heart pounded with anxiety—and she felt her temper rising. *He's doing this on purpose. To make me uncomfortable. To make sure I realize who's got the upper hand. Whose territory we're on.* Anger warred with embarrassment.

<I'm here.>

Heather swallowed, and waited.

After a few more seconds Khuharkk' stepped aside, waving her through the door. "Enter," he growled in Mizari (to Heather's vast relief). "By all means, enter my home."

When she'd discussed her plans with Hing, the older student had given her a rundown of possible responses to her request, and thus Heather recognized this one. It was a standard civil greeting, indicating his ownership of the territory, but that, for the moment, it should be considered neutral space. It was as good a start as she could've hoped.

She came inside, was immediately struck by the humid warmth, the heaviness, the spicy-musky Simiu scent.

"May I offer you some refreshment? A drink, perhaps," he offered graciously. He was being the perfect host, since his people rarely considered food consumption part of socializing, however, he knew that humans did. "Would you like me to change the environment for your comfort?"

"The environment is fine," she assured him, her throat constricting, "but something cool to drink would be wonderful."

He went immediately, bringing her back a short, squat glass filled with a clear liquid, ice, and herbs. She was startled to find it tasted just like lemonade. Perfect lemonade.

"Is it acceptable?" he asked, his voice carefully neutral. "Dr. Rob introduced me to it. It's become my favorite beverage."

"Perfect. Wonderful," she admitted honestly, taking a bigger gulp. The tart flavor seemed to open her throat.

"There is something you wish to discuss," he asked politely.

She put down the glass. "Yes. Honored Hing Oun has tutored me in your customs and traditions, but my knowledge is far from perfect, so I ask pardon in advance if I err, and I humbly request your patience."

He nodded graciously.

She took another sip of the lemonade and plunged ahead. "Honored Khuharkk', we met under the worst conditions. I was rude and ignorant . . . I dishonored you in front of others, and was too stupid to understand what I'd done. In my immaturity and ignorance, I blamed *you* for what happened and vowed vengeance against you. It was childish, and wrong."

The Simiu's glance was half-patronizing, half-suspicious. "Vengeance is best left to adults. How could a child like *you,* weak and toothless, hope to challenge and vanquish *me*?"

Heather focused her eyes on a tiny spot on the floor. "I didn't just hope," she whispered. "I did it. I wanted," she was stammering now, as she tried to make her mouth form the Mizari words, "I thought that . . . that is . . . I *did* . . . cause the . . . the malfunction . . . of your toilet! I'm sorry!" A shudder of real fear passed through her body.

He didn't move for a moment, then to her surprise she saw a twinkle of amusement in the violet eyes. "*You,* little one?" He gave the barking Simiu version of a laugh. "Small one, you have an excellent imagination! You may have *wished* that such a disgusting disaster befall me, but—"

"No," she blurted, knowing it was rude to interrupt him, but afraid that she'd lose her nerve altogether, give in, let him think what he wanted. "I *did* do it. I . . . can telepathically link with the computer . . . I changed a few things in the environmental system. I did it."

There was a long, uncomfortable silence, but Heather realized Khuharkk' was still just trying to believe her. *Believe it, hairball!* one part of her mind whispered, but she pushed her irritation down, controlling her feelings. *Doctor Blanket says I'm the only one that gets to tell me how I should feel,* she thought defiantly.

"Why the toilet?" Khuharkk' said finally. "Not that I necessarily believe you, but . . . why that way?"

"Because," Heather said, nakedly honest, "when you roared at me, I was so scared that I had . . . an accident. I wet myself," she amplified, seeing that he did not comprehend at first. "I was ashamed, and I wanted to make you feel the same way." She took a deep breath, "So I linked my mind with the computer, and I told the environmental system to make your toilet go backward."

"Who else have you admitted this to?" he asked finally, and Heather knew then that he now believed her.

"Dr. Rob. Janet Rodriguez." She wondered if that woman would ever trust her after all this. In some ways, that relationship would be harder to mend than this one.

"And they made you come to me, to apologize?"

She shook her head, then remembered to say, "No. I came on my own. They don't even know that I'm here."

"Who does know?" he asked quietly.

She didn't want to admit that Doctor Blanket was only a thought away, so she said, "No one. No one knows I'm here."

Slowly, he advanced on her, but she stood her ground. "You come here, alone, to my quarters. You invade my home. To gloat again over my humiliation. *You* have done this terrible thing to me, this degradation I will never forget! You, you tiny, insignificant, little human!"

"No!" she whispered, not looking at him, her face paling, her blood chilling in her veins. "Not to gloat. To ask for forgiveness. I know you probably *can't* forgive me, after what I did, but if your honor would be helped by it, I offer to do whatever you demand in the way of restitution. For your honor. Whatever it is, I'll do it." Her voice was quavering, choking on the syllables, and even her command of Mizari was faltering.

"Why should *I* allow *you* restitution?" the Simiu barked, making her jump. "I could kill you now, like a parasite, and stuff you in the recycler. No one would ever know."

He advanced another step, his mane bristling menacingly, but Heather suddenly felt a soothing calm settle over her. She met his eyes for the first time. "You would never do that, Honored Khuharkk'. Rob has told me about you. So has Hing. She told me how courageous you were in the face of danger, the honor you displayed during Greyshine's rescue. I know about your honor code. Only a completely honorless person would kill an ignorant, helpless child. I deserve the threat. But you would never dishonor yourself by such an action."

Khuharkk' looked stunned by her words, and eased back down on his haunches. "You have discussed me with Honored Healer Gable, and with Honored Hing Oun?"

"I needed to learn . . . about you . . . about your people . . ." Heather stammered. "To try and make up for what I'd done, I had to know . . ." She gulped air. "I'm sorry if I didn't say it right. I'm sorry if I made you mad, offering you restitution. But I had to try!"

"You have learned much, young one," he growled softly, and his violet eyes were suddenly soft. His crest was half-raised, indicating neither arousal nor depression. "And I must admit that your manners in coming here have been perfectly correct."

"They have?" Heather said dazedly.

"Yes. You have performed the proper greetings, behaved as a supplicant asking forgiveness. It takes time to learn these things . . . ways not native to your own. And you are right, too, in that I could never have harmed you as I threatened. I only did it to frighten the truth out of you. But I sense you have been telling the truth the entire time."

Heather dropped her eyes back down, tried to still her racing heart. "Then tell me how I can make restitution for the wrong I've done against you, and we can begin our relationship again, Honored Khuharkk'."

There was another pause and the Simiu asked softly, "Have you ever had an uncle, young one?"

Uncle Fred? her survivor-self sneered. *Yeah, tell him about Uncle Fred!* Heather tensed, wondering how he could know, then realized he couldn't know. He'd asked the question innocently, and maybe this was the first step in establishing genuine communication between them. "Yes, I had one," she admitted. "He was an evil man. He used to beat me up. I *hate* him."

Slowly, Khuharkk' came closer to her, and Heather held her ground, her heart racing. Then she felt the Simiu reach out, lay a gentle hand on her shoulder. "One who would beat a child is an honorless *dragkk',*" he said softly. "Especially one who would harm a child who has such spirit, such courage." The Simiu paused for dramatic effect. "Such . . . *honor.*"

Heather didn't know what to say. A moment later the leathery hand brushed her unruly curls with a feather touch. "Back home, I had a niece with a mane the color of yours," Khuharkk' said wistfully, stroking her thick mop with his knuckles. "She, too, had troubles, and needed my guidance. I am thinking, Honored Heather Farley, that you, too, could use a *true* uncle, an uncle who would be a friend and mentor. You would benefit from such an uncle, almost as much as this lonely uncle would benefit from such a niece."

Heather blinked, feeling her head spin at this sudden turn of events. He had called her "honored"! And he wanted to be her uncle! Hing had told her that an uncle was very special, a helpful big brother. That he would offer her this was an incredible honor.

She blinked, dazed. "I . . . don't deserve this."

"That may well be," he said briskly, returning to his old self as he stepped back. "But there is much I have to learn about humans . . . and I am curious about those things not taught in books. It would be a fair exchange. And I must confess, I would like to improve my computer skills. You could help me in that, couldn't you, little niece?"

She drew herself up, stood taller. "I'd be proud to, Uncle!" Then she added, "But only if we work strictly through the regular input modes!"

He glanced at her sideways. "This ability . . . to telepathically link with the computer. It is hard to understand. Do you do it often?"

She blinked, surprised by his curiosity. She shook her head, then glanced at the terminal in his room. Her terrifying experience was still raw in her mind. "No, sir. In fact, I've learned my lesson about that. I'll *never* do that again, not *ever,* and that's a promise!"

"I believe you, Niece," the Simiu said, and he inclined his head gravely to her. "Truly, you have learned a great deal!"

"We've discovered that the radonium in the vicinity of the school is breeding," Andrea Lynch said bluntly to the assembled StarBridge contingent. Jeff Morrow sat silent, not looking up, his face lined with misery. "You've *got* to get out of here, and the sooner the better."

Rob felt the blood drain from his face. "But—but . . ." he stammered. "Wait a minute! You said that everything here was all right!"

"That was a week ago," Lynch said bluntly. "It's breeding fast— and it'll continue to pick up speed."

"How long do we have?" Kkintha said, nervously pulling out tufts of her chest ruff. "Before it becomes dangerous?"

"A week, probably," Lynch said. "Maybe a little less."

"A *week*?" Rob slammed his fists against the arms of his chair. "Are you *crazy*? Do you know how long it's going to take to pack this place up, and *move,* lock, stock, and barrel? Just getting the kids to safety will probably take several days, now that one of our shuttles has been destroyed!"

"You'd better get started, then," Lynch said, her eyes flat and expressionless as a lizard's. "We're sorry about this, Dr. Gable, really, but it's not our fault. When radonium starts breeding, it's extremely unpredictable."

"This—this . . ." Rob sputtered at her, so angry he couldn't think straight for a second, then the red haze cleared slightly, and he was able to say, coldly and distinctly, "Just how long have you known about this, Ms. Lynch?"

The crew boss didn't meet his eyes. "Two days," she said flatly. "But we did a recheck to make sure we were right, and that was only completed today."

"You are certain of your facts, then?" Kkintha said in her soft, chittery voice. The little Chhhh-kk-tu didn't look strong enough to crack an acorn, but she was taking this much better than Rob though he knew she had to be equally upset.

"Yes, we're certain," Lynch said, her dark eyes grim.

"What about the star-shrine?" Ssoriszs said. "May we at least rescue that before we must evacuate? Serge told me that Cavern Two should be neutralized by now."

"Out of the question," Lynch snapped. "Cavern Two won't be safe for at least another week."

"I think we need a second opinion on all of this," Janet said, making no effort to hide her anger. "If only Andreiovitch hadn't—"

"I have taken care of that already," Kkintha said, interrupting Janet.

"You what?" Rob stared at the little alien, surprised. "What do you mean?"

"When Dr. Andreiovitch was killed, I knew we would need another engineering team," Kkintha said flatly. "So I contacted a nearby mining station where they mine radonium, and requisitioned their services. They will be here in three days."

"Whoa!" Rob gazed at the little alien in undisguised admiration. "You don't mess around, Kkintha!"

"No, Robert, I do not," she said in clipped tones. "This situation is getting to be, as you humans would put it, 'no longer within the grasp of the fingers.' So I determined to act."

Rob was bemused by her mangled idiom until he suddenly realized that she meant "out of hand." "I quite agree," he said tersely. "Ms. Lynch, I regard it as inexcusable that you didn't warn us the moment your instruments picked up even the faintest hint of radonium-2 near the school!"

"Frankly, I question that finding," Janet said. "I've been all over this immediate vicinity, and down in the bowels of these domes and my instruments don't register even a peep of R-2. How do you account for *that,* Ms. Lynch?" She leaned forward, her green eyes challenging the black woman.

"Our instruments are more sensitive than yours!" Lynch protested. "I told you that earlier!"

"So you did," Janet said, looking more than a little like a giant cat who is poised to pounce. "Tell me, just how much more sensitive *are* they?"

Lynch shifted uncomfortably in her seat, glancing at Jeff, who had scarcely moved, much less spoken, since he'd first sat down. "It's very technical . . ." she began.

"Don't worry about that," Janet purred. "I've boned up. I'm sure I'll be able to follow you, even if *they* can't." She indicated the other StarBridge staff. "I'll explain it to them later."

Lynch hesitated, then with a sudden grimace turned to Morrow. "Jeff, you led the survey team, while I stayed in the caverns mostly! *You* explain it to them!"

"Yes, Jeff," Rob said, trying to rein in his anger as he looked at his friend's haggard, drawn features. "You did lead the survey team. Is Lynch right? Do we only have a week?"

Morrow gave all of them a glance that seemed glassy, as though he'd received a shock. Remembering last night, Rob wondered whether the engineer had been drinking, but he didn't think so. Jeff looked extremely depressed, but he was clearly in full command of his faculties. "I told Andrea earlier that I thought she was being a bit of an alarmist," he said quietly. Lynch gave an audible gasp of indignation and looked daggers at her boss.

Morrow shrugged, spreading his hands out. "Well, I *did,* Andrea," he defended himself to the crew boss before turning back to the others. "Rob, realistically, I would say you had at least two weeks. It's possible that an evacuation won't prove necessary at all. My people are sealing off those areas as fast as possible."

"How many 'areas'?" Janet asked.

"At the moment, we've only found one that's within a hundred-meter radius of the school. There's another that's about a kilometer away. Both are small, and isolated."

"I'm surprised I didn't detect the hundred-meter lode," Janet said, her eyes never leaving Morrow's face. "I went at least a hundred meters out during my surveys. Sometimes considerably more."

"This one would be easy to miss, without the most fine-tuned equipment," Jeff said. "It's a tiny spot. *We* had to double-check it before confirming it."

Rob looked over at Andrea Lynch. The woman sat slumped down in her seat, her arms clamped across her chest, obviously defiant, defensive, and boiling mad at what she regarded as her boss's defection.

"If you didn't think the situation was as serious as Ms. Lynch indicated," Kkintha said, "then why did you condone her advising us to evacuate immediately, Jeffrey?"

Morrow ran his fingers through his lank hair. "To be honest, Administrator, there is *some* danger. I felt that you wouldn't want to take even the smallest risk, and would prefer to get the students out at even a whisper of danger." He regarded them all, one by one. "Am I right?"

Slowly, reluctantly, they all signed their agreement. There was no argument—the safety of the students had to come before any other consideration.

"We will begin putting my plan into effect first thing tomorrow," Kkintha said. "I will call an all-school assembly and brief the students. Janet, please arrange whatever transport you can to replace the *Fys,* as my plan was made before the destruction of that craft."

Silently, with heavy hearts, the StarBridge staff left the conference room to begin their preparations.

Very early the next morning, Hing walked rapidly down the corridor in the bottom level of the school, where the pool and gyms were located. She had promised Serge that she'd join him for his daily swim, and for once in her life, she was actually *on time.*

"Be on time, if that is possible," he'd teased her, when they'd parted shortly before midnight, after making love. Because it was Heather's first night back, Hing felt that she wanted to sleep in their suite, in case the child had any bad dreams. "Or you may be sorry."

"Oh, yeah?" she'd said coyly. "Why would I be sorry?"

"Because, if you are very late, I am apt to swim so many laps by the time you get there that I will be too tired for any other physical activity for the rest of the day," he'd replied solemnly, his sapphire eyes dancing.

Now, walking along the corridor with all possible speed, Hing glanced at her watch. "Hah," she muttered, "fooled you, Serge LaRoche! I can't wait to see your face!"

Of course, she'd promised herself that she'd be *early,* but she hadn't managed that. Still, she thought, managing to quicken her pace a tiny bit more, with a little luck she might reach the hall outside the pool area and be able to lean against the door before he came along, and then rag him that she'd been there for ten minutes and what had been holding him up, for goodness' sake?

Grinning, Hing gave in and broke into a jog. She couldn't wait to see him, even though they'd only been apart a few hours. She'd missed waking up with him beside her, one arm draped across her hip. Besides, she wanted to show him what she now wore on her left hand, for the first time in six months.

As she rounded the last corridor, she saw with a sigh that she'd missed her chance. Serge was already coming down the corridor from the opposite direction. He saw her, glanced at his watch, and then did a double take that was almost as satisfactory as Hing had envisioned. "Hi!" the Cambodian student called, waving her left hand at him. "Notice anything?"

He squinted at her, then his face lit up. "Wonderful! That is won—"

Hing never heard the rest of what he was going to say, because a dull boom resounded beneath her feet, half an instant before the floor surged upward as though punched by a giant fist. She screamed as she staggered, trying to stay on her feet, then she saw Serge fall to his knees.

Beside him, the nearest wall began a slow nightmarish topple, even as the muffled *thud* of a second, bigger explosion resounded below them.

"Serge!" she shrieked, wavering forward, trying to stay upright, praying the wall wouldn't hit him. "Serge!"

As she struggled, slipping to one knee, Hing felt the floor heave again beneath her, and then another giant fist slammed just below her, so hard that she had scarcely a moment to realize that the surface beneath her feet was no longer heaving, no longer plunging— it was no longer doing anything, because it was no longer there.

The floor beneath her had literally disappeared.

The student screamed wildly as she fell through the giant aperture that had opened up in what seconds ago had been the corridor. Using every bit of her strength and determination, she lunged forward, grabbing for the edge. Her fingernails caught on the ripped flooring and she scrabbled, kicking, clawing for purchase as she tried to heave herself up and out—

—only to fail.

And fall.

Hing had perhaps half a second to realize that she was hurtling downward, and that all was blackness around her—

—before the blackness slammed into her, and she was swallowed, engulfed . . . blotted out.

CHAPTER 14

◆

This Darkling Plain

Darkness. There had been darkness.

And fear.

And pain.

His head had hurt terribly—still hurt, though the pain was now a dull ache instead of throbbing agony.

The fear was also gone, though deep inside him, something shrank in terror from a searing knowledge that he stubbornly refused to contemplate—but that awareness was far, far buried, and he managed to ignore it.

And the darkness ... that was gone, too, because there was a wan light all around him.

Should he open his eyes? The effort seemed too much, too dangerous. Opening his eyes was a huge step—one he was not ready to take.

Sleep, that was what he needed. Oblivion, that was what he craved. He drifted off again, thankful that he hadn't really awakened. That was something he instinctively knew better than to do ...

But even as he slept again, he was uncomfortably aware that waking was inevitable. He could not put it off forever—no matter how much he wanted to ...

"Serge?"

He sensed that more time had gone by. The voice was familiar, and came from beside him. He awoke, but did not open his eyes.

However, his nose was busy, recognizing his surroundings by a faint odor. A hospital, that was it. He was in a hospital. Should he open his eyes?

No.

"Serge?" It was the same voice, the one some portion of his mind persisted in identifying as Rob Gable. "Come on, Serge. The monitor says you're awake. Open your eyes, son."

With a tired sigh, Serge obeyed, and the world rushed in upon him with the return of lights and colors and beds and neutral-colored abstract paintings on the wall. Reality returned, with a vengeance.

"Rob . . ." he muttered, eyeing his friend, thinking that the doctor looked terrible. The psychologist's eyes were red-rimmed and puffy, and his face bore new lines of strain and exhaustion. "Rob, you do not look well," Serge said, feeling his voice stick in his throat.

"You don't look too great yourself," the psychologist retorted with a wan attempt at a welcoming smile. "How do you feel?"

Serge put an unsteady hand to his head. "What happened to me?" He encountered no tenderness, no lump, but the generalized ache and a tightness, a tautness in the way his skin felt as it stretched over the planes of his face, made him realize that someone had been using a regen unit on him. "Was I unconscious?"

Rob was watching him intently. "You don't remember?"

Serge closed his eyes suddenly, as though there were something he didn't want to see. "Remember? No."

"There was an explosion down in the subbasement. It destroyed part of the lower level, down by the gym. Is it coming back now?"

Serge shook his head, still not opening his eyes. He was afraid to look at Rob's face. Something was there that he didn't want to see—ever. "I remember nothing," he said, though that was not quite true. Images were starting to trickle back, and he feared that trickle would become a flood.

Anything was better than those images, those flashes, so Serge opened his eyes again, sat up in bed, and made himself ask intelligent questions. "An explosion. Was it the radonium-2?"

"Nobody is sure yet," Rob said. "Of course radonium-2 seems like the most likely culprit, especially since Morrow and Lynch warned us thirty-six hours ago that it had been detected in this vicinity."

"Morrow . . ." Serge muttered, recalling his discussion with Professor Greyshine. "I attempted to call him . . . several times."

"He's probably pretty busy at the moment. He and his people

have been down in the bowels of engineering ever since the smoke cleared, working."

"Have they picked up any traces of radiation?"

"No, and that's the main reason Janet doesn't agree with H.U. that radonium is breeding beneath the school. She and Lynch have been head-to-head over this since yesterday."

"What exactly happened, then, to cause the explosion?"

"The main radonium power converter overloaded and blew, but we don't know why . . . yet. Lynch says some radonium-2, maybe just a little, got into it, causing the explosion. Janet doesn't agree." Rob rubbed a hand over his face. "I don't know what to think. All I know is, we've managed to evacuate sixty percent of the students to StarBridge Station so far. The rest will be gone by tonight. I hope."

"Is the school damaged? Did we lose pressure?"

"No, the entire explosion was internal, and the safety seals worked perfectly." Rob sat down on the edge of Serge's bed, staring at the younger man intently. "The damage is minor, all except for the lower level. The gyms are wrecked, and the pool is—"

Serge ducked as though Rob had aimed a physical blow at his head, throwing up a hand and making a strangled noise in this throat. "What is it?" Rob said, watching the young instructor closely, gauging his reaction with a therapist's trained eye. "What is it, Serge? Do you remember anything?"

"No," Serge said in a strangled voice that he had to force out. "No, nothing!"

"Nothing about the explosion? About a chunk of wall hitting you, then the rest of it collapsing on top of you?" Rob drew a deep breath. "About anything else you may have heard—or seen?"

"Non!"

"Well, that's what happened." Rob relaxed, sitting back a bit. "You were out cold, with a bad concussion, half-buried in debris. You also had a broken rib, but Dr. Mysuki took care of that, too, while you were out."

Serge rubbed his jaw, where he could feel a distinct stubble. "I was in regen," he said. "I can tell, because I was not due for a repressor application for another week or so."

"Right," Rob said. "Rachel says you can get up whenever you feel like it, but to take it easy, get plenty of rest, for the next couple of days."

"I understand," Serge said absently, wishing Rob would go away. He wanted to go back to sleep.

But the older man continued talking, still eyeing the patient with that alert, waiting look. "If it hadn't been for Heather Farley, we might not have found you as quickly as we did," he said. "Even though you were unconscious, the kid could still 'read' your location—especially with Doctor Blanket helping her focus her abilities. She was like a little bloodhound—we had to hold her back from digging you out with her bare hands."

Serge was no longer listening, because it was too much effort. He was so sleepy. He yawned widely. "Tired," he muttered, starting to slide down in the infirmary bed. "Need sleep . . ."

"No, Serge," Rob said firmly. "The monitors tell me that you've slept enough. I'm thinking that it's time you woke up—all the way."

Reluctantly, Serge straightened back up and opened his eyes again. Resentment and anger bubbled within him. He was *tired,* couldn't Rob see that? "Very well, I am awake," he said coldly, folding his arms across his chest, feeling the faint twinge of soreness in his left side. "Are you satisfied now?"

"Not quite," Rob said evenly, his bloodshot eyes still intent on the younger man's countenance. "There's something wrong with this picture," he said slowly, and Serge could feel his compassion, despite the stern tone.

"Oh?" Serge said, when what he actually wanted to say—actually, *scream*—was **Go away! Shut up!**

"Yes, there is. I think it's very odd that a kind, caring person such as yourself wouldn't ask whether anyone else had been hurt in the explosion," the doctor said quietly.

Serge's mouth seemed to move by itself—he certainly hadn't willed the words that emerged. "*Was* anyone injured?"

"A couple of students. We were lucky that it happened so early in the morning, and very few people were down there. A Drnian had his arm broken. One of the Mizari kids had to have an appendage amputated, because it was crushed by flying debris. Assorted bumps and bruises. If it weren't for one thing, I'd say we were fortunate . . ." He paused, as if waiting for Serge to ask what that "one thing" was.

The young instructor sat silent, but he could feel himself starting to tremble. Rob's eyes held him pinned like an insect in a collection. "Serge," Gable said very gently, "you can't keep running from it. You know, don't you?"

No! Serge's mind screamed as he squeezed his eyes tightly shut, shaking violently now. *No, I do not know, I do not want to know, don't tell me **anything**, I only want to **sleep**,* *let me sleep, let me hide*— He gasped, his chest suddenly hurting so badly that it was as if the entire school had fallen on it, instead of part of a wall, only the pain didn't come from the broken rib or the bruises, no, it came from—

"Rob," his voice was an agonized whisper, "*do not. Please.* I can't. I *cannot.*"

He felt Gable slip off the bed, felt the older man's hand grip his shoulder for a moment, "Okay, Serge," he said softly. "I understand, son. I'll have them give you something to make you sleep. You just take it easy."

Serge heard Rob's footsteps, slow and tired, as he headed for the door. Then he heard words emerge from his mouth, words that he hadn't willed, words that he hadn't thought he could think, much less speak: "Hing is dead. *Elle est morte, n'est-ce pas?*"

Rob stopped, then came back. When his shadow fell across Serge's face, the younger man opened his eyes in time to see the doctor nod, his expression a mixture of concentrated grief, frustration, anger, guilt, and misery. "I'm sorry, Serge, sorrier than I can ever say."

"I know," the young archaeologist said dully. "I know that you are, Rob. You . . . you loved her, too."

Rob nodded, then suddenly, as though his knees had given out, he sat down beside Serge with a thump, muttering in a voice that cracked, then broke completely, "She was so . . . special . . . my Little Friend . . ." He pressed his fists against his forehead, then ground them against his eyes, fighting for control.

Serge drew a deep breath, was surprised to find his own voice relatively steady. "Heather . . . how did she react?"

"She's devastated," Rob said, his voice hoarse, but once more controlled. "I think she may have cared more about Hing than about anyone since her mother died. I just wish the poor little kid would cry, get some of that grief out—but she's bottled so much up, over the years, that she can't express sorrow, even when she wants to. I'm worried about her."

"Did you . . ." Serge had to struggle to breathe, but his words came out in flat, even tones, "I remember very little. Did you recover . . . a body?"

"Yes," the doctor said. "She didn't die from the explosion, Serge, though it was almost instantaneous anyway, if that is any comfort . . . Oh, God!" he muttered. "Listen to me!"

"How did it happen?"

"She fell through the floor, where it buckled. Broke her neck . . ." Rob had to stop again.

"I want to see her," Serge said, still in that dead tone.

"Serge, son . . ."

"I *need* to see her." Slowly, deliberately, the patient swung his legs out of the bed, muscles protesting everywhere. There was a jumpsuit lying folded on the tiny bureau, one of his, and he picked it up and took it into the bathroom with him. Within a few minutes, Serge was back out, dressed. He slipped on his boots. "Take me to see her, please."

Minutes later Rob opened the door to the room where the school's two stasis chambers rested. "Wait here," he said, then went inside. Serge knew Rob didn't want him to watch while he opened the unit, removed the shroud, but he could see it anyway, in his mind's eye.

"You can come in now," he heard Rob call, moments later.

Serge walked in, his footsteps loud and heavy in the terrible stillness. Hing lay in the unit, her hair neatly arranged around her shoulders, her features composed and pale. Only a slight abrasion showed on her throat, and on one cheekbone, but there was no way her rest could have been mistaken for sleep.

Serge had never seen anyone who was dead before.

Putting out a hand, he tentatively brushed her face with the living flesh that began just above his wrist joint. Gently, he ran the soft skin of his forearm over her waxen cheek, stroking it. Cold, and not just from the stasis unit. Cold with the absence of warmth, of life. Dimly he was aware that Rob had turned away, giving him privacy, and was grateful in one part of his mind.

He thought of kissing her still lips, but he just couldn't. The woman he had loved was simply not *here,* and he could not bear the thought of kissing a dead body.

The ring he had given her still glittered on her left hand. Serge turned to Rob. "What does her Will say?" he asked softly. "Will she be going home to her family?"

Unable to speak, Rob nodded.

"Could you do me a favor, and ask them to let her keep the ring on? I—I think she would have wanted it that way."

Rob nodded again. "I'm sure they will agree," he whispered.

"Merci," Serge said, then he turned back for one last look.

Long moments later he turned away. "I am going now," he said, then waited outside while Rob returned the body to stasis.

When the doctor came out, Serge straightened up from where he'd been leaning against the wall. "If the school is being evacuated," he said, "you will need relief pilots. I am going down to Traffic Control and offer my services."

"Do you feel up to it?" Rob gazed at the younger man appraisingly.

Serge nodded. "It will help me to work," he said simply. "And if I have a free moment up at the station, I will check on Heather. I want to thank her for finding me."

Rob nodded. "All right, Serge. Whatever is best for you, but promise me, if you feel your concentration slipping, give it a rest, okay?"

"I promise," Serge said, and then they went their separate ways.

"That's better. I guess I'll live," Janet Rodriguez said hoarsely that same afternoon, keeping her voice low, as though she were afraid that someone might hear her through the locked doors of Rob's office.

When the Chief Engineer had first entered, several minutes ago, she'd been so pale and shaky that Rob refused to speak with her until she'd consented to eat something. The doctor had firmly sat her down, then stood over her until she choked down half a sandwich and a cup of heavily sugared coffee.

"Good," Rob said. "*Now* tell me why you came."

"I found out what caused the explosion," the engineer said, and for a moment the psychologist was afraid that she and her abbreviated meal were going to part company. He'd never seen the usually imperturbable Janet look so frightened, so *sick*. But she drew a deep breath, then, when she spoke again, she had regained control. "I know why the main radonium power-converter went up. It was sabotage, Rob. Just like Khuharkk's toilet. Just like the *Night Storm*'s crash. Sabotage, done deliberately through the computer."

Seeing her face, Rob didn't waste words asking if she was sure. "Another patched-on program?" he asked.

"I think so. But the traces of tampering had been almost totally erased, so I can't be positive that that's how it was done." She gave him a level look. "In other words, I can't be sure that it wasn't an *inside* job, if you get my drift."

"You think it was Heather?"

"No, actually I don't. If Doctor Blanket was right about why the *Night Storm* crashed, then my instincts tell me that what happened early yesterday is more akin to that incident than it is to the Khuharkk' one."

"Doctor Blanket has been monitoring Heather just about every waking moment, and seloz tells me that the kid gets panicky at even the bare thought of going back into the AI," Rob said. "It took her some time before she was even able to work at a terminal manually again. I can't believe it was Heather."

"Unless all three accidents were caused by her, but she only did the first one deliberately—the other two came as a result of her meddling, but they happened inadvertently, as a by-product of her financial wheelings and dealings."

"I don't think so," Rob said. "We haven't noticed anything else malfunctioning. This has been too *aimed* to be random."

She sighed and sat back in her seat, brushing her hair off her forehead. "I agree with you," she said. "I think it's Andrea Lynch's doing."

"Why?"

"I saw her face when I told her that I felt it was deliberate sabotage, Rob. If I ever saw guilt, it was on her face."

"That's not proof."

"I know."

Rob leaned back in his chair, looking at one of his holo-vid posters, which, at the moment, displayed *The Treasure of the Sierra Madre.* He felt a sudden *need* for a drink, for the first time in a long time—an urge so powerful that he held his breath until it passed. "Why would anyone want to do this?" he asked.

"I don't know. There are radical groups that oppose StarBridge Academy and all it stands for. Maybe Lynch is one of those fanatics. Or maybe she thinks that if she can frighten us off this asteroid, she can save the radonium and get some of it for herself. It wouldn't take many of those big crystals to equal a year's salary for someone."

"True," Rob said. He could almost taste the way a cold beer felt as it went down his throat in great, splashing gulps. With an effort, he wrenched his attention back to the here-and-now. "What do you think we ought to do about it?"

"I think we need to speak to someone from the League Irenics," Janet said. "Someone who could do background checks on Lynch, get some answers—and *fast.*"

Rob took a deep breath. "The moment the last kid leaves here, I'll make some calls. But until then, I'll need to help Kkintha supervise the evacuation. That's my first priority."

"I agree."

Rob hesitated. "I think maybe Jeff knows something's wrong about his crew boss," he said finally. "He looks like hell, and do you remember the way he spoke to her the other day?"

Janet nodded.

"I'm still wondering if all of this started when Lynch covered up some kind of error six months ago. Think about it. Who was on the *Night Storm*? *Andreiovitch*, that's who. A radonium expert. If anyone could have spotted a cover-up, he would have."

"But what about Jeff? Wouldn't he be able to spot one, too?"

Rob nodded. "I hate to suspect a friend, but . . . I've been wondering if Jeff didn't recently discover that Lynch pulled a fast one six months ago—but couldn't bear to expose her because it would mean disaster for his company." He ran a hand through his hair. "What if Jeff found out, then decided to try and undo the damage without saying anything—and now that things have gone *really* sour, he's afraid to tell, because Lynch's fall would take him down, too? Thinks he'd be charged with complicity or something?"

She considered. "Possible," she said finally. "It's one scenario that makes sense. You're right in saying that Jeff looks like he's been under an awful strain."

"That's putting it mildly."

Janet pushed herself out of her chair with a quick, decisive motion. "We can speculate all day, Rob. What we need is an investigation, by experts."

"You're right. I promise, the moment that last shuttle pulls out, I'll start. From what I've heard, they should be gone by tonight."

Janet nodded. "I saw Serge," she said. "He's piloting."

"How did he look?"

"Better than I would, under the circumstances. Brushed me aside when I offered condolences, saying, in essence, 'I'll think of that tomorrow.'" Her voice grew strained. "Every time I think about Hing . . ."

"Don't," said Rob firmly. "It took me nearly an hour to get myself back together after I talked to her parents."

"*Díos*," she whispered. "That must have been *awful*."

"It was pretty bad," Rob said dully, "especially when they told me that they knew the school had done everything we could, and thanked me . . ."

"Don't!" Now it was Janet's turn to say it. Seconds later she was gone.

Rob stared at the door sliding shut behind her, and wanted a drink so much that he bit his lip. Realizing that he actually might lose the battle this time, and knowing that he couldn't afford to take a chance on his own willpower, he hastily went into his bathroom, then pressed a small medical patch against his arm. The effects would last for a full month.

Then he sat quietly on the couch, eyes closed, until the medicine took effect. The urge was gone, but he felt almost as bad at having to resort to his medicine, as if he'd actually taken that drink.

Opening his eyes, the first thing the psychologist saw was his cat, sitting beside her empty dish. In all the confusion, he'd forgotten to feed poor Bast. When she saw him looking at her, she meowed pitifully, managing to look, despite her sleek, rounded appearance, like a poster-child from the late twentieth century.

"Sorry," Rob mumbled, and hastily fed her. He had to get back to the evacuation area, check on how that was going, give poor Kkintha a break. He was halfway out of his office when Resharkk' buzzed him. "Honored HealerGable, there is a personal call for you," the Simiu said.

"Who is it?" Rob asked, hoping fervently it wasn't another parent.

"She identifies herself as Angela Morrow. She seems very upset, and insists she must speak to you immediately. Will you talk to her?"

Rob slowly turned back to his desk. "Put her through," he instructed.

When the woman's tear-stained features and disheveled hair coalesced, it was all he could do to recognize the pretty, well-groomed young woman he'd seen before. "Angela!" he exclaimed. "What's wrong?"

"Rob," she said, controlling herself with an effort that was painful to see, "I've been trying to get through all morning! Have you seen Jeff recently?"

"Not since the day before yesterday," the doctor told her. "Why? What is it?"

"He called me last night, and he was drunk"—she bit her lip—"and he said awful things, *terrible* things about him and me, and about everything! He scared me, Rob! He was angry one moment, and so depressed the next that I was afraid of what he might do to himself! He respects you, Rob—he thinks the world of *you*. You have to try and help him!"

"Of course I'll try," Rob said instantly. "He's my friend."

"Oh, thank you . . ." She looked ready to burst into tears again.

Hastily Rob asked, "Have you noticed these bouts of depression before? And the drinking?"

"Yes, of course. His drinking was what split us up, mostly. I begged him to get help for it, to talk to a doctor, get on medication, but he wouldn't even discuss it. Then I thought that if I could get him into marriage counseling, you know, the two of us going together, the counselor might be able to help convince him . . . but he . . . Jeff slapped me when I asked him to go, said he wasn't crazy, that *I* was the crazy one! I moved out that night. My eye was black for a week," she said, her voice catching.

"That's awful," Rob said with a sinking feeling, remembering Jeff's version of the breakup. He knew that Angela Morrow was telling the truth—he'd stake his entire reputation on it.

"Then, when I knew Jeff was going to be working out there near the Academy, I got really scared," she said after a moment. "I mean, I still love him, and I don't want anything bad to happen . . ."

"Why?" Rob said, then at her startled look hastily rephrased, "I mean, why were you worried when you knew Jeff would be working out here?"

"Because every time he came back from there, seeing you, seeing the school, that's when he was so depressed that he couldn't even function. I worried a couple of times that he was having a nervous breakdown, or might . . . might . . . do something rash," she replied. "It was after a visit there that he first started really drinking."

"How long ago did all this start?"

"About six months after we were married. But it's only been so bad that I was frightened since he met *her.*"

"Who?"

"That woman. Lynch. After they met, they were inseparable. Went away on trips together, spent every evening together, talking—" She laughed bitterly. "Or at least that's what Jeff claimed they did. Talk."

Jeff Morrow and Andrea Lynch, lovers? Rob's mind boggled at the thought. He didn't believe it. "Do you think they were having an affair?" he asked cautiously.

"No, not really," she said mournfully. "I saw the way she looked at him, sometimes, when she thought no one was watching, but it didn't really have that kind of feel to it. But he's closer to her than he ever was to me in every other way."

"Well, listen, Angela . . . I'm very glad you called. I'm going to track Jeff down as soon as I can, have a long talk with him," Rob said, projecting as much reassurance as he could.

"Thank you again, Rob. You'll call me, won't you?"

"Count on it," he told her, trying to keep the grimness out of his voice. "Good-bye, Angela."

That "night," Serge stood in the docking bay at the school, watching the last shuttleload of students leave the Academy for the dubious safety of the station. He felt strange . . . light, almost empty, yet strangely filled with purpose. There seemed to be nothing left in life for him to do, except fulfill his promise to Professor Greyshine. *That,* he intended to do.

Focusing on keeping his promise (by retrieving the star-shrine and proving Andrea Lynch's guilt) was all that was keeping him sane and functioning. Only once since he'd left Heather today after trying to comfort the stunned, desolate—though still tearless—child had Serge allowed himself to think about Hing and truly realize that she was *dead,* that he would never see her again, never, ever.

When he'd done that, the resulting flood of choking grief and anger had been so frightening, so paralyzing, that he'd pushed the knowledge away, then resolutely kept his mind on his actions from moment to moment. If he did not allow himself to *feel* Hing's death, realize it, he could function, and function well.

The strategy was working . . . so far.

Moving quickly to the nearest terminal, he put through yet another call to Jeff Morrow. The man's assistant up at the station apologized for her boss's not returning Serge's calls, but said that Morrow was unavailable—again.

Serge smiled thinly. On his last trip up as a pilot, he'd checked in at the H.U. offices in person, and he had heard Morrow's and Lynch's voices. He hadn't been able to make out the words, but it had been obvious they were arguing. Now if only both H.U. officials would stay put up at the station for an hour or two . . .

Quickly loading the small borrowed shuttle with a few items of equipment, Serge changed into Janet's heavy-duty pressure suit that he'd worn before . . . the suit that was nearly identical to the one Lynch had been wearing.

Twenty minutes later he was at the site, his ship hidden in the shadows of the Cliffs, busily keying in Lynch's ID number into the airlock controls, holding his breath as he waited to see whether the code was still good. *If she has changed it* . . .

But the door slid obediently aside.

Calmly, Serge walked through it, carrying his equipment. Part of his nonchalance was based on the fact that he hoped to pass as one of the workers, moving quickly and purposefully to his destination, looking as though he had every right to be there. But the main reason for his calm was that he honestly didn't give a damn anymore. If they caught him, what could happen to him that was worse than what had already happened?

Cavern One was a mess. Serge frowned, seeing that deep excavations gouged the rock floor; all of the carefully outlined grids had been utterly destroyed. His lips tightened angrily as he glanced around.

Silver cylinders about two meters long were stacked against all of the walls except the back one. The archaeologist saw two men working down in one of the pits, and was immediately taken aback—they wore pressure suits, but had removed their helmets!

Perhaps the radonium-2 contamination never reached Cavern One, he thought, covertly eyeing the men and the destruction they had wrought on the painstakingly excavated site.

The back wall was gouged with deep cracks, and several of the huge holes, Serge saw, extended *beneath* the wall. During their surveys using the neutron emitter, Serge and the Professor had determined that the back wall gave onto another, very small cavern, hardly more than the size of a castle-sized bedchamber. The archaeologists hadn't had the money to consider pressurizing it so they could explore, and Serge was irrationally annoyed to realize that the little cave must be airtight, or the pressure would have escaped through those cracks and gouges.

As the young man started across the floor of the cavern, one of the workers looked up and saw him. The archaeologist's heart slammed as the man waved, and he attempted to answer with an equally casual gesture. With every step he took toward the airlock that led into the passage, Serge expected to feel a hand on his shoulder, but he never did. Lynch's code got him through again.

At the airlock leading into Cavern Two, Serge checked his sensor for radiation, but found none. Perplexed, he shook the instrument, then tapped it experimentally. Was it malfunctioning? It had worked perfectly when he'd tested it today!

For a moment he considered going back, but then he resolutely opened the lock and stepped in. He hit the controls to cycle it, then waited tensely.

When the door slid aside again, Serge held out the sensor, then frowned. *Nothing! This is insane!*

Even if Lynch and her crew had finished neutralizing the cavern, there still should be some background traces of radonium-2, not high enough to be harmful, but higher than normal. But this instrument recorded nothing of the sort!

Cavern Two was, if anything, an even bigger mess than Cavern One. The silver cylinders were stacked all over it. As he walked toward the ramp and the ledge leading up to the star-shrine, Serge was relieved to see that at least Lynch and crew had done *one* useful thing—the crevasse was securely covered with a sheet of plas-steel.

He stood at the foot of the ramp and looked up, shining his light, fully expecting to see nothing but a gaping hole where the artifact had been ripped away from the stone.

But the star-shrine was there!

Serge gave a soft grunt of satisfaction. *You waited too long, Andrea,* he thought as he clipped his instruments onto his belt, then, ponderously clumsy in his suit, he began crawling up the narrow, rough-hewn ramp.

He was sweating and panting by the time he reached the top, the narrow ledge the Professor had tumbled off. That was only a couple of weeks ago, and yet it seemed like another century. For a moment thoughts of Hing and this morning's awakening threatened to surface in Serge's mind, but resolutely he pushed them down again, concentrating on what was before him.

The star-shrine. It glimmered and flashed in the light of his torch, deep metallic blue-black as a background, with opalescent and colored gems studding it in the shapes of spirals and nebulas.

Quickly Serge took out his instruments and, without touching the artifact, took several quick readings. On the third one, as he analyzed the substance that had been used to cement the shrine into place, the archaeologist froze incredulously. He checked the material again, then a third time, only to see the same readings.

He could not be sure about the origin of the star-shrine itself, but the cement holding it in place was *modern* in origin.

Professor Greyshine's great discovery was a hoax.

But the other things were genuine! Serge thought, frowning in puzzlement and dismay. *We verified them! Were they planted too?*

Completely bewildered, the archaeologist reached out and touched the star-shrine—

—only to jump violently when the radonium-2 alarm immediately began resounding throughout Cavern Two!

Serge came within a hairsbreadth of falling, just as Greyshine had done, but managed at the last second to throw his weight forward, and stay on the ledge. Then realizing that the alarm would be bound to bring in the H.U. workers, he scuttled backward down the ramp as fast as he dared, then hid behind a pile of the silver cylinders.

He was barely in time.

The airlock door opened, and two fully suited H.U. workers strolled in—then calmly removed their helmets!

Then the puzzle pieces began to fall into place in Serge's mind, a few at a time, and he cautiously eased his own helmet off so he could listen to what the men were saying.

"What triggered it, do you think?" the taller man shouted as the short man took off his suit, then scrambled up to the star-shrine. Reaching up behind a lip of overhanging rock, he moved something, and the alarm abruptly ceased.

"Maybe some stray neutrons, given off by a passing ship," Shorty replied. "This thing has to be pretty sensitive to pick up the low levels put out by those professors and their toys."

Their conversation degenerated into a discussion of the newest holo-vid porn star and her charms, then the airlock door closed, and they were gone.

The cylinder nearest Serge had a bill-of-lading number stamped onto it, plus a product ID number. Serge grimly memorized both. He waited for ten minutes, giving the workers plenty of time to get out of the way, before he replaced his helmet, then gathered up his tools to go.

Ten minutes with the records at the station cargo docks should give me everything I need, he thought grimly as the lock cycled. *Then I will have to find Jeffrey Morrow before Andrea Lynch can return to the caverns. I know, now. I know why she did it, and how she is doing it . . . all I need now is the proof . . .*

CHAPTER 15

◆

Balancing Act

When Serge docked at StarBridge Station, he went directly to the cargo offices. They were fully staffed around the clock, as was necessary on a self-contained world that had to adjust itself to schedules from many planets.

By this time he was well known there as one of StarBridge Academy's pilots, and when he asked to check the records for shipping through the station, explaining that he needed to check on some archaeological equipment that had been back-ordered, no one gave him a second thought. Within moments Serge was hunched over a terminal, pulling up the data he needed.

First the product ID number of the silver cylinders. That didn't take long at all—they were specially padded containers for storing radonium crystals. Yes, *radonium, not* radonium-2—which confirmed what Serge had learned from Ssoriszs. The elderly Mizari had told him about Morrow's plan to vaporize the R-2, then collect it into tanks. Just to make sure, Serge pulled up a listing for a vapor-collecting tank, and found that it was a squat, bulky thing with a dull-gray finish and the CLS universal radiation-warning sign painted on each side.

It *was* possible that in order to get to the lethal R-2, Lynch had legitimately removed the "healthy" radonium—but Serge didn't believe it. That was where the bill-of-lading number came in. Quickly he pulled it up, then sat staring at the reproduction of the bill.

The silver radonium cylinders had been shipped to StarBridge Station about two weeks ago, which fit—but they had been originally *ordered* nearly *six months* ago! The cylinders had been stored at one of H.U.'s mining camps in a nearby sector, only a few weeks after the routine radonium-monitoring check. The name on the bill of lading as the person responsible for placing the order was . . . Andrea Lynch.

Serge grinned wolfishly. *I am getting close, Andrea!*

Still, it was possible that H.U. had simply reassigned existing supplies of the radonium cylinders when the emergency at the school came up. Serge quickly checked for an order having been placed by H.U. for vapor-collection tanks. After a few minutes, he found one, and his heart sank within him.

But a bit of further checking made him grin again. A communication had just been received today, saying that the vapor-collection tanks were on back order, and weren't expected to be delivered for another two weeks! He was willing to wager that the StarBridge staff had no idea that those tanks weren't even at the site yet. It wasn't *conclusive*—but it would do until he had the time to trace through the stolen-antiquities files to attempt to match up their "Lost Colony" artifacts with ones that had been reported stolen and were known to be on the black market.

Serge straightened up and flicked off the terminal. *Andrea Lynch, you have a great deal of explaining to do!*

Standing up, he gave a casual wave to the cargo office, then sauntered out. His strides increased in speed dramatically the moment he stepped outside, heading for Horizons Unlimited's offices. With any luck, Morrow would still be there, though it was getting pretty late. But he knew from his conversation with Jeff the day they'd had lunch that Morrow had an apartment adjoining the H.U. offices.

Jeff Morrow had supported their dig, had been sympathetic to their goals, and he was a good friend of Rob's. Serge felt he owed it to the man to discuss this with him before bringing it to the attention of the StarBridge staff, or the authorities. It was only fair to let Morrow know what was going on, so he could clean house in his own company, then help Serge bring Lynch to justice. The archaeologist was sure that Jeff would listen to him and agree that something was indeed rotten in Denmark—the pieces fit together too neatly for there to be any other explanation.

You will be sorry, Andrea . . . he thought grimly. *Every time I think of how we labored over those artifacts that you planted, only to have your own crew "find" them*—His steps came faster and faster.

*Lynch, I am going to make you **very** sorry . . .*

Heather sat brooding on her bunk in this cramped little room she had been assigned here at StarBridge Station. For perhaps the thousandth time, she wished she could cry. Hing had been dead for almost forty-eight hours, now, and she hadn't shed a tear for her friend. The well of grief bottled up inside her felt like a genie of legend that would burst forth and drown her.

Why? she wondered. *Why do things like this have to happen?*

The child was not expecting an answer, but out of the silence one came: <Because the universe contains forces we do not yet understand, little one.>

Heather was surprised to "hear" from the Avernian. For most of the day and evening, seloz had been busy counseling students (especially the telepaths) who were in a state of shock due to the explosion and their abrupt relocation.

Several times the child had reached out to the alien, only to sense that the fungus being was busy helping another student. But the new Heather (as she thought of herself) was not jealous of the Avernian's attention, as the old Heather would surely have been. Instead, realizing that she had received a great deal of seloz's time over the past few days, she'd resolved to be patient and wait until Blanket could again become her personal guardian angel.

Now she was filled once more with that sense of peace, the affirmation of seloz's love. After the events of the past day and a half, Doctor Blanket's warmth in her mind was like balm on a raw wound. Slowly, Heather relaxed and thought back to the question she'd asked, and the Avernian's reply. Why *did* things like this have to happen? What kinds of forces?

Are you talking about God, Doctor Blanket? she wondered. Communication with seloz was now so effortless that it seemed nearly as natural as talking to herself had been.

<Perhaps. God may be part of it, if God exists apart from the universe . . . but there are other forces, or binding laws . . . >

Like what? Despite herself, she was growing interested in this conversation. She'd never discussed philosophy with an alien before. For a moment she imagined Aunt Natalie's horror if she could see her erstwhile niece holding a silent conversation with a giant glowing fungus who rested in complete darkness half a kilometer away, and a hint of her old evil smile wavered for a moment on her face.

<Entropy, Gravity, Will, Faith, Destiny . . . there are many such forces.>

Are they all real? It seemed strange to think of Faith and Destiny being as tangible on some levels of being as Gravity was on others.

<At times . . . and wheres . . . >

Doctor Blanket, you're awfully smart, she thought.

<By your standards, I am 'awfully old,' little one. Wisdom grows with age, and an active consciousness. I have an active consciousness, even though to my own people, I am still barely past childhood.>

Really? How old are you?

<Rob believes I am about a million of what you call years old. We do not measure time, except by how many sporings we have made, so I have no way of knowing whether he is correct.>

Heather sat bolt upright. *Holy shit! You're a million years old?*

<So Rob believes.>

Doctor Blanket, how did your people get to be so smart when they don't have hands or technology or a written language or anything? The question had been growing in the back of her mind for a considerable time—ever since she'd known the Avernian.

<We were made to be as we are. Our intelligence, as you call it, was given to us before we existed in this then-and-now.>

Really? Where were you before you were in this then-and-now?

<OtherWhere.>

Heather was just about to ask where that was, when she looked up at her closed door, suddenly alert. Serge had just walked by—the girl knew it because of the distinctive brush of his thoughts, even though, as Blanket was helping her learn to do, she'd resisted actually *reading* them.

Quickly she pulled on her clothes, thinking, *I've gotta go see how Serge is doing, Doctor Blanket! I'm worried about him.*

<As am I,> the Avernian admitted.

Talk to you later!

She had no trouble tracking the archaeologist through the station, being careful to stay far enough behind so he wouldn't see her. Heather planned to let him reach his destination, then casually stroll past and act surprised to see him.

She really was worried about Serge. When she'd seen him today, he'd been so quiet, so overcontrolled, that she'd sensed he was hanging by a thread. And yet, even amid his own misery, he'd been concerned for her. Heather understood more than ever now why Hing had loved him. She only hoped that the Cambodian

tudent had gotten a chance to tell Serge how she'd felt before
her death.

Now Serge was nearing the Horizons Unlimited offices, only
o find them closed for the night. He turned purposefully away
nd strode toward the nearby bloc of apartments. Unseen, Heather
ollowed.

She flattened herself in a nearby recess, listening as he signaled
he door to Morrow's apartment. After a short delay, it was opened
y Jeff himself, a robe hastily flung around him. Heather saw the
gleam of a distort cuff on the engineer's ear.

Heather strained to hear the two men's conversation as Serge
egan talking excitedly, urging Morrow to accompany him down
o the dig site. From what Serge said, he'd just found proof that
Andrea Lynch had planted the artifacts six months ago, then rigged
a fake radonium-2 alarm, designed to be tripped when anyone tam-
ered with the star-shrine in Cavern Two. Lynch, Serge told Mor-
ow, was now using specialized containers purchased with H.U.
unds to steal StarBridge's precious radonium!

Holy shit! Heather thought. *This is just like* Teen Sleuths! *Serge
figured all of this out today?* She knew how the young man felt
bout Andrea Lynch—he'd spoken bitterly of her in Heather's
resence more than once. And today he'd told her that he
lanned to check on their precious star-shrine whether Morrow
llowed him on the site or not. Evidently he'd made good on his
romise.

Now Morrow was talking, assuring Serge that he'd come with
im as soon as he could get dressed, and that, together, the two of
hem would get to the bottom of this.

Serge shook Morrow's hand gratefully, thanking him for his
nderstanding. Heather, listening, suddenly shook her head. *No,
erge! Don't thank him! Something's **wrong!***

She had no idea what that "something" was, but she was sure of
what she sensed. Heather bit her knuckles as she considered what
he ought to do, but before she could decide, Morrow reappeared
gain, fully dressed. Together, he and Serge left the living area of
he station, heading for the shuttle docks.

What should I do? Heather thought, following them again. *I'm
ust a kid! Nobody's going to listen to me, and all I have are sus-
icions! If only he weren't wearing that damned distort!*

When the two men stopped at the docking area where the suit
ockers were located, the girl dug her fingers into her palms, took
deep breath, then deliberately *pushed* her mind at Morrow's,
eeking to read *past* the distort.

The pain slammed into her, along with the white-noise hum, the dizziness, the mental confusion. After a second she could stand no more, and had to pull back, leaning against the nearest wall for support. She came within a centimeter of throwing up, right there in public.

But she had succeeded—at least partly!

Now Heather *knew* that Jeff Morrow was lying, and that he intended nothing good toward Serge. Her friend was in terrible danger. She had to warn him!

Doctor Blanket! she "shouted." *Something terrible has happened! Serge is with Jeff Morrow, and Morrow's lying to him. I don't know exactly why, or how, but I'm certain he's in danger! Nobody knows they're together! I'm going to try and warn Serge. Please tell Dr. Rob what's happened!*

Ducking into the suit-locker section, she went into the women's storage area. With her computerpen, it took only a few moments to locate the smallest woman's suit there, and open the locker where it was stored.

Fortunately, no one was in the immediate area as Heather struggled to get into the suit and get it sealed properly. It was slightly too big, but she could wear it. Heather had gone through suit drill aboard the *McIntyre,* so she'd done this once before (with help) but it was hard to remember all the checks. She finally ended up "borrowing" the correct information on wearing the suit and getting it properly sealed from a woman several aisles away, who had no idea that her brain was being picked.

I know I promised I wouldn't do that anymore, the child thought, *but this is an emergency!*

Serge and Jeff Morrow were already down in the tiny terminal cubicle at the end of the docking tube where one of the H.U. shuttles was moored, filing their flight plan with Traffic Control. Heather sauntered past them, just another spacesuited (albeit a bit short) worker, then she bolted for the cargo airlock on the other side of the shuttle. Fortunately, it took her only a moment with her computerpen to open the lock.

Then she crouched in the cargo section, feeling her heart thud as the shuttle took off.

Now what do I do? she wondered. *I can't just go up to Serge in front of Morrow—I could've done that back at the station! No,* she had to get Serge alone, so she could tell him, then they could leave together. She wouldn't put it past Lynch or Morrow to play really dirty.

Heather made sure her computerpen was securely fastened inside the outer pocket of her pressure suit. If she could just get into one of H.U.'s offices on-site, she was certain she could rig some type of distraction to get Morrow away from Serge. She'd have to play it by ear.

Heart pounding, the child waited . . .

After tossing and turning for nearly an hour, Rob had just dozed off when the summons reached him. <Rob! Wake up, Rob!>

Eyes wide in the darkness, he sat up in bed, dislodging the cat, who gave an affronted grumble and jumped down. "Doctor Blanket, what is it?"

<Heather just contacted me. She is in trouble.> Rob groaned aloud. *Oh, no, not again!*

"What's going on? Is she in danger?"

<I do not sense immediate danger, no. But she says that Jeff Morrow and Serge are on their way to the archaeology site together, and she fears for Serge. She believes that Morrow is hiding something significant.>

"Is she right?"

<I do not know. Morrow was wearing a distort, as usual.>

"Then how could Heather know all this? Where is Heather now?"

<I do not know the answer to either question. I cannot reach Heather.>

"I've been trying to reach Jeff all day," Rob said, scrambling out of bed and nearly tripping over Bast in the dark. Hastily, he ordered on the lights, then grabbed his pants, pulled them on. His shirt and boots followed. "I'll call him again, right now. You say he's at the site?"

<That is where they were heading.>

"Do you sense anything wrong with Serge?"

<No, he was . . . not precisely *happy* when I touched his consciousness . . . > the alien groped for words.

"No, he wouldn't be," Rob said grimly, "not under the circumstances."

<But he was . . . satisfied. There was a strong sense of vindication within his mind, a feeling that he was accomplishing some goal that meant a great deal to him.>

"Can you still sense Serge or communicate with him?"

<No. Your mind I can reach at this distance, because we are strongly attuned after all these years. Serge I do not know well enough.>

"What about Heather? She's a telepath, too."

<I can no longer sense her on the station, but I cannot be sure
she is not here. She has a strong natural shield. If she is concentrating intently on something, it is difficult for me to "find" or distract
her. That is how she could invade the Mind without my knowing it
at first—until her concentration failed, I could not sense her.>

Rob frowned. "Well, we'll worry about Heather later. If you
don't sense any danger from her, we'll assume she's okay for
now. What I need is to get in touch with Jeff out at the site.
I'm afraid he's on the verge of a breakdown," he admitted. "His
wife called me today and said he's been acting very erratic for a
while now . . . which fits in with what I've observed these last two
weeks."

<I remember him from before. His mind when he left was in
chaos—blackness and hate poisoning the very real love he felt for
this school and those within it.>

"Hate?" Rob was taken aback. "I know he was depressed, and
angry, and frustrated, but he *hated* us?"

<His mind was in chaos, and he felt anger toward many things,
many people. But I sensed only deep affection for you, Rob.>

"I know he's very fond of me," Rob agreed. "We'll work together to straighten this mess out," he vowed, trying to summon a
positive attitude. If only he weren't so exhausted! Awake most of
last night, grieving for Hing, the pressure of the evacuation . . .
he sighed as he sat down before his terminal. *No rest for the wicked.*

Seven extremely insistent minutes later, the H.U. offices patched
him through to Jeff Morrow.

The engineer was apparently in the cavern rather than one of the
bubbletents, because Rob could see what appeared to be dark rock
behind him, rather than plas-steel. But Morrow had activated the
privacy shield, so details of the background were masked by the
distinctive glowing shimmer that surrounded him.

"Rob?" he said. "Listen, I'm really rushed right now. Can this
wait?"

"No," the psychologist said bluntly. "It can't, I'm afraid, Jeff."
Morrow, he noted, seemed calm enough, but there was an air of
feverish excitement about him that the doctor didn't like. Beneath
the rumpled hair, his eyes looked too bright in their shadowed
sockets. Far from being depressed, he seemed almost manic. Rob
couldn't tell whether or not he'd been drinking.

"Okay, then, shoot," Jeff said. "What's up?"

"Is Serge LaRoche with you?"

"Yeah, he's here. He wanted to get his star-shrine, was worried that old Lynch had designs on it. I told him that's nonsense, but he wasn't reassured, so we came down together so he can take the thing back with him. He's a nice kid . . . I don't want him to worry when there's no reason for it."

"Jeff . . ." Rob said slowly, "we need to talk. About Lynch, among other things. I'm willing to help you any way I can, you know that. Don't try and tell me that nothing's wrong, I know you too well for that. This whole situation is way out of hand—something is really wrong, and I think I know what it is. But between us we can work out a way to make it right. Let me talk to you. I'll grab a ship and come out there right away."

Obviously disturbed by Rob's speech, Morrow hesitated. "I'll meet you later up at the station," he offered finally. "Where are you staying?"

"I'm still here at the school," Rob said. "Janet's still here, too, with a few members of her crew."

"You're at the school . . ." Morrow repeated, as if he hadn't quite assimilated what Rob had told him. Abruptly he straightened in his seat, nodding. "Okay, you win. Come on out." Quickly he gave Rob the access code to the cavern airlock. "How soon will you make it?"

"I'll be there in thirty minutes, tops," Rob said, and broke the connection.

Next he signaled Phillips in Traffic Control. "Hey, Teresa," he said. "Have you got a ship and a pilot for me? I've got to get out to the Lamont Cliffs right away."

She shook her head. "No ship, Rob. All of the shuttles are up at the station. But for a point-to-point like that, you can use one of the little scooters. Can you pilot one?"

"No," he said, his heart sinking.

"That's all right. I've got a relief pilot down here, a Simiu named Khuharkk'. He'll take you out, I'm sure."

"I know him. Thanks, Teresa. I'll be right there."

Rob headed for the hangar dome at a fast jog, feeling his sense of urgency grow with each stride.

Hidden deep within the curtain of shadow cast by the cavern airlock, Heather watched the little scooter settle down near the entrance to the cavern where Serge and Morrow had gone. Who could this be? She recognized that the pilot was a Simiu—the four-footed stance was unmistakable. That argued that the craft was from the 'Bridge, because Horizons Unlimited was a human-owned and operated company.

Anxiously, she watched a spacesuited figure scramble out of the passenger's seat, then head directly for the lock. For a moment she almost stepped out and stopped it, but not knowing the newcomer's identity held her back. What if this was Janet Rodriguez? What if Rob had sent her to investigate? Janet would never believe anything Heather told her—the child sensed that the engineer wasn't even fully convinced that she hadn't caused the computer problems when the *Night Storm* had crashed.

While she hesitated, the figure quickly entered a code, then Heather felt the vibration as the doors slid back.

Too late now!

Cautiously, the girl crept out of concealment, then moving with exaggerated care in the strange gravity, she headed toward the spidery little craft, picking a path that kept her out of sight until she could peer at the pilot's profile. She thought there was something familiar about the way he carried himself . . .

A moment later she stepped into full view, waving to get his attention. Tapping her head, she shook it ostentatiously from side to side, holding a finger to her lips. Khuharkk' stared at her, uncomprehending, then she pantomimed again.

This time, he understood. She saw him turn off his suit radio, and did the same. Both of them leaned forward so they could touch helmets, and thus have a private conversation. "Honored Khuharkk'!" Heather said loudly, "I'm so glad to see you!"

"Honored Heather, what in the Name of Honor are *you* doing here?"

"I came down with Serge and Morrow, but I hid so they wouldn't find me. Who was that?" she pointed to the airlock.

"Honored Healer Gable," the Simiu replied, obviously bewildered by finding her at the site.

"Damn!" Heather scowled. "He's in danger, Khuharkk', I just know that he is! Something's wrong! Jeff Morrow is . . . he's not right, up here," she said, and tapped her helmet. "I'm sure of it. I think he might be having a breakdown or something."

"I will go in and check on Rob and Serge," the Simiu said, now alarmed. He started to get off the scooter.

"No!" Heather grabbed his arm. "Khuharkk', you've got to go for help! I'm going to break into that bubbletent over there and call up to the station, but just in case I can't get through, or they won't listen to me—grown-ups have a problem listening to kids, they always think you're screwing around with them—*you've* got to

go for help!" She gave him a pleading look. "Right now, Honored
Khuharkk'! The longer I stay here, the more scared I'm getting that
something awful is going to happen!"

"But Honored HealerGable told me to wait for him," the Simiu
protested.

"You can't! You've got to get somebody to help!"

"Honored Janet Rodriguez?"

"No, I mean somebody with authority—Station Security. The
cops! I never thought I'd hear myself say this, but we need the
police, or the Irenics—somebody who can help!" Heather was
almost in tears. Panic nibbled at the edge of her mind. The growing
sense of *wrongness* she felt was now almost unbearable. "Please,
Honored Khuharkk', *please*!"

The Simiu stared at her intently. She could see his violet eyes
narrow within the shadows cast by their helmets. "Are you telling
me the truth, Heather? Do you swear by your honor?"

"Yes, Honored Uncle, I swear to you with all my honor, on
my dead mother's honor, that I speak the truth," she said, raising
her hand solemnly. Hing had told her how Simiu revered moth-
erhood.

"Very well, I will do it," Khuharkk' said. "You must explain
to Honored Healer Gable where I have gone, and why." The pilot
looked up at StarBridge Station, seeming impossibly far away. "It
will not be easy to maneuver through the space lanes on this fragile
insect of a craft, but I must try."

Heather thought of how difficult that would be for him, and
almost told him not to try for the station, go to the Academy, but
then there would be lengthy explanations, and inquiries, and Janet
would be suspicious . . . "Go quickly, and in safety," she whispered. "Please be careful, Uncle!"

"I will, Niece."

Heather stood there watching as he took off. Then, computerpen
clutched tightly in her glove, she headed for the airlock of the
nearest bubbletent, her eyes the color and hardness of emeralds,
her chubby features set in lines of grim determination.

CHAPTER 16
◆
Zero Hour

Jeff Morrow stood gazing at the silver radonium cylinders (there were far fewer of them in Cavern One than there had been during Serge's reconnaissance), his lips tight with barely controlled anger. Slowly he shook his head. "I had no idea," he said bleakly, "no idea what was going on. I never dreamed that Andrea was capable of betraying me like this. You're right, it's time to call in the authorities. Horizons Unlimited is going to look very bad I'm afraid."

"Not if you help us apprehend her, and testify against her in court," Serge said. "After all, she did this, not you."

"No, but I should have realized what was going on. Andrea wanted to supervise the mining portion of the operation, letting me handle the survey and technical end, so I let her have her way. I enjoy the technical stuff more anyway. And then, once I began to realize what this crisis was doing to the school, I . . . well, I wasn't well."

Suddenly Morrow grimaced, then slammed his fist against the cylinder. "Shit, Serge, why lie anymore? To put it bluntly, couldn't handle the idea that it might have been my company's screwup that was costing StarBridge Academy its home. I didn't want to go down in history as the guy who put the school out of business, and I . . . well, I started drinking whenever I wasn't actually out with the survey team. I should have been checking up on what was happening here in the caverns, but I've been sloshed every night. I just . . . couldn't handle it."

Serge felt a stir of pity. "I understand," he said. "And Rob and the others will, too. But the important thing now is to stop Lynch, find out where she hid the radonium she has already stolen, then give her to the authorities and have them recover the crystals."

Morrow nodded. "You're right, and that's exactly—" He broke off as the communications link signaled with a series of beeps.

"Excuse me a moment, Serge, that's my priority code."

While Morrow took his call, Serge wandered around the cavern, examining the damage to their site, wondering why the devil he was bothering. There had been no Lost Colony visit. The whole thing had been Lynch's hoax to have them open up the caverns and pressurize them so she could get at the radonium.

Sadly, he pictured Professor Greyshine's and Esteemed Ssoriszs' reaction when they learned that, and shuddered. *This will devastate them,* he thought. *I'll have to tell Hing—* All thought stopped, then Serge felt his heart contract. For a moment he'd actually forgotten. *How could I forget?* he wondered, feeling as though he'd somehow betrayed her, or perhaps himself.

His throat was so tight that he could barely breathe, and tears filled his eyes. Resolutely, he fought them back. *Not yet. Not here.*

Morrow was still talking, surrounded by the glow of a privacy screen. Serge wondered where Lynch was.

Then the engineer broke the connection, and rose from the seat. "That was Rob. He understands the situation, and is on his way out here to talk with both of us, says we'll work something out together. In the meantime, you said you wanted to retrieve that star-shrine. Want to do that now?"

"I suppose so," Serge said, feeling a great letdown. It was almost over. "Even if the shrine is not from the Lost Colony, I am fairly certain it is genuine, and probably antique. I would like to run some tests, see if we can trace its origin, so we can return it to its rightful owners if it proves to have been stolen."

It was a delicate operation, but finally Serge stood with the star-shrine in his hands. Behind it, he'd found the connections where Lynch had wired it to the radonium-2 alarm, and anger made him grind his teeth together. *Perdition take her, the bitch!* Because of her, the Professor had nearly died!

When he and Morrow reached the main cavern again, the star-shrine with them, they found Rob Gable just removing his helmet to call to them. "Jeff! Serge! Where's Lynch?"

"We don't know," Serge said, carefully placing the star-shrine in one of the empty radonium cylinders. He had no stasis field, and the heavily padded container would protect the beautiful old object from harm. "She hasn't been here since we came."

"She's probably asleep up at the station," Jeff added. "That's what she was talking about doing when I last saw her."

"Asleep?" Serge stared at the engineer incredulously. "In the midst of the biggest theft of the century, you believe she is *asleep?*" He waved at the stacks of cylinders. "More than half of these are gone, since I was here earlier. Lynch is bound to be back for the rest of them at any moment!"

Rob was staring at both of them blankly. "Theft?" he said. "What about the cover-up? She screwed up the monitoring, didn't she?" His dark eyes fixed on Morrow's face. "You found out about it, didn't you? Jeff, you should have come to me—together we could have stopped her, before anyone died . . ."

Now it was Serge's turn to look blank. "Cover-up? Rob, it was Lynch, she is stealing the radonium! Jeff knew nothing about it!" He turned to Morrow. "What is he saying, 'before anyone died'? Was Lynch responsible for the crash of the *Night Storm?*"

"That's not all she was responsible for," Rob said in a choked voice. "The explosion at the school . . . Janet thinks it was sabotage, too."

"*Mon Dieu . . .*" Serge whispered. "Do you mean that Hing"— he could barely get the words out—"was . . . was . . . *murdered?* Like Rizzshor and Andreiovitch?"

"Andreiovitch was a radonium expert," Rob said bleakly. "She had to kill him, because he'd know right away that she'd screwed up the last monitoring check. And then Kkintha called in more experts, and we weren't evacuating the way she told us to, so she caused the explosion in the school . . . Hing . . . you and Hing just happened to be in the wrong place at the wrong time."

"And Rizzshor . . ." Serge's mind was racing. "Rizzshor would have been able to see immediately that the star-shrine was not from the Lost Colony, that it had been planted here, just like the other artifacts . . . the ones Lynch and her crew supposedly uncovered during their monitoring check . . ." He took a deep breath, feeling dazed at these additional revelations.

"Yes," Rob said softly. "It all fits, doesn't it?" He turned to gaze at his friend. "Jeff, how long have you known about Lynch? Did you suspect that she was responsible for the computer sabotage, too?"

"I found out last week," Morrow said miserably, sounding as if he were on the verge of tears. "Or I suspected. I didn't know what to do, Rob! I didn't want to face public disgrace—I ever considered suicide, but tonight I knew that I had to own up to it, and I knew you'd help me, the way you always have."

Serge froze, his mouth suddenly dry. *But Jeff swore to me that he did **not** know any of this. Was he trying to protect himself by lying to me? Or is there more than self-protection involved here?*

He glanced at Rob, saw the psychologist regarding Morrow uneasily. Serge caught the doctor's eye, then jerked his head slightly toward the airlock, in a "I need to talk to you in private!" gesture. Rob's eyes widened, then he nodded, his expression now carefully neutral. "Jeff, why don't you call Station Security, have them send down a team?" he suggested. "Lynch could be back at any moment for the last of the cylinders. Serge and I will wait in the airlock, make sure she can't get in until we're all ready to leave together."

Morrow nodded, walked over to the terminal. Putting on his helmet, Serge moved toward the airlock, and Rob fell into step beside him. They were almost there when Jeff yelled, "Wait! I just thought of something!"

"What?" Rob said, unsealing his helmet and turning back to face him. Serge stopped walking as the doctor froze, then, slowly, he, too, turned back.

"What's all this, Jeff?" Rob said, nodding at the gun in the engineer's hand. The weapon was up, and the muzzle pointed directly at Serge's head.

Morrow smiled pleasantly. "This won't take long, Rob. I'm sorry," the engineer added, now addressing Serge, "I had hoped this wouldn't be necessary. You might as well take off your helmet and save your air. You won't be leaving here."

Slowly, staring at the gun, Serge obeyed. He could almost hear the *clunk* as, in his mind, the last piece of the puzzle dropped into place.

Heather stared at her computerpen, then back at the keypad, then looked up at the screen. She didn't know whose system this was, but he or she was a helluva programmer. Even better than she was. She'd been at this machine long enough to have mastered its most intimate secrets, but she couldn't even get it to open up a communications channel! And the damned thing was acting all kinds of wonky, besides. For one thing, the chrono was running backward. Maybe the main brain had had a nervous breakdown.

She tried another overlay code, but it was rejected just like all the others. No way to call out. No one could call in. It was weird. She was suddenly incredibly grateful she'd managed to convince

Khuharkk' to go for help. She blinked, not wanting to think about him flying that little scooter out into open, endless space.

Frustrated, she stared at the machine, realizing that she was well and truly licked. Maybe, if she couldn't call out, there was something else useful she could do . . . Experimentally, she tapped in a new sequence, ran a few unique overrides, pulled up some deep passwords . . . ah, this might be something!

Horizons Unlimited's company files. Even crooks had to keep records, she supposed. Heather flipped through them looking for anything useful. Most of it was typical, boring memos, purchase orders, permits, stuff like that. But she kept looking.

Hey, okay! Here's the payroll for this project! Wonder what these guys are getting to rip off the 'Bridge?

She flipped through the list but it was amazingly short. She rolled it again.

I don't get it. There's hardly anybody on this thing. Just a handful—eight . . . Only eight employees down here at this site? I'd've thought they'd need dozens, at least. She looked for any name she might recognize, but there was none. *Andrea Lynch must be on here somewhere,* she thought and looked again. No Lynch.

She asked the computer to search for Lynch's name and was told her name was all over the purchase orders, bills of lading, permits, every other bit of business . . . but not payroll. Weirder and weirder. Maybe Serge was right in his suspicions . . . maybe Lynch wasn't her real name, and she wasn't a real engineer. Maybe she was an archaeologist, instead.

Then something else occurred to her. If this machine had sufficient safeguards to keep her from doing something as simple as making a call, then someone—Lynch, maybe—was good enough to program it that way. And if that was the case . . .

She mulled that over for a while.

Whoever was *that* good was probably also good enough to mess up the guidance beam, cause the *Night Storm* to crash. She shook her head in reluctant admiration. Whoever had done this was better than *good,* he or she was some kind of *wizard.*

Heather was so lost in thought that she didn't realize someone else had entered the tent until she heard the lock hiss shut. She jumped away from the machine, standing with her back pressed to the wall, knowing guilt was written all over her face.

A tall, slim, suited figure wrestled with its helmet, finally yanking it off with a grunt, and a woman's face emerged—a face she recognized from the flash she'd glimpsed in Serge's mind. Andrea Lynch. *This* was the infamous Andrea Lynch.

The black woman stared at Heather, obviously furious to find her here.

The girl felt her nerves turn to water, felt her knees buckle. The sensation was so much like that moment on StarBridge Station when Khuharkk' challenged her that she thought for a second she would piss herself again. But that was before. She was a different person now. She'd been through worse, Heather told herself. Nothing Lynch could do to her could be as bad as those plasma things inside the computer.

She made herself keep her head up, her chin stuck out, and refused to cringe. She was a person of honor, her uncle Khuharkk' had told her so. Heather thought of the Simiu, out in space even now on that tiny scooter, flying to save her, Rob, Serge, all of them. She had to be brave, too. If Khuharkk' could do it, so could she.

She drew herself up, staring at Lynch calmly, pretending that Doctor Blanket was in her mind, even though seloz was still on the space station, and couldn't "hear" her anymore. Seloz was in her heart. That would have to be enough.

"Who the hell are you?" Lynch demanded angrily. "And what are you *doing* here?"

Heather swallowed, not wanting her voice to quaver. "I'm Heather Farley. I'm from StarBridge Academy, ma'am." *Name, rank, and serial number. That's all you're getting from me!*

"*You?*" the dark woman sneered. "You're a damned *baby*. You're too young for StarBridge."

Now the girl felt her face flush angrily, but that was fine. Being mad didn't leave her time to be scared. "I'm an advanced student," she replied haughtily. "Special. *Gifted.*" She said it in a tone that said *not ordinary, like you!*

Lynch grimaced and yanked a gun from an outside pocket Heather hadn't even noticed. The youngster felt her knees weaken. "Yeah, well, for a *gifted* child, you sure did one hell of a stupid thing coming here."

Not as stupid as what you've done, you crook! Heather thought, but for once she managed to keep her mouth from living a life of its own.

Lynch strode over to the computer as Heather backed up, unable to look away from the woman's gun. The adult tapped something into the computer, then touched a button on the console. A mechanical voice rang out:

"Sixteen minutes two seconds. Sixteen minutes, one second. Sixteen minutes remaining in countdown sequence. Fifteen minutes fifty-nine seconds . . ."

"Ever hear a countdown before, *gifted* child?" Lynch snarled. "If not, you're hearing one now. There's a charge tied into the biggest radonium vein, and I can't do a damned thing about it. In fifteen minutes this whole rock's going to be *vaporized*. Understand me? Or am I being too simple?"

Heather's voice caught in her throat. She tried again, and it emerged in a squeak. Lynch was lying, wasn't she? Just trying to scare her? Wasn't she? But there was only truth in those cold black eyes. "You mean . . . like boom?" she whispered.

"*Big* boom," Lynch confirmed. "Major. Large. Ultimate BOOM. Got it, brat?" She latched on to Heather's arm, her grip like iron, hurting her, even through the spacesuit.

"What are you going to do to me?" the child asked, hating the tremor in her voice. She was really scared now, shaking. She knew Lynch was going to shoot her, leave her here, to be totally incinerated. *Remember your honor!* a voice inside her ordered. She took a deep breath and faced Lynch calmly. "What are going to do?"

"What am I going to do?" Lynch repeated, obviously on the verge of losing it entirely. "What am I going to do?" Panting, she tried to catch her breath, the pulse in her neck jumping. "I . . . uh . . ." she hesitated, startling Heather more than anything she'd done so far. "I'll *tell* you what I'm going to do. I'm gonna stuff you in the cargo hold of our shuttle. You're going to get in there and *be quiet*, you understand me?" She gave Heather a vicious shake, and the girl nodded rapidly in compliance.

"Yeah, that's it." Lynch was thinking hard. "You stay hidden, and after we're safe, I'll sneak you some food. When we're far enough away, at some port, I'll sneak you back out again, give you enough money to contact your people after we're gone. He'll never know. Yeah. That'll work. You got that?"

Heather blinked. She had no idea what the woman was talking about. "Who's *he?* You're not going to kill me? Leave me here?" She looked over at the console, at the voice intoning, "Fifteen minutes three seconds. Fifteen minutes two seconds."

"*Kill* you?" Lynch spat in complete amazement. "What the hell do you think I *am?*"

The girl collected herself, looked right into Andrea Lynch's eyes, and touched her mind for the briefest second. She was assailed with quick flashes of Lynch bartering for stuff . . . no, not just *stuff* . . . Heather remembered Serge's description of the artifacts they'd found here. Lynch had bought those things on the black market and planted them here. She glimpsed the memory of Lynch buying and installing the star-shrine. Oh, this would just *kill* Serge! She saw snippets of other memories, too, in the brief touch. Lynch loading radonium onto a ship.

"You used to be an archaeologist," Heather whispered, terrified, but unable to say anything else. "But now you're a thief . . . and a liar."

The woman flinched, then grabbed her ear as if searching for something.

Her teledistort, Heather realized. *It must've gotten yanked off when she pulled her helmet off so quick.*

Lynch barked an ugly laugh. "All that and more, kid. But I'm no killer. I've never killed anybody, and I'm not starting with a kid, even a mind-reading snotty little brat like you."

"But it was you, wasn't it, that tampered with the guidance beam?" Heather blurted. "Lots of people died because of that . . ."

"No!" Lynch shouted, her voice cracking. A muscle in her cheek jumped. "That wasn't me. Not me." She shook her head, the grip on Heather's arm easing up, becoming almost a caress. "I didn't do that, didn't know he was going to do it, either. Not till after it was done. All those people, dead . . . he's gone too far . . ." She almost whispered the last, her face drawn into a terrible mask of grief, anger, and desperation.

"Who?" Heather asked softly, making her voice as childlike as she could.

"Jeff," Lynch murmured morosely. "He's gone too far, he's losing it . . . he's over the edge. If he finds you, he'll *kill* you!" This last was a fierce whisper and she shook Heather again, her resolve crystallizing. "I can't let him do that. I have to keep him safe, protect him, or he'll get caught. So you do exactly like I say. Into the cargo hold. C'mon, there's not much time."

Heather grabbed her helmet, her mind racing, the countdown voice distracting her. "But . . . we just can't *leave,*" she said plaintively. She had no choice, she'd have to trust this woman. "We can't leave Rob and Serge here to die!"

Lynch's eyes widened. "You mean you're not alone? Those jerks brought you with them?"

The child shook her head. "They don't know I'm here. But they're talking to Mr. Morrow right now, in Cavern One."

"Oh, *shit!*" Lynch groaned and glanced at the console, listening to the countdown. "I'll never make it! If I take you to the ship, then go back for them . . . I'll need time to convince Jeff . . ."

"You can't leave them, *please!*" Heather babbled, panic-stricken. "Don't leave them to die! I can get myself to the shuttle. Just tell me the access codes for the airlock, I'll let myself in! I'll find the cargo hold and go hide. But *please* don't let anything happen to Rob and Serge!"

Lynch hesitated for just a second. "Okay," she said finally in a defeated voice. She looked ashen, gray, suddenly old. Heather knew all her hopes, her plans, were crumbling around her, that she was desperate to find a way to make everything work out. "Maybe I can convince Jeff to take them as hostages . . ." She reached over for an H.U. computerpen and manipulated the controls, then handed it to Heather. "This'll get you into the airlock. Since you're *gifted*, I'm sure you won't have any trouble figuring it out. Now, get your helmet on and GET GOING! I MEAN it!"

Heather nodded her head so hard she nearly gave herself a headache, reaching for her helmet as Lynch barreled into the airlock. With one part of her mind she heard it cycle, but most of her attention was arrested by the countdown.

"Fourteen minutes remaining in countdown sequence. Thirteen minutes fifty-nine seconds . . ."

Heather walked over to the console, stared at it. *You can stop it,* an inner voice assured her smugly. The child nodded, and stared at her own computerpen, then at the one Lynch had just given her.

*Not **that** way,* her survivor-self sneered. *That's the **hard** way. You know what I'm talking about.*

Heather shook her head. No. She was not doing that. Not now. Not EVER.

We're talking big boom here, kiddo, the voice whispered. *Bye-bye Academy at StarBridge. Janet Rodriguez and a whole crew are still working there. They'll die. And what happens to you when there's no more StarBridge? Guess it's back to foster homes, huh? Normal school. Full of **normal** people, who just **love** having telepaths around them? That's okay. You can handle it. You've done it before. It'll only be **ten more years** until you're a legal adult . . .*

Dr. Blanket! Heather called desperately in her mind. There was no answer. *DR. BLANKET!*

This is hell, kiddo. No guardian angels here. Just you. Serge. Rob. And the bad guys. You going to let them do this to Rob— destroy his school? After what he did to save you?

She stared at the console, shaking. "No," she said aloud, in a firm voice. "I'm not going back in. Not EVER. I can't. I'll find another way."

Grimly, she grabbed the computerpens and started working out codes that might break through Morrow's programming, and all the while the countdown rang hollowly in her ears . . .

Only when he was staring in horrified fascination at the gun Jeffrey Morrow was pointing at his face did Serge begin to realize how very much he still wanted to live.

Ever since he'd awakened today, to find that the woman he loved more than anything in the world was dead, Serge had been playing in the back of his mind with the comforting thought that when he had fulfilled his obligations to Rob and Professor Greyshine, if he truly found that he could not go on without Hing, he could arrange to die.

After all, it was easy, out here in space. The environment would be happy to kill you, and often did, whether you wanted it to or not. Just step into an airlock and "forget" to seal your helmet or your gloves properly. Or hop aboard one of the scooters and aim it at a cliff, or at one of the deep holes that pockmarked the ground. Millions of ways.

But now, he realized, he didn't want to do any of those things, and it looked as though he was going to die anyway. Life was certainly odd, wasn't it?

"Jeff," Rob was saying, "what the hell do you think you're doing? Whatever Lynch did, it isn't worth something like this. We can—"

"Rob," Serge said quietly, "look at him. Lynch didn't do it. He did. Didn't you, Jeff?"

Morrow nodded. His eyes in the glare of the overhead spotlights were a washed-out gray, and his face was greasy with sweat. "Finally figured it all out, didn't you, Serge?" He smiled with seemingly genuine regret. "I'm sorry about this, you know. I really liked you. But I'm afraid you'll have to stay here. I'm taking Rob with me, of course, but I can't watch two of you at one time, not effectively. And you're a pretty husky young man, not like old shorty over there." He gave the psychologist an affectionate glance.

"Jeff." Rob's voice was calm now. Therapist mode, Serge realized. "Let's talk about this. You must put the gun down. You mustn't do this, it would be very destructive. It's not too late to undo things, fix everything. The radonium can be recovered, the radonium-2 can still be stop—"

Morrow smiled tolerantly, and gestured with the gun. "Rob— Rob, you're being rather obtuse. Tell him, Serge."

"There is no radonium-2, Rob," Serge said flatly, feeling as though he were a computer with a human voice, obeying a programming command. "There never was. The radonium-2 crisis was as false as the idea that the Mizari Lost Colony came here. They needed to keep us away from the site, while they took the radonium, so what better way than to declare it off-limits, because it was contaminated? They planned this months ago, Rob."

Glancing over at the psychologist out of the corner of his eye, he saw Gable nearly stagger as the truth sank in. How would it feel, Serge wondered, to have one of your best friends betray you so ruthlessly?

"Jeff," Rob whispered, "*why?* You have more money than anyone can reasonably hope to spend in a lifetime, you told me so. *Why?*"

"You can never have too much money, Rob," the engineer said, his eyes gleaming fanatically. "You'll find that out, when we take in all the worlds in first-class style. You won't have to worry about this place anymore. It was sucking you dry, draining you like a damn space vampire, but I've fixed *that,* too."

Moving lightly, quickly, the gun still pointed directly at Serge, Morrow backed over to the terminal, then hit a button. The computer began to speak: "Sixteen minutes remaining in countdown sequence. Fifteen minutes fifty-nine seconds, fifteen minutes fifty-eight seconds . . ."

The engineer smiled proudly. "See? It's all taken care of. No more StarBridge to slowly kill my best buddy, Rob. I did it for you."

Mon Dieu, Serge thought, feeling so sick that for a moment he was afraid he might faint, *we are dealing with a madman. Jeff is crazy, completely crazy!*

"Jeff," Rob said soothingly, "this is not productive. Put down the gun, and we'll discuss this. If you want, we could go somewhere together, sure. But there's no need for you to do this . . . blowing up the school will just make you feel terrible, later, don't you think?"

Give it up, Rob, Serge thought, seeing Morrow's sweaty face and glittering eyes. *You cannot reach him . . .*

"No, I won't feel terrible," Morrow said, sounding a bit petulant and impatient that Rob didn't appreciate the gift he had planned for him. "That place kills people." He jerked his head at Serge. "Like it's killing him. It sucks the students dry, then spits them out. I won't let it kill you, too."

Rob took a step toward the engineer, and suddenly the gun moved, came to bear on the psychologist, who stopped short. "Besides," Morrow said, and now his voice was as hard as the vacuum outside, "the radonium was making those damned Mizari rich, and now *they'll* have to buy from *us*—from Earth—and we won't be threatened any more, held down, treated like second-class citizens."

"Jeff," Rob said, "that's not you talking, that's Mike, your dad. Remember how—"

Behind Serge, the airlock hissed open, and they saw Andrea Lynch silhouetted there. The gun in her hand was pointed directly at Morrow. There was no way that Jeff could turn and fire at her before she would be able to shoot him; the angle was all wrong, and Serge saw Morrow realize that. Slowly, he lowered the gun.

Moving deliberately because she had to do it one-handed, the woman removed her helmet. "All right, Jeff," she said reprovingly, "this has gone far enough. Put the gun down. Move slow."

Obediently, the man responded, laying the gun down and then straightening slowly back up. "Andrea—" he began.

"Shut up, Jeff!" she snapped. "I'm calling the shots now, and you do what I say. We'll both be free and safe—and rich, just like we planned. Now you stop that damned countdown. You're not killing anyone else!"

One part of Serge's mind registered what she'd said, but he was too preoccupied with the drama that was taking place before him to focus on it, and its implications.

"All right, Andrea," Morrow said. "Maybe you're right."

Slowly, keeping his hands away from his sides, he moved to the terminal and keyed in a password, then a command. The monotonous voice abruptly ceased.

There was a palpable easing of the tension in the cavern. "That's better," Lynch said, and managed a halfhearted smile. "God, Jeff, I thought you were coming apart on me. Don't scare me like that again, okay?"

"Okay, I guess you're right, Andrea," Morrow said, returning her smile. "It'd be a damned shame to waste all this good radonium, wouldn't it, honey?"

She smiled at him like a fond parent, then they both chuckled. "Now"—Lynch waved her gun at Serge and Rob—"what are we going to do with *them*?"

"I don't know," Morrow said, still standing by the terminal. Slowly he began walking toward the woman, still moving cautiously. "We can't kill them."

"Damn straight," agreed Lynch fervently. "There's been too much killing. "But we can't leave them free, either. They'll call the cops on us."

"What about if we put them in the bubbletent and then take their suits?" Jeff suggested, walking over to idly run his fingers along one of the radonium cylinders. "They'd be fine there, plenty of air, a servo—but we smash the communications equipment. Sooner or later, they'll get around to looking for them, and find them there, safe and sound."

"Sounds good to me," Lynch said. "Come on, the ship's fully loaded."

"Don't we have time to get another load?" Morrow gestured at the radonium stacked around them. "After we lock these two up, we can—"

"Lynch," Rob broke in suddenly, urgently, "don't trust him! He's a borderline personality, and he's breaking down—undergoing a psychotic episode. He's delusional, and paranoid. Don't trust him! He's conning you!"

"Shut up, Gable," she said. "Don't give me that psychologist's mumbo jumbo. Jeff was just a little overeager, but he's fine now."

She really cares about him, Serge realized sickly. *I believe she is in love with him. She cannot bear to recognize that he is mad, because she loves him . . .*

"Rob is right, Ms. Lynch," he said. "When he was talking to us before you came in, he was nearly raving! Do not trust him! He will hurt you!"

"Shut up!" Lynch snarled, turning the gun on the two prisoners. "Jeff and I are partners, and soon we're going to be so rich—"

Serge saw Morrow bend over beside the cylinder, glimpsed a large chunk of slag in his hand as he came up, arm swinging, and yelled, "Lynch! Look *out!*"

But instead Lynch whirled toward Serge, and that error was her undoing. Rob yelled hoarsely as Morrow struck the side of her head viciously with the rock. Serge heard it crack against her skull.

Dazed, her skull probably fractured, Andrea Lynch dropped the gun and fell forward. In a second, Morrow had pounced on the gun, grabbed it, then stepped back to cover all three of them. "Too bad, Andrea," he said calmly, scarcely breathing hard, "you should have listened to them."

Slowly he backed around in a circle until he was beside the terminal again, then he turned the countdown back on. "Six minutes forty-six seconds, six minutes forty-five seconds, six minutes forty-four seconds . . ." it was saying.

Lynch could barely move her head, but she was watching Morrow, the look of wounded betrayal in her eyes as eloquent as any animal's. "I turned the *sound* off, Andrea," Morrow said, as if speaking to an idiot, "not the countdown itself. You lose."

Then, to Serge's horror, his finger moved on the trigger, and a deadly spurt of energy lashed out, turning Lynch's head and half her torso into a charred, smoking horror.

Gagging, Serge fought the urge to vomit, and all the while the computer was chanting: "Six minutes eighteen seconds, six minutes seventeen seconds, six minutes sixteen seconds . . ."

Serge realized he was going to die, knew it as surely as he knew now how much he wanted to live. He had so many things left to do—so much music he wanted to write! So many treasures he wanted to discover!

"*You* caused that," Morrow said accusingly to his prisoners. "If you'd kept quiet, I probably couldn't have got the drop on her like that."

Serge groaned softly, shaking his head, saw the gun swing toward him again. "Sorry, Serge," Morrow said, and his finger moved—

With a rush that amazed Serge, Rob Gable left the ground in a flying tackle, then he and Morrow were struggling for possession of the gun. The weapon went off, and a lance of energy struck the back wall, leaving the smell of ozone almost overcoming the odor of over-cooked meat. Even as he rushed to help Rob, Serge held his breath, expecting them to lose pressure.

Rock spurted, crumbled, then, with a slow, majestic ka-THUMP, a huge chunk dropped down into the pit H.U. had dug.

But the pressure held, and Serge then remembered the small chamber beyond. The little cave was indeed airtight, *Grace à Dieu!*

As Rob and Jeff struggled wildly, Serge reached the other gun that was lying on the floor, and picked it up rather gingerly, thumbing the setting down to stun. "Stop it!" he shouted, and his voice sent more rock dust cascading. "Stop or I will shoot!" Grimly, he thrust the end of the muzzle against the back of Morrow's neck. "Drop your weapon!"

Slowly, Jeff's fingers loosened on his gun, and it clattered to the floor. Rob Gable was bent over, fighting for breath. "Tie his hands," Serge said, backing up to the terminal desk, then handing Rob a length dispensed from the roll of plas-steel cord that still sat in the corner, a mute reminder of the vanished archaeological site.

Quickly, efficiently, Rob lashed the engineer's hands behind him, then stepped back.

"Three minutes twenty-nine seconds, three minutes twenty-eight seconds, three minutes twenty-seven seconds . . ." the countdown was saying.

"The helmets!" Rob yelled. "We have to get out of here!"

Jeffrey Morrow 'began to giggle. "You'll never make it," he chortled. "Never, Rob! This wasn't the way I planned it, but at least we'll always be together, won't we?"

"Shut *up*, you sonofabitch!" Rob screamed at him, slamming the helmet down over the engineer's head, then sealing it with a jerk.

Moving with frantic haste, the doctor handed Serge his helmet, then donned his own. Grabbing the unresisting Morrow beneath his bound arms, they hauled him to his feet and started toward the airlock.

"Three minutes remaining in countdown sequence," said the computer. "Two minutes fifty-nine seconds, two minutes fifty-eight seconds, two minutes fifty-seven seconds . . ."

One stride short of the airlock, Serge stopped, then shook his head, thinking of how far it was across the slagged plain to the landing area. "We will never make it, Rob," he said, knowing it was true.

Rob stopped, then nodded.

Slowly, Serge took off his helmet again, and Rob did the same. They let go of Morrow, and the engineer backed away, tripped, then sat down hard on the rocky floor. Serge could see the man's lips moving, and was glad he didn't have to listen to him anymore.

"Two minutes remaining in countdown sequence," said the computer. "One minute fifty-nine seconds, one minute fifty-eight seconds, one minute fifty-seven seconds . . ."

Serge took a deep breath, then, catching a whiff of Lynch's still-smoldering corpse, he walked over to the terminal, grabbed a dropcloth they'd used for collecting rock samples, and threw it over the body, hiding it. He really didn't want *that* to be the last sight he ever saw.

"One minute seventeen seconds, one minute sixteen seconds, one minute fifteen seconds . . ."

Serge smiled at Rob. *"Au revoir, mon ami,"* he said, holding out his hand to the doctor. "It has been a pleasure—and an honor—to know you, Rob."

The psychologist solemnly shook hands. "Same here, Serge,"

he said. "To quote one of my favorite films, 'Bye . . . see you on the other side.' "

Serge shook his head ruefully. "But I do not believe in the other side," he said.

"Fifty-five seconds, fifty-four seconds, fifty-three seconds, fifty-two seconds . . ."

Rob raised an eyebrow at the younger man. "We'll both know, soon enough," he said. "And if I'm right, Hing and I will have a good laugh at your expense, when we all get together."

The archaeologist smiled. "Then I shall hope that you are right, and I am wrong."

"Forty-seven seconds, forty-six seconds, forty-five seconds . . ."

This is it, Serge thought, fighting panic, wanting to die with dignity. He realized that Rob was still gripping his hand.

"Thirty seconds, twenty-nine seconds, twenty-eight seconds . . ."

"Oh, dear God," Rob whispered, and then, by mutual unspoken instinct, the two men grabbed each other, holding hard as though the feel of another living person could stave off the inevitable. Serge could hear the doctor rapidly whispering a prayer.

"Nineteen seconds, eighteen seconds, seventeen seconds . . ."

Hugging Rob against him with all his strength, Serge closed his eyes. Would he see Hing again? Was Rob right? If only he could believe . . . but he couldn't.

"Nine seconds, eight seconds, seven seconds—"

If only I could have finished the Starburst Symphony . . .

"Four seconds, three seconds, two seconds, one second . . ."

Serge heard a *click,* then an unmistakable giggle. A sweet, high-pitched voice cried, *"Boom!* Fooled you, Mr. Morrow!"

Completely bewildered, Serge raised his head, only to realize that he was still in a tight embrace with Rob Gable, and that their faces were only centimeters apart. Embarrassed, both men hastily stepped back just as the airlock door slid aside.

A diminutive figure stood within the small cubicle. It removed its helmet, and a mane of curls blazed forth. "Hi, Dr. Rob. Hi, Serge!" Heather said breezily. "I got him good, didn't I?"

Serge was just beginning to realize that he wasn't going to die. "*You* stopped the countdown?" he demanded.

"I sure did," she said proudly. "Morrow entered his password, and that gave me the opening I needed. I had to go *inside,*" she grimaced with distaste, "but if I hadn't, we'd all be dead now, so I guess that's okay, huh, Dr. Rob?"

"I suppose so," Gable said feebly. "But don't do it again."

"Don't worry, wild horses couldn't drag me," she said, then looked around curiously at the cavern. "What happened to Lynch?" she asked, suddenly uneasy.

"Jeff killed her, I'm afraid," Rob said. "Heather, tell me one thing . . . how did you get the countdown to keep going, but not blow up the asteroid?"

"Oh, I stopped the *real* countdown a couple of minutes ago," she said with pardonable pride. "That was just the voice recording talking. I thought Morrow might get suspicious if that stopped, and come looking for me."

"Morrow . . ." Serge whispered as memories suddenly rushed back. "What Lynch said. He was the one—"

Before Rob realized what he was doing, Serge was across the cavern to the bound engineer. Quickly he unsealed his helmet, then viciously yanked it off.

"What are you doing?" Morrow gabbled. "No, no, I didn't, it was the computer, I didn't—"

His words stopped as Serge's inhumanly strong hands fastened around his throat, not exerting much pressure, but enough to keep Jeff from speaking.

"You killed Hing," the archaeologist said softly, between his teeth. A crimson haze seemed to be drifting across his vision— or was it his mind? It felt wonderful, more potent than any drug. "You killed her, and I will never see her again," he snarled into Morrow's pale, sweating face. "And now," Serge said, his voice calm once more, "I am going to kill you. One crunch"—he gave an experimental squeeze that made Jeff gag—"and you will be dead. How do *you* like it?"

Rob stepped forward, one hand held out. "No, Serge!" he said. "Don't! It won't help! It won't bring her back!"

Serge hesitated. "But he *killed* Hing," he said after a moment. The red haze was thickening, and Morrow's flesh felt very fragile in his grasp.

"I know he did, but this won't help, Serge!"

Suddenly, Heather was before Serge, her small stubby hand going out to rest on the archaeologist's shoulder. "Serge," she whispered, and he saw tears in his eyes. "*Don't.* Please. Because Hing . . . Hing wouldn't like it."

And then Heather Farley began to cry.

Serge was never sure exactly what happened over the course of the next few minutes. He realized dimly that he had let go of Morrow, and that Rob, gun in hand, was shoving the stumbling engineer over to the terminal, then thrusting him hard into the chair. Looking down, he saw Heather in his arms, sobbing against his shoulder. His own face was wet . . . were they her tears, or his own?

Later, he was aware with some faraway portion of his mind that the airlock had opened again, admitting the security force from StarBridge Station . . . but mostly he was aware of Heather, still burrowed against him, weeping. Cautiously he stroked the carroty hair, murmuring to her softly in his own language.

Serge realized that he could now think of Hing without wanting to kill himself from the pain. It still hurt, it would hurt for as long as he lived, but he *would* live, he knew that now. The terrible, devouring void inside him was gone.

Much later, when he raised his head, he found Rob standing beside him. Lynch's body was gone, and so was Jeff Morrow. "You okay?" the doctor whispered.

Silently, Serge nodded.

In his arms, Heather, who had been quiet for some time, suddenly wriggled free. "What's *that*?" she asked, still hiccuping and gulping a little. She pointed at the back wall.

Something was glowing inside the small chamber.

With a soft exclamation, Serge got to his feet and walked across the cavern floor, with Heather and Rob in his wake. Reaching the hole that Morrow's stray shot had made, he knelt down and peered through.

"Oh, my God," he heard Rob Gable say softly. "How long has it been there?"

Serge did a quick calculation. "It must date back from the time when this was part of a planet," he replied, his voice barely above a whisper. "Roughly two hundred and fifty million years ago. At least."

"Wow," Heather whispered. "Holy shit!"

"Watch your language, young lady," Rob admonished. "I think this place *was* sacred ground, at one time."

The thing within the chamber most closely resembled a dais, with steps leading up to it, but it was obvious in a single glance that humans had never made it. The colors and angles were all wrong, the steps not shaped to accommodate a human foot. Colors cascaded off it in gentle sheets like rippling water. Atop the dais was a glowing field that obscured what lay inside, but Serge thought he could make out a long, shrouded shape there.

"A burial?" Rob guessed.

"It must be," Serge said. "But of whom? The planet must have been inhabited by intelligent life before the comet destroyed it."

He gazed reverently at the artifact. "All these years, that terrible cataclysm, and it is still functioning," he breathed. "What kind of people build things to last for two hundred and fifty million years?"

"Wait until Professor Greyshine sees this," Rob said.

Serge, awed in the presence of such ancient death, could only nod. He was tired, yet somehow an aura of peace reached him from the shrouded figure. Peace and inner calm.

Finally, Rob threw an arm around each of his companions. "Hey, let's go," he said softly. "It's time to go home."

"Dr. Rob?" Heather said, leaning back against Serge to look at the psychologist. "Do I *really* have a home?"

"You sure do, honey," Rob said. "For as long as you want to stay, you sure do."

Epilogue

Rob Gable sat alone in his office, brooding. He'd just received a call from Angela Morrow. Jeff was now in a hospital, the best money could buy, but his doctors, so far, were not hopeful. Rob knew they were right to be cautious. Borderline personalities seldom recovered on a permanent basis.

The engineer would probably never stand trial for his crimes.

The doctor wished he could care more about whether Jeff got well or not, but he still felt so bruised from his friend's betrayal that it was hard to summon up genuine sympathy. One part of him still cared a great deal, but whenever Rob remembered Hing, the rest of his mind quenched those warm feelings in a flood of cold anger.

Maybe time would heal this wound, too, but it would have to be a *long* time. Not two hundred and fifty million years, of course . . . but close.

Serge and Greyshine were back at work out at their dig, examining the artifact, measuring it from every angle, recording it, and doing all the other things archaeologists did to strange burial sites. They'd discovered that each "step" leading up to the dais was equipped with visual and mental images. So far, they hadn't been able to make much sense of it, though Heather had been able to help them "translate" to a small degree. No doubt the team that was coming out from Shassiszs next month would be a big help.

Heather went out to the dig nearly every day with Serge, after they'd both finished class. Serge had announced his intention to Rob of finishing up all his schooling, then asking to be reevaluated on his fitness as a potential interrelator. Rob had a feeling he'd make it, this time.

But he also frankly wondered whether Serge would ever have time to take on a diplomatic job. Between his work at the site and his composing, Serge was an extremely busy young man. In addition to his "big-brother" role with Heather, and his archaeological work, he'd finished the Starburst Symphony three weeks ago. The second movement, based in part on his tone-poem, was now an unforgettable threnody in memory of Hing.

Serge's symphony was due to be performed for the first time at the end of this week. The New York Philharmonic, under the direction of Maestro Antonia Zelinksi, was currently on tour. When Zelinksi, an old admirer of Serge's, had heard that the young musician was again composing, she'd arranged a special stop at StarBridge Academy. The Starburst Symphony would be performed for the first time in the newly dedicated Hing Oun Memorial Theater. Serge would be joining the performance as the pianist in the percussion section.

Rob sighed as he thought of Hing. He still missed his Little Friend of All the World, missed her every day. But he thought she'd have been pleased about the theater dedication.

His intercom signaled. Rob flipped it on. "Yes?"

It was Resharkk'. "Honored Healer Gable, there is a ship coming in at the hangar dome, and Honored Serge, who is piloting, requests that you be present to greet its passengers in person. He says they are distinguished visitors."

"Really?" Rob hadn't heard that any were due, but the school did have occasional drop-ins, mostly when eminent diplomats or leaders had a layover at the Station and wanted to kill a few hours. "Okay, I'll be right down."

Quickly he went over to his closet, combed his hair (*should I do something about this gray?*), and put on a jacket.

On his way through the corridors to the hangar dock, he couldn't help glancing around him with preternaturally aware eyes. He couldn't forget that he'd almost lost this place forever. *I'll never take you for granted again,* he thought, trailing his fingers along the wall. *No how, no way.*

When he reached the observation deck, he found Ssoriszs waiting there, too. "Esteemed One!" Rob exclaimed. "What are you doing here?"

"I was summoned by young Serge," the Mizari said. "He said important visitors were arriving, and I should be here to welcome them personally. So here I am."

"He sent me the same message. I wonder who it is?"

They spent the moments waiting for the ship to glide in and dock chatting about the genuine archaeological discovery. Although Ssoriszs was understandably disappointed that he had not found his ancestors, his faith that someday the Lost Colony would be found was undaunted.

"Here it comes," Rob said, and together they watched the ship come in, then settle down into its bay. A perfect landing.

Serge and Heather came out first, and the girl's red hair was even more unruly than usual. She waved excitedly, started to yell something. Serge abruptly clamped a hand over her mouth. Unruffled, she plucked it off, then stood back to make way for the first passenger to disembark, a slender young woman with a long brown braid of hair and a wide grin.

Before she was halfway down the ramp, Rob had bolted down the stairs, vaulted the railing, and was running down the length of the docking bay. "Mahree!"

When the ecstatic hugging and kissing finally died down, ("Yuck" had been Heather's comment), Rob gasped, "Why are *you* here? Why didn't you tell me?"

"Because I wanted to surprise you," she said, smiling at him, stroking back his hair.

"Oh, no you don't," he said, reaching up to grab her hand. "Don't you go on about my gray, too."

"I wasn't going to!"

"Yes, you were."

"Was not!"

"Were too!"

The argument continued back and forth until it was halted by another round of kisses, this time of a more intense variety. Heather gazed wide-eyed. "Holy shit," she whispered to Serge. "I didn't know old people kissed like *that*."

Serge gave her a mock-stern glance. "Your language, Heather, remember? And what, no 'yuck'?"

"They've gone far past a 'yuck.' That one's a 'yeuchhh'!"

Ssoriszs flowed down the ramp toward the next passenger. "Grandson!" he greeted Zarshezz. "What in the name of the Star-Spirits are you doing here?"

The young Mizari affectionately entwined tentacles with his grandsire. "I wanted to talk with you, to say how sorry I was about that day," he said. "Then, when I heard about the sabotage, I was worried for you, so I came to see that you were all right." Zarshezz peered into the old Mizari's face. "*Are* you all right, Grandfather?"

Slowly, the elderly Liaison inclined his head. "I am now," he said simply. "I missed you, too, Grandson."

Rob, his arm around Mahree, turned to leave the docking area, heading for his quarters. He had so much to tell her!

"Hey, Gable!" It was Janet's voice. She was up in Traffic Control, he saw, waving down at him. "Wait! Look!" She pointed.

Following the direction of her finger, he turned, then let out a glad whoop. "*Shrys!*"

The Drnian student was undoubtedly vastly surprised to be violently hugged by a human, but since he had learned tolerance at his school for other species' strange customs, he did not draw back. "Dr. Rob, I am glad to see you, too, of course," he said when the psychologist finally released him, "but your welcome . . . is it not a bit extreme?"

"Not for someone returned from the dead," Rob said fervently. "Why didn't you call?"

"You never told me to," Shrys said with a Drnian's typical literalism.

Mahree stepped to his side. "Are you going to introduce me to your friends?" she prompted.

"I certainly am," Rob said, and hastily presented her to the Drnian. Then, as they once more headed for the ramp, he added, "But, darling, I have to warn you . . . everyone in this whole school is my friend, so if you want to meet *all* of them, you'll have to stay for a long, long visit."

She smiled at him. "I've cleared my schedule for the next two months," she said. "By that time, you'll be sick of us."

"Us?"

"Shirazz and Claire are coming next week."

Rob glanced over at Heather, who was chattering animatedly to Serge, and thought of his own chestnut-haired, extremely bright, telepathically adept daughter. He paled slightly. "I just hope the old place can stand the strain," he mumbled as they started up the ramp again, hands entwined. "Claire doesn't still love messing around with computers, does she? Tell me she doesn't!"

"You know she does," Mahree told him. "She takes after me."

Rob groaned theatrically. "See that redheaded kid over there?" he asked, nudging Mahree and pointing with his chin.

She nodded. "Nobody could ever miss that hair! Why? What about her?"

Rob kissed Mahree again, then smiled wickedly. "I'll tell you the whole story of how I was privileged to visit the innards of our computer, the time Blanket and I had to rescue that little redhead from the monsters in the AI," he promised with a gleam in his eye. "But it's a *long* story, my love. It'll take me all night . . ."

She grinned back. "I can live with that."

Afterword

Sometimes I think I must be part Avernian. No, I don't appear particularly fungal (except before I've had my morning coffee), but sometimes I seem to be on a shared mental wavelength with my readers. For example, just about the time I took a deep breath and launched into the final rewrite of this book, I received letters from a number of StarBridge readers asking me when I was going to feature Rob Gable as a character again. They also wanted to know when I was going to write an entire book set on the StarBridge asteroid so they could see more of the day-to-day life at the school! So, as Mahree Burroughs would caution, "Be careful what you wish for—you might get it."

As to future books—after helping me out in a pinch by writing seventy or so pages of *Serpent's Gift* (can you guess which ones?), Kathy is only a chapter or two away from completing the first draft of *Silent Songs* (yes, it's *Songs*, plural); we're excited about this story and hope you will be too.

Many people have asked me if I'd consider doing a novel about the legendary "Sorrow Sector." If the series goes beyond five books, that will definitely be a theme I'd like to tackle in future—I'm curious myself about what it's like!

Thanks again to my readers for all the warmth and encouragement you've shown in support of the StarBridge series. You make all the hassles and hard work worthwhile.

—Ann C. Crispin
October 1991